NIZ THOMAS COLLECTED

VOLUME ONE: CRIME STORIES

NIZ THOMAS COLLECTED
BOOK 1

NIZ THOMAS

COPYRIGHT

Niz Thomas Collected
Volume One: Crime Stories

COPYRIGHT

Family Tree

CONTENTS

Also By Niz Thomas   xi

Introduction   xvii

QUICK HITTERS

BURN OFF

Chapter 1   7

Chapter 2   14

Chapter 3   20

Chapter 4   26

THE TWO O'CLOCK KILLER

Chapter 1   33

NO CONTROL

Chapter 1   47

Chapter 2   49

Chapter 3   52

Chapter 4   56

Chapter 5   58

Chapter 6   68

SLOW BURN

LANE CHANGE

Chapter 1   77

Chapter 2   95

Chapter 3   100

Chapter 4   114

THE BAD GUY

Chapter 1	129
Chapter 2	131
Chapter 3	137
Chapter 4	140
Chapter 5	142
Chapter 6	147
Chapter 7	151

RED TEMPEST

Part One	163
Part Two	201

DARKLY TWISTED

WHEN SHEDS TALK

Chapter 1	217
Chapter 2	223
Chapter 3	226
Chapter 4	229
Chapter 5	235
Chapter 6	238
Chapter 7	240
Chapter 8	242
Chapter 9	245
Chapter 10	247
Chapter 11	249
Chapter 12	250

RAY RAY'S STOOP

Chapter 1	257
Chapter 2	269
Chapter 3	274
Chapter 4	278

THE VOICE OF RAGE AND RUIN

Chapter 1   293
Chapter 2   298
Chapter 3   302
Chapter 4   306

ELDER HUNGER

Chapter 1   315
Chapter 2   320
Chapter 3   323
Chapter 4   328
Chapter 5   331
Chapter 6   337
Chapter 7   341
Chapter 8   343
Chapter 9   348
Chapter 10   351
Chapter 11   355

SERIES STARTERS

THE OMEGA DINER

Chapter 1   367
Chapter 2   373
Chapter 3   379
Chapter 4   385
Chapter 5   388
Chapter 6   393
Chapter 7   396
Chapter 8   399

THIN AIR

Chapter 1   411
Chapter 2   414
Chapter 3   419
Chapter 4   423
Chapter 5   426

Chapter 6   429
Chapter 7   432
Chapter 8   434
Chapter 9   436
Chapter 10   437
Chapter 11   441
Chapter 12   442
Chapter 13   445
Chapter 14   447

CALL ME BETSY

Chapter 1   455
Chapter 2   487

CALL ME GERTRUDE

Chapter 1   493
Chapter 2   529

Afterword   533
Exclusive Sneak Peek   535

FAMILY TREE

Chapter 1   541

Join the Mailing List   549
Also By Niz Thomas   551
About the Author   555

ALSO BY NIZ THOMAS

For a full list and links to purchase, visit:

NIZTHOMAS.COM/BOOKS

Nizpatches

Volume One: Crime Stories

Volume Two: Twisted Crime

Niz Thomas Collected

Volume One: Crime Stories

---

the Ledgerman series

The Omega Diner: A Ledgerman Story

Razor's Edge: A Ledgerman Novel

Thin Air: A Ledgerman Story

Last Ride: A Ledgerman Novel

---

the True Name series

Call Me Betsy

Call Me Gertrude

Call Me Aileen

NOVELS

Family Tree

Door Number Five at the Memory Motel

And The Moon Is Full And Bright

Election Day

SHORT STORIES

A Refraction of Kind Light

A Void of Ascendant Light

Becalm This Mighty Sea

Burn Off

Burn Together

Cheers

Elder Hunger

Fiona's Mercy

First Light of Every Morning

How to Commune with a Futurist

Lady Death

Lane Change

My Bleeding Kansas

No Control

Paint It Thrice

Rail Music

Ray-Ray's Stoop

Recidivist History

Red Tempest

Ships in the Night

Songbird

The Bad Guy

The Climb and The Glory

The Forever-ish Flame War

The Imminent Fire

The Impassable Way

The Light Alone

The Two O'Clock Killer

The Voice of Rage and Ruin

Upon Your Dreams They Prey: A Lullaby

Vanguard

Vida's Sixth Trip Around the Sun

When Sheds Talk

NIZ THOMAS COLLECTED

INTRODUCTION

I've been thinking a lot about structure.

(As one does).

What sort of structure, you ask?

The structure of a day, maybe? That single unit of measure which seems to me about the maximum amount of time a human being can truly hold inside their head. It is the one True Unit, perhaps, besides the very simple Now (though nowadays, nobody can much focus on Now)–for there are no yesterdays and no tomorrows, only todays.

Or maybe the structure of civilization. That constantly shifting alchemical mix of people, places, things. The distribution of capital, of wealth, of equality.

Perhaps the structure of a life? That almighty spine upon which we humans can walk, or tiptoe, or stomp along to ensure our lives Mean Something, that we leave this pale blue dot a better place than how we found it?

No, not that kind.

The structure I had in mind was far less weighty, far more pedestrian–though also quite practical.

And since you are holding this book in your hands—or your eReading device is holding it for you (the files are in the computer?!?) and you hold *that* in your hands, or you are listening to this, in which case the words are bypassing your visual cortex altogether and shooting mainline into your brain stem (though perhaps, if you're a visual thinker, ending up in your visual cortex after all, if by a circuitous route), or perhaps you are in some near future (because it doesn't seem so far off, given the realities of the day) where we've figured out a way to bypass those fleshy biomechanical processes altogether and you are simply one with the book, a mind-meld of a sort—but *anyway*, since you're consuming the media in whatever way you are, I would hazard that you might be interested to know about the structure that I had in mind. And more importantly, he says by way of filling up a word count for this Introduction, how that structure might affect you.

It was the structure of this book.

I had all manner of ideas. You see, there are fourteen stories enclosed within. Some people would just line them up in order from best to worst (metaphorically, of course; there are no bad stories here!). Some people would weave them together so that the highs of one wend into the lows of the next. Some people, when it comes to short story collections, are real artists.

Or as I like to call them, showoffs.

As you may have guessed from looking at the cover, or the spine, or the back cover—hey, maybe you're even one of those people (like me) who looks at the copyright page—you may have noticed this is the first collection of stories put out under my new series *Niz Thomas Collected: The Short Fiction of Niz Thomas* (you'll never guess where we got the name).

That's not to say I'm a total novice here. I've got a separate series of short fiction collections called *Nizpatches*, which are shorter, more tightly focused. There's overlap, sure, and if you came here from *Nizpatches*, write me. I'd love to say thanks and even give you a free, exclusive short story for being such a loyal fan. But *Niz Thomas*

Collected: The Short Fiction of Niz Thomas is intended to be all-encompassing. At the end of what I hope to be a very long life (heck, I just read in the newspaper they put a pig heart in some guy from Russia), someone with all the *Niz Thomas Collected: The Short Fiction of Niz Thomas* series will have a large chunk of my corpus—a phrase that sounds a whole lot worse than it should. Maybe a large chunk of my *oeuvre* is a better way of phrasing it (no, that sounds weird, too).

Hopefully you get the gist.

But back to the artistry of a collection of short fiction. I hope some of that was done already, in the picking. I think we done picked a solid lineup here. We've got eight-and-nine-hitters who could hit clean up. And best of all, we've got fourteen hitters in the lineup!

But as far as sorting all the stories out, well, fourteen *is* a bit unwieldy. Nine hitters in a lineup is one thing. But add most of your bench players into that mix and you need a lineup card to keep it straight most of the time. So I did what everyone that writes on the internet does.

I broke it up with section headers, baby.

(Hey, it works for the AI chatbots who write most of the crap on what used to be your favorite blog).

Since this collection is themed around crime, I probably could have gotten away with just skipping this step (and probably should have gone a little lighter on the weighty existentialism in the opening). But before I was a writer, I was a reader. And I know as a reader, sometimes it's looking ahead to that next section break and knowing you can get there before you need to eat or use the bathroom or get called into that appointment you're sitting in the waiting room for that keeps you moving forward.

And anyway, crime is such a wide swath of fertile ground, isn't it? You've got murderous crime—both solving it and perpetrating it. Detectives and serial killers, cops and ex-military bank robbers, newspapermen and the paranoid assassins who target them. Then, of course, there is crime of a different form. Thievery, grifters, people running a scam. We can't forget the desperate, either. Or the crazed. The unscrupulous. The moral vacuums. Sometimes, we turn to crime fiction to find the best and brightest who face the dark. Sometimes it's to get sucked into the vortextual black hole of evil. Ideally, you get a little bit of both in each story.

It's wide-ranging, though. That's for sure.

I had initially come up with a bunch of crazy crime ideas for how to break these stories up. I could group them, comparing each story to a serial killer, I thought. The smart, intellectual, pinkie-up stories that were sharp as a scalpel could be the Hannibal Lecters. The evil-or-crazy-which-one-is-stronger could be Jason Vorhees stories. But it got too down in the weeds. And all it takes is one person to not know a character before the comparison made no sense to them at all.

So in the end, I went with something a little more straightforward–though, I hope, no less interesting.

Because while the stories that follow all fall under the umbrella of what I dub as "smart suspense for a stupid good time," there is certainly some distinction.

There are the "quick hitters"–stories that are shortest in length and pack quite a punch.

There are the "slow burn" stories. Whereas the quick hitters have a kind of frenetic pace about them, the slow burns build through character revelations, arriving at explosive climaxes.

There are the "darkly twisted" stories. Perhaps my favorite of the lot. These all contain character studies with people who perhaps have a few screws loose. Or can't even be found in the hardware store at all. While that description could certainly apply to other characters throughout this collection, it most certainly is true of the characters in this particular subset of stories.

And finally, we have the "series starters." Stories which feature a series character in two different series–the Ledgerman series and the True Name series. You get two stories from both characters. If you like them, there are more on the way (or already out in the world, depending on when you read this).

So I hope you enjoy what I selected in terms of the structure of the stories that follow.

I sure had a lot of fun working on it.

Niz Thomas
March, 2024

QUICK HITTERS

quick hitters

[kwik hiterz] *noun*

_____

a frenetically paced short story that grabs you by the throat and won't let go

BURN OFF

NIZ THOMAS

BURN OFF

ONE

The road back from Jackson rattled Gideon's nearly thirty-year-old 1989 Ford F-250 pickup the same way a grizzly bear might handle a lame jack rabbit that limped into the wrong den once spring had sprung.

He grimaced against mounting pain in his hands, wrists, and forearms. Knowing for certain it would spread and get worse. Knowing that even as bad as it was, knocking him out of the damn workforce a little over a month ago, it wasn't nothing compared to life's true pains.

Gideon checked the clock on the dash. About the only part of the F-250 that worked properly, even though it was twelve minutes fast, showing a reading of four fifty-eight in the afternoon, meaning it was actually about quarter-'til five. Meaning they'd be cutting it close to arrive by nightfall. It wasn't a dealbreaker, but this truck didn't generate much from the headlights to guide their work should it have to happen too long after the sun went down.

He tried to do some simple calculations as he gazed through the speckled glass windshield onto the desolate, open land ahead: they were near the southern portion of the Gros Ventre Wilderness now, a place so pristine that it served a constant reminder that a more God-touched area did not exist in this world. Heading south away from it. Forty miles left to go. Good, clear conditions, nothing around to slow their route except for Angus and Hereford cattle that dotted the landscape and the fact his truck was near old enough to file for Social Security. The grass on either side of them was the same color as the Mountain Dew label (not the toxic sludge in the bottle) and stretched off in all directions until the silver sagebrush took over, then gave way to bur oak, then to dense copses of quaking aspens and thick, dark-green pine trees that seemed to blot out the last of the light on the western skyline. Off to the southeast, out his driver's side window, the Wind Rivers loomed in their dark grey countenance, still a ways off in the distance.

Whack. Whack. Whack. Each of the bones in his arms getting an aftershock from the road below like it was San Fran, 1906.

Gideon had modded the pleather steering wheel covering with hockey tape snagged from one of his nephews about eight years back– one strip wrapped at ten, another at two, both faded from white to "aged" (if one were kind with the descriptors). Family really was everything around these parts where the weather could be harsh, the wilderness unforgiving, at times cruel, and the work available to a man was rougher than anywhere else on land (if at sea, maybe they could talk).

So right then, as the rattling car went south down the solitary two-lane Route 191, Gideon was happy to have benefited from little Gabe's kindness to his uncle all those years ago. But the tension inside Gideon made it so he was gripping the wheel the way his grandfather gripped hold of the life raft in the waters off the Marshall Islands once the sharks started to circle and the wake started to rise and fall with approaching storms. Maybe that tension had never left his line ever since that moment. Maybe it had always been there to start.

Family really was everything around these parts. For better, for worse.

Driving now back from Jackson, the light of afternoon just beginning to fade to dusk as the bottom of the sun dropped behind the tips of the Tetons on his right, he recognized his truck was ready to be put out to pasture.

The deep ache had already settled into the places up his arm that he knew from experience would take days to fade. But he just tried to focus on their destination: the abandoned spot south of Pinedale where natural gas bloomed out of the ground like pollen from a dandelion in a spring wind. Gideon silently cursed himself. These bum arms and hands were the whole reason he was in this mess to begin with. And if he wasn't careful, they'd be the thing preventing him from getting out of it.

Assuming, of course, a way out existed. That remained to be seen.

Gideon's eyes cut to the rearview, to the bed of his truck.

A seismic quake of a jolt from a three-inch deep pothole the size of a manhole cover brought his attention directly back to the road.

At times on this drive back, he felt like he was back on the job, working his six-ton NPK hydraulic hammer attached to the long arm of his excavator, opening the earth below looking for pockets where natural gas flowed. He'd always been sensitive to what the subtle changes in vibration coming off his hammer told him about the land and the potential treasures below. A rise in the frequency meant harder rock, maybe shale—Cody or Mowry. When the vibration lessened, maybe rhyolite that gave the Wind Rivers their ghost-like color. Or just some soft sediment that had too much water from a nearby underground source. They had fancy radar on the computers these days that could identify that stuff, too. But he'd always done it by feel.

"Maybe try a straight line, 'hon," Trish said from the seat next to him. She had her seat pushed all the way forward, the upper part reclined so far back it was almost to bedding (much as you could get out of this pickup anyway, even with the extra cab room). Two long, toned legs caught his eye (mercy—always had). Two bare feet out the open window already with a light dusting of road grime, and they were only thirty-five minutes outside town headed home.

Gideon didn't catch her face but he could tell her eyes were closed. Resting. He'd never seen anybody able to rest in conditions like this. Not even back in the service (though to be fair, he'd been part of the generation of plant eaters who served after the Gulf War and checked out before round two in the sandbox). Her chair had even less padding in it than his, and if it weren't for the pounding his arms and hands were taking, his back would be making itself better known right now.

Something behind him, beneath the bed of the truck (he guessed, though he was practiced at diagnosing the truck's problems by sound alone), was loose. It whistled with the high whine of ungreased metal against metal. Gideon's eyes once again fluttered to the rearview, toward their cargo: a rectangular metal frame about three feet long by one-and-a-half feet wide and tall, four long, rolled-up rubber hoses, and three loose connector wires affixed to ... what had the dweeb in Jackson called it ... a *mother*board? It was the green status light Gideon keyed in on, though. It was how he knew the rig–what was basically a computer attached to a homemade generator with some very specific modifications–was still operational. As long as that light stayed green, they had a chance.

Well, as long as it stayed green *and* they got back in time.

The truck's left tire jerked. The whine now taking physical form. Felt like someone put a cue ball in a sock and slapped him with it. *This* was the pain that had caused him to start missing work.

"Like I said, 'hon. Straight is the way to do it."

Gideon grunted. Very funny. She always had been. Beautiful with those long legs, smart as a whip, funny as all get out. That's where Brett got it from, no doubt (except the beautiful part. The kid was cute going on boyish-handsome, but no son of Gideon's would ever be *beautiful* in the way Trish was).

Gideon checked the rearview again.

"It'll be fine, Gid. Thing is made of machined metal as thick as my tibia. And you sure spent enough time tying it down."

"Kid like that," he started, trying to find the words.

"Kids like that are sending people to the moon, old timer. I think he can make a generator and a computer work together just fine."

Gideon grunted. He'd spent years working with roughnecks out on the high plains drilling for natural gas. Guys that were one bad decision away from prison. Plenty who already belonged there, but they were able to skate by with work in remote places where cops didn't feel a need to visit much. Some good men, too, like Gideon. Stable. Sober. Fellas who worked a hard job in a hard way, kept themselves and others safe as they could.

Ain't a single one of those men looked like the dweeb kid from Jackson. David, was his name. Sat half-slouched in his chair with clothes that were bewilderingly tight around his crotch. A sweatshirt big enough to take up into the Tetons to camp with, maybe fly it down the side of the mountain when he was done. Like those X treme athletes in the squirrel suits. Didn't look like any man Gideon had ever worked with, ever trusted. Certainly not one that had ever manufactured a piece of useful equipment.

But Trish said to trust the kid—he knew computers, knew a way to turn something Gideon and Trish could get into cash.

When Trish looked him dead straight in the eyes and says, "Trust," Gideon did exactly that. That was family. That was bond.

It would all work out. Had to. Assuming, of course, they could make it back before true dark. And before David the Dweeb's vague deadline was up. "Before the other guys ..." was all he'd said.

"You're setting back your jaw like a pit bull got whiff of chicken fried steak," Trish said. "What is it?"

The pain didn't help none. But Gideon said nothing. Cut his eyes at the rearview again. David the Dweeb's equipment was still back there fine. Green light switched on.

The road was otherwise empty again. Not even a distant headlight around.

He wondered whether the kid was bluffing about the others.

Trish wasn't thinking about that, apparently. Wasn't like her to leave something alone to fester. And true to form, she didn't. "You don't agree with the plan, say something. It's awfully late to do so, but it ain't *too* late."

The plan could work. He could admit that. But it needed to go off without a hitch. He'd never experience a plan like that before. Plans were freaking hitch magnets.

"Not the plan you disagree with, huh?" Gideon knew without looking that his wife's one eye was open now. Watching him. Waiting for a reaction.

Or about to create one.

"It's the *kid*, isn't it? Not the plan. It's the kid you don't agree with."

Honestly, everything was the problem at this point. Pain was the one at the forefront of his mind, though. It was enough to make winning the lottery a grim event in his life right this second. Inside him, somewhere deep in his soul, he hurt even worse. Brett, their poor son, at home. Injured. No. Paralyzed. Didn't help none to pretend otherwise. Fell off a rock outcropping one day playing out back behind the house. With Gideon unable to work and the rough-neck who replaced him falling asleep on the job and damn-near decapitating one of the other fellas on the crew, the small drilling company he worked for went under. Scary to think how thin of a margin so much survived on in this life. But that was the way it went for roughnecks in a rough place. Wyoming sure ain't New York or Miami Beach.

So this plan was born from Trish's internet research. Contacted David the Dweeb, kid who apparently had pioneered some technology that used flare gas to power computers to mine something called *cryptocurrency*. Gideon didn't know a thing about it, but it seemed lucrative given how much David was willing to pay. Flare gas was something the drilling companies needed to burn off when they found gas somewhere that didn't have a pipeline close to it. It was essentially waste product, which was not only dangerous, but also a bit like burning piles of cash all day, every day. Now that the company had gone under, the burn off was done for. Nobody to maintain it. And the site was abandoned.

Meaning the flare gas was free for the taking.

"Well, Gid, say *something*, would you? Heck, say the first thing enters your mind."

They'd played this game before. It felt to Gideon like shaking up a bottle of pop for thirty, forty years and then cracking the top.

Gideon exploded. Smacked at the dash and instantly regretted it. A lightning strike of pain shot through every nerve ending in his arms. He saw yellow spots at the edges of his vision.

Trish sat up. The half-rolled passenger window beside her knocked against its track inside the door.

She touched his arm, gently rubbing it like she had so many nights. Only thing kept him from the bottle or the pills or (like so many others around) the crank. Her, those touches, and Brett.

"Ah, 'hon, c'mon. You know once this is–"

Gideon turned his head toward his wife, so sudden did she stop speaking.

Trish's eyes were straight ahead. "Watch out!"

Right in front of the windshield: a massive crow. Nearly as big as a baby fawn. Hovering there as if suspended in time and space.

Gideon slammed the brake.

The truck, bless its weary, Tin Man heart, didn't just come apart at each and every seam in the old beast. But it seemed to come as close as possible under the circumstances.

Luckily, the dust settled atop the roadway wasn't so thick and the brakes (Lord mercy what was left of them, anyhow) bit, sliding the car to a stop. Safe.

The crow, unfortunately, wasn't so lucky.

TWO

It probably wasn't more than a minute.

A full sixty seconds.

Gideon sat there in the driver's seat of his raggedy F-250, the quiet of the valley completely blotted out by the pulse in his ears.

The windshield was spider-webbed with crimson. It felt like both he and Trish sat there for a long night of the soul, considering their complicity in the act which had just befallen them.

Gideon stepped down from the truck and surveyed the damage.

It was mostly the windshield, though the damage there was significant enough that it would require some finesse before driving further. Finesse, in this instance, wouldn't be so hard to come by—he had a tire iron somewhere in the back, he could use that to bash out the windshield and they could ride home getting bugs stuck in their teeth if need be.

From the outside of the truck, it appeared as if the crow had somehow collided first with the windshield before denting the hood of the truck in several areas. A trail of blood marked the way. Nothing critical, especially to an old beast like the F-250, but curious nonetheless.

About twenty feet away, the crow lay motionless, glass-eyed, its feathers ashen with the slick oily texture of a Louisiana bayou. Part of it seemed to have exploded out, but he was happy to find it was the part facing opposite where he now stood.

Whether they could drive the truck home was an open question, though one he was certain would be yes.

But he was more interested right now in the generator.

"Bad omen, to be sure," Trish said.

He and Trish were all alone out here now. Nothing new there. Ever since he had to stop working because of his hands, it had been them against the world. They had enough squirreled away to survive on for quite a while if things went off without a hitch.

They just never worked out like that for Gideon.

Without Gideon being able to work, his health benefits would run out soon.

Once Brett got injured, the razor's edge got sharper. At first, they thought the paralysis was temporary. Would clear up. Maybe. It only bonded Gideon and Trish closer, being there for their son. In a way, him being off work was a blessing. He got to be there for everybody, physically, emotionally.

But the money was tight. Getting on some government plan would be their next best option, but that just made their margin for error even tighter.

Then things got noose tight once the doctors changed their story. Long-term care. Rehabilitation. Specialists. The numbers the social worker at the hospital had been quoting them seemed made up to him. Game show numbers. Christ, he cloned himself three times over with good, strong hands he couldn't afford those bills.

So to David the Dweeb they'd gone, once Gideon told Trish about the company going under.

"Thank God," Gideon said, leaning over the truck bed so he could see the generator. "Still operational."

Wouldn't be but a few minutes until purple dark arrived, setting their valley to the darkness, to the night.

"Now we gotta get back," Trish said.

As if on cue, the hitch in the plan emerged right then.

The back left side of the truck dropped about six inches lower with a crash of scraping metal. It didn't pop out the back left tire so much as it crushed it down beneath the weight of the truck. Whatever part of the truck he'd heard rattling around before had finally given up holding on. Gideon rushed up and into the truck bed, grabbed the jack, and got the back of the bed up off the ground so the tire didn't give out fully. The road underneath the jack was, of course, cracked and potholed, so the jack's hold on the truck seemed precarious at best, but it was the best he could do with what was at hand.

They wouldn't be driving the truck any further. Bad omen, for sure.

"No service here, I bet," he said, wasting no time now complaining about what had just happened.

Trish leaned across the driver's seat and grabbed her phone. "Bingo. Probably not for a few more miles."

"That figures." This was a known dead zone. Perfect place to get your car pelted with crows.

"Uh huh."

To Gideon's right, a flash of light caught his attention. "Well, would you look at that." A car was coming from off in the distance, same way as they had. If that wasn't something like good fortune, he wouldn't know what was.

"I'll flag 'em," Trish said. "You might want to hide, old man. Wouldn't want to scare any of these nice folks off, eh?"

Gideon smirked. He'd never been what you might consider intimidating, but he couldn't argue with the logic of Trish flagging down a car instead of him. Heck, she was beautiful enough to flag down an airplane.

He watched as the truck slowed a few hundred yards up the road, as if only now just seeing them stuck there. For a second of panic, he thought maybe they'd been spooked. Like they looked ahead up the road and saw danger. A trap. Please Lord, show some mercy.

He held his breath. Please don't turn back around.

The truck picked up speed again, red-lit dust kicking up behind it from taillights just turned on. Gideon and Trish would have a chance at a ride, it seemed. A tow was probably out of the question with the tire. But a ride they could do.

"Looks like some kind of utility truck," Trish said. "Big enough bed in the back to house that thing."

"You think we're getting a ride back, cargo in tow?"

Trish smiled and winked and it about exploded Gideon's heart. He loved this woman. He couldn't imagine being in this situation with anybody else. Where he was weak, she was strength. With any luck, they'd live out the rest of their days without her recognizing his deficiencies with what he brought to the table. Her face still visible as the last fingers of sun stretched through the tops of the mountains off in the distance, she said, "If we do, we can ride the four-wheeler out to the site. Hook this thing up, confirm it works, then David said he'd wire the money straightaway."

Wire the money. Gideon had never even heard of such a thing prior to their meeting. Trish had been prepared, of course. Had given David the Dweeb all the details, the kid nodding and tapping away at his computer like he was playing piano.

"Could have this whole thing behind us here shortly. Brett'll be getting the care he needs by week's end." She made it sound so easy.

The utility truck pulled up beside them. New truck. An interesting one, too. Municipal electricity in Pinedale, according to the logo on the passenger's side door. But it also had a U.S Postal Service decal stuck along the truck's bed, which was covered by a hardtop camper shell. This truck did double duty, as some did out this way. And it seemed the driver was pulling in two clean incomes, too, as very few did out this way.

"Carl Lyle. Is that you?" Trish asked as the truck's passenger side window rolled about halfway down. Inside the cab was dark, the light in the sky so faint now that it didn't provide any illumination inside.

Carl Lyle. Gideon breathed a sigh of relief. It seemed fortunate smiled upon them, indeed. Trish wouldn't have to flex too much charm for them to get a ride back. He didn't know Carl much, but he knew Denny, Carl's older brother, from working together. Denny was a roughneck all the way through. Both the good qualities and the bad. One of those fellas who lived at the edge of the prisoner line. But smart, too. More so than most. Denny knew some things about the world. How he learned them was anybody's guess. But he had enough smarts to make something of himself in the world. Why it was such a shame he hadn't. Or wouldn't.

Carl was the good egg of the family. Would know Gideon's name, even if he didn't remember meeting him once or twice at one of the local bars.

"How do you know him?" he said to Trish.

"He delivers our mail."

That made sense, what with the Postal Service decal and everything.

"Howdy, Trish. Gideon." Carl's voice boomed from inside the cab.

Rather than get out or roll the window all the way down, he reversed the truck and did a wide circle around so that his truck's back end came up close to the back end of the F-250.

The driver's side door of the utility truck opened. Out stepped Carl–a thickset man with fiercely black hair, dressed in jeans, work boots, and an olive-green fishing shirt.

"What in the world happened here?"

"Attack of the crow," Trish said, flashing her warm smile. Even in the approaching darkness, it was a megawatt smile.

"Something else, huh?" In that moment, Gideon tracked something odd about Carl.

A second appraisal called more into question. Though he had always been a thickset fella, his face was now thin. Almost gaunt in the deepening shadows of dusk. Eyes seemed a bit sunken, though they were alive with an energy that scared Gideon in that moment.

He realized, too, that the clothes were made for a thicket fella, but a thickset fella wasn't wearing them.

Standing before them was a fella who used to be thickset.

And around these parts, a sudden weight loss isn't usually a good thing.

In fact, it almost only ever happens when the person losing the weight starts using.

Trish's back went straight. Like hackles on a cat.

Something was wrong here.

The passenger door opened.

Out stepped Denny Lyle. Looking for all the world like he was here to cause wreak havoc.

Gideon's heart started hammering in his ears, the pain in his arms receding only slightly due to adrenaline but reminding Gideon that his arms weren't strong enough to take on Carl or Denny Lyle, let alone both of them.

Family really was everything out there.

THREE

Carl took another step closer to Trish, his movements twitchy.

Gideon reacted, closing the distance between himself and his wife so that he could at least get between Carl and Denny and Trish. He got a feeling he might need to fight these boys, and he already knew that wouldn't end well. Besides both being a head taller than Gideon, he wasn't sure he could hold tight on a fist at the moment.

David the Dweeb's words came bounding back like a shout from Zeus at the top of the mountain. "Before the other guys ..."

Now Gideon realized what it was about that statement that struck him so cold.

There was competition for David the Dweeb's money.

Out here, money wasn't an especially easy thing to come by.

Especially not the sums David had thrown around.

Had Gideon thought more about it, it would've made sense the competition was from someone familiar. This wasn't a big place. Industry here wasn't like in the big cities, millions of people buzzing about like bees. Here you could fit the population of all the oil producing counties into a New York City apartment, probably.

Gideon might not have chosen Carl and Denny as the first competitors, but they were as likely as anybody else. David the Dweeb was here, after all, in Wyoming. If he had someone interested in West Texas, likelier than not he'd have gone there.

"No need to make a big scene," Carl said with a tight jaw, waving Trish away from where she stood. "Two of you just stand right there so I can see you both close. This'll be quick, don't worry."

Trish stepped backward until she was about even with Gideon. She put an arm around him and pulled herself closer to him. Protected. Though what that meant with a gun pulled on you was anybody's guess.

Gideon tried to pull her tighter against his body, but he flat couldn't. He wondered if she noticed. Her husband was about as strong right now as a babe.

"How'd you find out?" Trish asked.

Carl smiled something dark and mischievous. "Noticed the bills first. Thought you all were either flush with cash or needing some pretty quick. Overheard you one day babbling about it on the phone. About setting a meeting in town, how you had access to a pocket of natural gas, how it wasn't even being used right now but your fella was the one to find it. So, we followed ya."

Denny stepped up to Gideon. "Help me put that thing in the truck. Or are you too weak even to do that?"

"Might be, Denny. Honest. I could barely hold the wheel."

Denny's eyes blazed with the fire of the lost soul. "I wasn't planning on killing ya. Don't make me change my mind."

For some reason, that comment actually made Gideon feel lighter. Denny knew Trish and Gideon couldn't go to the cops once the generator got taken. What they were trying to do wasn't exactly legal, so there'd be no crime Gideon could call up the sheriff and pin on Denny. Not without implicating himself. And Denny knew Gideon well enough. The old driller wasn't the criminal kind—current situation notwithstanding. Some of the roughnecks they knew, those old boys would string you up if you even thought of robbing 'em.

Gideon simply would not retaliate in that sort of way.

Denny knew it. Nothing Gideon could say or do here to make him think any different.

And that, too, pained Gideon. Meant he'd once again let down his wife and his boy.

Meant they were back where they started. Unable to care for the kid who so needed them right now.

"You're not taking that generator, Denny. You neither, Carl. Kill me if you need to. But we ain't leaving here without it."

Denny smiled. Almost like he relished the thought. "You go that route, we ain't gonna just kill you."

That sent a shiver through Gideon.

"Please, Denny. The money ain't for us. It's for our boy."

Carl cut his eyes over to his brother. Denny didn't flinch. Told you something. Even through whatever hardships had fallen on Carl to make him find the dirty path that so many around these parts walked on, he still had some humanity in him.

Denny apparently didn't share that.

Gideon stepped closer to Denny. Gun be damned. Maybe Carl wouldn't pull the trigger.

Denny stepped to Gideon. "You want me to show you how it's going to be?"

Anger welled up in Gideon. And just like the company was doing with the blooming natural gas pocket, it burned off. In its place was only despair. "I got no choice, Denny. Please."

Denny got close enough so Gideon could smell the wintergreen chew tucked inside Denny's mouth. Probably the cleanest vice the roughneck had. "And what makes you think I do?"

Gideon looked straight into the man's eyes. All he saw there was a deep, empty well of nothing.

"Get your ass to the truck and help me carry that generator,"

Denny said, knocking his shoulder into Gideon and pushing past toward the back of the F-250.

Carl kept the gun on Gideon. His eyes went colder and he nodded for Gideon to follow his brother.

Without anything else to do, Gideon turned back. As he went to his truck, he couldn't bear to meet Trish's eyes.

Gideon went to the opposite side from Denny, the side where the truck had dropped lower, twisting the metal of the underside into a mangled mess.

Denny smiled. "Something loose on that side of the truck?"

Gideon understood. The Lyles made it so the F-250 was never making the full trip back to Pinedale. They were always going to take this generator, presumably leave Trish and Gideon stranded on the side of the road. That just pissed him off more.

Denny hopped into the bed and unlatched the numerous ways Gideon had secured the generator in place. "Ain't got all day," Denny said. He hopped down and held one side of the generator. Gideon tried to ball a fist around the other side but the effort shot daggers up and down his forearm. Instead, he just kept an open palm around one of the pieces of metal framing, matching where Denny had grabbed on the other side.

They pulled the generator off the back of the truck.

Before he took a second step, Gideon dropped his side, unable to stand the pain and unable to fully close his fingers around the metal framing. The generator wasn't particularly heavy, but it was awkwardly-shaped.

Denny got in Gideon's face. "What the hell, man. I need to have my brother put you and your bitch wife in a ditch or something?"

Gideon's face flushed hot.

"Get over here, Carl. They ain't doing nothing to stop us."

Carl came over and took Denny's place so the larger Lyle brother could now hold one side of the generator and still keep eyes on Gideon and Trish, both standing frozen now beside the F-250.

Denny bent down to pick up the side Gideon had dropped. "You weak little pus–"

Gideon snapped his foot out like he was kicking a hundred-and-fifty-yard-long field goal attempt. His work boot knocked Denny straight across the jaw, whipping the roughneck's head around with a kinetic snap that turned Gideon's stomach. He was no pansy, had seen plenty of fights around the job sites. Been in a few scrapes with fellas who deserved it. But this brush with violence was both surprising to him and unsettling.

Carl stood there in shock, unable to process what had just happened.

When he finally did, he looked bug-eyed at Gideon, as if he was processing in slow motion from an instruction manual of what to do next.

Gideon saw the light behind his eyes go out.

Carl raised the gun toward Gideon.

Trish came out of nowhere and slammed her body into Carl's side, knocking him off-balance and coloring the Lyle brother more than a little confused. Carl tripped over the edge of the generator and fell to the ground, the pistol knocking out of his hand and skittering a foot away from his outstretched hand, coming to a stop just beyond the place where the F-250's back tire was bent at its weird angle on the car.

Carl hit the ground with a grunt but didn't seem shocked anymore.

He army crawled for the gun, reaching his hand out to grab it.

Gideon put his work boot onto the back left bumper of the truck and pressed against it with all his weight. Trying to knock the truck's jack out of place.

It gave, but not all the way.

Trish ran in beside Gideon and lent her weight to the effort.

Gideon heard metal against concrete. Carl's hand and the gun.

The truck–bless its dinky heart–finally gave way, the unsteadiness of the jack working in their favor. As the F-250's weight slammed back toward Earth, the sound that erupted from beneath them was haunting. A thousand lemons all crushed by the world's biggest lemon squeezer. Trish screamed out. Gideon, in too much shock, simply swallowed back against the rising bile in his throat.

As darkness finally fell over the mountains, the scene went once again silent.

And it was just Trish and Gideon and the generator, whose green status light now glowed.

FOUR

Five minutes of excruciating pain later, Trish eased the utility truck in a loping circle back in the direction of Pinedale. Toward their forgotten pocket of natural gas.

Gideon sat in the plush leather passenger seat, sweating, the pain from helping Trish move the generator into the covered back of the utility truck's bed now engulfing so much more than just his hands, wrists, and forearms. He had to close his eyes and breathe deeply against the new throbbing rolling in waves into his shoulders and upper back.

The adrenaline was fading, but he still felt jolted to attention with what all had happened.

Trish said, "So what was the deal with that crow?"

Gideon thought about that. Thought about Denny's unconscious form as Trish dragged him out of the road and onto the shoulder. Thought of Carl's head going water balloon pop beneath the F-250's weight. Gideon shuddered.

"I guess it was like you said. Bad omen. Just not for us."

They were both silent for a while.

Eventually, Gideon was able to open his eyes. The pain receded, only slightly, but under the conditions, it felt like a great reprieve. Trish flipped on the utility truck's brights. "Should be enough light to see us through," she said. "Seems they've come a long way in the lights department in the past thirty years. I can actually see out the window."

Gideon smiled even despite the pain. "Smooth ride, too."

"From here on out, let's hope."

Gideon doubted it would be. Though they might not have competition, they still needed to get the generator working. They would need to deal with the fallout from the Lyle brothers, one of whom's death would be difficult to explain. And even then, assuming they got past that and Denny didn't come out seeking revenge, Brett had an uphill battle to climb, though the specialists had been optimistic about everything except Gideon and Trish's ability to pay for the necessary care.

But whatever might be ahead for them, Gideon knew the woman seated beside him would make it survivable.

They couldn't afford to fail.

And Trish wouldn't let them.

THE TWO O'CLOCK KILLER

NIZ THOMAS

THE TWO O'CLOCK KILLER

AN ORIGINAL CRIME STORY

ONE

Stimble stretched out in his silver Chrysler sedan. Enjoying the extra legroom of the personal vehicle, having decided against bringing a station-issued one with him to this stakeout. Given he was in a residential area—small but manicured lawns, respectable-looking homes (not exactly your typical stakeout destination)—he hadn't wanted to attract any unwanted attention with something screamed cop.

His gaze had shifted away from the single-level house tucked into the corner lot and toward admiring his vintage Patek Philippe Nautilus watch, rubbing his fingers along the scuffed leather band and the patina at the edges of the round face, absentmindedly thinking about when his Daddy had given it to him all those years ago.

Thinking about the past. And about new chapters. Standard for a stakeout where your mind doesn't have much else to do but wander.

His reverie was broken when his bird—that's what he called his phone—chirped on his hip.

He sat up in the plush driver seat and took the call, keeping one eye on the house. He'd been sitting on it for the last hour, parked just far enough away and in the shadows so if anyone was inside, they couldn't see him move.

"Yeah?"

It was Teddy, his partner. Lead detective on this case. On most cases. Some people called Teddy the Beagle, on account of his eager pursuit of all things investigative. Teddy was the kind of guy that took that as a compliment. Stimble was the Robin to his Batman. It suited him just fine.

"I'm twenty-five minutes out from your location," Teddy said as Stimble glanced at his watch. "Got tied up with this creep Anderson."

Anderson was a shady guy, a lead that Stimble told Teddy wasn't worth running down. But Teddy was by the book. And so he had Stimble come out here to the suburbs and sit on this other lead—this Tim Murdoch, who was supposed to be living inside the single-level home—while Teddy checked out Anderson.

"Wasn't him, huh?" If Teddy was still coming here, Anderson wasn't the guy. But Stimble already knew that.

"Don't say I told you so."

Stimble didn't. He'd jab Teddy with it another time. Instead, he said, "It was the clock was missing, wasn't it?"

"You gonna make me put a notice in the paper: *STIMBLE WAS RIGHT*?"

"Maybe just a spot on the radio. A full thirty-second one, though. Don't get all cheap on me."

"Play your lottery numbers, you lucky bastard."

"Lucky's better than good, sometimes."

"Smartass. Anything moving on your end?"

"Doesn't look like anybody's home. But I got a hunch about this one." Stimble had done some homework on Murdoch. And he liked him for this. Seemed like he could be the guy they were after.

"Sit tight 'til I get there, huh?" Teddy said.

Stimble clicked off. Looked at the house. Nothing doing.

Lights punctured the dark street. Halogens. Blinders, was what

Stimble called them. Bright white and blue like they were shining down from heaven, last thing you see before you go into the light. Whatever happened to being able to see on the road?

The car approached from the north, like someone coming home for the night. Pulled into the driveway of the house, opened the garage, parked inside next to a wall of neatly arranged power tools. Stimble's eyes finally came to. A blurry figure in the shadows went to the inside garage door and into the house, the outside garage door closing as he did so. Lights went on in the house, then off. On, off. On, off.

Like an SOS.

Stimble exited his vehicle and walked to the door. Neighborhood was quiet, not even any dogs barking. Not surprising for nine-thirty on a Wednesday night. School night. Kids were already supposed to be in bed.

As he walked toward the front door, intentionally stepping on the grass rather than the neatly placed stone walkway, he noticed the low hum of porch lights and the stronger hum of the occasional spotlight in the yards along the street, lighting up front facades with some blinding, garish yellow light meant to make the house look majestic but really just casting odd shadows around the yard.

Tim Murdoch's house didn't have any lights on outside.

Stimble knocked on the door.

More interior lights turned on. Footsteps moved toward the door. The porch light overhead went on.

"Yeah?" Tim Murdoch said, opened the door. Forty-eight. Single white male. Five-nine, one-sixty. No kids, despite the neighborhood. Shaved head. Nothing special, was how Teddy described him to Stimble after pulling his info. Stimble had said it was always the normal ones who turned out to be monsters.

"Detective Stimble." Flashed the badge, watching for that flicker in everybody's eye. The one where they inventory their whole lives, wondering what they did wrong. And why Stimble was on their doorstep.

He loved that flicker.

"Mind if I come in and ask you a couple questions?"

"About what?"

Stimble stepped in. "I'll be asking the questions, Tim."

Murdoch stepped in and out of the way. Not sure what to do.

"Let's talk in the living room," Stimble said, closing the door behind him.

Tim Murdoch obliged him.

"Can I get you anything?"

"Warm water with lemon."

Murdoch looked put off by the request, which made Stimble happy. Eventually, the suspect padded into the kitchen. Glasses started clinking.

Unlike the movies, Murdoch didn't call out over the clinking sounds. Didn't try to make small talk. Which suited Stimble just fine, since he was already checking out the living room.

There wasn't much to the house. Looked about what he'd expected after watching it for hours. Nice but not sprawling. From the living room he had a good (not great) view at twenty-square-feet of backyard, both bedrooms, the office. Only the kitchen and hallway bathroom weren't visible from Stimble's vantage point.

The vintage bulbs were the first thing that caught his attention, though. How could they not, glowing yellow-orange like a collection of dying flames?

They were positioned on a mantle above the room's lone unlit fireplace. Edison bulbs, though those were easy to come by. Just table stakes for collectors, as Teddy had told him after doing a deep dive online. But Murdoch had others. Amber-hued bulbs the shape and size of an avocado. Smoky Chandeliers with twisted, ornamental filament designs.

Tim Murdoch had quite a collection here.

Stimble checked his watch. Ten minutes until Teddy arrived.

This collection was part of the profile, oddly enough. *Obsession with vintage items highly likely—lightbulbs, radios, cars,* was what they'd gotten back from VICAP. After Teddy had found trace elements of tungsten on one of their first victims, they'd narrowed it down to lightbulbs. Was a weird obsession, Stimble knew. Twenty years on the job, never saw it in any profile before.

Wasn't particularly happy to see it in this one.

The rest of the profile—the age, sex, location details—were already hits for Murdoch, which is why Stimble was here in the first place. He and Teddy had basically been working down the list of antique lightbulb collectors since making the connection with tungsten a week and a half ago.

Since that time, there'd been three more victims.

Stimble had been busy.

He'd also been the one to suggest they split up their efforts, try to catch the killer double quick. He'd be happy to leave this all behind him now. It was this case that had him thinking about chapters ending back in the car. And what all might come next.

"My guilty pleasure," Murdoch said from behind him.

Stimble turned. Murdoch was close, almost too close. Definitely uncomfortably close, at least. Stimble grabbed the glass of warm water with lemon from Murdoch.

"The filament bulb, Thomas Edison. The appeal of that time period. The *craftsmanship*, even on the bleeding edge of technology at the time. For some reason that just does it for me, you know?"

"Sure."

Stimble put the cup down on a side table. Gestured for Murdoch to sit down on the couch.

"So what was it you needed to speak to me about, detective?"

The guy was cool, collected. Almost too much so.

"I'm part of the task force tracking down leads on the Two O'Clock Killer," Stimble said, using the obscene moniker the papers had come up with. He didn't like doing it, but it was how the general public knew the guy, so it helped with the shorthand.

"Oh."

"And your name is next up on my list."

"My name?"

"Your name."

"I don't see how that's possible."

"Luckily that isn't part of the criteria we consider."

Murdoch sat forward in his seat. "Listen, officer—"

"—Detective."

"Detective. I don't know a thing about the Two O'Clock Killer, save what I've seen on the news."

Stimble nodded, letting his eyes wander around the rest of the living room. The strange thing about the profile was it had identified three components that likely would lead to the killer. *Likely* being the operative word. Unfortunately, a VICAP workup was as much art as it was science. Just because it said the guy was forty-eight didn't mean he couldn't be forty-six. Five-nine could be five-eleven (though not usually taller than that). It was all more a landing zone than bullseye.

"Would you be surprised to hear that our profile of the killer includes a layman's obsession with applied mathematics?"

Stimble nodded toward the corner of the room. Murdoch had a reading chair setup. Worn-in leather recliner with a side table next to it. One of those arc lamps, bathing the space in a warm, peach-colored glow from the radio-style bulb. Stacked on the floor next to it were mathematics textbooks, as tall from the ground as the armrest of the chair.

Murdoch sat back on the couch, put his arm on the rest. Looked genuinely surprised. "Just because I—"

"You're a numbers guy, I see."

"Not really," Murdoch said. "Mathematics is more than that. A way to think about the world. Logic and reason that underpins the very fabric of our reality."

It was almost as if Murdoch wanted to make Stimble's case for him.

The math stuff was strike two. VICAP said the suspect had a meticulous mind. *Obsession with numbers, logic, mathematics likely.* A mind capable of planning something all the way to the end.

Like a murder. Or ten of them, and counting.

Stimble checked his watch. Five minutes until Teddy arrived. He felt his heart flutter a bit in his chest, his cheeks warm up.

"What is it you're not telling me, Detective?"

Stimble said nothing. Kept his eyes moving around the room. The words from the profile flitted through his mind like fireflies. *Obsessive. Meticulous.*

Murdoch was a surprisingly strong candidate for the Two O'Clock Killer.

Except for one key element.

"Listen, Detective," Murdoch said as he stood up, "I wish I could be of more help."

"I don't think I asked for your help."

Murdoch put his palms up. Surrender, sort of.

Neither of them said anything for several ticks of the clock.

Three minutes until Teddy arrived. Stimble could practically hear the tires on the pavement outside.

"Wait a second," Murdoch said. "If I'm the Two O'Clock Killer, wouldn't there need to be some clocks here? I mean, I've got one over the kitchen sink. A digital one next to the bed. But check the whole house..." Murdoch's mind seemed to be working, trying to play catch-up. A logician's mind. No doubt there.

He was right, though. The lack of a vintage clock collection was problematic. As stupid as Stimble thought the name was, the Two O'Clock Killer got it for a reason. It was another thing from the VICAP report, though Stimble thought that bit of it was fairly obvious.

Ascribes symbolic meaning to time or timekeeping.

"...I hardly even know how to tell the time on a clock..."

The Two O'Clock Killer left behind some type of time-keeping device at every kill scene. A clock. A sundial.

A watch.

"...so you see, I couldn't possibly be him."

"I think you'll do just fine, Tim."

Murdoch stared back questioningly.

Stimble pulled out his service weapon and shot him in the chest.

Murdoch fell back onto his couch but missed, fell onto the floor. Gasping for breath. His hands were up near his chest, as if trying to plug the leaking air hole.

Stimble checked his watch. One minute until Teddy arrived.

He bent over Murdoch's body as he faded away on the floor.

"You almost checked all the boxes, Tim." Stimble closed his eyes, letting the familiar feeling of a job well done wash over him. Felt the triumph of death tingle on his skin.

Murdoch flailed on the ground and gasped for a breath that just wouldn't come.

"I was worried you might not have an acceptable clock, though." He raised his wrist to show Murdoch the Patek.

Recognition in the near-dead man's eyes. Then terror.

Stimble put a gentle finger to the crown and used his nail to pull it out to the second position.

Took a deep inhale, savoring the moment for a single second longer. Not knowing when he might once again feel this. The investigation had gotten too hot, too much attention. And now he'd have to adjust his process to keep this story going.

The Two O'Clock Killer was now dead. Thereabouts at least. Would be a real red flag if he kept killing people same as he'd been doing.

Stimble wound the dial around until the clock face read two o'clock. Wiped his own prints off the thing, not worrying about the DNA that would be excluded for being at the crime scene. Knelt down and slipped it into Murdoch's pocket as the dying man's eyes went wide with protest.

Death's warm embrace ensconced Stimble, smothering Murdoch for eleven more glorious seconds before Teddy banged on the front door. Stimble called him in.

Murdoch's eyes went wide one last time as he saw another officer of the law enter the room. Stimble knew those eyes were dying to scream the truth.

Dying being the operative word.

Teddy took in the scene, gave Stimble a surprisingly calm raise of the eyebrow.

Inside, Stimble felt like he'd just mainlined the high he usually felt from Death. His partner in the room as his victim died was like nothing else he'd ever experienced before. Nirvana of excitement and anxiety.

What if Murdoch ekes out one last word?

What if Teddy somehow reads the room, feels some of Death's juju lingering in the air like summer static just before it rains?

What if Stimble loses it, hops onto Teddy the Beagle like a feral jungle cat and strangled him while mawing at his carotid in a fit of crazed hunger?

Stimble turned back to Murdoch, the man's eyes recognizing the futility of their plight. It was like what Stimble figured it felt like to watch a baby be born, or one of those once-in-a-lifetime comets shoot across the night sky. He could barely contain his inner trembling, less worried now about his victim unmasking him as he was with crying with complete ecstasy at the beauty of this moment.

Stimble took two quiet breaths. When he spoke, he couldn't tell whether this voice was calm or like a ten year old's who just saw his first naked lady.

"He..." his voice trailed off. He wasn't yet ready to speak.

Teddy put a hand on Stimble's shoulder. Did he feel the energy surging through? Like a supercharged electric fence for cattle.

Stimble swallowed. "He made a move," he said again, this time confident his words sounded normal. He shrugged, gestured around the room as if to say, *can you believe that VICAP profile?*

Teddy knelt next to Murdoch and checked his pulse. "He's dead."

Stimble let out a deep, relieved sigh that he had no trouble faking.

"But look at this." Teddy showed him the watch.

"Figured we'd find at least one of them in here, once he got squirrelly."

Teddy shook his head. "Wound to two o'clock and everything. The sick bastard."

Stimble shrugged his shoulders, the high of death beginning to drain from him. Usually it lasted for a while, until it once again got too great for him to keep control over.

After this, though ...

He wasn't sure how much longer he could go through life without feeling this again.

"Wonder what it meant," Teddy said, handing the watch to Stimble to take a look at.

Stimble stared into his Daddy's old watch, memories and emotions flitting around on the dying wave of adrenaline inside his body.

"Whatever it meant," Stimble said, "I guess that chapter's closed now."

And another one would soon open.

NO CONTROL

NIZ THOMAS

NO CON-TROL

ONE

I always liked driving—that nowhere-to-go, nobody-to-see, ambling aimlessly along the highway kind. Cruising, as the young bucks say.

Not for the reasons most people like it, though. Never was so interested in the myth of the "so-called" Open Road™. Don't care to make a cross-country trip, or follow Route 66 straight off into the ocean like an idiot (I'm not even compelled to drive west to California, let alone all the way across country). And I definitely don't need to see the world's largest ball of twine, or whatever other silliness is out there. Driving for me isn't an act of rebellion. I'm not *pulled* away, looking for something better, wanderlust all in my nether parts.

I'm just not built like that. Don't much care about the wind in my hair or the music turned up loud like some high school kid trying to show off at Make Out Point.

My hands are very nearly almost at ten and two. I drive the speed limit. I brake thirty to fifty feet before my turn and most always use my signal. I'm just as comfortable with talk radio as I am with an oldies station—and I frankly don't give a bit of a dang what anybody else thinks about it. The kids can have their fancy satellite radio (I'll never figure that one out) and their MP3s, or whatever the acronym of the day is (heaven forbid they say all the dang words they mean, since everyone knows they're in *Such. A. Rush.* what with their whole dang lives still ahead of them).

I like things traditional. I drove a Ford Taurus, old enough not to have all the silly bells and whistles on it, like seats that shuck and jive like they got dance fever on a Saturday night. Cloth seats, a working air con unit, though I hardly use it much for the improved miles on the gallon, much preferring the fresh air passing through the cabin to keep any funky smells at bay (cloth tends to pick up more than leather). Radio turned only about one-fourth of max-volume, maybe a little less. Low enough where you can hear yourself think, without some ridiculous rumble cube in the trunk rattling your brain like a Rock 'Em Sock 'Em Robot. But not loud enough where anybody in the car (at least in the front seats) feels they want to start talking.

That's another thing I like about driving. It doesn't invite conversation. Not for me, anyhow. When I'm driving, I'm focused on what's ahead of me, even as my brain is off in Who-Knows-Wheres-Ville. The smooth road beneath my treads tends to lull me into a kind of waking sleep.

Which I guess is how I ended up getting pulled over. Too much going on upstairs and not enough attention paid to the road. Because one minute I was thinking on a news report on NPR about how the twenty-six richest people in the world had more loot than over half of the world's population (*twenty-six!*), and the next thing I knew, I had John Joseph Law riding alongside the highway next to me, chirping his siren and bullhorn (which I could hear, since my radio was at a respectable level), flashing his lights, and telling me to pull over.

A bit pushy, I thought, but I figured maybe I had a taillight out or something.

And anyway, I was in no rush to get Mother back.

TWO

You may be wondering what in tarnation you just experienced.

I sure did.

And I'd be working in some kind of other job were it a case I could summarize in a succinct manner, *as the lawyers might say. Maybe I'd be President. Or one of those technology tycoons you see out here from time-to-time. Taking a joyride in their custom Ferraris or McLarens on their way through the mesas and the flat, vast desert strips of road where the speed limits rise until—depending on how far out you go— they disappear altogether. Heading to some of the tranquil places, where you can supposedly feel the auras of the earth. Or, more likely, to take some newfangled designer drugs outside of the public eye, at their villas and compounds.*

Could've been all manner of professions I might have gone into, were I able summarize the above and the below. Or even wrap my head around it.

As I lean back with a creak in my wooden office chair and settle my old bones into the cushion-less seat, the empty hum of a municipal office is all I can hear. The purr of fluorescent light and computer towers—even the lone vending machine. The steady under-

current of volts and data delivered on wires and through the air. A world that not so long ago would have seemed inconceivable. A science fiction.

It's late at night, naturally. In here, where I've got all the lights turned up, you wouldn't know it. My office isn't glamorous. Not situated near any doors or windows, either.

Not that there is any glamour here at all, in the three-room municipal offices of Morristown, Arizona. All of that went to the post office and the school. Technically, Morristown, Arizona doesn't even exist—we are what's known as a census-designated place. Which is a fancy way of saying we are a statistic only. At least in the eyes of the U.S. Government. It's a long and awfully boring subject, but suffice it to say, it means more than a few people live here but we aren't a town or a city or any other sort of incorporated place. We are un-incorporated through and through.

Sounds a bit like the Old West itself. Lawless. Roguish. But it ain't. We're just a patch of chaparral and saguaro nestled directly between a bunch of other, bigger, and more significant places (in the eyes of the U.S. Government, at least). There's a city nearby, called Surprise, that is eventually going to annex us. But they don't seem to be in too big a hurry. And I expect we aren't, either.

And yes, I know what you're thinking. Surprise. Sounds made up. It isn't. Real name for the place. So-named, according to the record books, because the city's founder said she'd be surprised if it ever amounted to much.

But hey, this is Arizona. Where our ancestors were the people too crazy, maladjusted, or ambitious to stay in the areas of the country that already had roads and houses and people. They needed to venture off where it was hot, dusty, and filled with stuff that could kill you quick and painful or slow and miserable. All just to make their way in this life. Me, I just woke up here one day and kept going. They were the ones made the choice.

So yeah, Morristown, isn't much. All 227 of us, in case you were wondering. Lot of stuff we don't have. One of everything else.

If I haven't put you to sleep yet with the history and civics lesson and you want to know more, go ahead and look it up. It's all real.

But that's not what I'm doing here. You want to learn about any of that stuff, there's better teachers than me.

So what am I doing, then? What is it you're trying to say, old man?

Why am I up so late, even despite that it looks like daytime in this room I call an office (which I'm sure might actually exist beneath all the stacks of paper piled atop every visible surface)? Not that the time matters. I know it's late because I feel it in my bones. I'm awake. Alert. Not just because of what I just read, either. Always been a night owl. It suits me.

So maybe that's part of it, what I'm doing. I got access to this file, one of the rarest of rare documents. A monologue of a transcript which I believe to be the closest thing to a genuine tap into another person's thoughts, for all the good and bad of that exercise. About to clear it off the top, file it away in my Done pile, whenever I can find it amidst the rest of the papers. It's a case that still haunts me—though not because of the wild twists and turns in the investigation. This thing was as open-and-shut as it gets.

Like O.J., except the lawyers got it right.

And maybe 'cause it's late and I'm alone, it's got me thinking back to my days in the Scouts. Hiking, camping. Setting up tents for the night, grabbing anything dry enough to burn hot and stay that way against the cold desert nights.

Ghost stories. Only those all made sense.

And they were fake, even if we didn't know it at the time.

This one, I saw the aftermath with my own two eyes. It was all too real for me.

Sorry for sharing, if you think it's too much.

But I always found it was more helpful to know about evil so you can be ready for it.

Much better than it walking in your midst, you unsuspecting, and it comes for you before you even understand what is going to happen.

THREE

Rolling my window down was like opening a hatch to a coal-fired pizza oven, only without the inherent delicious promise. Outside my window was the currant-dusted landscape of the desert along Route 74. Rolling hills and distant mountains looming like geeks at a high school dance.

The cop sure took his time getting out of his car. Me and him, we went through the whole rigamarole of exchanging paper and pleasantries and then he said, "Sir, do you have anything in your trunk?"

His voice cracked when he said it, the way a teenage boy's might. He seemed tentative, standing arm's length from the car and sorta behind me, so I had to lean out the open window and turn all funny. It stretched my back out.

I told him no, which wasn't exactly true (I mean, does anybody have an *empty* trunk?), but I didn't figure any harm in a little white lie.

He gave me a bit of a funny look when I answered. The sort of look he might've made if I told him that aliens existed or I just crudded up my pants. But he didn't say anything further, just walked back to his car in that way all cops did. Self-important like. As if I had all the time in the world to wait on him—though with more pep in his step than on his first mosey to my window.

While he was gone my radio kept talking. War and peace and all the rest of it. I didn't much pay attention (turned the station, actually), and got to thinking about her.

And I guess I should also mention it, since I didn't before. The thing I like about driving. Got a bit off topic, telling my tastes and preferences when I'm steering in the cockpit of this here vessel. Maybe vessel isn't the right word to describe *my* car—it's pretty Plain Jane, though that's what I like. It's not new, clocking in at fifteen years old. No bells and whistles like the things they're running on down the assembly line today. *Those* are vessels. Spaceships, if you sit in them (which I don't, but I peek inside new cars along the street from time-to-time). Doodads and gadgets and computer screens is the norm these days.

I wouldn't have the faintest idea how to even start the things. Apparently they don't even come with keys.

My taste in vehicles (that's what police call them, did you know? *Vehicles*, not cars) is pretty vanilla, I guess you might say. I like my Ford. Beige, 'cause that was cheapest. Stays cool in the heat. Reflective. Plenty of miles on the thing now, not a single problem since I got her—except the odometer broke, which I actually find soothing. Something about the numbers cranking higher and higher raised my blood pressure. Distracted me from the driving. If it hadn't broke, I probably would have broke it myself, honestly.

I looked up in the rearview. The cop was out of his car—I mean, his *vehicle*—and had the radio held in front of his mouth. The little tangled phone cord was pulled tight, like when you try to take a phone call from your kitchen line in the toilet.

He was tense, this cop, I could tell that much. Young fella, clean-shaven (or maybe he wasn't even up to shaving yet). Knees bent a little bit, shoulders hunched forward. Ready to strike, was the phrase ran through my mind.

His other hand (the one not holding the little radio) rested on his hip, right by his gun. Gunslinger, was another phrase ran through my mind. But this here gunslinger wasn't liable to in any matinee anytime soon. He was anxious. Hesitant. Almost like he was ready to do something but wasn't entirely sure how to go about it. Maybe didn't want to do anything without backup. The sort of gunslinger in the TV movies who got dead real quick, before they even hit the first commercial break.

I couldn't tell what he was saying—nor did I much care, under-stand—but I was getting a little tired of waiting. I didn't set out that afternoon to drive across Route 74 from northwest Phoenix out to Morristown and back again to be sitting on the side of the road, watching all the other drivers enjoy themselves and me just sit tight like a bump on a log.

No sir.

The cop turned away, looking somewhere behind him. A millisecond after, I heard what he must have heard.

A pandemonius symphony of destruction.

On brass: a big, metallic crunch somewhere behind us. Then another.

On strings: a half-dozen car horns, joined together in eerie symphony.

On percussion: A few tons of metal slamming into something hard and immovable, but still organic in some way. Something that seemed "of the earth," if you will.

It sounded like a Big Bad Accident, the kind of thing that would make the news. Certainly the sort of thing that would make a commuter about pull his hair out before he even got home. Imagine that—busting your hump all day at a job you don't like, then finally settling into your car afterwards, sweat still on your brow, a chafe developing along your underwear line, with one, lone goal in mind. Getting home. Home, home on the range. That illustrious, far-off place just out of your reach. Because of the Big Bad Accident, you can't even make it bless-ed on home, for crying out loud. You just sit, and sit, *and sit*, and ... well, you get the idea ... traffic building up in front of you, behind you, emergency vehicles riding up along the shoulder (all important-like, taking priority), flashing lights as the sun settles behind the horizon for the night, the bruise-purple sky turning to red-and-blue flashing amidst the dark vastness of outer space. All the while, you're just itching to get out, *get ANYWHERE* but inside your danged car. You want to be home. You need to be home. Out of your clothes. Into the shower. Crack into a few drinks (oh please tell me we're not out of the strong stuff) so you can hopefully get to sleep, since you're now so jacked-up with fury about a thirty-minute drive taking you ninety minutes. All so you can go ahead and do it again the next night day.

And all because some fool didn't bother to pay attention to what he was doing. Probably had the radio turned up too loud.

The cop's back was to me now. At least, was to my rearview mirror, which was how I was looking at him. So take that for whatever it's worth. It's just to say that I had a good (albeit mirrored) look at what happened next.

Poof. A silent picture in eyeball-shattering technicolor film. A fireball like something out of Dresden plumed up into the sky. It took another millisecond and then the sound of the explosion rocked my car practically down to the studs (not really, but that's how it felt). I felt the heat wave through the open window, even though the flames didn't get anywhere near me. I bet that cop's face was redder than a Jersey tomato, though.

The cop dropped his little microphone. Both hands went instinctively to the top of his head like he couldn't believe his eyes. He probably couldn't, come to think of it. He hadn't handled my situation particularly well. It was fine for me (heck, the last thing I needed was for the Police Detective of the Year to pull me over). But looking back, it wasn't by the book even a little bit. Lot of rookie mistakes, I must say. A young fella, too. And his awkward tone—unsure and lacking in confidence. You know they say this generation coming up is pretty soft. Too much coddling from their mamas.

I believe it. Every word of it.

FOUR

Up to this point, every word in this transcript is true. Sounds crazy, I know. But that accident did really happen. That cop really was a rookie. And he plum didn't know how to handle the situation.

I'm only a half-cop, really (since we are un-incorporated) and even I know that.

But that accident was some sort of act of God. Why God would have any say in letting this scenario go on any longer, I haven't the faintest. Could have had that car crash happen another hundred yards up the highway and it would have taken out the right guy, in my opinion. Made everybody's lives a whole lot easier. Especially mine, since here we are ten years later and I'm still dealing with the paperwork.

But like I said, the importance is in the telling. No clue what other sort of darkness exists out there in the world. Probably some that's buried even deeper than this all was. Hidden so deep inside that even a transcript of a man's last words wouldn't be enough to dig it out.

That's the sort of darkness we all need to be vigilant about.

But it's the brazenness of this case that scares me. And hopefully scares you, too, else you might want to get yourself looked at.

Evil exists, folks.
Don't say I didn't warn you.

FIVE

The pipsqueak of a cop was framed perfectly in my rearview. Hands overhead. What I'm sure was a mouth that could be described as *extremely ajar*.

Behind him was the big kahuna of car wrecks, I'd bet. Saw it later in the papers. A fiery blast from Hades, is what it was.

Reminded me of a show I watched once about active volcanoes all over the world. You know how many of them there are? Fifteen hundred. That's fifteen hundred chances around this globe that could end all life as we know it. Or at least end paradise, since so many resorts and beaches are within spitting distance of the dang things. The most beautiful things come at a price, I guess. But you get a big enough 'cano, the thing could spit so much ash into the sky to make the first Ice Age look like a weekend trip to Death Valley in July.

All that pent-up rage and raucous energy, simmering beneath the surface. Earth, the mean-spirited parent who whips on their kids a little too quickly. Or doesn't bother to say they're disappointed, just goes on and leaves them at the department store after they've been bad.

And it just *flows* beneath the surface, like. Some kind of subter-

ranean river of hot lava and coal ash, ready to spew if even the teensi-
est, tiniest little thing gets out of place. A reckoning from up high and
delivered from down below. And not a dang thing anybody on this
planet could do to stop it.

All out of our control.

But I guess that's how it goes sometimes. Control isn't given,
it's taken. Thinking of it in those terms was a little depressing,
really.

So I decided to take me some right there.

I flipped my ignition from park to drive. Punched my foot dang
near through the floorboards. Peeled out, burning rubber like a South
American tire tycoon, back before the WTO got involved (don't get
me started on what that evil cabal of jerks had done to cripple us
regular folks here back home, those Ivy League, ivory tower sons of
crud).

The screech of tire against the loose rock as my trusty Ford struggled for purchase atop the pavement of the highway's shoulder was
even louder than the explosion. My car fishtailed, back sliding from
left to right and back again as I shot, bug-eyed and bushy-tailed, back
into the slow lane of traffic, which by now was like pickup day at the
nursing home, folks looking all over tarnation and nobody focused on
the road ahead.

In the rearview, the cop barely even got his head around from the
explosion before I could no longer see him.

On my left side, a hideous red convertible honked and screeched
out of the way, causing a ripple of other cars to do the same. I saw
most of that in my side view mirror, having been too excited to get
back going again to check for oncoming traffic.

That was when Mother almost rolled off the passenger seat,
spilling onto the floor in front like I was taking a pizza home and had
to stop short.

I reached across—still quick, but not as spry as I used to be—and
palmed her head, stopping it from rolling onto the floor in front of
me. Her tongue lolled out from between her lips, eyes knocking

around inside her skull like a couple of marbles dropped into a tank of petroleum jelly.

I kept one hand steady on the wheel as this all happened. Not sure who or what else I might have disrupted, as far as traffic patterns go, but I was able to careen my trusty old sedan back into a straight line of traffic. My dalliance with reckless driving was over.

It was once again just me and the road.

And her.

I guess maybe I should mention about her now. Only, maybe not, on account of what happened next.

I couldn't quite say how much more time passed between when I pulled off the start line from where the cop pulled me over and when the boys in blue finally caught back up to me. Sorta like how it went before I got pulled over, I guess. One minute I was zoning (this time on a sweet jag of smooth jazz tunes) next thing you know, I heard helicopter blades overhead. Of course, it was because my radio wasn't turned so loud, so I could hear them even before I saw them. But they came into view eventually, riding on a perpendicular route across the highway. Plain as day. Impossible to miss. Like the cavalry coming into town. The 'copter must have banked around or something, because its rotors deadened against the hum of the road, and it banked up and out of my vision. I knew it was still up there somewhere, but the road took over in my perception.

It took some additional number of minutes before I saw the rest of the law. Riding and rumbling up behind me on the highway like a scene out of *Mad Max*, only these fellas were keeping their distance. Like that was doing anything. It felt like we were the only people driving across the earth. The planet's curve creating a subtle horizon line that the police stayed just ahead of. Me setting the front of the line. Blazing forward like Christopher Columbus.

I checked the mirror one last time, trying to count them all. Six of their cars (excuse me, vehicles) in total, that I could make out. All lined up one next to the other, charging up the highway behind me like Valkyrie storming the gates. Likely another row of them just behind the first, so we'll call it an even twelve. At least that's how I woulda done it.

The boys in blue must have called ahead or something because once I hit the next exit, the rest of the traffic was practically nil. No cars going on the highway in either direction. Each diversion off the highway marked by a single police vehicle parked perpendicular to the exit or entrance, blocking entry or exit. Real disrespectful to any of the lunks trying to get home from work, but I suppose John Joseph Law doesn't much care about that.

I'll tell you. As someone who appreciates a nice drive, I sure as heck found it to be a pleasant experience.

None of those low rider grease mobiles or the ridiculous trucks with spotlights and gun racks and thirty-five inch tires—the blacked-out, middle-finger-sticker-plastered, Punisher-mobiles that looked like they rolled off the front lines of the war (almost twenty years and still at it, no wonder the taxes are so damn high; surprised more of the top twenty-six richest aren't involved in warfare as their business, though I expect all those fellas had long ago gone private, took their names out of the proverbial running and decided to do laps in their swimming pools filled with money—but I digress ...).

No, after a while, it was just me and the highway. The subtle asphalt curve of this world. Tire tread grip making sure I didn't leave and enter orbit.

I couldn't imagine a better feeling.

And now that I've had some time to reflect on it, I think I know why.

See, the thing I like about driving is *the control*. Just me, the steering wheel, and a couple tons of steel shooting around the road like one of those NORAD missiles.

Only I got the control of it, not some bureaucrat out in Washington.

I might not have been the brightest bulb in the shed, nor the richest farmer in Kansas. There were way more than twenty-six folks who had more money than I'd ever be able to count to. But when I got my mitts on a steering wheel and my puppies started getting heavy with lead, there wasn't a single place else I wanted to be—police-chase be damned, I say.

I turned in my seat, let one hand fall from the wheel. This was Easy Street now, I figured. No real harm getting a little lazy. It was all over for me, in a manner of speaking, so no real reason to be playing it safe. No cars around me, nothing but a straight shot for as far as I wanted to go before taking a leap.

Or maybe I'd already taken one.

Mother was next to me.

I guess it's finally time I should mention her. She is the reason I'm in here in the first place, I suppose. Let's see ... yeah, I guess. I already told you about the driving and the cops and the explosion. And I explained about control, too. That's important. And later on, I'll mention about the preacher.

So, who was she?

Mother. Next to me.

At least, the part of her I'd been most keen of.

Mother was always a rush of energy. A life force. Not the sort of person you could ignore, no matter how old she was—and I was old enough to make her pretty doggone old. The life force of any party she went to. Beautiful. Modern, yet classic. As sharp a dresser as she was a tongue-lasher if you didn't mind your manners. Hair always done perfectly, not a strand out of place. Like she lived inside a magazine ad for hair products. She was a supernova dressed like a star. My sun. And just like the sun, as capable of ending the hopes and dreams of so many—and just as quickly and ruthlessly as that gaseous ball in the sky, should she become disturbed in her celestial perch.

Mother was nobody to trifle with. You could ask Father, only he's dead.

And yet—what would you call what I'd just done with her?

I guess I'll get plenty of time to think on the right word for it.

The easy way out would be for me to say it was all Mother's fault. That I was raised like this. That maybe what I'd done, she'd had coming. I think some of those things are true. Maybe all of them. But there was something else, too, that was important.

And I think it all comes back to control.

We'd been taking our normal Thursday drive. On up the highway from Mother's nursing home (and may the Good Lord Jesus forget all the aspersions she cast upon me when I put her in that place! And it wasn't like I locked her up and threw away the key, either. The facility had not one, but *two* golf courses for crying out loud!) to a little roadside cafe she liked (but referred to as a "trashy diner"). Rita's, was the name of it. She insisted we go each and every Thursday. There could be nowhere else. It was a place that, frankly, didn't suit her gravitas or her tastes.

But then again, she said she made us go there because it fit my own.

Rita's was empty, as it usually was. To describe it as a shoe box would be overselling it. More like a tin can. Shaped like one, too. In fact, that was part of what always confused me about it. You see all over the fancy cable TV networks (which I don't watch, but Mother always had on in her home whenever I went to pick her up) a real resurgence in this country for shipping containers. You've seen them. Corrugated steel siding. The kind of thing carried behind a giant eighteen-wheeler truck, or on the deck of a cargo ship. Literally just a metal box meant to protect whatever was inside from the elements. These days, apparently, people set them down in their yards and paint 'em, decorate 'em, set out furniture. Whatever other silliness you can do to make people forget they're inside a box that used to carry fertilizer from China to the Eastern Bloc, or cheap plastic toys from India to Canada, or whatever else needed to be transported from one place to the next. Maybe humans, smuggled overseas by some European organized crime syndicate. I don't know. But anyway, the idea is that people "reclaim" this crap and "recycle" it, as a way to be trendy. Which is to say, we used to aim a little higher in this country—didn't take trash out of the dump, put some lipstick on it, and call it the prom queen.

And it's a wonder why the next generation is so soft. Maybe it's a blessing I'm getting a breather from all of it. Doesn't seem like my viewpoint is much represented these days, anyway.

But what confused me most about the place was that it was *spherical*. It wasn't a shipping container. Not like the ones you see on the TV, anyway. More like a giant oil drum. Or a septic tank. Repurposed, I guess (it didn't *smell* like a septic tank, but looking at it, you could occasionally get a whiff). But from the apparent age of Rita's, I had a sense they didn't decide on this major architectural decision to be trendy.

Maybe a giant tin can was all they could afford.

Rita, or whoever, had done a decent enough job of dressing the place up on the inside. Cut a few holes in the siding that passed for windows. A long acrylic counter hugged one wall, stationary barstool seats with vinyl coverings. Another half-dozen booths hugged the other wall, ostensibly four-tops, but unless you were a little person, you weren't comfortably sitting beside anybody in those booths. It was the sort of place where they don't set down the placemats down until you sit. A table in the corner had three people at it, the third being a child (and even he looked miffed at the lack of space).

So, go figure.

The clientele was trucker-chic, with a sprinkle of underprivileged long-distance drivers, probably heading to-and-from Mexico looking for work (something that, in this old bird's opinion, should be celebrated instead of denigrated in this country, for crying out loud). A few regulars, which is to say, people that lived around there. Desert people, I guess you might call them.

I'd never seen the table with the kid before. But they didn't exactly look like the Rockefellers stopped in from off the highway on their way to Disney.

We'd had lunch, Mother and I, as we usually did. We'd been going there long enough where neither of us needed to consult the menu.

Pancakes and eggs for me (they called it the Flapjack Friendly

Breakfast), side of grapefruit juice. For mother: black coffee and a heavy extra helping of disrespect and nasty comments.

"Still wearing those ugly glasses, I see. They make your face look like it wants to get punched."

"Eighty-nine years old, Mother, and your vision is still holding up. Cause for celebration, I think."

"Not from my angle, it isn't."

Mother was always a conversational marvel.

She simply stirred her spoon against the porcelain of the coffee mug, perfectly coiffed hair (not a single patch of thinning, the devil!), watching the black vortex of hot liquid.

Watching me.

"Have you seen the sun recently? You live in Arizona and you can't even *say* suntan."

To which I said, "I work in an office, Mother. You remember work, don't you? Oh, that's right, you just lived off Dad's insurance money."

"Pancakes with that flabby belly. Should we take you shopping for new clothes after this? I saw a double-XL store back off the highway."

To which I said, "How about a scarf for you, too? I could shove it right on down that throat, Mother."

At least that's what I think I said. Honestly, some of it got a little fuzzy after that.

The next thing I knew, I was cruising back down the highway, looking for a channel on the radio dial. I knew it was then that everything came through, became clear, metastasized, if you will, because Mother (who always *always* ALWAYS talked incessantly when we drove to the diner) hadn't said a single word the whole drive. It had let me fall into the predictable low-fi pattern of my mind wandering off from me as the road extended on beneath my treads, soothing me off into the land of driving.

First, there was the preacher station. I don't much like those. Too much hot air and shame for my taste, sprinkled on awfully heavy.

Like salt on the takeout Chinese food. Though at the time, I let the fired-up Bible thumper talk for a while. Probably because Mother was so quiet, it wasn't so bad hearing this phlegmatic man wax poetic about the Power of Christ™ and how all of us heathens were headed for a fiery, everlasting death if we didn't get with the program.

"And what's the program, you think, Mother?" I said this out loud —I remember that much. Breaking my own rule of the road. Just because I wanted to hear the silence of her lack-of-response.

True to my expectations, she didn't say a word. Not a peep. Not even a nod of the head (thought, admittedly, that was a little hard to gauge under the circumstances- a bump in the road created some confusing head movements).

Instead, the preacher kept on with his fire-and-brimstone pitch, and by now, I was getting into it. Fired up myself, with no particular reason behind it and nowhere else to take my frustrations other than the road ahead. My apparent swift act of ... justice? ... hadn't relieved all the pent-up aggression of years and years of abuse from that woman. So I punched down the gas, let the Ford Taurus live up to its celestial namesake and gallop us on down the paved road toward Hell.

And wouldn't you know it, that was exactly where it took me.

Because the only other thing I remember, really, if I'm being honest, was that somewhere in that pious screed disseminated across the good ol' airwaves (here I wonder: do they have the word of God in the satellites?), the answer to my question to Mother was answered.

And I quote:

"And let me tell you, unwashed ladies and gentlemen of the afternoon, if you are listening to this—if you *ARE REALLY LISTENING* —then God Himself has deigned to smile upon you this fine day. Yes children, you should feel God inside of you. Let him get all up in there. Because you are bad, bad, capital-B Bad boys and girls. You must give penance or risk living the rest of your miserable, SOILED lives as part of the legion of darkness that the Great Satan has cultivated since Time Immemorial. And yet—there is another way.

"Because ladies and gentlemen of the Sinful Jury, I stand before you today, a Servant and Counselor to the Lord and Savior Jesus Christ, and I offer you this one FINAL CHANCE at Absolution. And if I may be honest with you children—and I hope we've built enough trust in one another now that I will do exactly that—I must keep mine own-self from breaking one of the Ten Commandments at this very moment. Perhaps let that be a lesson to you: Sinners never prosper. And Satan—all curses be upon him—never quits. For now, I am actually feeling quite ENVIOUS of you. You at home, or you in your car, or you at work. You who is LI-STEN-ING. And why should I be envious, dear children? What have I to envy from a group of Sinners, those too blind to have not yet taken the salvation that Christ has, in his beneficently glorious wisdom, bestowed upon you?

"Because you have this one moment to save yourself. Or forever it may be that Satan can claim you as one of His Own.

"So praise be this opportunity. And make concrete your commitment to the Lord and Savior Himself, by calling this toll-free number and making a donation to the Army of Christ ..."

I remember smacking that steering wheel right then. "I told you it was coming, Mother."

Only she never said a damn thing again.

SIX

The funny thing—if you can say anything about the whole affair was funny—was that all that spilled out of Jeffery Aaron Jackson's mouth in response to the state-appointed administrator asking if the convicted had any last words.

As you can see, there was no contrition. Nor any attempt to at least plead innocence. I'm not even sure you could call it an excuse.

It was nothing more than a fictitious world spilled forth from inside of him and onto an unsuspecting (and, from my experience in this world, woefully unprepared to deal with this sort of problem) public.

Part of the reason I thought it worthwhile to tell this story aloud.

Used to be a time in this country when even the most heinous crimes and criminals never exceeded a certain level of indignity and savagery. They were bad. But they weren't casually bad. They didn't separate their parents' heads from their bodies and take them for a little joyride.

Not that I can remember, at least.

How I ended up here, well that's a story that might be less interesting than the history of my town. Suffice it to say, nobody wanted to touch this case with a thirty-foot pole. And since our jurisdictional boundaries are fuzzy at best, that meant I was in charge of the case. Nobody but me gave it much thought after that.

Not until the evidence was in, that is.

I'll admit, something about the gruesome nature of the killing shook me in my bones. I worked everything perfect. Even took a few books out of the library (the one over in Surprise—pretty well stocked) about murder case work and forensic procedure. Might have been that nobody else gave a damn about the case, but I wanted to work it clean and put that creep away in a dark cell and throw away the key.

Turned out, I might have done too good a job. When I handed the thing into the County District Attorney, his eyes went bright like I just put the lucky quarter into his slot machine. I didn't know him well (no district attorney before or since has taken much interest in Morristown, since we can't vote him in or out of office and there isn't much in the way of sensational crime cases), but could tell straight away he was an ambitious one. And he was pretty good at the sort of political math you needed to make it big in his line of work:

+ A slam-dunk forensics case

+ A criminal with no political clout or standing to push back

+ The murder of a woman over the age of 70

= A straight shot to the lethal injection chamber

And here in Arizona, voters are two things, if they are nothing else: charged up over executions, and often on the wrong side of the halfway mark of their lives.

The case practically ran itself. And the District Attorney almost landed in the Governor's seat before the judge even made his ruling.

I'm sure most everyone associated with that circus has moved on to bigger and better things.

Can't much in this life get any worse.

Me, I'm set to at least move on to better, but given our standing here in Morristown, likely not a whole lot bigger.

And that's just fine.

Moving on from that case once and for all will be like waking from a long, recurring nightmare with assurance from the Sandman that such horrors will no longer plague you.

That's enough for me.

Just as soon as I find that darned Done pile.

SLOW BURN

slow burn
[slo bern] *noun*

----

a story that builds in anticipation and tension through, capped by an
explosive revelation or climax

LANE CHANGE

WRITERS OF THE FUTURE AWARD FINALIST

NIZ THOMAS

LANE CHANGE

AN ORIGINAL CRIME STORY

ONE

As far as Arthur was concerned, some things about Miami didn't feel like they'd ever change. Top of mind at the moment was the fact that the city was crawling with scumbags who deserved far worse than Fate (or whatever one believed in) seemed capable of doling out.

One thing that *was* different, though–and something Arthur could really get behind–was that snipers never had it this good.

Arthur was in the prone position on his belly, floating in opulent luxury aboard his thirty-meter yacht just offshore Downtown Miami's coast. It was late-October after the hurricanes had drifted out of everybody's consciousness and the temperature was just as perfect as you could imagine–especially now in the early evenings.

Conditions were so perfect–both for comfort and for what Arthur was there to do–that he would hardly need to account for much to ensure a smooth, accurate shot.

The veranda of the Masquiatt Grille was centered on a long cement outcropping which jutted into the dark downtown Miami water like a short chin, the waves of the unprotected shoreline lapping against the faded and erosion-smooth concrete like tired kitten paws against their owner's calves.

Arthur noted the falling sun—a problem at the moment as it descended just above the roof of the Masquiatt, a red Spanish tile slant which covered much of the veranda in a long shadow punctuated only by fingers of blinding light leaking through toward the veranda, the water, and most crucially, Arthur's vantage. The sun's light was blood orange and red as it leaked through alleyways on either side of the restaurant and a sliver of space in the roof that had crumbled long ago into the sea, never to be replaced, giving the place a certain Mediterranean flair.

Picturesque, no doubt.

But for Arthur, it was little more than a blinding nuisance. And so he settled in to do what all successful snipers did better than anyone.

Wait.

The Grille was not crowded but nor was it hurting for patrons. Ten tables on the veranda, eight full, one two-top open with a pending couple at the hostess stand deciding on indoor or outside dining. They'd be wise to take it inside, Arthur thinks (they're wearing white in an area soon to encounter a forecast of pink mist), but he just watches as the woman hems and haws and finally decides it's just divine out and why not watch the water while they dine?

That's alright. After all, Miami dry cleaners have plenty of practice with far worse stains than what's in store for that couple.

The restaurant serves fish, of course, though it has no smell to Arthur. It wouldn't fry anything—heavens no, not with this lean, beautiful clientele—but Arthur had no sense for how anything else might be prepared. He might be able to smell a fry kitchen from here, but fresh fish prepared well? No chance unless the limp wind picked up and did a one-eighty. Grilled halibut? Smoked salmon? Butter-roasted cod? Impossible for him to say from this distance. But what he was here to do didn't leave him with much appetite.

A quick scan of the tables could tell him, but Arthur knows this was not the sort of detail that would help him in this situation.

Whether they were eating fish and chips or diamond-encrusted caviar mattered not.

All that mattered was what he was there for.

There, of course, was a bit of a relative term. The restaurant was *there*. Arthur was somewhere else. Four hundred thirty-three yards away on his yacht called *Terminal*, elevated roughly ten feet from the water and six feet from the front of the concrete chin (depending on how high or low the light chop of waves beneath *Terminal* kept the ship in their buoyant embrace).

Arthur lay flat. Hidden in the folds of the ship, so to speak, though not overly so. Anyone on land doing countersurveillance would likely have seen him without much trouble. Wearing clothes– white linen pants and a white seersucker shirt–on a yacht off the shores of Miami would be the first tip-off. Most wore skimpy speedos or thong bikinis or absolutely nothing at all. Even people who were as aged as Arthur, though he kept in far better shape than nearly everyone twenty years younger (often–and this was a sad fact for humanity at large, but certainly down here in Miami–the older and in-worse-shape-one got around here, the less they gave a hoot what others thought, so you got some *really* interesting clothing choices from people dressed like they weren't just angry at the rest of the world, but in fact wanted to maim and to injure the psyches of those they came into contact with by providing a free, unsolicited show that nobody wanted to see).

The other tip for the discerning viewer, aside from Arthur's clothes, would likely be the very cleverly named M2010 Enhanced Sniper Rifle steadied atop its included bipod and set on a piece of white rubber car floor mat Arthur had procured from an auto body shop that catered to the high-end cars (for most places, though not necessarily for Miami). Arthur had gotten the floor mat especially for this occasion, and bought the good stuff to ensure the rubber legs of the bipod did not come into contact with the fiberglass of his boat. Despite the bipod's rubber legs, there was always a chance of slip-page against such a perfectly shined surface as this yacht. Any floor mat would have done that fine, but the good stuff–thick, rubberized, and coated for all elements–would hold better against the fiberglass, even if a storm moved through and produced humidity or precipitation. The rifle was also pressed tight against the fleshy part of Arthur's shoulder for stability when firing.

If he took his shot, it wasn't going to miss because it slipped from his grip.

So either the clothes or the roughly five-foot-long rifle would make it so anybody paying attention would know something nefarious was afoot atop the *Terminal*.

But nobody was. Paying attention, that is.

Nobody had any reason to.

Arthur glassed the veranda and the surrounding area. Counter-surveillance did not concern Arthur. And not because he was careless–though a *strong* case could be made that not taking the time to properly canvas the kill zone prior to getting himself lined up for this shot was as careless as one in Arthur's position could get. The World's Strongest Man sort of strong case.

Arthur just didn't think the scumbag twenty-something kid had much in the way of funds, operational background, or lived experiences for security. Certainly not the sort of security that could deter a sniper team with the sort of experience aboard *Terminal*. Nation states and the highest levels of wealth had failed to stop them. And so Arthur didn't figure this kid–though surely privileged from birth–possessed the sort of resources to prove dangerous.

He sure had enough in the way of funds for this dinner, or for the club he would inevitably hit afterwards, or the late-night spot after that. Maybe not yet enough for a yacht like Arthur's, but from what Arthur knew of the kid, that hadn't ever stopped him from enjoying himself. *Rich thoughts, rich life.*

The prick.

Being enmeshed in genocidal geopolitical situations abroad, in civil wars, in counterinsurgencies hadn't bothered Arthur.

But something about this bastard prick kid sure did.

No—not *something*. Just the one truth that rose far above all the rest of the things Arthur knew about this lowlife scoundrel.

Sometimes it only takes the one thing before you can say for sure somebody deserves to die.

A multi-faceted existence be damned.

While his temperament was hot, the gentle breeze coming from his back did make things more palatable from a comfort standpoint. Low humidity on the day. Unusual for Miami. Arthur's hands were dry, his brow free of any dripping sweat or cracked skin. Not like most of the places he'd pulled the trigger from. He could even still smell the citrus lotion he'd applied earlier this morning, which someone managed to cling to his skin all these hours later without being even the slightest bit greasy. He would need to tell the wife that she'd made a fine selection for his birthday present this year. Fine indeed.

"You're having second thoughts?" Right on time and on target, as he would expect. The soft voice came from just beside Arthur on the ship's deck, so quiet that had he been any less keyed up, he might have thought he imagined it. As it was, when Arthur took to his rifle, his senses amplified all the way to eleven. He often felt he could hear the heartbeat of his target despite them never being closer than a few hundred feet. Out here on the water, it was actually sort of nice because the water allowed for him to more or less tune everything out as being nonessential for this shot.

"No," Arthur said, though he knew the words coming from Maggie were never spoken without purpose—especially not in a situation where guns were hot, so to speak.

Maggie did not move beside him (her ability to stay still was legendary), but Arthur *felt* her shift, emotionally speaking, as if preparing for something. "You should be, if you aren't. I certainly am."

"Well *that* is exactly what I was hoping to hear before putting my finger on the trigger."

"He's a kid, Artie." Maggie was the only one who could get away with calling him that. And even just that use of the pet name, something she'd been using since their first date all those years ago, was enough to raise the hackles on the back of his neck and arms. Back then, he'd almost walked out of the date entirely. Were it not for Maggie's impenetrable blue eyes, her amazing beauty, and the moxie to not just call him Artie, but to then double down and call him that again once he told her not to, then Arthur would have left the intimate jazz bar in Paris they'd selected as their first date venue and never looked back. In the intervening twenty-seven years, Maggie had loosened up on her use of *Artie*, but she'd never truly given it up. He could still keep steady aim and fire a perfectly placed round through this prick kid's forehead from three times as far away as he was right now, but use of the name *Artie* made that more difficult.

And Maggie would know that.

Maggie *did* know that.

"Kids are innocent, Maggie. Kids are *good*. You think this animal is either of those things?"

"Already fully 'othered' him? Impressive." There was no audible tone in the quiet of her voice, so maybe Arthur imagined it or projected it, but he felt like he heard his own wife shed some respect for him in the span of five words.

"Othering" someone was a term that he and Maggie both used, one that gave credence to something that every leader of men (and women) in combat had known since time immemorial: that it was easier to kill something who you thought of as *less than* human. It was a dark reality of the art of the sniper or the soldier or the hitman that they look at the craft of taking another's life as both a job (to be done professionally) and a service (to make the world better). Othering helped to make the latter more palatable. It allowed people like Arthur and Maggie to sleep at night, knowing they themselves were not monsters, but just people operating in an unjust and nasty world. Ridding the world *of* monsters, really.

Anybody who didn't need a little help on that front wasn't fit for this type of work. Too sociopathic, too thirsty for blood. A person like that might like this type of work, but nobody else in their right mind would want to work with someone like that.

Arthur chose to ignore her comment. "And another thing: kids are supposed to be protected from the world. By their parents, other adults, the world at large. Goddamn if everybody isn't wearing a big fat failure chain around their necks that this *kid* is walking around upright, sitting at his high-end restaurant ready to take in a fine dining experience. You think *he* needs protection, Maggie?"

Maggie said nothing.

"I didn't think so," Arthur said, pointlessly spiking the argument ball like a 'roided-up D-lineman who just picked up a fumble and took it back to the house. And for good measure: "There's someone I know who needed protection from him. That's for damn sure."

It wasn't usual that a husband and wife operated as sniper and spotter. Was, in fact, highly *un*usual. But that was how it went with Arthur and Maggie.

And sometimes that meant little spats like this one when they were out on a job.

Though this wasn't *exactly* a job, was it?

Arthur took a breath in through his nose and held it for the slightest of moments, steadying himself as the boat continued its gentle rock on the quiet ocean water. Box breathing. In for four, hold for four, out for four, hold for four. The ritual of it calmed him.

He had to focus if he was going to do this right.

And Arthur never did anything any other way.

But laying here glassing down this kid, something didn't feel right. Even though it felt *good* in this moment to think about the .300 Winchester Magnum cartridge enter and exit this prick's chest cavity, sending his innards on a mad scramble for the exit the same way an airplane passenger's body would if somebody threw open the emergency exit at thirty-five thousand feet–it still didn't feel *right*.

And that was where Arthur was experiencing a bit of dissonance.

Maggie had picked up on it. Was obviously feeling it herself. Gave voice to it, too.

Arthur, on the other hand, used his rather common male skill of ignoring this feeling, putting it away to fester and smolder like kindling.

And he plunged forward with his pre-shot preparation.

"Wind?" he asked Maggie.

Typically Jane-on-the-spot in terms of immediate response, Maggie hesitated.

"C'mon. We're not going to do this the whole time, are we?"

Maggie said nothing.

"I know you're used to being in charge," Arthur said, referring to the common misconception of The Sniper as either lone wolves or God-level force multipliers. The truth was, when they were in the field and he was behind the gun, Maggie was the team leader. Sniper teams were certainly lonelier than most other units and they could multiply the forward operating element's power (at least back when they served, before they both went private), but it was a team game between the two of them—and you could even argue it was a scale balanced in favor of Maggie. This time was different since they didn't have any kind of official (or even unofficial) mandate.

This was personal.

"Wind." Not a question this time.

"Hardly any."

Arthur nodded. Not exactly the answer he was looking for, but an answer nonetheless. He concurred with the assessment—the wind was almost negligible today, especially from such a relatively short distance. He adjusted his Leupold M5A2 scope accordingly. It was programmed and dialed-in to such an extent that it would allow him to fire at what appeared to be the prick kid, even though Arthur's rifle would actually be aimed elsewhere. Otherwise there was too much imagination involved. He'd be "aiming" at open space.

"What about humidity?"

"I don't think we should do this," Maggie said with a measure of both finality and an invitation for Arthur to share his own opinion. "Too rushed. Too reckless."

Arthur stretched his neck ever so slightly, though he did not lose visual through the scope.

"I agree with half that." It was certainly rushed. Arthur had learned of the prick target's actions only two days prior. In that time, he'd setup some very basic target monitoring–a fraction of what he would have done for a High Value Target in the field. He'd procured the weapon, which screamed Army Sniper, enough to lead the cops to the conclusion Arthur wanted them to draw. Recently in the news there was intimation that Central American narcos had linked up with a rogue element of the U.S. Army on logistics. Reading between the lines and intercepting traffic (both things Arthur and Maggie were exceptional at doing) told a clearer story: a small cadre of Army punks–dishonorably discharged due to suspicion of illegal activity while in uniform–had traded in their disgraced names for the desperado lifestyle by helping the cartels bring in drugs and smuggle out money, guns, and most likely women. The cadre was ex-Special Forces (or could at least talk the talk) because the same skills taught by one of the world's foremost tactical schools were arguably even more valuable to the narcos as they were to the Army itself.

So Arthur's use of this weapon to eliminate the prick kid would lead to suspicion of the kid being a player in some cartel drama– something the cops would certainly chase down, given the death at an upscale restaurant like this, but it would never blow back on Arthur or Maggie. Which was another skill part of the successful sniper's repertoire. Awfully hard to do the next job if you got caught on the one before.

Still ... he hadn't done the same kind of due diligence he was used to. While this prick was no High Value Target, it wasn't an excuse to cut corners.

But that was exactly what he was doing, wasn't it?

Arthur took a deep breath. He wasn't cutting corners on this one. He was just working fast. It wasn't reckless to kill this little shit.

It was street justice.

In this world, sometimes that was all you got.

And sometimes it was just enough.

"Humidity I've got clocked at fifty-two percent," he said, answering the question for Maggie. If he was wildly off base, she could tell him. But as much as he might have been rushing this, he didn't much want to lollygag through. While he was sure he could do this and not get caught (hence this not being a reckless move), there was no point in putting himself in the danger zone for longer than necessary.

The temperature was light and fresh, not unheard of for Miami in late-October, but much appreciated, surely, by all the residents on a day as beautiful as today. His Casio Mudmaster watch told him it was seventy degrees on the dot.

And that would do just fine.

Arthur, for his part, also appreciated this temperate weather. While he'd been in plenty of jungles or sandboxes or even places where it was so damn cold he had to adjust several feet in elevation of his shot because the cold bullets move slower than hot ones, he didn't mind cleaning up the world's scum in the beautiful clime of his adopted hometown of Miami. And today? Well, *today*, all he had to do was make calculations so small in nature that he almost didn't need Maggie for anything else but a confirmation of his own reads.

And part of him wondered whether that was all he *would* get from her.

"I'm not saying you're wrong, Maggie. But I still think this is the right thing to do."

She said nothing.

And after a time, Arthur returned his focus to the veranda.

Of the eight (soon to be nine) tables, Arthur was of course only interested in one—a three-top round table that housed two women and one boy-man prick kid asshole (Arthur could not think of him as simply *a man*, though he supposed that is what society called boys of this age and this level of immaturity these days). Prick kid would probably do just fine for the small amount of time until Arthur made him a *former* prick kid.

All three patrons wore stylish, professional attire (even *boring* attire, considering this was Miami), and drinking a round of rather pedestrian iced teas (or perhaps Arnold Palmers). Arthur had made sure of that much, following the waitress as she walked the order to the outdoor patio bar and then the bartender as they mixed the fresh juices together, adding nothing else that might have corrupted Arthur's job out here today.

Or from corrupting any of the patrons seated at the table with the prick kid (Arthur noted, trying to keep the hot-acid bile from circulating through his body and mind and composure).

In the foreground out over the water that lapped against the veranda's front chin, seagulls dipped and fell, their bodies going from white-grey shapes to dark silhouettes against the light of the sun. Arthur noted their upturned wings only allowing them to coast for a moment before they were forced to beat their wings, using their own effort to stay adrift. There was no hidden wind movement here—no sudden changes in air pressure which might affect the M2010's shot once Arthur put just the slightest of pressures onto the trigger.

Perfect shooting conditions.

And not a cloud in the sky or indication that would change.

But Arthur watched for several minutes nonetheless as the wind went from a whisper to nary even a gentle out breath, the massive palm leaves on either side of the veranda sitting as still as statues in their giant porcelain planters, the water going momentarily glassy. As if the entire scene was an animal waiting, waiting, waiting for that moment when prey enters the kill zone, unaware of the dangers lurking.

A good time for Arthur to complete his task.

Do it now. Be done with it.

Even through the dying light, he could have pulled the trigger.

He'd shot many a rifle in situations far more chaotic and with far less visibility than this one. The sunlight was a problem with how low it sat along the backdrop which framed this scene. But it was not insurmountable. Nor would it keep him from doing what needed to be done.

Something *would*, however.

And it was a mixture of a nagging conscience and the fact that his wife–the person he trusted more than anyone else in the world–was nestled into a fold of their yacht not more than a few feet away from him. And despite the fact she hadn't climbed over and physically stopped Arthur from yet shooting, he could tell she was considering it.

He cursed. Didn't want to hear from Maggie another comment about why they should probably not be doing this right now. But that was like saying he didn't want to eat greens or moderate his intake of alcohol. He had no choice in the matter (so long as he wanted to keep himself a productive member of society) and was only the better for listening.

"Alright fine. What do you suggest we do, then?" He hadn't pulled up on the trigger or the scope, but he felt Maggie's invisible hands massaging his psychological shoulders, easing the tension and pressure of the pre-shot reality that Arthur was about to kill someone. A reality amped up even further when considering how it was all going to go down. On a non-combatant.

It wasn't exactly that it would burden him. It was just big time stakes in a game that very few people ever got comfortable playing.

Maggie was quiet for some time and Arthur wondered if perhaps she had only been playing games. Maybe this Socratic dialogue had only been to see whether Arthur could stick to his guns and shoot this kid. Like maybe if she could talk him out of it, he shouldn't have done it in the first place.

Or maybe Maggie hadn't thought far enough ahead to answer the question. That would be unlike her.

But then again, sitting a few hundred feet from a non-combatant ready to put a round through his body was pretty unlike Arthur. You kill someone in their line of work, they deserved it. They were "inplay." Maybe they weren't shooting at someone, per se, but they were pulling strings that resulted in someone getting killed, somewhere.

Or worse.

"We'll do what we always do," Maggie said.

It was almost as if Arthur himself had been shot through with a round. Only this one was imaginary and instead of cutting through flesh and bone and arterial walls, this one cut directly to the small semblance of himself that one might have considered a soul. There were plenty of times when he didn't think that still existed–if it ever had. Maggie always told him otherwise, though. And her constant presence as his spotter brought to him a measure of safety and protection against the acid so prevalent in all men who spent their lives ridding their world of others.

The one strong enough to dissolve who one is and everything they stand for.

"I don't know if I can do that." He meant it, though it may very well have been more a statement to prop himself up than a truth.

"All of us have the chance to make things right, no matter what has come before."

"This *is* our chance to make it right." Arthur bit his lip.

"It's not our place."

"When has that ever mattered before? Was it our place to decide the fate of O'Reilly in Belfast or Harlova in Ankara? How about the ones we took out during the purges in Zimbabwe or any of the countries in the Maghreb? Was it our place when we took those shots?"

Arthur sighed. Beneath him the boat rocked gently. Above him the fading sun turned to an awe-striking evening sky. All around him there was peace.

Even the birds were quiet.

And for one long moment of the soul, so was Arthur's mind.

But still he did not pull the trigger.

"This is what we do," he said.

"No. It isn't. Not really."

"So what happens if I do it? What then?"

It was Maggie's turn to take a long hard think about the situation and all its repercussions. As she did, the sun fell further in the sky, the very last rays of its light still visible from behind the restaurant, but only just. The lights on the veranda had come on, illuminating the diners in a warm glow that was powerful enough for Arthur to see everything through the scope of his rifle. Where before he could make out faces and features, now he could see even the tiniest of micro expressions on a patron's face. Despite everything in his body telling him otherwise, he trained his scope on the two women with the prick kid all seated together at the table. All three had blonde hair and accompanying light features. All three had similarly confident jawlines and sharp blue eyes. One of the women was perhaps three years older than the target, the other perhaps three years younger. All of them were a picture of youth, health, and wealth.

Arthur realized in that moment that they were family. Siblings. He hadn't a chance to properly clock them yet–a realization that shook him to his core. To have been ready to kill without identifying those inside the kill zone was a cardinal sin of sorts. Arthur was a good enough shot to get away with such an oversight, but still ...

He was being reckless. Maggie had said so, but seeing it for himself jolted Arthur from the brink of his quiet, seething rage.

The younger woman at the table stuck her tongue out at the target, who laughed with a genuine tenderness for the apparent ribbing from his sister. The eldest sister, while the more stoic of the three, smirked, the edges of her puffy pink lips turning up and revealing not even the faintest of wrinkles anywhere around her eyes or forehead.

They were quite a picture, these three. And seeing the prick bastard target in this comfortable element only served to humanize him against Arthur's own efforts to do the opposite.

"Family affair," Maggie said, as if reading Arthur's mind.

"Nice looking family," Arthur said.

They watched for a while, only the ocean's gentle soundtrack to accompany them.

"You never answered me before," Arthur finally said. It would be fully dark soon, and Arthur wanted to have a final decision locked in before then. It wasn't so much he needed it as he sort of felt a roiling sense of discomfort inside him. Like he just ate fish and found out it was days old. The sick hadn't set it in yet, but sometimes just the knowing was worse. "What would happen?"

The waiter came to the target's table, all smiles and gentle deference.

"Don't do it, Arthur." Maggie suddenly using his proper name. "It's like that Ghost of John song."

Arthur didn't know that one and said so.

"It's a nursery rhyme."

"Naturally."

Maggie sort of hum-sung it.

> Have you seen the ghost of John?
> Long white bones with the skin all gone
> Ooh ooh ooh oo-ooo-oooohh
> Wouldn't it be chilly with no skin on?

The little tune sounded familiar to Arthur but he sure couldn't place it. Sort of like a distant memory, long ago forgotten, but not totally lost to the strange architecture inside the mind.

Maggie spoke in two ways—either direct and exacting or in metaphor.

The former was impossible to miss in the same way a bullet through your abdomen was (and Maggie's directness could often feel exactly that way).

Often, the latter was several steps removed from Arthur's ability to leap from one concept to the other. It was a quirk of his wife, some-thing he had long ago learned to love ever since she'd explained to him that firing a sniper rifle was like paint by numbers at long distance. Since that day, for whatever reason, Arthur hadn't missed a shot out in the field—and he never once took a shot without first thinking of that tidbit. The metaphor and the way she explained it was one of those things that simply clicked for him, and he forever after *just knew* how to do it right.

"I'll bite. And what about this situation would be like that song?"

"The question of the song is very simple. It's not about the ghost, nor about his temperature. Rather, the question the song brings forth is: who, exactly, was this John? And what kind of person ends up with no skin?"

"His ghost has no skin, though, right?"

"Ghosts don't have skin anyway. Not like you and me."

"Is that right?"

"That's right. And so the missing skin isn't really a ghost thing at all. It speaks to who John was as he lived. And, very likely, how he died."

Sometimes Arthur marveled at the types of things his wife thought about. It wasn't as if she were some housewife with all the time in the world on her hands. She often did as much or more research as Arthur for their missions. She trained with all the same weapons and held all the same proficiences—better, even, in many ways.

And yet she somehow found time to philosophize about things like this, then shoehorn them into relevance out here in the field. On their first few missions Arthur had thought it was just something to pass the time. Like a way she could keep their minds sharp and focused during the interminable downtime that sniper work required. But after a while, he recognized it more as a sort of subconscious sense of communication. Like there was something inside her that she couldn't turn off, even if she wanted to—some past-life educator, maybe. Maggie contained multitudes, as the saying went. And Arthur was just happy to have her, to know her, to love her—and for all those feelings to be reciprocated back.

Maggie said, "My money goes to John being a traitorous bastard–

perhaps a pirate, a real scallywag, given the likely origins of the song in a late-middle century wharf town. So let's just say he's a pirate. I think he was probably tortured and skinned alive before finally passing to the other side. And forever after, those who did the deed sang about this John, not about how he died, but about what sort of thing haunted even John in the afterlife. It's maybe the origin story of every ghost who ever ... uh ... lived. And it served a purpose."

Arthur was at least following now. "Uh, okay? And?"

"And, the fact that his skin is all gone is not simply some temperature control problem for John. No. It is an eternal problem. Something for which he will pay forever after, due to how he lived in his mortal life. It is not deliverance from evil, but comeuppance for it. And it haunts John. And in the singing of this song, it's a lesson to all the folk of the wharf village not to live like John did, else your undying soul will never rest."

"Is that so."

"That is so."

Arthur took a moment with that. He wasn't sure he was putting the dots together. But some vague notion emerged ahead of his thoughts. "And you're saying I'm John?"

"Not yet, hon. But everybody has the capacity to be if they don't do what's right. That's how a song survives dozens of generations. It's universal."

Arthur bared his teeth and could taste the salt of the sea spray. Did Maggie just tell him his own conscience and eternal soul was on the line here? "Quite a statement from someone who helps to put down wrongdoers for a living, no?"

Arthur was uncharacteristically bristling from that deep analysis. Ready to put all that out of his mind. Whatever scant bit of wind there had been was now gone. He could see better, though the sun was not entirely gone beneath the horizon line. And, most importantly, the target presented himself toward Arthur's position at full mast—chest forward.

Asking for it.

A better target did not exist outside of a shooting range.

Screw it. Arthur was sick of the conversation.

He didn't acquire these skills with a rifle to be more diplomatic.

He sighted the kid.

Say goodnight, you fake-tough little bastard.

TWO

"Hold up," Maggie said. Arthur had a mind to flat ignore her and pull the trigger, but something in her tone told him not to.

He also hadn't gotten this far in life ignoring his wife.

"What?"

"White elephants," she said. Their code phrase for police on the scene. "In the parking lot."

Arthur took one last look at the smug face of his target, then the broad open spot of chest on the white button-down shirt, and finally with a blooming annoyance slowly scanned right away from the veranda and toward the parking lot situated to the right and just inland beyond the restaurant. From his vantage, a police cruiser crept into the parking lot. It drove low-rider slow through the rows of cars parked enjoying their meals, but it didn't stop yet. If it was looking for something, it hadn't yet found it. Or, if it was just cruising around killing time rather than arresting the punk criminal stuffing his face with the seafood tower, they didn't seem to be in any rush.

"Not a meter maid," Arthur said, tracking the cruiser, which was half-unmarked. It was a Charger sedan in dark blue with the windows tinted darker than was legal, even down here in Miami, but it had the dash and grille lights installed and an antenna that looked like it could summon extraterrestrial messages on the back. Arthur never understood why a car would take half-measures like this. It seemed, to a sniper's mind, antithetical to all sense. One either wanted to be seen as a show of force, in which case one opted for a tried-and-true cop car—something nobody would misunderstand. Or one wanted to blend in, be hidden amongst the populace, in which case didn't it make more sense to drive something inconspicuous? Perhaps a Honda Accord or a Chevy Equinox? But no, even cops had to show off and show out. Much to their detriment, Arthur figured it.

Either way, this development put Arthur squarely back in the waiting game.

And the measure of victory in this game was, of course, overcoming paranoia.

A less experienced sniper team would find this coincidence hard to overlook. A cop shows up to the scene of an execution, you tend to wonder who else might know what is going on.

But Arthur knew that only he and Maggie had any foreknowledge of what was going to happen here.

And there was not even a shred of a question about whether she would have done anything treacherous with that information.

Besides, even if he doubted her, she was on the hook here just as much as he was.

"Doesn't seem to be waiting for anybody. So I doubt very much they've suddenly uncovered the crime that brought *us* here." No cop in his right mind would ever rush an arrest like this in a restaurant without backup. And none seemed imminent.

The Charger looped around the lot again and idled beside a walkway that connected the parking lot to the front of the restaurant. Arthur had no line of sight to see who might have been coming in or out from the front door, nor what all might have been going on there. That didn't make him feel good about the situation. It was an unfortunate reality he'd had to accept if he wanted to relative safety of the boat and the water to ensure someone didn't accidentally stumble upon their sniper hide, but it sure did suck right about now. But he didn't panic yet. He and Maggie had been in far worse situations than this and lived through to the other side. They still had plenty of time and could easily pick up and be gone from sniper prone position and overwatch in a matter of seconds, sailing this yacht that nobody would ever be able to trace back to them back into the ocean. Worst case, a trained and astute cop would radio in to the Coast Guard, but the route Maggie and Arthur would take to return would cut out that possibility like a plastic surgeon looking at a lipo patient. Ditto their anti-radar capabilities. And really worst case, they would sink this thing to the bottom of the ocean, remove all trace of themselves, and be gone under cover of darkness faster than any Coast Guard–even one with the sort of skill and training as the Miami branch–could combat.

Arthur didn't move.

Neither did the cop car. Not for a long while.

"Something feel weird to you?" Arthur asked. If it did, he was somehow missing it. In the waning light, the cop's taillights had drawn a glow around where it was parked, an almost halo, as if to say that the car itself was not subject to the same rules and regulations as the rest. It wasn't just Arthur's sniper skills that tagged this thing as cop. It was everything about the damned thing–from the way it was parked to *where* it was parked, all the way down to the windows so dark they could blot out the daylight.

Maggie didn't answer immediately. Which Arthur took to mean she didn't think anything was wrong, either–even though a development like this should feel that way.

"Can't say it does," Maggie said. "Should feel like Ramadi, but it feels like a regular walk in the park."

Arthur hadn't thought of Ramadi in quite some time. And he was happy to keep it far from his mind.

"Funny coincidence, though, no?"

That prompted a snigger out of Maggie. "Coincidence" was a bit of an inside joke between them. It was common knowledge *there was no such thing as coincidence.* But try telling that to someone who once army crawled into a nest of venomous snakes, or who got planted in-country and had to hunker down while a once-in-a-life-time rainstorm poured down on them, closing off all possibility of assassination during the only period of time it could go down, or who found themself stuck in an airport that was suddenly devoid of planes because of an outbreak of wildfire forty miles away that threatened to overtake an entire Saharan village if not tended to immediately.

If you were in the game long enough, coincidence was an impos-sible acquaintance to avoid.

"Far as I can tell, they're either biding time or here for takeout."

"Keep an eye on them, would you?" Arthur asked. He swung his rifle back toward the veranda where the waiter was clearing the last of the three plates from the target's table. The entire back half of the restaurant and the water were now engulfed with the darkness, a promise of night even despite the patio lights draping just enough twinkle on the place so that Arthur could clearly see faces up close. He centered the rifle again on the target and considered whether this shot was worth taking, whether the risk was worth the squeeze and all that.

But no, it wouldn't be.

Would it?

After the dinner course was half over, Maggie finally said, "They're still parked out front, if that's what you're asking."

Arthur blew out a breath. "Wasn't what I was asking. I asked what I was asking."

"Maybe you *should* be asking questions like that, since it looks like you're scoping down a, what, twenty-five-year-old kid out to dinner with his sisters while a police car waits out front. And maybe if those things don't register any alarm bells for you, you might consider whether *any* red flags exist that might give you pause for this mission."

Arthur bristled. He kept his eye on the glass, able even to see the day-old stubble on the target's face as he rubbed his palm against a cheek and smiled at his youngest sister. He didn't need Maggie trying to throw him because they were close to the end zone now.

Even if the line-to-go might be impossible to reach.

"Let's keep our morals about us, Art. Let the authorities handle this."

"The authorities had their chance already."

"Yeah and one guy blew it. But we could talk to them. It isn't written in stone."

"We could also just take care of this. Not rely on those thumb-suckers to do their jobs. Just because they get paid double pension doesn't mean they're any good at what they do."

"That's not what we do. Not like this."

"Maybe the way we do things isn't all that important, Maggie. Maybe it's just the things we do that matter."

That seemed to quiet Maggie for a bit.

And it was a bit longer than that before Arthur felt bad.

"Sorry," he said. "Attitude doesn't belong here."

Maggie sighed. "Nobody's perfect. I accept your apology."

They waited.

And still Arthur did not shoot.

THREE

The target held his glass up, indicating to both sisters that whatever he was about to say would be wise and worth listening to.

Arthur rolled his eyes. He wondered whether either of the sisters were sick of the kid's shit, his pomposity, his know-it-all attitude. Arthur had got enough of a taste of that doing his light recon and signals intelligence interceptions. It was a study in insufferability.

It did nothing to dissuade Arthur from the course of action upon which he now embarked.

The kid didn't seem able to exist without bristling anybody who wasn't similarly situated—meaning, anybody else who wasn't a total dickbag.

Arthur was pissed now. Growing agitated with each passing second that the target lived. The growing risks as the Charger idled. For all they knew, the cops were up close waiting for the hit on the target. Maybe somewhere behind them the Coast Guard or one of the maritime police units were closing in. A snare. Pulled slowly. Ever so slowly. Until finally it was too late to remove one's neck. Had Maggie never brought this up, Arthur would have already pulled the trigger and they would have cut tail, maybe even been halfway home by now. After apologizing to his wife, he'd sat there and watched the kid eat dinner. Luckily for the kid's longevity, Arthur could not actually hear what was being said. They might normally try and drop a wire on target, or utilize either ears in the sky or some kind of powerful directional mic, but it wasn't necessary for this operation. Nor was there time to get it figured out. And anyway, there was nothing the kid could say that would change Arthur's mind. They knew he was guilty. And it didn't figure he'd be discussing the topic with his sisters, anyway.

But since Maggie had gone and spoken up–and really even before that–Arthur'd felt strange about what he was about to do.

The waiter came by with the bill and dumped it with the oldest sister. Arthur's blood boiled thinking of this prick and what he'd done. In fact, just the faint thought of it sent Arthur's finger to twitching. As if some cellular synapse inside him was firing, trying to out-will his mind into pulling the trigger and putting this piece of trash down like the rabid animal that he was. The fact he wasn't picking up the tab shouldn't have mattered. But it did. And it did.

By god it goddamn did.

The waiter came back a few moments later and picked up the check, scurrying back to the card terminal to process it so the restaurant could turn over the table and get another diner on the docket.

It was this chance that Arthur would perhaps not get again. The bastard target sat there between his two sisters in a moment of quiet conversation, no doubt basking in his acquired confidence that a criminal feels once the dust settles on his crime and nobody has come a-knocking. He'd done something illegal, wrong, befitting scum of the earth–and he had gotten away with it. And maybe–if he was the sort of scum that stuck to your shoe and never really went away, but rather just picked up imprints of all the other muck and dirt and grime you stepped near through the rest of your days–then maybe he even *liked* what he'd done.

Liked it and now knew there was no one in this civilized world who would ever stop him from doing it.

Nobody except for Arthur.

The one unfortunate part of killing the kid now would be that said kid would never know who it was had gone and rubbed him out. But that was something Arthur had always contended with as a sniper. Usually it made no difference to him. The bad guy got dead, that was the important part. But for this job, Arthur wished for a little more poetic justice.

The waiter came back all smiles and niceties, no doubt trying to leave a pleasant taste in everyone's mouth aside from just the dinner. Tips could be legendary in this town, and even though his patrons were young, they were the sort of top breed that wouldn't even think it strange to open a menu and find eighty-dollar entrees.

Everyone at the table looked up at this waiter as he set down the check with the credit card run. He had interrupted some engrossing conversation, surely full of sophisticated tastes and intellectual curiosities.

For that moment, everything in the entire world went on pause.

And yet still Arthur did not pull the trigger. He willed himself toward it. Thought of young Annabelle, the girl who lived down the street in the gated, private community that Arthur and Maggie called home. Seventeen years old now. Not hardly a girl. Though they had known her since she was roughly seven.

Arthur and Maggie never had kids—their lives, their work, did not really allow for such dependencies. Dependencies that made it so holidays, extended family, even friends had to fall by the wayside. They were married to the job, as Maggie used to say. Their kids were the operations they sometimes spent months planning, sneaking behind enemy lines, living amongst the enemy, fading into the background before pulling the trigger and putting some problem of the world to bed. For good. But Annabelle was someone that Arthur had taken a shine to. Such a beacon of light, airy goodness as a seven-year-old girl who'd someone managed to get into Arthur and Maggie's backyard, despite all the hidden surveillance and countersurveillance measures in place, without tripping all but the last alarm (Arthur thankful to have such a harmless intrusion by this little girl so they could tighten up their security; much worse to find a disgruntled brother of some former target who decided to come pay a visit). Annabelle who had unknowingly overcome sophisticated security in search of her lost puppy who had run away earlier that day. Annabelle who, when Arthur spotted her in the backyard, looked up to him with the innocent doe eyes of a little girl and said, "You have a *lovely* home," like some sophisticated old maid who'd just come for a visit.

That Annabelle.

Over the years, Arthur couldn't say he'd gotten to know her. But he'd watched her grow up from afar. He was made aware of her around the holidays (the ones he and Maggie found themselves at home alone for, anyway), one year feeling tears form at the corners of his eye watching the ten-year-old Annabelle sing Christmas carols with a few other kids in the neighborhood. Christmas in Miami was always a weird thing—no snow, no cold, no seasonally appropriate trees—but that year it had felt like the most right thing in the whole wide world. Maggie, too, had a taken a shine to the girl. One year when Annabelle was maybe fifteen, Maggie watched from down the street as Annabelle snuck back into her own property at an hour that was surely far past the girl's bedtime. Maggie had been on a midnight walk around their gated community. Something to help her sleep after a mission had left her jet lagged and a little stir crazy. And it was the recognition of something like a kindred spirit that tugged at Maggie's little heart string in much the same way as those doe eyes had done to Arthur.

The target cornered her, was what she'd told the police. It was a party, sure. But she didn't want to party *like that*. Hearing the little girl that was still very much alive in Arthur's head speaking like a mature woman was a mindfuck that Arthur had not expected. Of course the little girl was grown up. Maggie so much as found that out when they almost crossed paths on the midnight walk. Arthur had known as much. But to hear that girl's voice sounding like a woman's, using words like *drugs* and *sex* and *torturous*, well ... something inside Arthur broke that day.

He hadn't been looking for this. God no. Even someone as jaded and eye-clearingly weary as Arthur would never have dreamt to wade into those waters.

But he and Maggie kept a close eye on everyone living on their private island community. And that included the cops. Not because they were nosy, Arthur and Maggie. No, no. Just because they were careful. Certainly they were the very opposite of reckless. And because of this close eye (or in this case, ear), that was how Arthur came to hear the conversation between the sleepy detective Zack Tilson and Annabelle, as the former took down the complaint and resultant report by the latter.

Anybody who had half a brain and lived through the past two decades could have written it. A kid at a college party. A girl too young to be there but too brash and independent to realize that fact. The kid cornered her in a hallway of the house, drinks flowed. He pressed himself up against her until she opened the only door she could access, and then found herself alone in a room with said kid. Alone in a room with a closed and locked door, once the kid got through doing that. Alone in a room while he smiled lasciviously (another word that spun Arthur's head, he heard Annabelle saying it).

"He licked his lips like some sort of ... wild animal ... predator," Annabelle said to Tilson between gasping sobs.

Alone in a room while the target did what it was he'd done that eventually sent Annabelle to the police.

"T-T-There ... was nothing in his eyes ... but coldness."

Christ. If there was ever a time for Arthur to finally act like someone his age and just drop dead where he stood, it would have been then.

And maybe it would've been a mercy.

But no. No mercy on that day as he sat stunned to stillness in his office, listening to Annabelle's voice, Arthur wishing he could crawl through the thick jumble of telecommunications equipment and stand in the room with her, hug her, comfort her, do any such thing that might make the girl feel even the slightest bit better.

Instead all he could do was listen and try to keep calm enough to keep his heart from exploding.

Listen to just how alone Annabelle had felt.

Alone and scared.

When it was done—all twenty-five minutes of it to give an idea of how thorough Tilson was (Arthur having had haircuts that lasted longer). In front of Arthur there were four broken pencils in a heap and a splotch of blue India ink staining his leather desk mat from where he'd bent the nib of his Montblanc Steinway until it burst open. Arthur vowed to do the same to the prick bastard of a kid. Until Maggie patiently listened to Arthur's rant and finally talked some sense into him. There was no way even Zack Tilson could screw up an investigation like this, given how eloquently Annabelle had spoken, how clearly she'd described the assault on her. *There was just no way. Just have faith.*

It was a moment of staggering naivete from a woman who was anything but.

But Arthur had listened. Surely, something would come from the investigation.

Two days later, Annabelle was back in the station. Arthur was listening. And this time, he was watching, too. Now that he knew what to look for, he had practically been standing guard on the precinct house's surveillance and security systems, having tapped into them shortly after Maggie had pulled him back from the precipice of the scorched earth doctrine. He hadn't noted a lot of hustle up from Tilson, but maybe, just maybe, there was something had slipped through the cracks of Arthur's surveillance.

From the first moment of the conversation between Annabelle and Tilson, Arthur's blood could have boiled the oceans.

"I'm wondering, Annabelle," Tilson started off and his tone, his goddamn tone, was already more aggressive than any cop investigating this kind of crime ought to be. Ever. Unless he was speaking to the perpetrator of the crime. "What were you wearing that night? I went through my notes twice and it seems you never mentioned it."

"That's cause you never asked, you lazy sack of shit! Not that it makes any bit of goddamn difference!" Arthur was up at his desk. Luckily there were no more pencils to break. But he was about as cool and collected as a prisoner on steroids who just initiated a jailhouse riot. Arthur had been in conflict zones his whole life and could never remember raising his voice the way he had to the grainy video feed on his computer as he watched Tilson start off this follow up conversation.

Maggie entered the room shortly thereafter. She turned off the hacked video and audio feed not long after that, knowing all too well it wasn't doing a bit of good for Arthur. Not to mention the questions were even pissing Maggie off–something hard (and strictly inadvisable) to do. It was there, in Arthur's office, that they decided to take matters into their own hands.

And now here they were. Ready to do it.

At the table on the veranda, the older sister signed the receipt without hesitation–without even hardly looking at the damn bill–and they were, all three of them, through the veranda's doorway and lost in the intimate darkness of the inner sanctum of Masquiatt Grille seemingly as quickly as the round from Arthur's rifle could reach them.

"You made the right choice," Maggie said once there was no chance Arthur could confidently take a shot.

Arthur grunted. He wasn't so sure about that. What he *had* done was let a target walk when he could have been buried dead. And unlike some of the people he'd been charged with taking out, this one was confirmed to be a wrongdoer. Way wrong. Who knows? Maybe the kid had plans later to find another girl and do with her what he'd already gotten away with once. Maybe he'd take it even further this time, the way so many first-time criminals do, since there didn't seem to be any blowback for such behaviors.

The way Arthur himself almost just had, perhaps.

"Damnit." He already felt shame and that strange feeling when put up against a hard choice to only come away having selected the spineless option. "Goddamnit."

"It was right, Arthur. Just. And now we help to work it the right way."

"The right way just evaporated when that prick walked out the door."

"Now, now Arthur," Maggie said, tiptoeing on the precipice of chiding and caring. "Don't get all hung up on one target."

Plenty of husbands would have snapped at their wives after a comment like this, but Arthur was the opposite. Getting all hung up, making things personal out in the field ... well, that was the way dead men operated. Anything besides clinical, exacting, and ruthless efficiency was dangerous.

Deadly.

Besides, it was only the true lowlife husbands who did things like this, bickering with their wives, or putting them down for having something approaching an opinion. Arthur had never been like that. He liked to think of it virtuously, but it very well could have been due to the fact that his wife was just as (if not more so) dangerous than he was.

Now that the target had walked through that door and out of sight, Arthur frankly felt a potent cocktail of strange emotions surrounding this particular job. Or failed job, was how he now thought of it. First, he felt an intense pressure inside his chest—something often times relieved once he saw pink mist downrange. This wasn't so much nerves (there was likely some of that, sure), but rather the tension of a job unfulfilled having finally been completed. Snipers had a strange dichotomy to account for. On the one hand, they had the most clearly defined and consequential target known to man. Kill another. And yet, on the other hand, snipers also had the ultimate task opacity. Hardly ever was the target to be killed a certain way or from a certain place or with any specific weapon. All that ambiguity—security, approach, escape—was left to the shooter and his spotter to decide. It was pass/fail at the highest levels of consequentiality. So that undone task was what created this knot of tension inside of Arthur. He often didn't sleep more than a few winks each night until the job was complete.

And after going toe-to-toe with this prick bastard, he might not sleep right again ever.

But there was also an intense sadness inside Arthur. And he felt actually that it stemmed not from deciding against taking the shot but rather the fact that he was close to taking the shot in the first place.

"You were right," he admitted to Maggie. Plenty of husbands made it their life's mission never to say those three words to their wives, but Arthur wasn't one of them, either. Frankly, if husbands ever put their literal lives in the eyes, ears, and minds of their wives the way Arthur did with Maggie, they would show a lot more gratitude and sweep a lot more of the stupid stuff to the side of the road and just continue on.

Maggie said, "So now we just need to figure out how to hand deliver him to the cops."

Arthur swung his rifle to the right and glassed the parking lot. He wasn't done with this prick bastard yet. He hadn't considered the opportunity before him until just this moment.

The cop car still idled outside of the restaurant in the same spot it had parked when it finally came to rest.

After a few moments, Arthur spotted the blonde trio as they emerged from behind the restaurant's structure. Thye'd taken the walkway leading away from the front door, hugging the lone place on that side of the parking lot which Arthur could not see from his vantage point. These three weren't military-trained, otherwise it might have irked Arthur they'd done this. Might have spooked him, like maybe they weren't just the luckiest sonsofbitches in the genetic lottery, but also had some innate skill, too.

But no. They were just the luckiest sonsofbitches in the genetic lottery.

And for all the things that was—unfair, annoying, envy-creating—it damn sure wasn't illegal.

And as far as Arthur was concerned, it didn't justify killing.

"Damn I've gone soft," he said to himself.

As Arthur's scope found the wide, darkened void of the parking lot, he swept it from one way to the other over the sleek metal forms of Porches, Ferraris, Range Rovers. This was Miami, after all, where being ostentatious with your wealth was practically a prerequisite to going out in public.

Says the guy laying just shore aboard his yacht.

Maybe that was why Arthur had taken so much to Miami—because for all his actual work as a sniper, as the proverbial grey man, blending into the environment and being absolutely invisible through taking the shot and beyond, to the evasive maneuvers required to disappear inside a foreign country that was now on high alert looking for you, once he was off the clock, he wanted to loosen up on some of those tendencies.

Maybe he wanted to let his freak flag fly a little. Even if his "freak flag" was a bottle of Clos d'Ambonnay, a car so expensive it came with its own driver, and a boat that—while modest—still cost more than triple the average home price in this part of the world.

But there'd be plenty of time for all that later.

After a slow walking of the scope from left to right, he found the golden-haired trio approaching their car, a rather modest Mercedes G-Wagon in a matte white wrap and with tires big enough that Rommel himself would have been jealous. But here in Miami, such a vehicle was akin to driving a beater truck down in West Texas or a beater Toyota Landcruiser in the Middle East. One hardly even noticed.

All three of the golden throuple ascended into their white chariot—the esteemed target doing the driving. The G-Wagon pulled out of the spot and headed toward the parking lot's exit. Almost gone from Arthur's sight. Almost out of his capable hands.

"The cop is still there," Maggie said, notes of confusion and foreboding interlaced with one another in her voice.

Arthur said nothing.

Then with a little more fear in her voice, "This shot isn't the shot, Arthur."

Again, Arthur said nothing.

Maggie was not quite close enough to do anything about whatever it was Arthur was going to do next. But it didn't stop her from trying. There was legitimate panic frothing up like white caps along shore during hurricane season. "Arth–"

He exhaled and put just enough pressure on the trigger during his respiratory pause so that the rifle fired with the sort of precision that any expert craftsman seeks in their pursuit of the thing in which they find beauty.

And fire that rifle did. It fired at a rate of approximately two thousand eight-hundred-fifty feet per second, the round traveling the full distance from the yacht over water, over land, over the dark parking lot and directly perfect into the target Arthur had imagined as little more than paint by numbers in his pre-shot routine.

It would have been another moment until the crack of the rifle's report made landfall, rolling over the open space of the parking lot with something like a whimper from this distance, especially with the open ocean and the ambient noise of the city. Arthur had a Titan-QD Fast-Attach suppressor on the end of his rifle, which did little in this scenario, but it did provide some relief on the sound aspect of things. It still sounded like a gunshot to anybody who'd been around guns, but it would make it more difficult for a lay person to identify where the shot came from or whether the sound they heard was a shot at all.

The round tore a sizeable hole in the perfectly wrapped matte of the car's skin in much the same way a grenade stuffed inside someone's abdomen might do.

The G-Wagon slammed immediately on its brakes, giving the impression the truck had actually bunny-hopped forward. Like how a person might when walking behind someone through a doorway who suddenly stopped short. Then the G-Wagon sped up, peeling out and fishtailing against loose gravel beneath its hefty weight, before again stopping short.

What someone in the biz might call *panic*.

In the field, a sniper's job was to shoot and a spotter's job was to manage the situation. If they were there to kill someone and the sniper's first shot missed, the spotter noted the particulars of the miss—high, low, wide left or right—and called out an adjustment on the read. Out of instinct, Maggie did just that.

"Must be elevation. Kick it up a few meters. We're close enough, I'm surprised your reading was off."

"It wasn't," Arthur said and fired a second shot, this one even lower than the first. Rather than ripping a hole in the matte white, this round blew a neat hole inside the G-Wagon's front tire, instantly deflating it from the pressure and the massive weight of the vehicle above. It likely put a decent dent in the tire's infrastructure, too. They were too far away to clearly hear anything—especially with the rifle's report still clinging to the air around them—but Arthur figured the tire's sudden release of pressure and crush of steel probably made enough noise to bring anybody in the parking lot onto high alert. Followed by the gunshot's echo, anybody over there would certainly be looking around, even if they could not place the sounds.

The G-Wagon lurched but didn't go anywhere. It was now a bottleneck at the mouth of the parking lot, blocking incoming and outgoing traffic. So just in case the cop's were blasting show tunes or whatever else they got up to inside their tinted out half-incognito mobile, this would have eventually gotten their attention. Or at least the honking horns would have, from pissed off people prevented from making their dinner reservation on time or leaving the premises once done.

Well, objective achieved. The disturbance from the G-Wagon's sudden maiming curried enough attention that the red and blue check of the lights on the police car flooded the semi-dark parking lot like the first dance at the disco. Arthur pulled back from the changing colors in his spotting scope and gave the entire scene a long look, letting his eyes re-adjust to normal vision and his mind stay open to whatever was out there. This was the work of the predator who did not bring predisposition to any situation, who simply acted and reacted with lethality based on whatever they found in front of them.

The police car that had idled for the past twenty minutes was apparently interested enough to mosey itself on over across the parking lot to see what was going on.

Finally about ready to do something about a problem which had been flying under the radar far too long, if Arthur had a say so.

And while he figured he didn't have one–not really–if he wasn't willing to take his shot, it didn't mean he had to be entirely passive and silent on the situation. A man with his skill set and experiences rarely was much of either. Well, silent maybe–but only when conducting an operation.

"Just what did you do, Arthur?" Maggie's voice half-grinning.

"You said before I was rushed and reckless. At the time, even I had to agree. But now I see it different. I was quick, not rushed. And I was reckless only in my thought. Was lazy, too." Now it was Arthur's turn to use a metaphor, though his tended to be simpler and less obtuse than Maggie's. "I'd been looking to use my hammer to solve a problem that really only needed a screwdriver."

The Charger parked behind the G-Wagon. Behind it at the best angle they could squeeze in to ensure a clear approach without giving whoever was inside the broken down vehicle an opportunity to spray gunfire at them. Was a shame cops had to think about things like that, but it was reality. And it showed to Arthur two things: that these cops were evidently competent enough to know some basic tactics, which boded well for what Arthur had in mind. And, perhaps more importantly, that they approached the situation with the G-Wagon with the right eyes–eyes that saw a potential threat.

Two figures emerged from the Charger and approached the G-Wagon with guns drawn but pointed at the ground. Not a great tactic, honestly, but most cops tended to be pretty unskilled with their service weapon. So if you only went shooting the mandatory minimum amount each year to keep your licensing, it was better to point the thing away from people lest you make a mistake that was impossible to take back.

When the closest cop saw the gunshot wound flayed open on the car's exterior like a zit on the prom king, he said something over the G-Wagon's tall body and both cops raised their guns to a more serious, threat-assessment level.

"What did you do?" Maggie asked with a sly smile in her voice.

"We should probably go," Arthur said. "No sense hanging around until they ask where the bullets came from."

FOUR

Despite their relatively conspicuous sniper hides (as compared with, say, some of the woodland and jungle theaters they had operated within, with wandering countersecurity, enemy booby traps, and mortar units ready to rain down terror from the skies), Arthur shimmied himself backwards from his perch and behind the yacht's border wall. He crouched low, bringing the spent rifle with him in the process. Immediately, instinctively, he began to disassemble the M2010 with the sort of expert precision gained from a lifetime working with weapons systems. Truth to tell, Maggie was even faster and more adept than he, but she had other tasks to perform here.

She crouched behind the yacht's border wall, too, giving him a cat-like look. Said nothing, though, just crouch-walked toward the yacht's captain's quarters will the smooth assurance of the operator conducting the physical movements they'd played out in their head a hundred times before the actual chance to do them.

As Arthur unscrewed the suppressor from the end of the rifle, he let out the heaviness inside his chest in the same way one might drop an anvil into the ocean. By the time he had broken down the entire M2010, he felt an even greater sense of relief, somehow, than on a mission where he'd executed on the intended target. Perhaps because this time he'd both completed the task—the *true* task—*and* avoided taking a life in the process.

It was ... nice. Almost.

"Whatever," Arthur said, using an Allen wrench to unseat the screw and bolt that allowed the rifle's stock to fold in on itself for ease of carry.

The quiet idle of the sea broke with the yacht's raising of the anchor, Maggie having made good time already as the deep-underneath engines came to life, too. Arthur went to stern and hefted the anchor into its pocket, shooting a flash of his flashlight to let Maggie know. She answered with two quick flashes of her own flashlight. As soon as the second flash was extinguished, the yacht was in motion, Maggie's expert captainship on display for exactly no one besides Arthur to witness.

At least that was the hope.

They were halfway back out to Biscayne Bay when Arthur had half the rifle chucked over the side at irregular intervals. By the time they entered Fisherman's Channel, he'd gotten rid of all of it, and with it, the last of the physical items that could connect him with firing those rounds into the G-Wagon—evidence that would put him in prison for a stint far longer than the rest of his expected life (even if Florida). Once he took a shower and wiped himself of any and all forensic evidence, he would be totally in the clear. He would do that, of course, but not just yet.

Overhead, the moon had emerged, bulbous and shining in amber in the sky. All around the yacht was the beauty that only an ocean moonscape can bring, with the waves growing larger, though still tame given the mild conditions. Arthur took a few deep breaths of the salty air as they rode farther out to sea, where at some point Maggie would navigate them through Norris Cut and toward the private island community they called home.

A light ocean breeze blew over the deck, enough to chill Arthur. It was perhaps the end of a very short window of temperate weather in South Florida. In conjunction with the loss of the flood of adrenaline which always came with a mission, he shivered, the hairs standing up on his forearms. It was nice, though, the quiet and the view of the moonlit ocean, and the few solitary moments he kept for himself.

After a time he joined Maggie in the captain's quarters. She stood at the controls, their charted course visible on one of the yacht's many control room screens. It wasn't a long journey, but it was always mapped on the GPS system beforehand, to be deleted by the computers immediately following completion of their journey, followed by Arthur taking the memory chips from the computer and throwing them into his masonry furnace, followed by a sojourn over the water where he released the ashes into the ocean. Yet seeing their charted course was a comfort to Arthur now, as the waning energy flowed from him.

"Tea?" Maggie asked. Another inside joke.

"Dirty water? No thanks."

"You planning on telling me what you were up to back there?"

Arthur grabbed an aluminum cup from beside the captain's desk and filled it with ice from the miniature refrigerator-freezer combo seated beneath the captain's desk. He then grabbed a Diet Coke and a pre-sliced wedge of lemon. He mixed both into the cup of ice and sipped long enough so that the bubbles and cold tickled his throat.

"I've been meaning to tell you," Arthur said, finding himself in a bit of a silly mood. "The lotion you bought me for Christmas? Very nice. Doesn't have any greasy feel whatsoever."

Maggie rolled her eyes. "Well your shot spread would say otherwise. I was worried your finger slipped. Lucky a little old lady didn't wind up catching lead."

Arthur smiled and the bubbles tickled his top lip.

"But seriously, Artie, don't change the subject. What was all that about?"

Arthur smiled as he took another sip of his soda. "You said before I had moved rushed and reckless." Arthur said this again and still the words felt strange to him. They almost hurt, coming from Maggie and talking about him. He wasn't any of those things. And yet he *had* acted in a way that could be construed as both or either. That stung. Because it wasn't the sort of operator he was. So it begged the question of *why?* A question now he was just beginning to grapple with.

He held up a finger from the aluminum cup. "I said you were half right. But now as I reflect back, I think you were all the way right. And also wrong."

Now it was Arthur's turn to talk opaque, apparently.

Maggie turned away from the controls for a moment and gave a look to Arthur that he'd seen plenty over the years. One that said, very simply, *you're an idiot, but I still love you, but you're mostly an idiot.*

Arthur continued, spurred on by the fake sugar and the caffeine and the sense of completion he felt.

"In my *methodical* preparation for this mission, I did something so stunningly smart that I hadn't even realized it until it was almost too late. As you know, in our pre-shot planning we had a not-insignificant problem. If we succeeded, there was the intended outcome that our target would be shot dead in the middle of a crowded restaurant. Naturally, police would ask questions. While we had no reason to fear those questions, nor was there any reason to leave ourselves vulnerable to them. And so was born the drug angle. The rifle used—determined if the police had enough sense to analyze the rifle rounds—would lead police right where we wanted: to this apparent group of defectors who worked logistics for the cartels."

Maggie swung the yacht in a wide, loping arc around Fisher Island and the southern tip of Miami Beach. The immaculate moon reflected almost perfectly in the rising and falling of the waves.

"And that was probably good enough. Or at least it would have been—for someone *reckless*."

This prompted a smile from Maggie. Despite her not turning around for Arthur to see her face, he could tell by the slight change in her posture that she was starting to get where this was going.

And liked it.

"But what I did earlier today before we set out on the yacht was take a little drive. Since I didn't know much about the target, I wanted to get a feel for him in his natural habitat. Call it one last peek before putting him down like the dog he is." Arthur was still Othering the target, but he didn't care. He'd been the angel of mercy on this job and now he could do whatever the hell he wanted with the target's avatar, that thing created solely by a sniper when tracking, hunting, killing his prey.

The chop of the oceans stayed tame as Maggie plunged the yacht forward, raising the speed until they were cruising smooth enough through the water to make even the most seasick-prone comfortable.

"What I found was the target whipping around in that same G-Wagon that just found itself with a sudden flat tire."

"And a punctured exterior," Maggie added.

"That, too. So I tailed the target on what seemed to be a morning of leisure. Coffee at some place with twenty-dollar lattes. A haircut at a membership-only men's salon. A trip to the high-end gym that's all the rage these days. Even a green juice afterwards at a place with the same branding as the coffee place but apparently no actual business relationship–I looked."

"Really dug deep, huh?"

Arthur smiled. "Am I the only one who thinks all these hip new places with their corporate responsibility schtick look the same? It's like they all ordered logos from the same company. Can hardly tell them apart."

Now Maggie smiled. Almost pitying her curmudgeonly husband. "But you digress."

"But I digress. Anyway, target goes home to shower up and do whatever silver spoons like him do for leisure after their leisurely errands have been run. And so I took it upon myself at that point to approach the vehicle."

"You're not serious."

"Serious is exactly what I am."

It wasn't necessarily out of bounds to have done this, but Arthur knew it was a risk at the time. A risk that had paid off, of course, but there was no way to know it at the time. No way to know with how little prep he'd done before putting the target in his crosshairs.

Arthur cut it off at the pass, though. "Before you get all pissed, it was always a play toward the alibi."

Of course this would only serve to piss off Maggie more.

"What did you do, Artie?"

"I put a few kilos of uncut smack in the wheel well of his car."

Maggie turned, quick and full of daggers. "*That's* what you've been doing these past two days?"

Arthur appreciated he had a wife who didn't bother to ask, "Where'd you get a few kilos of uncut smack?" but rather simply went straight to the fact that he'd obviously gone out and procured it using all the skill set that made him a good sniper. "I thought you said it was the papers and our usual ring of sources that confirmed the Army rumors."

"It was. But then I double confirmed with a little intel expedition of my own. Didn't get very far. Didn't need to, really–though it might be worth sticking our beaks back into if the cops can't tie it back to where I found it. I just figured some smack planted on our target would eventually be found upon his assassination, and then the conclusion we wanted the authorities to arrive at would be so forgone that not even the thickest local yokel deputy could connect the dots."

Maggie didn't smile but her tone softened. Because she was coming to the same conclusion Arthur had when he was on the gun. "And when you didn't take the shot on the veranda, you figured that half-marked cruiser in the parking lot could mosey on over and eventually find the same stuff you were figuring would get turned up after the fact, during the murder investigation."

Arthur smiled. "Like I said, it was a perfect, non-lethal setup."

"You're smarter than you look," Maggie said. A favorite inside joke between the two of them, something that harkened back to a certain advanced sniper tactical school they'd both gone through during their early years of training.

Arthur did a faux bow. "Why thank ye, m'lady."

"Though a truly smart person might have planned this from the jump. So we didn't have to come out here and play are-ya-gonna for over an hour."

Arthur waved an arm at the temperate outsides. "And miss such delightful weather?"

"The cop was a nice tough, though."

Arthur's smile dimmed. Enough so it was clear he'd tipped his hand.

"Oh, gosh. You didn't even plan that?"

Arthur said nothing.

"Better lucky, I guess," Maggie said and turned back to the controls. They were nearly home now and soon this would just be another mission under their belts—albeit one that went a little different than convention. "And maybe it's better this way. Annabelle can see justice was done, but without having to put herself under the public scrutiny that a case like that would bring, especially against a kid from a 'nice' family."

Arthur nodded. It hadn't even crossed his mind. Frankly putting the kid dead and gone to the next world was the only thing he'd had on his mind. Just didn't feel right. Maggie's point was a nice silver lining, though.

"Something about that kid got under my skin," Arthur said. He was a kid now, again. Twenty-something. Punk, for sure. Committed a heinous crime. But plenty of people Arthur came up with—good people, community-arch-stones—had done worse in their heyday.

It just wasn't that kind of world anymore.

"She means something to you. To us. It's understandable."

Maggie was right about that. On both accounts. Annabelle *did* mean something to Arthur. Not as much as a child, naturally. And perhaps not even in that way. Maybe she was just a reminder of all the good still in the world while he and Maggie went out and did the worst to some of the world's worst. It was understandable, wasn't it, that someone who meant that much to you would cause feelings when they were put in harm's way.

To this point, only Maggie and a select few teammates with whom Arthur and Maggie had worked with over the years would fall into the category of able-to-elicit emotions from Arthur.

Maybe he was just getting old.

Or maybe ... just maybe ... he was starting to evolve. Something he and Maggie had talked about a lot recently, as they both got older (not old, mind, just old*er*). About how to shift gears from the only life they'd ever known to something closer to normal.

Whatever that meant.

"Well it probably doesn't mean shooting people," Maggie had once cracked to him as he'd mused aloud.

Perhaps not.

But perhaps it did mean something else.

"Hey, I had an idea," Arthur said.

"Famous last words. And before you say something you'll regret, why don't you get that cute behind out there and tie us onto the dock."

Without Arthur realizing it, they were finally home.

Before the relief could settle in, he made his way toward the bow to heave over some lines onto their dock. Maggie was a pro at maneuvering this watercraft, and she could seemingly keep the thing against the dock without ever touching. Once Arthur had tied up the front, he repeated the task at the back of the boat.

Within a few minutes, both he and Maggie were walking barefoot along the fifty yards of perfectly manicured grass which stretched from the pool off the back of their house to their dock off the back end of their property where the yacht was now parked. Their glass-and-stone-encased home loomed before them, tastefully lit up, the view from the back edge of their property framed perfectly by matching rows of palm trees on either side of the grass, each side bowing ever so slightly inward toward one another. Arthur had to pinch himself sometimes, whenever they docked the boat along their own private bay space, because the home was something out of an *Architectural Digest* cover shoot (something he secretly wanted but knew would never happen on account of their anonymity being of paramount importance to things like their continued ability to live).

Both he and Maggie touched the smooth, like-new paint on "their" Adirondack chair–a quaint nod to their upbringings, both having grown up in the Northeastern part of the country. The chairs were set about three-quarters down toward the water along the lawn, close enough that if they ever sat in them, they would be able to hear the waves lapping sleepily along the sides of their yacht. This was sort of a ritual, this touching of the chair. It was the only time they *ever* touched them, since Arthur refused to ever sit in the chairs, telling Maggie that perhaps he was paranoid or perhaps he was smart, but only someone who had never taken out a sitting duck who got too lax on security would be caught dead sitting in the chairs.

Dead being the operative word.

They held hands as they crossed the rest of the grass in quiet, their feet through the natural fibers of the earth the only sound.

As they walked around their massive infinity pool, Maggie spoke. "You said something about an idea."

Arthur had indeed. An idea about whether it was time to hang things up. Maybe use their skills for other things besides killing people. Like being a supplement to real law enforcement. Force multipliers for good.

But something inside Arthur told him it wasn't the right time.

Soon, perhaps.

But not now.

So instead he pulled up his free hand to his nose and gave it a long sniff. "Yeah I was thinking that next year, I might need a bigger container of that hand stuff. It's just divine."

Maggie looked at him for a long moment, knowing full well Arthur's thought had been something far more serious than this feeble attempt at humor.

But she didn't press it.

Rather, she slid open the back glass slider door that separated their patio from the cavernous living room. A few of the automatic lights brightened on their dimmers as she did so, welcoming them back home.

"It was a good gift," she said.

"That it was," Arthur agreed.

And he already–finally–felt a little bit better.

He just hoped one day soon Annabelle would, too.

Whatever that might mean for her.

THE BAD GUY

NIZ THOMAS

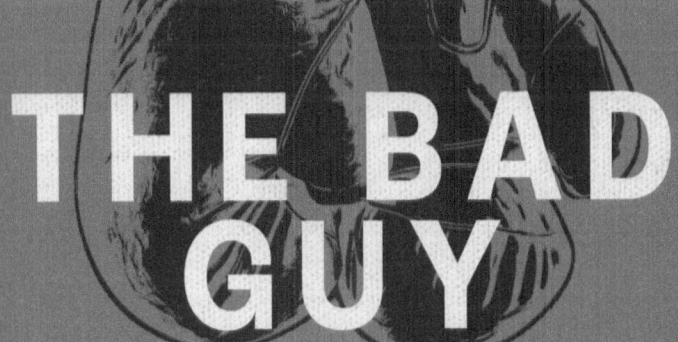

THE BAD GUY

AN ORIGINAL CRIME STORY

ONE

Usually, Teddy Pemberly couldn't even remember a passing score of the 5 Ws about one of his fights. Not Who, What, When (and sometimes), not even Where the whole thing was going down.

Just another match, another venue, another sweaty, petroleum-jelly-slicked, bruised and bloodied opponent set up before him for some predetermined number of rounds. Inside the ring, bright lights and darkness all that could be seen on the periphery. It didn't much matter usually who it was standing across from him. Fighting came natural to Teddy. The way most people breathed or ate junk food or took a crap.

Tonight, he knew more answers than most nights.

But most importantly, he knew Why he was doing it.

The crowd's chanting rained down on him like fire arrows in a medieval fantasy movie. Blocking out the sky. Fight in the shade type shit. For most people, this environment would make them crumble up. A beer can smashed against some doofus frat guy's head, trying to make the girls swoon (and allow the neurologists of the world to send their kids to graduate school). Teddy had plenty of experience with head trauma, what being a boxer and all.

He just didn't think any fancy-pants doctor was going to save his sorry excuse for a brain. It was probably most of the way to pulped blood orange by now.

And maybe that was just as well. Since nobody in their right mind would be caught fighting inside a place like this.

It was cramped. No A/C. No amenities to speak of, really. Packed-tight gymnasium, those cheap metal folding chairs that only got sold in packs of a hundred—not bad for a graduation. But absolute hell for the thirsty-for-blood spectators of tonight's fight. Hot enough to make your sweat evaporate, but too humid for it to actually happen. *Muggy*, was the word edumacated people would use.

Hotter than Hell was how Teddy experienced it. And in a church no less, Lord Have Mercy.

To most people, the sound alone would have drummed them straight into the ground. Hammer, meet nail. Here on this side of the cheap rubberized flooring (horse stall mats) beneath his boxing shoes one minute. Sleeping with the worms, or the fishes, or whatever else was beneath this church gymnasium the next (hell, it could have even been Hoffa).

But that was why Teddy was who he was.

And everybody else wasn't.

Few understood what it was to be the bad guy.

Teddy Pemberly knew what it was like to be The Bad Guy™.

He practically wrote the book.

Tonight he was going to finally show everyone just how it was done.

TWO

The walk to the ring could be long for some. Not nearly long enough for others. No matter whether it was a gym or arena or (in this case) a church gymnasium in the Bronx, if you walked the path and didn't want it to end, you were already dead to rights.

Teddy walked over the first of the black rubber horse stall mats. This was the first time in forever he felt like that. Usually he was about ready to go all rabid Doberman on whoever he might find at the end of this pathway.

Tonight though ...

Well tonight was different.

Some jabroni from seats good enough to make you wanna double-cross your mama butted into Teddy's headspace. Teddy happy for the distraction (another thing he'd never experienced).

Jabroni was either tipsy or letting out all the steam he'd accumu-lated over a lifetime of loserdom (except for whatever he'd done to get these seats). Jabroni spilled his beer over the little fugazi metal guardrails setup to separate the crowd and their folded metal chairs from the fighters as they entered the ring. Keeping the crowd penned in like bovine on the farm. Or maybe it was the other way around. These were the same mats they'd use on a farm after all.

Teddy's boxing shoes tip-tapped out of the way of the moisture, their soles gripping the rubberized flooring. This guy, this jabroni prick with a whisper-thin gold chain tangled up in an untamed wilderness of dark chest hair, all spilling out of a five-button shirt with three buttons undone, made from either silk or satin (but in any respect, tacky). Jabroni screamed whatever pain was inside him at Teddy, pretending like the guardrails were permanent, immovable forces instead of loosely connected pieces of scrap aluminum barricade dragged into place by a fat union crew member. Like he couldn't easily get in Teddy's actual wingspan if he wanted to as badly as he was pretending. The jabroni's face got as purple as Teddy planned to make his opponent's, just with more pressure behind the eyes. Mouth open wide enough that a well-practiced doctor could feasibly give the guy a colonoscopy. At least you figured with seats like his, he could afford the insurance.

He was unloading everything he had onto Teddy, but none of it stuck. At least *that* was the same for Teddy. It all slid off like Teflon, swept away with the rest of the boos and hisses and expletives that had turned the church gymnasium into the Devil's playground.

"We fighting in a church?" Teddy had asked his manager, Louie Bernadino, once he told him the details a few months back.

"Amen," was all Louie said.

"Is that like ... legal?"

Louie laughed, chomped down on the fat cud of chewing tobacco inside his cheek. "Is it legal to beat the ever-living snot out of somebody?"

Teddy shrugged. He was never much of a legal scholar anyway.

"It's a big church, anyway," Louie B said to someone on the phone a few days later while grunting out a deal. Louie was always on the phone, working on some deal, spinning up some story about how this match or that fighter was the next train to Gravytown. He cupped his hand over the phone and leaned away from this makeshift card table in the corner of the rundown boxing gym he ran. Teddy was busy hitting the speed bag. "Big enough you can finally get that pool you been dreaming of." Teddy didn't even remember saying anything to Louie about that. Louie dropped his hand and went back to his phone call, to whatever greaseball dealmaker on was on the other end of the line. "They hardly make churches this big anymore, you know? It's practically like we're fighting in the Vatican."

Teddy continued his slow walk toward the ring. He'd read the Vatican had ceilings hand-painted by some of the greatest painters ever. This church didn't look like it had ever painted the ceilings at all. Not even with the stuff you'd use to seal in the insulation.

A faceless crowd on either side of him. In these moments, he was both here and not. The crowd was a single organism hell bent on crushing his spirit.

As if they were the first to ever try doing it.

Some small-hands, small-Johnson loser tossed a bag of popcorn over the guardrails. This from seats that would make your mama simply shake her head in disappointment at you. "You ain't made something of yourself, son," she'd say. If she was in the grave, she'd be rolling over in it. Probably call you collect, too—no reason for her to go through all the trouble of a full-blown haunting just to tell your lazy, bum ass what you already knew.

The popcorn bag hit the ground with no sound, having gotten swallowed up in the rest of the melody of malaise that Teddy had come to appreciate over all his years fighting. Had come to *love*.

If you can't make 'em feel anything, then nobody's ever going to pay to see you fight. Was what Louie had always said, anyway.

"That means *zero* pools." The spray of tobacco juice turned the coffee-stained card table into a flood zone.

"Thanks for spelling that out," Teddy had said.

Louie waved a hand. "Hey, how long I been with you?"

Teddy shrugged. He'd lost track of the years.

"Since the beginning," Louie said, screwing up his eyes and face in a *the-fuck-you-serious?* face. "And believe me, during that time, I observed you. Smarts isn't really your thing, champ. Don't start pretending like it is now, huh?"

The popcorn hit the rubberized flooring right in the spot where the ramp declined slightly toward the ring. Last mile of delivery, or something like that. The bag tumbled forward a few steps in front of Teddy. Not the first thing ever thrown at him, but what kind of idiot tosses six bucks on the floor like that? Especially one with loser tickets like his? A guy in the front row can toss whatever he wants. Even in the Bronx, even in a church gym, the door was raking in cash.

Teddy could just barely smell the butter as he stepped up to the popped morsels. His face was already covered in enough grease and sweat that smelling anything else was a true testament to butter's willpower. Belonged in some kind of Seven Wonders list. Right there next to Wonder Bread, Wonder dark beer, and the wonderful contribution to mankind that was the deep fryer.

The familiar scent of hundreds or thousands of people sweating, exhaling, spraying their noxious anxieties out into the closed-air gym. Petroleum jelly. Vicks VapoRub that his team made Teddy huff on before he left the locker room—all the better for him to breathe.

Breathing was good in the fight game.

Hard to imagine *anything* having enough sniffing power to cut through all that. But butter on popcorn did it.

"Watch your step," Wallace said, pushing past Teddy and clearing a path with his foot. He used his beefy shoulder to give the stand-back-ace to another screaming punky who'd leaned over the railing, enough spit sprayed from his mouth to grow a few weeds when all was said and done here.

Wallace was Teddy's corner man and trainer. "Don't need you slipping in the ring on that shit, huh?"

Teddy nodded.

But then he stopped.

"Hey, champ!" Wallace said, grabbing at air where Teddy's right arm shoulda been.

Here's where it happened. The big transformation. Every time, near abouts. People had wondered as time went on. Fight game writers had pontificated as Teddy progressed through his long and often arduous career. Announcers—back when Teddy was young enough to have them cover his fights—had speculated:

Was it Teddy who fell into the trap? A guy who just couldn't get out of his own way?

Or was it everybody else who got twisted up in *his* game?

Teddy honestly wasn't sure.

Like Louie said, smarts wasn't really his thing.

Teddy threw back the hood of his robe. At one point, his robes had been silky smooth. Like the jabroni's shirt, only a lot classier. Shining beneath the bright lights of Madison Square Garden, the Vegas lights. Even a few international venues. He'd shimmered beneath those flash bulbs like a phoenix out of the ashes.

Now, though, his robes were plain vanilla in a cup. No sprinkles. A lightweight cotton material. Black cloth. Woven tight so as to keep his body warm on the walk from the locker room down to the ring. Hood big enough so that Teddy's face was shrouded in shadow as he approached.

So that whoever was inside the ring felt like the Reaper himself was on his way.

Now Teddy's face was out. Glaring up at the crowd. All he saw was a single blob of shadows punctuated by white-hot spotlights. A chimera of all of man's worst things: vice, misplaced emotion, avarice. How many of these people had placed bets against him, wanting so desperately for him to finally get his true comeuppance? Laying 4-1 odds, it was the sort of boxing bet that a lot of degenerates had been waiting for. Almost too good to pass up.

Teddy glared up at the ring first before doing anything. Looked at Nate Galero. Typically, Teddy didn't care who was in the ring. Lately—due to fatigue of the grind, or age, or whatever jelly was starting to slosh around inside his noggin'—he was embarrassed to admit he just couldn't keep it straight.

Tonight though, he knew.

Tonight was different.

The past-his-prime Bad Guy stepping into the ring against the new up-and-comer Golden Boy. Everybody loved Nate Galero–even the whites who so often turned their backs against any brown-skinned brother trying to make it in the fight game (at least since Iron Mike).

Everybody wanted in on that.

But there were still a few minutes until the bets would close.

People could still lay down some cash at 4-1.

Teddy Pemberly would see to it that they did. The bad guy, making sure everybody has a good old time tonight.

He bent over, using both gloved hands to pick up the half-empty bag of popcorn, kernels and fluffy white popped clouds hovering down to the ground like snowflakes as he did so. Not an easy task to do, picking things up, with boxing gloves on.

Teddy held the bag up as if to challenge whoever it was had thrown it. That small Johnson loser. Bring it, chump. Enjoy this.

Teddy held the bag up now, higher. As if to challenge every damn person inside this church. As if it were the Holy Grail, and he was the one person to uncover the damn thing.

And now he was going to gloat about it.

Show them what they were missing.

He turned the bag up from the bottom and let the greasy, salty popcorn pour out.

Straight into his damn mouth.

He smiled as he chomped away at it, the scent of it overpowering his tastebuds. It tasted amazing. Smelled even better. The crowd's hissing and booing went from Led Zeppelin to Slayer, which heightened all of it. Made it all the sweeter.

It was nice, eating some chow before the big fight.

But most of all, it felt good to be the bad guy.

THREE

Teddy sidestepped a left jab that could have taken out a small village in Africa.

As he did so, a strange slow-motion moment of clarity: cameras flashing, blinding lights in the crowd turning every face into an apparition. The church thumped, an indistinct bass line hovering beneath the surface like Jaws. The twin-scented coppery bloodstains all over his body and shorts–his and his opponent's.

For that moment, Teddy felt in another dimension.

Despite the thrum of his heart and the adrenaline so thick inside the church that Christ himself would get jealous, it seemed to Teddy that he'd sidestepped himself out of the ring and into some other dimension.

Nifty Nathan Galero tried another attack, this time opting for a right hook. Nice try, Nate. Teddy ducked beneath it with so little space between impact that the *whoosh* of the air was like a tornado passing through a trailer park in summer. Any closer and Teddy's face would have to be picked up off the unkempt vine and weed-tangled yards.

It was the fourth and second-to-last round. Once upon a time

Teddy had gone twelve rounds. Back in the title fight days. Back *before*. But when you fought in a church auditorium in the Bronx—even when it was packed to the gills like this one—people didn't have the attention span to watch twelve rounds. And nobody wanted to see the sad sight of a has-been like Teddy trying to hug his opponent to keep from tipping over.

Louie had pushed for the fight to be six rounds 'cause they could have upped the ticket price a buck-fifty at the door. But, "These fucking priests don't like that number!" Something about the Devil or something.

So five rounds it was.

Right now, Teddy was winning the fight, midway through the fourth. Probably. One of the things about boxing, you never really knew. Yeah, the scorecards were put up on the TV when you watched—but nobody was broadcasting this fight. And the judges weren't exactly the pick of the litter. They were about as shady as everybody else involved in the proceedings here, so it was anybody's guess which way they'd go.

Even still, anybody with half a brain could see it was all Teddy Pemberly in this fight. He'd had two knockdowns already in rounds two and three, respectively, and had Nifty Nathan up against the ropes for most of the fourth so far. Even if you paused everything right now, one look at their faces would sum the whole thing up.

Teddy probably still had butter around his mouth from the popcorn.

Nate's face looked like someone had just pounded a piece of steak with one of those mallets you see at the carnival. The High striker, or whatever it's called. High striker sizzling steak.

Delicious.

But Nate was nothing if not persistent. He started working his feet like he should have from the beginning. Cutting off Teddy from working his way around the ring. Keeping Teddy on the defensive. Not a half-bad strategy. Had he started it in the second round, it might have worked. Nate knew it. Teddy certainly did. So it wasn't such a surprise to Teddy when Nate tried what he tried next.

The guy needed to make some noise.

Rumble, young fella, rumble.

Nate approached Teddy from the side, sliding those young feet like Fred Astaire, if he was desperate to get the part. Teddy saw him– hell, the whole place saw Nifty Nate coming.

But Teddy saw something else, too.

Right behind Wallace's brick-wall frame was the kid. All four-foot-seven of him. Big brown eyes like saucers, the creamy whites of his eyes as innocent and pure as cats drinking their milk.

What the hell was he doing here?

"Stop wondering, start punching!" Louie and Wallace's voices both echoed inside Teddy's head. Weird catchphrase they had at their gym. Someone had even spray-painted it on the wall. It made sense though, Teddy figured. Louie always said Teddy wasn't the brains behind the operation, to leave the thinking to Louie and Wallace.

So what was Teddy wasting his energy wondering for now?

Louie was never what Teddy would consider *wise*. But maybe on this one point he was.

Because that's the thing about wondering when it comes to boxing.

It typically doesn't end well.

FOUR

The kid shouldn't have been there for a million and ten reasons. How did he even get in? He wasn't with a parent, wasn't there on some Make-a-Wish thing. Kid that age shouldn't have been sold a ticket—not to something like this. A big time fight, bright lights—if a kid his age could swing that, or get someone to bring him, then that was alright.

But not here. Here lies the seedy underbelly of the sport. Complete with every seedy character who came along with it. A fleet of clown cars full of them packed into this gym tonight.

Wasn't anybody taking care of this kid?

Wasn't anybody responsible?

No adult presence to accompany him, at least?

Those eyes—those honest, good-natured, wide eyes—were now watching the bad guy in action. They were in the bad guy's world now. This might have been a church, but Teddy didn't think it was a particularly Christian thing to do to a kid this age. He was twelve, maybe thirteen. Grew up around here. Good kid—as most are at that age—but he wouldn't be for long if he hung around places like this.

Couldn't anybody see that?
Why didn't anybody care?

FIVE

Teddy fell hard. Like tree. Like forest.

Teddy fell hard like Rome.

He did something he hadn't done much of in his career: touch the mat with his face. Having done the thing, it wasn't hard to see why you'd want to avoid it. For one: the mat wasn't forgiving. Not at all. The canvas slapped back. A woman who just found out you were sleeping with her sister. The mat was vengeful. Just another foe boxers had to face.

For another thing: falling down in the fight game meant you weren't doing it right.

Meant you might never get a chance to be the bad guy, maybe 'cause nobody ever got invested enough in your career to care whether you were good or bad.

They simply wouldn't even know you existed.

"The fight game is a fickle bitch," Louie said a million times if he ever said it once. "My first wife could tell you all about that."

"That why you left her?"

"Left her?" Louie scoffed, coughed, and brushed himself off before chomping back down on his ball of tobacco leaf. "I'd skin myself alive and let you make a jacket out of me for another night with her." He scoffed again. "*Left her*. Ha!"

Teddy didn't know what to make of that, so he hadn't said much else at the time.

Still didn't know what to make of it now, but it didn't seem so important when his brain was pounding away at the insides of his skull like someone buried alive in there.

Either his vision was going white at the edges or the flashbulbs outside the ring were blinking out like galaxies on their last legs. He didn't hear anything except for the Teddy Pemerbly's Brain High School marching band (specifically the percussion section) doing their darndest to breach a new threshold on the decibel scale inside the auditorium of his mind.

Plenty of people would say Teddy had lost a step. Anybody who just turned up would have a hard time refuting that statement, what with Teddy practically stone-cold dead on the mat and all. Hard to argue reality, that.

Only they'd be wrong.

Teddy might be on the mat.

But it was exactly where he wanted to be.

Black sneakers square-danced around to right next to his position–prone, bruised, and with a half-wit smile trying to peek through his thicker-than-a-bank-vault mouth guard. The sneaks stopped, assessing. This would be the referee. Teddy knew–from experience standing *up* in the ring while his opponent lay on the mat like a schmuck–that a countdown would be underway.

One, two.

The referee would be talking it out loud, letting the downed fighter know how much time he had before he needed to stand up or shut up.

Three, four.

For the life of him, Teddy didn't hear a damn squeak out of the ref though. Not unless the guy was talking in a single-frequency, high-pitched whine that seemed to emanate from an unknown cavern inside Teddy's skull. Teddy imagined one of those cave explorers (the kind who goes a mile deep into the darkest abyss looking for bats) taking a journey inside his fractured head, surveying the scene, and sending word up to base camp that things are even worse than they all feared. "Send help," they'd transmit up to those who might be able to do anything about it. Unfortunately for those intrepid explorers down below, base camp would get nothing coming up through the communication channels but that high-pitched whine. In fact, those explorers had been left for dead ages ago, the people up top already having mourned, performed their memorial service, and moved onto other things.

Those down below abandoned. Swallowed up my Mother Nature's insatiable appetite.

Spelunkers, was what they were called. The cave explorer guys. Teddy had looked it up once—taking care not to strain himself too bad from the effort. It even involved picking up a book. He'd learned about a cave in Vietnam that stretched almost six miles underground. Sơn Đoòng cave. Epic shit.

Five, six.

The bad guy lay prone on the mat, all of these leaching pains feeding off his energy stores. Teddy wasn't out of it, not by a long shot. The good guy in the fight—in life, hell—would have hopped right up, smile on his face, a double-glove-tap (I'm ready, Coach!) and an 'attaboy emanating from inside his soul like the chipper prick he was.

But the bad guy wanted to milk this moment.

Because in this moment, something was happening out there in the arena. Something boxers weren't supposed to think about when they were inside the ring. *Stop wondering, start punching.* These people here to see him lose smelled blood. They knew the bad guy was hurt. Was down. A little over a round left to go, too. Maybe there was still time to get in a bet on Nifty Nate? The odds were bad, but hell, it was a sure thing, wasn't it ...?

The high-pitched whine of Teddy's inner ear dissipated. In its place, another ringing sound.

A cash register.

Seven, eight.

A bunch of them, actually. Almost like a walk through the Vegas slot section.

In-match betting would be going on here. You don't wind up at a boxing match inside a church auditorium with a nightly matchup card like this one if you didn't like to gamble. And pre-fight gambling simply wouldn't cut it for you, either.

There were too many chances to lay out some more action to pass up.

Teddy got to a knee, then to his feet.

He stood up and looked the square-dancer ref in the eyes.

"I'm good," he said through the mouth guard.

"You good?" the ref asked.

"I'm good, motherfucker," Teddy said, scowl on his face, his voice loud enough so that Nifty Nate could hear. The bad guy didn't mess around.

"He's good," the ref said to the ringside crew.

The crew nodded and said something back to the ref.

Further out, the crowd murmured. So close they'd been to getting what they wanted. The bad guy had been down.

Now he was up.

Did he look shaky? Tired? Fucking concussed?

Yeah, yeah, yeah.

And maybe still, he'd go down in a heap of his own making.

Everybody wanted to see that.

Just to be sure the crowd got what they wanted and then some, Teddy figured he'd give 'em a show. Let 'em see exactly how much he valued their opinion of him.

The bell rang to end the fourth round.

Some—*most*—felt it came just in the nick of time for old ass Teddy Pemberly.

And those that didn't soon did. Because Teddy walked toward his corner and climbed the post. He raised his arms overhead and beat on his chest, giving the crowd his best come-at-me, I-dare-you stare.

The crowd roared in disapproval. Once again they shifted and swayed with unseemly aggression. They tossed a few beers toward the ring, but their pansy-ass pitchers didn't even have the arms to reach.

The bad guy was here. And he wouldn't let the people forget it.

Only one round left. The fifth.

They'd see.

They'd all see.

SIX

Jab, jab, hook, jab, hook, jab, *HOOK*.

Nifty Nate wasn't the golden boy any longer. Not when his back was up against the wall.

Now he was a savage. A caged animal. Fighting like he caught rabies.

The crowd murmured, cheered. Their collective heartbeat grabbed a quick flight down to Colombia for party favors and flew all the way back up on their own beating arms. They grit their teeth with a whine, gnawed their fingers down to stubs. Sweat and spit and vapor floated in the air like a summer rainstorm had just come through.

All the while, Teddy blocked, blocked, ducked, shifted, blocked, ducked, *ATE IT*.

Another knockdown. Another song that only he could hear. A requiem for how his brain used to be.

The mat was no more forgiving this second time. Teddy didn't just lay on it in the prone position, he melted into it. This time struggling to keep his eyes from crossing up like Iverson. He was pretty sure he was still breathing, but Nifty Nate had served him up with something nasty–ten thousand pounds of pressure on his chest.

Maybe they'd call him that after this match: Nasty Nate. The former golden boy.

Nate was now a wild, dangerous individual. Wanted in three states. Considered armed and extremely likely to make everybody a boatload of money on tonight's fight.

Could even be the new bad guy, huh? Maybe was being groomed to be just that.

Teddy–through an electrical surge of pain rushing down his spine and neck–turned slightly to look over at Wallace.

Toward the kid.

Wallace sat like an eclipse on his stool, one hand on his hip bone (like something an archaeologist might dig up), other hand on the very edge of the mat outside the ropes. He was nowhere near the action, which (so much as it even was action at this moment) was at the approximate middle point in the ring. *There lied Teddy Pemberly, former boxer, about to cross over to be with Jesus.* Wallace's eyes were still and cold. Two pits staring out from the dark side of the moon. As if he were watching his best friend betray him.

Teddy figured that was a pretty good approximation for what was going down.

Behind Wallace, the kid was barely visible. Daylight on the horizon. Peace at the frontier. The kid stood pressed up against the cheap aluminum barricade that kept the sweating, screaming, unwashed masses from charging the ring. Another few inches, the kid might get turned into string cheese squeezed through the slots.

Even still, the kid stood expressionless. Hands not even white knuckling the metal as he held it, his knuckles bruised and battered like he knew a thing or two about fighting himself.

Maybe because he did.

Maybe because Teddy had him hitting the speed bag twice a week. The heavy bag every other day. Jump rope twice each day, along with calisthenics to beef him up a bit. A way to keep some of the rougher elements of the In Christ We Believe Orphanage, where the kid lived, at bay.

Teddy heard the ref's countdown this time. A miracle on par with their current location in a house of worship (or at least next to one).

Six, seven.

Teddy didn't hear a peep from Wallace. The big man seemed to get what he was witnessing. Maybe he wasn't happy about it, but he wasn't going to say so. "It's your fight once you step in the ring," Wallace was fond of saying–less an abdication of duties than a way to keep Teddy focused during the grueling months of training.

Teddy heard Louie, though. Inside his skull, but still. "Might be your last payday before we send you to the glue factory. Let's get that winner's fifty-percent take from the door and you can finally get that pool."

Eight, nine.

Louie didn't have enough sense to recognize Teddy lived in an apartment in the city. Nothing fancy. Just enough for a guy with soup for brains to spend his days, plenty of delivery places for when his knees went to shit, plenty of ladies for when he got lonely, and plenty of floors below him in case the darkness inside of Teddy ever got too deep and menacing to flee.

There was no pool there.

No.

But there was one at the In Christ We Believe Orphanage.

Or at least, there would be, once Teddy got done being counted out.

The ref hesitated.

Teddy let himself fall into the mat. His whole career, his entire self-worth falling in with it. He was a spelunker tonight. Taking a dive, getting as far into the murky dark as any fighter could ever go.

He just hoped that in the end, it didn't swallow him up whole.

Ten.
Ding, ding, ding.
The bad guy lost.

SEVEN

Only, the bad guy didn't. Not really.

Teddy's whole body was swollen. The locker room quiet, dark. Loser-lonely. Lockers almost big enough to get stuffed into, like the weakling loser he now was.

"We should have put you out to pasture after the last one," Louie had said right after. Some people might have been able to say this kind of thing in a *mea culpa* way. *I put you in this spot, Teddy. That's on me.* Somehow Louie made it seem like Teddy had been the one at fault. Like he hadn't been the one laying it all out there inside the ropes.

Teddy didn't mind. His head hurt too much to mind. And besides, he'd done the bad thing.

Fitting for the bad guy.

Louie paced around like an aardvark on a coke binge. Teddy still had stars in his ears and ringing in his eyes, but he could see that Louie was, uh, a bit agitated. Smell it, too, the nervous sweat fuming off his manager like a chemical spill.

"FUCK!" Louie slammed an extra folding chair against a wall of lockers. Slamming it again and again and again, punctuating each creative combination of cuss words as he did so. As if the lockers were the ones who'd just lost the fight.

Yeah, he was maybe a little more than agitated. Teddy was having trouble coming up with the word. But it was a strong one, whatever word you wanted to use.

The little bit left of his mind hovered somewhere above the whole scene, detached from the throbbing pain of the rest of his body. Still feeling it, but also seeing it from somewhere else, too.

"You were expecting something different," he said. "A different outcome."

"A different outcome? The hell is this, Shakespeare? I was expecting you to come through for me! To win the damn fight against that two-ply golden boy out there."

Louie picked back up the chair and continued tapping out the beat of his anger on the lockers.

Teddy lowered the ice pack from whatever part of his face it was in contact with. He'd stopped being able to feel awhile ago. "Guess that will be something you can talk to Nifty Nate about, now that you manage *him*. Though I was thinking, you might want a rebrand. Get ol' Nifty mad, another side of him comes out."

Louie stopped mid-slam with the chair. He looked at Teddy's face, searching–probably in vain–for the fighter's eyes.

"Nasty Nate, maybe." Teddy shrugged, unable to come up with any other nicknames. "I don't know, something to think about."

A small bomb might have gone off somewhere inside Louie. But on the outside, nothing doing. Like maybe somebody hit the pause button on him.

Teddy had little control of what was going on with his face at the moment. But he hoped he smiled.

Hoped his eyes said, *Yeah, fuck you, too, Louie.*

Teddy thought they might have done just that, because Louie threw the chair halfway across the room. It broke into pieces after hitting the wall. Then he stormed out, huffing and puffing, saying something about never working again with rent-a-fighters, that he was going to finally take his talents to the big time.

Yeah, yeah, yeah.

Wallace had wandered in and out after Louie left. A mass moving through the post-fight pity party. Like a celestial body revolving around the imploded dark star of its galaxy. Wallace didn't say a single word, just tended to a few of Teddy's cuts and changed out his ice. If he knew what went down, he didn't say.

That suited Teddy just fine.

Eventually even Wallace left him alone.

So Teddy was left to think about it—all of it—by his lonesome. His conclusion (as best he could come to one with pea soup for brains): *Shit. All that for nothing.*

The kid appeared from the dark corners of the locker room. He'd disappeared into the crowd once the bell went off. Now he stood amongst the shadows thrown off from the yellow incandescent light flickering above him.

"What the hell?" was all Teddy could manage. The inside of his mouth hurt like he'd gnawed on glass. Ribs and lungs didn't feel so hot either. The rest of him would feel like shit later on, once the real soreness set in.

But the burn of the bad guy never dies. Even for a washed-up has-been like himself, something had been at stake here.

Burn, burn, burn.

The bad guy isn't so happy. "You show up here alone? Was that part of the plan, kid?"

The kid instinctively stepped back. Half-a-step. Maybe less. Even a mangled and mauled Teddy Pemberly could strike fear in a kid.

Only for an instant, though. The kid's eyes went from saucers to daggers. He balled his hands into fists.

He stepped forward into the yellow light, which seemed to flicker again. This time like it was almost cowering.

The kid said, "Dennis got into that stuff again. He could barely tie his own shoes three hours ago when I left him. How you think he was gonna do once we got here?"

Dennis was the third leg of their whole *fecocked* plan. Dennis worked at the orphanage. A social worker who shouldn't have been— too much social and not enough worker. He had a good heart, but he couldn't turn down a beer or a pill to save his life, and most of the time he didn't seem to care so much about said life to even bother trying. And once Dennis started, the rest of the night was as inevitable as death, taxes, or brain damage for a guy like Teddy. Shoe tying would seem like quantum physics compared to his capabilities.

Teddy's burning rage smoldered and flamed up. "I took a fuckin' dive, kid! You have any idea what that means?"

A smirk. Tightening of the eyes.

"Something funny?"

The kid jumped up on one of the locker room benches. The bulb above him flickered, but somehow burned brighter. "Oh, ye of little faith." Unlike Teddy, the kid was pretty smart.

He produced three betting slip receipts from one pocket of his hoodie.

A stack of folded cash as thick as an encyclopedia from the other.

"How the hell–?"

"Told some creep he better put in the bet for me."

"Oh yeah?" Teddy said with a relieved sigh. Behind his eyes, the pressure of a thousand storms was building. "Why would this creep do a thing like that?"

The kid smiled. "Told him I'd scream he was a dick diddler if he didn't." The kid was young still and couldn't help but giggle at this.

"I'll be damned," Teddy said.

Only he figured he wouldn't be. Or if he was, it would be for something else he'd done. Plenty to choose from after all.

Tonight, though, he was pretty sure he'd done the *right* thing for once.

The bad guy cashed in for the kid.

"Was hoping I might see your manager on the way in," the kid said, looking back over his shoulder toward the locker room entrance. The kid peeled a bill off the fat stack. "Maybe give him a little tip."

"Easy. Don't get so confident now." Last thing Teddy needed was the kid turning into a two-bit hustler.

"What? He was trying to play you."

Teddy sighed. Louie was definitely doing that, yeah.

"He goes down in the fifth," Louie had said on the phone after he thought Teddy had gone to the showers. It was the night before the fight, in the gym, Louie doing what he always did: talking on the phone.

It was all Teddy could do not to slam through the locker room doors and set Louie straighter than Wilt Chamberlain. If he thought Teddy was taking a dive, he had another thing coming.

Only ...

"Yeah, the golden boy will be our golden goose. Odds are opening their legs for us right now, ready for us to stick it in, baby. A bet like ours—if placed strategically at the right time—could be lucrative. More so than my first divorce was for my wife. You understand?"

Teddy couldn't believe it. His *opponent* was going to take the dive? *That* fact might have been even more insulting. Nifty Nate would hit the mat alright. But it would be by Teddy's hand.

But instead of barging into the gym and playing speed bag with Louie's face, he listened.

Listened as his little slime ball manager cupped a hand over the receiver and hunched his back forward as if he could smother the sound of his own voice.

He might have had better luck just turning his lazy ass around and making sure nobody was around to hear.

What Teddy heard from all this listening was Louie drawing up a scheme to profit off Teddy's bad guy image. "Nifty Nate is the golden boy. Young, but too green to win this fight. Teddy is old, but tough as they come. He won't let this pretty young thing take him down unless he catches a heart attack in the ring. And let me tell you, he might be shaking like an earthquake and sipping his meals through a straw in a few years, but one thing Teddy Pemberly's got is heart."

Instead of being flattered or getting angry, Teddy decided to just take the advice Louie'd been giving him for about as long as they knew each other. He'd been telling Teddy for years that smarts weren't really his thing, after all.

Well it didn't take a genius to see an opportunity like this one.

"People eat up the *story*," Louie said, taking his hand away from the phone to unleash a tobacco-soaked loogie. "Nobody wants to bet on the bad guy. They all want the golden boy to win. Early lines are coming in at three-to-one in favor of Nifty Nate, and our street team marketing in the next twenty-four will kick it up a notch. That's our chance. We bet Teddy to win by knockout in the fifth. Then we start slumming it on yachts in Saint-Tropez."

The strategy was sound. People would bet heavy on Nifty Nate because they wanted him to win. Everybody wanted to hitch their wagon to a rising star, not the aging bad guy. And whatever anybody ever tries to tell you about gambling, don't let 'em say they do it with their brain.

Heavy betting on Nate to win meant the odds would shift. Payouts for people who bet the other way, on Teddy, would grow. That was exactly what Louie was trying to tap into.

And Teddy's typical antics in the ring—even before he hammed it up tonight for the crowd—would only drive more people to bet on the golden boy, driving odds up even further.

But the bookie needs to even out at the end of the day. He wants an equal amount of money on both sides of the bet. Living off the vig, that's the bookie life.

So that same bookie would be more inclined to take an asteroid-sized bet once Louie placed his own. The way it would work was Louie's big money wager on Teddy to win by knockout in the fifth would create an imbalance. To re-balance things, the bookie would need to change the odds to make the Teddy-to-win-in-the-fifth bet *less* attractive to bettors. Meaning its opposite–a Nifty-Nate-to-win-in-the-fifth bet–would become *more* attractive.

That represented the opportunity Teddy needed. Other than betting on himself to win–something he pretty much already did with his health, life, and future welfare each time he stepped into the ring–there was no other play that would deliver big money. Betting on Nate to win *before* Louie placed the bet would simply have the same odds, which weren't great since so much money was riding with Nate. And there was no guarantee that Teddy *would* win, even if he did bet on himself. Least of all in a certain round. Boxing matches were hard enough to win on their own.

No, it had to be a bet placed on Teddy's knockout right after Louie's bet created the imbalance of money for the house. The void would need to be filled with something.

Besides, that outcome had the added benefit of screwing over Louie, who was apparently managing both sides of this fight without ever having mentioned it. Convenient.

Up until Teddy slammed into the mat in the fifth, everything had been going exactly according to Louie's plan.

It had also been going according to Teddy's.

"How much you get?" Teddy asked. "All twenty?"

The kid smiled again. This time his eyes went big. Sơn Đoòng cave big.

"What?" Teddy's mind working in freeze-frame. Did the kid not have enough dough to bring this thing all the way across the finish line?

"I got forty-seven."

"Forty-seven? Thousand? How'd you manage that?"

The kid smiled but didn't say.

"Guess you'll be getting the Olympic-sized pool, then, huh, kid?" It would be above-ground, so maybe not *quite* that big. But bigger than the zero square feet of pool the orphanage currently housed.

The kid nodded. "Maybe even a hot tub. Invite some ladies over."

"Easy, kid." He didn't need the kid turning into a player, either.

But despite himself, Teddy sat back against the cold steel of the lockers and smiled. Or tried to. His pain already fading.

He sensed his face was too swollen and tight for the smile to actually come through.

Better that way, anyhow.

Bad guys were only supposed to enjoy being bad.

And for once, Teddy did good.

RED TEMPEST

NIZ THOMAS

INSIDE EVERY INVESTIGATION
LIES A STORM

RED
TEMPEST

AN ORIGINAL CRIME STORY

PART ONE

The unopened bottle of wine sat alone between us out on the moonlit patio like all the tension that'd bubbled up over the past few months. My fault, I admit—no sense pretending otherwise.

I sat in the typically comfortable high-backed patio chairs (that cost some ungodly amount of money, I imagine) of our "secret" seven-bedroom beach house along the Jersey Shore. Bayhead, NJ. One of the towns without public beaches to keep the riffraff away. Certainly a far cry from my own experiences growing up and coming to the shore, where a free soda from Jenks on the boardwalk made not just my day but my whole year. Bayhead was a stone's throw from an ocean that too often made me shake my head in amazement, the fact I owned property so close to it. "Owned" in theory, at least.

House fully dark. To keep up appearances. We weren't really here, after all.

I stared at the bottle, as if doing so would make all my problems go away. But I couldn't get myself comfortable out here, under the moonlit clear sky with the soothing lullaby of the Atlantic Ocean. Not even a little bit.

And that, for me, should have been a sign of how bad things were.

The ocean always calmed me.

The wine bottle was sweating atop our massive acacia wood patio table.

My current predicament had me doing just the same. Except I also had the pleasure of being screwed to go along with it.

So I guess once we opened it, the wine and I would be in a similar place.

Beyond the eerie blue glow of our forty-foot pool and the patio within which it was nestled—which stretched ninety-five feet from the bottom floor of the house, an almost unheard-of length for a back-yard in this area—the ocean waves crashed along an unseen beach. Only the fresh, salty spray visible, its scent surfing on the wind's back and toward us. In front, the tops of the dunes glowed white beneath the moonlight. The dunes being a surprise treat levied onto us by the town after Hurricane Sandy hit.

Not that I minded. We weren't here that often, anyway.

Two dim candles on either side of my wife, Nancy, sent angular shadows scrambling to grab hold of something, anything, on her perfectly smooth face. And they made the combination of dark green bottle and blood red wine flicker with mystery. It was a fourteen-year-old Artisan. Not exactly vintage, though it was getting there.

When I first purchased it, it was only about two years old. As much as I could have afforded back then.

The label turned away from me, I only saw the bottle's ghostly glow. Like dark kryptonite. This varietal was called *Tempest*. A Napa Valley pinot noir that I'd been looking forward to since before we even bought it. The mystery building and building over the years.

Once a symbol of personal accomplishment—on my salary, expensive wines had never really been possible. Now, given the strange impulse when I'd gone down to the wine cellar to drink it tonight, its original meaning felt much different. More ominous.

Definitely a downer, compared to when I bought the damn thing.

Having removed it from the wine fridge downstairs twenty minutes earlier to adjust up, slightly south of room temperature, I'd made the mistake of bringing it out onto the candlelit back stone patio and never wrapped it up in a napkin or a towel to catch the condensation. Despite the cool temperature, made even cooler by the light breeze off the ocean, the air was just humid enough to make the bottle sweat.

I resisted the urge to get up and fix my mistake, something I knew Nancy would have rolled her eyes at. She was always saying how I worried too much about the little details, the things that most people were able to ignore or sweep under the rug. Things that in the grand scheme, probably didn't matter. It was true, of course. Not so much about the details not mattering—in my line of work, they mattered. Mattered more than anybody on the outside could ever know.

But I sweated the small stuff. Big time. Stuff I *knew* didn't matter, really, in the grand scheme of things. Just couldn't let it go. Not a great trait, but it had its upsides. The thing was, in investigations, it was always the overlooked detail that could have solved you the case sooner.

In my investigations, that could be the difference between life and death. And recently, there had been enough death that I was beginning to think that I was losing my knack for detail.

The heavy lump of tension inside my chest told me I still had the sweating the small stuff tact down pat.

But just like every wife's criticism of her husband—true or not—I didn't have to like it. Especially didn't have to like it now, during this shitstorm I was in.

I could hardly pull my eyes from the ring of moisture forming where the naked wine bottle touched the wood table that sat twelve. At other times in our life—simpler, more joyful times—we'd been forced to cram even more than that. Now it was just the two of us, hiding out, me sitting at the head and Nancy sitting to my right. And more than a few empty chairs looking back at me.

A reminder of those I'd lost by not seeing enough of the details. Failing to put all the pieces together.

So instead, my eyes and mind focused on the one small thing I could control but didn't want to with Nancy watching me. Like the permanent wood stain this damn bottle of wine was creating.

I knew Nancy didn't give a damn about wine. Early on, at least, she'd indulged me with the interest. We'd done Sonoma (the best), the Bordeaux region (stuffy but beautiful, like most of France). Even South Africa for Pinotage (breathtaking but a pinch guilt-inducing, what with that whole former-Apartheid-state-turned-segregated-settlement thing). Nancy could always afford it—the wine and the trips—which was probably why it held no allure to her. Being a high-powered attorney came with perks—the most prevalent one being the boatloads of cash backed up to your doorstep on an annual basis.

The stunning house, beneath whose shadow we both now sat, was another. I'd have to work overtime raiding the evidence cache just to clear half of what it was worth.

But Nancy?

Purchased entirely with *one* of those cash boatloads.

Which is what made it a perfect place for us to be now. The theory being (and like most theories, to paraphrase Mike Tyson, it held up for now, until someone punched me in the face) that since nothing was linked to my name, only a small, select group of people knew we were here. And *group* was probably too strong a word for it.

More like a half-full poker game.

I looked at the Artisan bottle, remembering how it had once been like a trophy. Proof of an accomplishment which seemed great at the time but now, after all these years, seems like table scraps compared to the problems of the day. The bottle was a present to myself. Stubborn enough was I to insist I pay for it myself, rather than have Nancy do it.

She'd wanted to get the *already* vintage varietal, despite having no actual idea the difference between the two.

But I had my meager eyes on the Tempest.

Now, with what was surely to be my last investigation set before me—then ripped away in a befuddling mix of details, lack of clues, and sheer emotional uppercuts all packed into one traumatic bombshell of an investigation so utterly fucked that it would make Jenna Jameson blush—it seemed as good a time as any to indulge.

This bottle of wine was now to be my participation trophy. Like I was some Gen-Z four-eyes, picked last for dodgeball, getting a pat on the back because of how well I'd shown up. Didn't even let my precious allergies stop me from leaving my safe space or nothing.

I dabbed my fork in the garlic-scented hummus we'd been enjoying (correction: I'd been mindlessly eating and *Nancy* had been enjoying), forgoing the freshly baked bread that Nancy made. Not wanting to allow anything in my stomach that would soak up the alcohol I planned to drink. The bread was a new hobby, one that I hadn't given her much credit for. Hadn't bothered to understand. Or really even notice outside of mindlessly eating the stuff once it was out of the oven. Not when she'd bought the yeast or the flour. Not even the bread oven, a strange looking red and black instrument that now sat atop our Calacatta marble countertop here (I guess to go along with the black one we had at our normal house—a penthouse apartment in the Gramercy neighborhood of New York City) and took up too much room to justify its existence.

The bread smelled amazing. No surprise. Nancy did nothing half-baked (no pun intended) and she was as skilled in the kitchen as she was working on the '78 Porsche I'd bought for her thirty-second birthday a few years earlier (I had to buy Ike Jones, the ring man in charge of the repo auctions, drinks for three months to conveniently *miss* the bids coming from two collectors in the back of the open-air bidding ring). Most people—myself included—tended to struggle juggling a full-time job and having a life. My *life* consisted almost entirely of my full-time job, which is to say that I juggle about as well as a blind guy with no arms. Part of me—the part I often wielded as a lens onto the darkest psychology humanity can produce—knew my attention to detail developed out of a need to control things. The less mess I left behind, the less maintenance my life required to stay in control.

So yeah, not much of a hobby guy.

Nancy, though, was some kind of prodigy when it came to hobbies. When it came to most things, actually. Despite working seventy-plus hour weeks at the firm, she still managed to be virtuosic when it came to the complexities of sourdough, rye, or three-liter rear engines. And those were just the two hobbies she'd developed in the past year. She also rock climbed, went scuba diving, and trained in judo and Brazilian Jiu-Jitsu. I'd often joked with her that she should apply to be a member of Mensa.

She just kind of looked at me like she'd run circles around those people.

The breeze off the water, mixed with the constant, gentle thrashing against the shore, ripped the bread scent away from me. Good thing for me, too, because it was started to crack my resolve. In its place wafted the wonderfully weird smell of salt water. Confusing, in that it didn't typically smell that great, but it carried with it so many other memories and sensations that it somehow made itself into something better. Tricked your mind into thinking dead fish smelled good. Ah, the complexities of man.

At least half—and an actuarial assessment would come in far higher—the reason we bought this house in the first place was that smell. We both fucking loved it.

The candles flickered, sending their golden glow drifting about with the whims of the breeze. Nancy's blue eyes shone above those smooth high cheekbones, staring at me. I was sort of just staring, though I noticed her lone piece of skin poking out from beneath her oversized white shag sweater (looking dyed blue from the pool's light) carefully draped off one toned shoulder. The sweater, hard as it tried, wasn't nearly baggy enough to conceal her feminine muscles and bronzed skin. The six-times-weekly gym routine enough to hold all excess weight at bay, even despite all the bread she made.

Our patio suddenly felt chilly. Though Nancy didn't seem to mind. The ocean's breeze had done me in, maybe. Or maybe it was Nancy's gaze that had given me the chills. My wife was a knockout. And she was looking at me intently. I could feel it.

She was the sort of woman that you'd trip over yourself to talk to if she walked in off the street, un-showered, wearing a circus tent big enough for Barnum and Bailey.

When she was dressed normally, sometimes it was hard to catch your own breath around her. Those eyes ... God. They were deep enough and sharp enough to kill.

She cut her eyes at me, the baby blues mixing with the red and orange glow of the candle. Reminding me of the center of a flame. Old-timers, guys who'd been in the job for a decade-plus, always talked about how they got stale on their wives after a while. How the passion went away. I guess most of it was kid-related, something Nancy and I didn't have to contend with.

Or, you know, the fact that those guys spent more time sitting down to dinner with John Jameson at O'Malley's or Leggett's than their own wives.

Goddamned if those eyes didn't still do it for me, though, like twin magnets and I was the perfect opposite pole, unable, by the mysterious laws of nature and physics, to resist. Even through the recent tension we'd had (which was definitely my fault). No matter if we were fighting, eating, or playing gin rummy, those eyes cut through me like nothing else I'd ever seen. Still capable of taking my brain and sending it down into Neanderthal levels of cognitive func-tion with a certain kind of look or wink. Because I'll be damned if my wife wasn't some kind of world-class winker. Tim Weathers, my old partner on the job, used to say that with a wink like that, it was lucky Nancy let me keep my paycheck (not that she needed it). Because she could turn me into an ape who donated his bananas if she truly wanted to.

But tonight, something didn't feel right to me. No surprise there. To be expected even, given what was going on with the investigation.

"Should we open the wine?" I asked, uncomfortable now in my own skin from her gaze. I never would have wanted to face those eyes in court. Would have had me pleading guilty for crimes not committed if it was what she wanted.

I reached across for the bottle placed between us, its red wax seal dripping down the side of the bottle like drops of blood on a recent crime scene.

I spun the bottle around so I could see the label. It was crème colored with a subtle, raised texture. Almost as if the paper had been crumpled first before the adhesive backing was applied to stick it against the glass of the bottle. Red, feathered lettering to match the wax's color. *TEMPEST*. A picture of an angelic woman floating in space in the upper right-hand corner. In the foreground, a different woman gripped both sides of her head, as if her own internal thoughts were too agonizing to bear. Despite the fact I liked to tell myself I had a sensitive palette for wine, I couldn't ignore the fact that the labels did a lot to sell me a bottle.

And the fact of the matter was that this one looked pretty damn cool.

Taking another look at it, it was startling how much artistry there was in the woman's face in the foreground. An attention to detail that I could appreciate. Part of the reason I liked the brand at all. A black and white pencil drawing, or at least it had been at some point, probably before they scanned it into whatever computer they used to design the label entirely. The whole thing had a very textured and tangible feeling. Three-dimensional despite being pasted-flat on the bottle. Shadows perfectly drawn to the point they almost looked etched into the paper, just so you could make out every curve and crevice on the woman's tortured face. Her mouth open, the shadows darkening and spiraling down into complete blackness as they wound their way down her throat.

Pain like hers wasn't easy to come by.

And there I go again, empathizing with the damned.

"I'll get it," Nancy said, her manicured nails clinked against their glass before I could grab hold of the bottle. The corkscrew appeared in her other hand immediately, as if she slipped it down her sleeve like a magician. As if she'd somehow been waiting for my word. "Wouldn't want you to spill on your white shirt."

It was a joke. During our fourth month of dating, we'd gone on a weekend away in Boston together. I had to go for the National Behavioral Analysis Conference, a multi-agency criminal forensics gathering, and Nancy had been able to get off work and join me. Hotel room was already paid for, so she just needed to spring for the Amtrak tickets.

Everything then had seemed so exciting. It wasn't just the sex. Each habit and new revelation was its own journey.

But the second night we'd gone to a nice dinner at a Brazilian steakhouse near Copley Square, just the two of us, having been able to sneak away from the other conference attendees. After gorging on red meat for an hour, we were too stuffed to make any true effort at the bars with my colleagues. So instead we grabbed a bottle of red from a nearby liquor store and planned to pop it open in the hotel room.

Come to find, corkscrews don't come standard at a run-of-the-mill Marriott.

So Nancy says she knows a way to open wine bottles without one. She describes the method to me—placing the base of the bottle inside a sneaker or other thick-soled shoe and knocking the shoe's sole against a wall. Essentially trying to jar the cork loose bit by bit. To my surprise, it worked.

But she forgot to tell me what happened when you took the cork off.

That night, I was wearing a white shirt. No surprise, as I was at an FBI conference. White dress shirts were practically standard issue. They come with the gun.

So what Nancy forgot to tell me was when you finally remove the cork from the bottle, you need to account for the buildup created inside.

When the bottle exploded everywhere, I learned that last part the hard way. Blood spatter, was probably how it looked. Luckily it was only the five-year-old Cab I'd gone to three liquor stores that night to find and dropped about fifty dollars on, something I thought would impress the high-powered attorney who I had somehow tricked into dating me. You know, the one who couldn't tell a rare vintage wine from Two-Buck Chuck.

So the Cab soaked my shirt through like I just knifed a grape lattice.

We had laughed and laughed about it, Nancy having "forgotten" about that last part. I still wasn't sure if that was some sick practical joke or if she'd really forgotten. But knowing how little ever truly got past my wife, I had always presumed it was the former.

Nancy's toned shoulder poked out further from her sweater as she twisted and worked the corkscrew from the bottle. This time using the *traditional* method. It exited with a satisfying *pop*, something that reminded me of my last day walking through the FBI classrooms, my jubilant ass acting like everything else in the world, from that point forward, was going to be alright.

She smiled at me and poured a thick stream of blood red liquid into my glass, the only difference being the slight bubbles as the vino rose. Real blood only bubbled right at impact.

Nancy poured herself a glass, then tucked a foot underneath her butt on the chair.

"Cheers," she said, raising her glass.

I clinked against hers without even thinking. A wife acts, a husband reacts, I guess.

"What are we cheersing to?"

She shrugged. "You remember when you bought this bottle?"

I nodded. It had been the same weekend as that conference, after I received a surprise award for my use of a new forensics methodology to clear a rash of cold cases, all linked (unfortunately) to a long-dead serial killer who'd terrorized the Boston Harbor area for an eight-month period during the late 1970s. It was unfortunate because it was the first time anybody had been able to put a face to some of the unspeakably evil murders that had occurred and gone unsolved for so long. Luckily for the politicians and citizen of Boston at the time, the murders happened to the sorts of people who didn't garner a lot of media attention. It was a sad but true phenomenon. Serial killer victims often tended to be from marginalized communities who wouldn't—or couldn't—cause an uproar once their people started going missing.

While it was good to clear these cases off the dockets, the unseemly underbelly of the investigation was the unspoken one that made everybody uncomfortable: hanging fifteen cold case bodies all on one man—one horribly evil man—served to remind that society contained evil in its purest and most unadulterated forms, walking amongst us, blending in, never captured, but only able to be stopped by dumb, blind luck or hard-earned (and with demand far surpassing supply) investigation. The former like when the killer, named Brendan Alex Masterson, finally succumbed to some unknown disease during the winter of 1979, putting an end to his horrid deeds once and for all. And the latter like when I came along nearly a half-century later and figured the case out.

The wine had been a gift to myself—both as a reward for the recognition bestowed upon me by the conference committee, and as a kind of panacea after the brutal months of trying to climb inside the mind of Brendan Alex Masterson in an attempt to find more threads we could pull on. It was one of those cases that grabs hold of you and doesn't let go. A pet project that I stumbled on during training in Quantico and didn't give up on until it got solved a few years into my actual law enforcement career.

"I was so proud of you, Cam. You'd set a goal for yourself and accomplished it. It was quite a turn on." She winked, which almost sent me into a mental tailspin.

Somewhere behind me, the ocean slammed down along the Jersey coastline like it had stolen something. And that noise had broken through my brain just enough to keep it focused on the present moment.

"But it seems to me that you've lost your way a bit."

Ouch, that one hurt. More so because, as usual, Nancy was

completely correct. I'd seen her wield this accuracy in court like a scalpel. And today, apparently, was going to be no different.

I took a giant swig of my wine, forgoing all manner of pomp and circumstance typically surrounding the ritual. Daddy just needed to numb the feelings.

And the feelings were legion.

I took another sip of the wine, its aroma catching me in the back of the throat. Flushing my face and neck with its gentle heat. It struck me, too, in the front of the head, making my eyes swim a little from the thick punch of its powerful oak and berry scent.

Nancy either didn't bother to see my reaction to her words or had decided she wanted to twist the knife a little further. "Because the thing of it was, you used to be such a brilliant investigator. A true visionary in the field."

What was she getting at?

She continued. I eyed her glass, which sat beside her untouched on the table, apparently waiting for the moment when she got done eviscerating me. "And now you've got four dead agents on your conscious and as far as I can tell, not a single viable suspect."

I was not unaware of the reputation my wife had developed inside the courtroom. Often, with exacting people—those who wield clarity of thought and logic the way Musashi wielded the katana and wakizashi—their aggressive veneer and tone can rub people the wrong way. Known—and this is probably the kindest descriptor in existence—as a bit of an Ice Queen, Nancy could cut right into you with her directness.

It was by no means her only form of communication. But it was the one you remembered the most, if you were ever on the wrong side of it.

Nancy leaned across the table and grabbed my hand, a tight, pained smile crossing her face. I couldn't read her eyes.

I just fell into them.

But then she smiled and showed me there was apparently some mercy left there in those baby blues.

"You know what I remember from that Boston weekend?" she said, crouching down to get her eyes level with my downcast ones.

"What's that?"

"Finchy."

Fuck. "C'mon, Nancy, I'm not in the—"

"Shhh. We don't honor the dead by pretending like they didn't exist."

I wanted to honor the dead by catching the fucker who killed them. But I guess in the absence of that ...

"That was the first time I met any of those guys. And Finchy was about the most protective guy I could have gone toe-to-toe with."

I waved my hand at her. "Oh, please. You could have run circles around him if we took both your legs off and replaced his with Usain Bolt's."

Nancy puts up a finger. "*Could have*, yes. But that would not have been a wise course of action. Brett Finchy is not a man who took humiliation lightly."

Took.

Goddamn.

"I didn't realize the conquering Nancy Ashe concerned herself with the wise course of action when vanquishing opponents. At least not when pomp and arrogance stood in her way."

She shrugged. "I was soft back then. But anyway, that first night out, before the conference even started. We all got pizza somewhere downtown before hitting the bars. Stumbled into some Irish Pub, naturally. You remember that?"

I could still smell the liquor and see the long, dark wood bar that seemed to stretch on forever, like our bright futures.

"Sure. J.J. Foley's. Place is legendary. And old. I think that was where the Boston PD voted to strike back in the early twentieth century. Thousands of police got canned as a result."

Nancy rolled her eyes. "A fitting place to tar and feather your new girlfriend."

"At least they had Guinness."

"Anyway, Finchy kept pressing me. Asking me police interrogation 101 questions. 'What brings you up here with Cam?' and, 'What are your intentions for this trip?' Not a warm welcome. Frankly, not even a welcome that anybody would recognize as such. Not anybody with manners or décor, anyway.

"I think he even asked, 'What sort of future do you see with my friend here?' It wasn't clear to me whether I was dating his friend or his daughter."

I smiled despite myself. Mostly against the pain. "Finchy could be a bit protective." A pang of guilt bloomed inside me at the thought of that. Felt like getting slowly poisoned.

"Well naturally, my answers were flawless. The shots of whatever nasty well whiskey they were serving us that night didn't hurt, either. Took the edge off for me. And it put Finchy into Grinchy Finchy mode."

That memory made me laugh out loud. Back then, Finchy was a bit of an angry drunk. Never malicious—the occasional fistfight with another guy who'd had too much and had the same kind of pent-up anger notwithstanding (though, as a law enforcement professional, this was considered with far greater latitude than nearly every other kind of civilian).

But mostly, Finchy just got mouthy. *Fuck this place*, or *screw that idea*. Talking about his precious New York Mets was like listening to an Andrew Dice Clay record. But less clever. And a whole helluva lot sadder.

"Grinchy Finchy," I said. "Wow. Been a while since I heard that."

"Been a while since I thought about it. He started mouthing off, I forget what about."

"More likely you drowned it out after the first ten minutes."

"Probably. But later on, we were probably six, seven shots deep. The mouth was starting to go on cruise control for him. It was nearing the point of reckless driving for me."

"He always could hold his liquor," I said. I'd left him at plenty a bar after hours and heard stories about him closing the place down. Then saw him bright-eyed and bushy-tailed the next morning.

"That he could. An amazing talent," she said, rolling her eyes. "So anyway, at one point he's *f-ing* this and *f-ing* that, really getting on a hot tear. I guess I was standing in his way or something and he leans in, gets his face an inch from my own. Stares me down. Eye-to-eye like we were weighing in for a prize fight. And he says, 'Don't mess with my friend.' Dead serious. Stone-cold sober-like. Like a moment of clarity amidst a drunken storm of Grinchy Finchy."

I nodded, trying to keep the reins on my mind instead of letting it run wild off into the dark corners up there. Here and now with Nancy? This was a nice story. A fond memory. Everywhere else? Not so much.

"We just looked at each other for a while. Probably a second. But seemed like a lifetime." Nancy's eyes drifted off, the reflection from the flickering candles rippling across the moist blue surfaces of her eyes. It was only then I realized she was crying. Or, at least, tearing up.

"Nancy—" I said, suddenly pulled from within myself out of concern for her.

"No." She squeezed my hand and used her other to bat at the edges of her eyes.

The scent from the ocean drifted up on the back of the wind. Behind us, the house creaked and swayed—something I'd been surprised to find out happened even in expensive homes.

I let my hand linger on the warmth of Nancy's.

After a long, windswept moment of quiet, I said, "So what happened next?"

She smiled and it was almost as if the sadness disappeared at the snap of some imaginary fingers. "I don't know. He kept staring. I stared right back. Nothing else seemed to move, everything else fell away. There was some godawful music playing. But it went silent. It was like he was appraising me or something. Trying to take my temperature.

"And just as suddenly as he slipped into that clarity, he emerged from it and said, 'And who do I gotta blow to get a fucking drink around here?'"

"Classic Finchy."

"Yeah. But in that moment, I felt like he really saw me. Strange and cliché as it sounds, I felt as though his gaze opened up my mind and walked on through its labyrinthine corridors. Opening doors, peeking inside rooms. It was really … weird, to be honest with you. But given how protective he had seemed of you, and the fact that he never once again asked me questions about my *intentions* with you, I guess he got whatever he was looking for."

The truth of it was that Nancy and Finchy—while they got along just fine superficially—were never particularly close. Of all my friends, Finchy was probably the one who kept her most at arm's length. But he was—fuck, *had been*—a bit of an emotional rock himself. I was kind of surprised the Ice Queen experienced such an odd emotional connection with the guy. Doubly surprised she was moved to tears thinking about it.

"I wonder what he'd have to say about it now," she said, her voice kind of trailing off into the darkness. Not sad, though. Genuinely curious, maybe. "I never did get a chance to ask him about it."

"You know him. He probably would have either played it off like he didn't remember or made it into some big joke."

"*Nancy's got a crush on me!*" she said, slurring her words the way he would have if he'd been drinking. Laughing.

"Oh, God. I'd never hear the end of it. He'd be giving me shit for weeks about how my wife was ready to leave me, shack up with him."

Nancy smiled again, though it didn't quite touch her cheeks.

That smile reminded me of the pain underneath that story. At least the pain I felt. It was all-encompassing. An eclipse of the emotions. Like when you were sick and suddenly could not imagine feeling well again—or ever having felt well in the first place. Between that story and all the others I'd lived through recently, it didn't even seem possible to feel anything else.

Nancy raised her glass. "Another toast then."

I clinked with hers.

"To Finchy," she said. "May he enjoy heaven as much as he did J.J. Foley's."

"Here, here."

We sipped in quiet.

"So," Nancy said, letting the single word float out between us. I knew she was marching toward something. She rarely spoke without purpose. "How's the investigation going?"

The words hurt. Not as bad as the others. Less cutting and stabbing. More like getting squeezed tight in a pressure point. With a bruise. It was the sort of comment only a wife could make, she was trying to injure instead of nurture. Body blows.

The investigation, to put it mildly, was going like shit. Four agents dead already.

After two, my boss told me it was an historic black eye for the agency.

At three, it was an embarrassment.

He didn't bother to contextualize the fourth with words. Suffice it to say, it was a five-alarm fire. And I was asleep inside the house as it burned to charred ash all around me. Worst of all, my whole family was inside, too. Screaming at me to wake the fuck up and do something.

Nancy knew it wasn't going well. Had to. My lack of sleep and short temper would've been dead giveaways. The bags under my eyes and the terse responses. Only dregs left in the coffee pot when she gets up at five-twenty in the morning. I don't even think she knew about the extra three fingers of Macallan I'd been drinking each night.

Or the three more after that, when the first round didn't quite do the trick.

I took another sip of the wine, vaguely conscious of the fact that I was clearly trying to avoid my feelings. It was a classic scenario I saw at work. And just like most scenarios people saw at their place of work, it took me a while to diagnose its existence in a new and different environment. Just like when you run into a co-worker in a benign, safe space away from the office. Takes you a few moments to recognize them. Unless you just look the other way and pretend you didn't see them at all.

With those I study—killers, mostly—their inability to process the trauma of their lives causes them to lose themselves. Or perhaps to discover their true selves, if you're one of those people who believes Big Evil exists. Since I'm not, my belief system stems from the fact that the repressed traumas of peoples' lives force them toward coping mechanisms. For some, like me recently, that manifests in a drink or two after work to numb this pain (numbing, of course, that ignores the true root cause of the problem, yes, I know, and thanks for the concern).

But for the subjects that come across my desk every day—or worse, those I need to cull from the massive troves of personal data the FBI has at its fingertips—these same coping mechanisms manifest in much different ways.

These thoughts all floated just beneath the surface of my mind like bodies trapped beneath a thick layer of ice, their faces obscured by the frost and snow. I felt as if I were standing atop the ice, feet unsteady, watching as these things tried to reveal themselves to me.

Yet still, I recognized that some larger giant lurked in the dark waters that I could not see. A secret revelation that simply did not want to show its face near the ice's surface.

Such was the experience of investigative work.

Hard to tell if this time was different or whether the victims—those men I considered brothers-in-arms at the Bureau—just heightened the usual feelings that came along with trying to catch a killer who seemed to always stay one step ahead of your ken.

"Not so good, huh?" Nancy said, the stark blue accepting eyes frowning ever so slightly. Like a puzzle master trying to figure out how to fit in the last piece.

"Brody is pretty upset," I said. Brody was my direct supervisor.

Great guy, practically a clone of Captain America. Best man at my wedding and vice versa. But all this had taken a toll on him.

"When was the last time you spoke to him?"

I sighed, swirling the remaining blood-red wine around in the thick bottom of my glass. So much had gone on in the past twenty-four, forty-eight hours, I truly wasn't sure the answer to Nancy's question.

"He won't return any of my calls," I said, at least knowing that part to be true. I'd dialed Brody a baker's dozen, at least, since this morning. Word was that maybe he'd gone to the brass to do damage control.

Realistically, he'd probably gone, hat in hand, ready to cut my ass if necessary.

Of course, that would not be necessary just yet. As bad as it might be that four of our guys died—probably all at the hands of the same killer—it would have been a whole lot worse to cut bait and start over now. Data-sharing was a whole lot easier these days at the Bureau, easier in the sense that it was actually possible now, if you wanted to do it. But this wasn't a case anybody wanted to inherit. Even Bureau guys didn't make enemies they hated bad enough to drop a shit-sinker case on someone like the one I've got.

No, no, no. The brass would let me sink this ship all on my own. At least until the body count grew to double-digits. Seven on the outside.

Yeah, this was my shit pile to lord over until the end. Plenty of time to pin the blame on me once it was all over with.

Besides, although everyone would do their best to help me out, there wasn't anybody else better suited to solve this case than yours truly.

Of course, and this what the sick part, the part that really would spin a two-bit shrink like me—focused on uncovering some of the sickest and cruelest killers who ever walked this earth—in circles like Scooby Doo after he busted a Sinaloan grow field: I didn't mind the fact that all this crap was getting dumped on me. Or would get dumped, at least. Some point down the road. Dump away, was how I looked at it. Dump, dump, dump. Because I'd never been in this game for the politics.

I only ever cared about putting bracelets on bad guys.

Since this would almost certainly be my last case, somebody smart and centered would accept the bad—revel in it, even. One day, maybe, I'd miss it. I was kinda sick like that.

But I'm not so centered or smart.

I'd never before needed any motivation to accomplish the goal of catching killers.

But now, with the pressure coming down from on high to clear this sideshow off the streets, I had more than enough.

Maybe more than I could handle.

All four guys dead were my friends. And it was becoming increasingly clear the same person did all the killings. In fact, with the fourth body—I was trying my hardest not to think of it as Brett Finchy, my former partner, a guy I went to the Academy with—had made the connection between the first three murders all but impossible to ignore. Even the stats nerds had told me it was more likely the universe implodes in on itself than a "disinterested or disconnected party," (nerdspeak for "someone else") killed four of my FBI brothers.

So why the hell was I here with Nancy when I should have been tracking down leads?

I sipped my wine and clenched my jaw at the thought of that.

Brody might have had a different opinion than me. But the reason was a bunch of political bullshit. I'd grated and ground against the politics of my position many times before. But this time was a battle I couldn't win. A true Kafkaesque maelstrom.

I was the person in the best position—perhaps the only person—who could solve this case.

Yet they didn't want me anywhere near it. Or, at least, not until it had received the solemn head nod from on high. The executioner's nod, you might say. Brody needed to cover ass until he received that nod, when he could put me back onto the case on a lease so short you'd be hard-pressed to see it. Then they'd ride me all the way into the ground before putting me under it once the case got solved and this whole thing blew over.

Go puzzle that one out for me.

Part of me wondered if the FBI wanted this case solved at all.

That was mostly hyperbole, of course. People on the front lines, at my level and a few levels above me, all wanted it solved. Double-quick.

But I had my doubts about the upper echelons of the Bureau food chain. Anybody that was enough of a political animal to get into positions like that could spin a big spectacle like this—even one that had the high likelihood of embarrassment—into fodder. Bait for their own whims and goals. Because now people were finally *watching*. And once they were watching, it wasn't a stretch to convince them that the FBI required more resources to catch the cold-blooded son of a bitch capable of killing four of our best and brightest in cold blood.

So far, at least. Four so far.

And from what I could tell, getting resources was the number one highest aim of everybody that worked at the upper echelons of our organization. Of any government organization, really. Because once you got it, it was double hard for it to be taken back away from you. Nature of Washington, D.C., I guess.

"You've always had a lot going on inside, Cam," Nancy said. A slight breeze picked up off the ocean and made the candles dance atop their wicks. Long spindles of hot wax dripped down the sides like slow tears. "Even now, I can see the wheels turning up there."

"Sorry. Sometimes it's just hard to turn off. The gift and the curse, right?"

Nancy pursed her thick, wet lips. The flames danced on the tips of her eyes, the moonlight casting her in its milky white glow. The food in front of us had grown cold by now. It made my stomach turn. Nothing but acid inside. And now, alcohol.

"You always had the knack for investigations, Cam."

"To the detriment of everything else," I finished for her. It was true. A common complaint over the years. I was too much in my head, spinning through fragments of information on my investigations. Turning them over in my mind like I was looking for half dollars beneath rocks. While I should have been paying attention to my wife. To my friends.

Four of whom were now dead.

"Why don't you talk it out?" she said. "Maybe it will help you process some of the info."

"Won't do me any good, anyway. Brody iced me from the case. I'm no longer able to investigate in any official capacity. Was told any unofficial investigating would be considered highly renegade—until I get the green light. Prematurely re-entering the arena would 'affect my future employment and pension.'"

"So they'll fire you?"

"I'll be fired either way. They're going to dump this whole thing on me and not even give me the opportunity to solve the bastard in the end."

"You've never been one to give up before. And if you're giving up now, then it's pretty piss-poor timing, no? Given everything that's at stake."

She was right about that.

"Who cares about a pension, anyway?"

And that, too. We hadn't bought this beach house on FBI money.

"Maybe talking it out will jar something loose for you. It worked on the Red Stream case."

I shuddered. Dark days I had hoped were behind me. Only come to find that they weren't nearly as dark as things could really get. At least *that* hadn't been personal. The Red Stream case was something best left as far away in the past as was possible.

"I'd hate to kill the mood, babe," I said. Wanting to avoid talking about this case. Talking about it just didn't feel right. Red Stream, I couldn't help but discuss it with gentle prodding back then. It had enveloped my mind, wandering inside like a worm to an apple.

This case? I just wanted more wine, less feeling. Less thinking. Less talking.

"The mood is dead and buried, Cam."

I grimaced. Plenty of my friends were dead these days. But not all of them buried, yet. The pace of their deaths coming so fast and furious it would have made the genius ATF gun walkers blush.

"Sorry, poor choice of words." She saw me eyeing the Pinot and got up, refilled my glass. I'd never been a huge talker, but she must have figured the best way to get me going was to put a few heavy pours in me and hope for the best. "Here you go. Country club pour," she said, handing me an almost-full glass.

I smiled, watching her lithe body move with incredible grace along the moonlit patio. Like an actress in a '50s musical. The breeze from the ocean carried with it the light scent of lavender, my beautiful wife's signature scent for early spring. Wild thoughts danced quite a bit more primitive and hungry behind my eyes as I got lost in the cool scent. The flush of wine over my face wasn't the only thing that was warming up right now. The adrenaline of the case, the anxiety, the rising tension ... Christ. It all needed an outlet.

I often wondered what it was about me she stuck around for. Maybe she pitied me.

Nancy was whip-smart and a born litigator. Her knowledge of the law, and of people, was spot on. Probably better than my own. I joked with her that if she had preferred far less money, recognition, and professional freedom, she would have been an ace field agent.

She always said she didn't have the stomach for all the blood.

I didn't buy it. She seemed like she had the stomach for anything I could handle—plus a whole lot more besides.

Nancy stayed standing, glided around behind me before I finished taking my first sip. She was a quick one, her body moving almost faster than my eyes could follow. Had been an athlete back in her high school and college days. Ran track. And not the kind that look like they swallowed a tapeworm. Her pictures from college made it clear she could have been a model just as easily as an athlete.

She placed a hand on either side of my neck. Started massaging her thumbs into the backside of my traps. "Maybe I can help you out."

Her hands kneaded my neck, hitting tension spots I hadn't even noticed yet. One of Nancy's hobbies, some years ago, had been massage work. There had been a brief, but quite luxurious, phase where I was her test subject. Relaxation massages like shiatsu and hot stones had done wonders for my golf game—as much wonder as playing four rounds a year allowed for. I did reach new levels of flexibility that I hadn't even known existed, though. Which helped in other places.

But once she got keyed into the deep tissue and sports rehab portions of her curriculum, my enjoyment level as her test dummy plummeted way down. Even now, visions of pressure points and the remembered shock of feeling like my muscles might pop under her prodding still lived only slightly beneath the surface.

Like all things Nancy did, she'd come at massage from all angles.

Right now, I was back firmly in the not-minding-it camp.

"You haven't been doing the stretches," she said, referring to the protocol a doctor put me on two years earlier after I'd developed a splitting bout of migraines that he claimed stemmed from stress.

Turns out trying to nail some of the world's most disgusting violent criminals tends to raise the old heart rate.

"Stretching doesn't calm me," I said, feeling the deepest muscles in my neck tense and then loosen beneath the pressure of Nancy's fingers. Her hands (and I think maybe even an elbow, so lost I was in the sensations) danced along, knocking all the muscles back into place like a game of whack-a-mole. She'd somehow gotten stronger at this since she last experimented on me.

"I know, Cam," was all she said. Not bothering to add the thing we both knew to be true. That stretching wasn't supposed to calm me. It was just supposed to allow my muscles to move freely instead of twisting in on themselves into knots that eventually sent me into a tailspin of pain.

But mercifully, Nancy decided we didn't need to talk about that right now.

"What characteristics would make the perfect lead suspect?" she asked, probably realizing if this conversation were to get going at all, she'd need to pepper me with questions and massage. Make me forget what was going on.

I took one long, big sip from the wine before putting the glass back on the table. A deep breath helped push away all the shit cramped up inside my head. Just for a minute. The fragrant mixture of lavender, clear air, and mist of saltwater doing just enough to keep me from getting too worked up.

Then I fell away into the simple bliss of investigator mode.

"Organized, first and foremost. Scary organized. Each kill was meticulously researched and planned for. Willis, for instance, was killed during church, for shit's sake. Plenty of possible witnesses. Not a single one of them saw anything helpful. No security footage available, obviously. Except for three places in the church. Two of which were possible entry and exit points. And what would you know? But the killer didn't use either of those, instead finding a relatively unknown doorway not even accessible without some legwork."

"What does that tell you?"

"Killer isn't noticeable. Or, at least, is good at blending in. Possibly a regular of the church, someone nobody would associate with a strange sighting at mass."

"What else?"

"He did his homework. Anybody else would have used the doors with the cameras—both of which were well-hidden. I'm an investigator and I didn't even see one of them."

"And you canvassed the church's records, right? Got a list of all their parishioners?"

Two of Nancy's fingers zeroed in on a pressure point midway between my Adam's apple and the cord of muscle running down the side of my neck, their kneading and twisting sending shockwaves of perfectly placed pressure into the deepest recesses of my neck and down my spine. It felt the way I imagine nirvana might.

"It was one of the only things the brass gave me any help with, actually. Smoothed it over with the archdiocese and everything."

"Because of that whole, *freedom of religion* thing, huh?"

I laughed. "Yeah, something like that. Only trouble is, its congregation is more than thirteen thousand people all in. The largest church in the tri-state area, if you can believe our luck."

"But you can eliminate a lot of them, can't you?" Nancy let up for a moment and I reached back for the wine. I shrugged and took another big swig.

"Theoretically, yes. But that takes a lot of analysis. The techs are working on it, but the overall population of the church also adds to the other confounding factor."

"That the suspect could have slipped in unnoticed." I could tell Nancy was doing the thing she does every time she helps me analyze a case. Squinting her eyes, like she's trying to make the images appear right before her. It's incredibly cute. And she's got the type of dynamo personality where sometimes I'm actually surprised when the clue doesn't appear right in front of us. "So the parishioner list is probably chock full of people who wouldn't know the name above or below them. A church like that one, in the city, new people show up all the time. So I guess that doesn't help as much as you'd like."

"Ding ding ding," I said, watching the wine circle the glass. Nancy let me take another sip before continuing on with the massage.

"What else?"

"The organization is the main thing that stands out so far. You see it so infrequently out in the real world. But the killer is also calm under pressure. Every crime scene showed clear signs of the killer pausing. Taking his time. Never rushing anything. Even with Willis —in a *church*—there was a preternatural calm.

"With the Padrino killing, the medical examiner said it was likely

Raul was alive for close to twelve hours, getting bled out like a fucking cow."

I bit my lip as Raul Padrino's dead body flashed before my eyes like two headlights speeding around the bend. If Nancy thought she'd have a problem with the blood I see on a regular basis, she would have had no chance at that crime scene.

She started working to the right of my spine, pressing her thumb and forefinger against a band of tissue running down that side of my neck, which felt like a steel support beam right now. But Nancy's fingers felt good. Like they could melt steel if given enough time. Popping knots and who the hell knows what else that got twisted up in the flesh.

Exactly what I needed, though not enough to really let the tension out of me. I tend to get tight when reliving the details of four of my friends being murdered.

"So, organized in preparation," she said. "Calm during the act itself. What does *that* tell you?"

"That we're dealing with a very dangerous individual. Probably the least likely kind of killer. The one everybody in my position hopes to never draw on their bingo board."

"What's that?"

"An apex predator."

A little squeeze from Nancy's fingers told me the description shook her. Of course it did. She was more than just smart. She understood the types of crazy investigations I'd been a part of. Most serials, spree killers, or violent crimes were committed by people who were disorganized, impulsive, and had practically no chance of really getting away with it. They did so by preying on the weakest and most vulnerable portions of society—marginalized communities, the disabled, kids. Absolutely disgusting. But true. Every once in a while, though, you had a calculated killer who slipped through the cracks— not as much anymore with all the forensics, but it still happened.

This, though, was different. This killer took out four FBI agents.

And did it in gruesome ways. *Skilled* ways. Which was a term I hadn't ever needed to use in any past case.

One that I still wish I didn't need.

"An apex predator?" she said, her voice tight and nervous.

"Basically. Like a lion roaming around inside our playpen. But replace the giant mane, long teeth, and a jaw capable of crushing a car door with the lethal traits that only a human predator possesses: cunning, wit, persuasion, focus, commitment ... "

My voice trailed off. When I said like that, finally verbalized the challenge I was up against, it made me lightheaded.

It sounded damn near an impossible case to solve. One of the unsettling things about the killings was that these weren't four people who couldn't stand up for themselves. I'm not saying they were all MMA fighters, but not a one of them had let themselves go. And most of them trained semi-regularly in tactics. They could fight.

Which meant our killer was either a bad ass fighter or could throw one hell of a surprise party.

Or ...

"Commitment to what?"

"I'm not sure," I said, my voice sounding to me like it had gotten caught amidst the churning waves of the ocean. If only I could lose my troubles in there, too. "But that's what I need to find out."

"Have you considered the likelihood that you know the killer?"

"Yeah. Seems almost impossible for that *not* to be true. Other than all four of our guys being field agents, there was almost no other link between them."

Nancy had finished kneading the left side of my neck now and moved her fingers to my shoulders. I hadn't noticed. But her fingers started working the same sort of unseen and unfelt knots, just in different places. "Almost?"

My body tensed up involuntarily. I didn't necessarily look forward to the fact I needed to tell my wife something uncomfortable. Something I hadn't yet shared with her until now. Something I was very desperately hoping would become irrelevant, or a moot point. Preferably because we'd caught the killer. Or killed the bastard.

But each death made it more impossible to ignore.

And we hadn't caught shit yet.

"Well, the thing of it is, Nancy," I said, working on keeping my voice steady. Not loud. With any luck, it would wash out against the sound of the waves. If they had been churning a few minutes ago, they were thrashing much harder now. The calm and peaceful sound giving way to nature's rage. A reminder of its power and the fear and respect which it should be given.

Something I hadn't yet considered when dealing with serial killers. Just one more of nature's shitted-up, shitted-out creations. One more thing that can kill you.

Nancy's fingers stopped moving along my shoulders. "What is it, Cam?"

Nowhere else to hide. "The biggest commonality between all the victims is me."

As I opened my eyes, everything still looked almost exactly as it had before. The moon's glow was glaring off the smooth, polished surface of our table. The candlelight danced, too. My wine swirled ever so slightly inside my glass. The bottle with its artistic layer sat just past my reach, still sweating on the table. But everything seemed a bit ... whiter. Blurrier, though. How long had my eyes been closed?

I knew that despite the appearance of similarity, behind me stood a wife who might very well be different now that she heard those last few words.

And if she were smart—and damned if she wasn't brilliant—she might be looking down at me now like the massive liability I knew myself to be. If she was anything, it was pragmatic.

"What does that mean, exactly?" she finally said as another wave crashed onto shore.

"George Willis worked directly with me on the Trenton Prison project," I said, referring to a research assignment the two of us had conducted to study the efficacy of a new kind of personality test on violent criminals. "Padrino was my AIC for my first four years on the job before he got kicked up the chain and migrated over to organized crime. Winters got his interview on my recommendation."

"And Brett Finchy was your partner for two years," Nancy said, finishing for me. Probably she knew I would've had trouble saying that last one myself.

"Right."

"And you haven't made any other links between all these victims? I mean, didn't they at least know each other?"

I shook my head. "That's the thing of it, Nancy. They really didn't. Maybe in passing? Sure. Might nod and shoot the breeze for a few, they ran into each other at Leggett's or McGrady's. But they didn't have much else in common. Not besides me."

I took another sip of the wine, realizing with only mild surprise that I was almost done with *this* glass, too. My face was warm, flushed, and I guess I was getting a little bit buzzed because it all felt happier and lighter than before, even though my eyes felt a bit heavier beneath the lids. This case was really starting to wear me down. Maybe getting canned wouldn't be so bad after all.

But something else was lurking beneath the surface of my mind, too. I let out a deep breath and buried my head in both hands. A storm of a headache was approaching, something I knew had the possibility to rage harder than the ocean water I loved to watch so much.

"I don't know. I'm pretty beat, Nancy." I didn't add in the fact that I was worried, too. About whether she was even safe. Whether I was. Some brass had assigned two troopers on the block, undercovers. Which must have been because one of those ass-kissing, King-Kong-climbing pricks had gone long on my career over/under. Plenty of guys wash out of the ranks. The job swallows them whole, especially in the land of what I do. I've heard twelve years is where they pin guys. So I'm guessing we only have undercovers on the block because somebody had me and the over. I wouldn't hit twelve years for another month.

So we were "protected," I guess you could say. Especially since we were at the shore house. And it was under Nancy's name, which wasn't even the same last name as mine.

But given the sort of skill for killing on display at the crime scenes of my four friends, that didn't exactly calm me.

My gun on my hip? That helped a bit. This wine was helping, though it might be a death sentence should the killer really come after me. We figured he wouldn't strike again this close to Finchy, having been only two days. And even if he'd had a bead on me, my routine has changed significantly since then.

So I was worried, just not so much about right now, tonight. My three (to six) fingers when we went back inside and Nancy went to bed would help ease the anxiety for tonight. After that? Who knows. I'm sure I could scare up some pills from one of the guys at work, If I could catch them outside the office. It was made quite clear that I was no longer welcome inside.

I'd seen some darkness in my lifetime. Enough for two lifetimes, actually. But the murder of colleagues and friends was a lot to take on.

Being on the sidelines was its own sort of punishment.

"I worry about you, Cam. I really do." Nancy's words were quiet, spoken just at the edge of my ears. Her lips caressed my earlobe, sending a shiver of delight down my spine. Finding its way to a certain area that I hadn't even thought about since the murders had started.

Her fingers worked expertly on my neck. Despite myself, I relaxed, my body falling back into the chair. The wine was working itself into me, almost like I could feel it coursing through my bloodstream.

Only it felt funny. A little bit like I was slipping into a sleep I couldn't pull myself out of.

I lifted my head up. Tried to, at least. My head didn't move.

"I really worry about you, Cam." Nancy said again. This time, her words were different. More edge to them.

Alarm bells went off in my head. The same way they did when I got some new hot lead on a case. Or when interviewing a suspect and realizing they were the ones who committed the crime.

"You're looking for a killer that's organized, calm, blends in, and enjoys to kill. Someone who knows you, probably. Or knows the others in a way that isn't yet clear."

"Pretty much," I said, the words feeling jumbled on my heavy tongue. Maybe I wouldn't need those three fingers after all. The events of the previous thirty days, since Willis got killed, swirled inside me like the waves out on the beach.

Anger and frustration were the catalysts. But they paled in comparison to the hurt and shame that came with not being able to solve the case before *more* of your friends got killed. Every scrap of self-doubt materialized before me, weaving together into a horrific chimera, getting life breathed in from the darkest recesses of my psyche. Jung called this *the shadow*. And right now, I couldn't conceive of a better name for it myself.

"Know anybody like that?" Nancy asked, stepping around to stand before me.

When working cases, I often envisioned a watch. Not the digital kind, nor the cheap quartz or battery models. I'm talking the high-end mechanical ones. The type of watch that contains hundreds of minuscule parts, all moving and pulling together in unison. A profile of a potential killer are the screws and studs and levers that hold a watch together. The foundation. Without them, the watch would fall apart. But they are hardly the total package. Atop that, I lay the case details—evidence, interviews, working theories—which represent the various wheels and balances that work beneath the surface to turn the dials.

And as the facts of the case change, and we uncover more evidence, the hands on the watch face march around the dial. The second hand represents small achievements—clearing suspects who fit the profile but definitely did not commit the crime. The minute hand represents the revelations that drive us close to our target—

when we narrow down an occupation or general area where the suspect lives.

Until finally, all the hands come together.

And line up at perfect midnight.

I looked up at Nancy. Her blues eyes radiated from the nascent light of the backyard. She stood with both arms at her side, her figure still as taut and perfect as ever.

But in that moment, I found that I was not attracted to her. Not at all. I was actually ... repulsed. In a way. She seemed far less feminine than I remembered. As if the thought of how she had always been the entire time I knew her drifted off like smoke on the wind.

I experienced that perfect investigative midnight.

She had a smirk on her face. Like she'd been reading my face, waiting for me to come around to it.

No.

No, it wasn't ... couldn't be possible.

I tried to stand. My head suddenly weighed about a million pounds. Compressed my spine to inert. My body felt just the same. Neither arms nor legs responded against the extra weight.

Like I'd swallowed Jung's shadow.

My eyes wouldn't focus. Blurred at the edges. Awash in the blue glow from the pool.

The wine glass fell from my hand in slow motion. But I could do nothing to stop it.

The screaming, tortured woman on the wine bottle's label.

The Tempest raging in her head, just like in mine.

I reached for the bottle, suddenly desperate to hold something I knew was real. Something I could use as a weapon.

Except ...

The shattered glass startled me. It was only after it broke that I realized the clumsiness of my attempt. The difference between what I had tried to do and what actually happened. Blood red wine stained the dark stones of our patio. My hand fell, heavier than all the stones combined.

I was so very tired just from that one attempt.

"S ... s ... shit," I said. My mouth was full of sand, maybe. Or marbles. I couldn't talk over them.

"Oh, that's alright, Cam," Nancy said, her voice a pitched sing-song of *strange*, given the situation.

I tried to get up, to lean forward and kneel. To start cleaning up the shattered glass. No idea why that urge came over me. As if picking up the mess would put things back to how they were just before perfect midnight.

Instead, I rocked forward and against the table as I fell against it, the light of our patio blurring in my vision like a time lapse photo. My legs gave out beneath me. The thick wood table held me upright, half-in and half-out of the chair.

I was a fumbling mess of a man. Had I already gotten this drunk? I'd had some wine, but not *this* much wine.

"Don't you worry about all that now."

I put my arms on either side of the chair, trying to turn in my seat and see Nancy's face. My head was so heavy, though. Took too much effort.

Instead of turning, my arms bents at the elbows like cooked spaghetti, losing all possible leverage.

I fell to the ground and landed amongst the shattered glass. I braced for pain. Tried to. Even though my reactions were dulled, I knew the bracing came far too late in the process.

But I hardly felt a thing.

What the hell was going on?

A nudge against my side. Then I was looking up, the moon high above me. Massive. Like it was ready to drop right on top of us all.

Nancy's face appeared. The candles had no trouble throwing their shadows across it now.

I never interviewed any victims of the killers I'd investigated in my career. Crazy to think about, but true. Unfortunately, no case I was ever on had any living victims. But I'd done my fair share of research, reading transcripts and watching interview footage of other people's cases.

In the more infamous cases—your Dahmers and Bundys and Pichushkins—surviving victims often spoke of a moment just before or during the attack when the assailant physically transformed. In Dahmer's case, an escapee spoke about how the physically unaffecting Dahmer suddenly transformed into the Devil, his body growing taller and wider during the gruesome attack. As if the killer had drawn power from the prospect of violence. As if Dahmer embodied the true evil that existed inside him.

Lying still on the patio, unable to move, I now understood that anecdote in a way I could never before have imagined.

Nancy's eyes were thin slits, their powerful, sexy blue still visible but smoldering beneath something much darker, like dying coals on a fire. All the surrounding features that made her stunningly beautiful were still there—high cheekbones, the small, perfectly shaped nose. But she was no longer pretty, face contorted into a slight frown, brows furrowed. Reminded me of a desperate, dominant, hungry animal.

An apex predator.

The oversized sweater draped down. But she looked bigger beneath it, as if ready to spread her wings and truly become reborn in the guise of Satan.

She stood differently. Not stooped, exactly, but as if there was a coiled live wire inside her, ready to explode. As if she could reach out and wrap her dangerous arms around the whole goddamned world until she smothered it right where it lay.

The suddenness of this change was so startling to me that I tried to blink it away. But even the simple act of blinking now felt impossible. My eyes were hooded and heavy. Whatever was happening to me, whatever this was, it seemed to be kicking into a higher gear now.

"Right under your nose this whole time, Cam," she said, shaking her head slightly and clucking her tongue. "The answer has been right in front of you."

"Nancy ... what the ... *fuck*?" I think I managed to get out. I now realized I was not drunk.

What I actually was? That was anybody's guess.

"Twelve long years together. At first it was fun. The sex was *great*. And then I thought it would be useful to have a husband in the FBI. And it was. Always hearing about the latest and greatest methods for catching killers. The best working theories from the alleged best minds in the crime fighting community. You were so generous with your information. A little lipstick and lingerie and you practically taught me how not to get caught."

The flushed feeling in my face spread. Down my neck, slowly, creeping along like a spider. Then to my shoulders. My biceps. My forearms.

"Oh, I'm so sorry. *You didn't know*." She laughed and laughed. A disingenuous, haughty laugh that turned into something far more sinister, given what she was laughing about. The sound drowning out the waves from the beach. Growing. Multiplying. Piped in directly, down from the giant moon. The one which Nancy eclipsed from my vision like the celestial body she revealed herself to be.

"P-please, Nanc—"

She cut me off. "But, Cam, the last few years? Well, the job really consumed you. You grew isolated. Stopped sharing, so you weren't as useful anymore. Your effort in bed was less than stellar. While I was branching out, growing, becoming stronger, learning new things? You, sadly, were not."

"H ... he ... help. Please."

Nancy ignored me. "The final straw for me was that you were losing your edge. Was it the extra drinking? That would get my vote, personally. I don't think you have dementia. Would be a little early for that.

"And so I devised a way out of this marriage, Cam. I'm sorry to say it. You were either going to catch me, which would have been interesting. Would have given me a new challenge to chew on, as unlikely as I figured that outcome to be. Or this would happen."

The flushed feeling grew warmer. Less like a pleasant drunk. More like putting your hand inside the open door of an oven. "So you ... poisoned me?"

"Don't be so dramatic. You know, I thought about just disappearing. Vanishing without a trace. I figured that would have been hard on you."

"And ... " I coughed involuntarily. As if the poison had seeped into my lungs now. "You thought ... it would be easier to just ... confess? To killing ... four ... friends?"

"*Easier?*" Nancy let out a laugh. "Heavens no! I thought this would be more painful. I'm not one to let somebody off the hook, you know. I nail them to the cross *and then* make them drag it." She shook her head and kneeled beside me. I could smell the lavender on her. The scent made me gag now. "*I thrive on pain,* ex-husband. Sick, perhaps. I'm sure you could diagnose it. But I've always needed something a little bit ... *darker* ... to occupy my mind."

I shuddered. Probably from whatever poison Nancy had given me. The edges of my vision blurred and narrowed, closing in. The blue light from the pool, the candles, the moon. They all morphed together into one shimmer of light.

But they couldn't stop the slow crawl of darkness.

My mind raced. But clumsily. How could I have been so blind as to not see Nancy as a suspect? How could this even be fucking happening?

"And I'm not a feminist, either. But the fact you *always* think only a man could kill the way I do? It's a little insulting."

"St-st ... stat-is-tical probability."

"Look at me, Cam. I am a statistical *im*probability. You've always known that. You just chose to ignore it."

The last bit of light in my field of vision was surrounded on all sides by the coming darkness. The hot sting enveloped my body.

This was how I would die.

"Goodbye, Cam." Nancy's voice came from somewhere amidst this haze.

It was the last thing I heard.

PART TWO

I look up from the dusty mason jar, filled to the brim with house red which is about a stone's throw away from rotted grape juice. The bartender clearly hadn't known what else to do with my order. Not that I blame him. Might be that I'm the first person to have ever ordered a red wine in Pete's Watering Hole, a name which is oddly less quaint in a shithole like this.

The bar smells like regret. Which is to say, it suits me fine. Low, Styrofoam-paneled ceilings with either water damage or water damage which had turned to mold. Yellowing lights which threw off enough heat that this place should have been deemed a fire hazard—which would have been a more merciful ending than it deserved. Nearly empty. Not quiet, a Johnny Cash song plays too loud, piped in through tinny speakers that have a slight reverb when his voice gets to its deepest baritone.

It probably says a lot about me that the environment feels perfectly right for me, right now. Everything I was looking for in a place to relax for a bit. Everything I felt I deserved, certainly.

Except I would have preferred a better wine selection.

The bartender stands down the other end of the rough and

mortared bar top, busy stacking wet, empty glasses he just ran through the soapy water bath next to the tap. At least I hope there was soap in it.

Next to me, the only other patron in Pete's Watering Hole, is Ernest. Goes by Ernie, if you can believe it.

Ernie is one of those guys who can somehow sleep while sitting atop his barstool and yet not fall over. Best I can tell, he's been doing it the whole time I've been talking to him, only occasionally reaching out for his shot or his Schlitz and taking a big, thirsty gulp. He never opens his eyes when he does this.

Some people have a real talent.

Ernie is my kind of guy. Discrete. Somewhat secretive. Wouldn't even tell me his name (the bartender mentioned it—though how *he* knew will have to be a secret between them). Whether these secrets are due to Ernie having no ability to speak clear English or his likely deficiency in being able to form coherent thoughts, I suppose I'll never know. His lisp, and what I can only imagine as years—decades, maybe—of hard-drinking, have turned his speech to something slurred and sloshing, a jumble of odd sounds all blended together. I suppose I can't say for sure what his mind is like, but I'd put money on it being not much different than the frozen slushie machine you'd find in Cabo or Cancun on college spring break—all exotic disease were it not for the paint-peeling quantities of liquor involved.

Ernie just gives you the sense that, you tell him something, he won't go around sharing it with others.

Which is why he's been such a pleasure to share my story with. To get everything off my chest. To talk through it all in a way I hadn't yet been able to.

It's been four months since Nancy's big reveal to me out on the patio of our house. All the forensic evidence, when looked at through a different light, supported what she told me—that she'd killed my FBI brothers. There was very little, of course. Evidence. She was meticulous. So much so that most of the evidence we uncovered was only identifiable once we knew the likely culprit. We sort of had to back into a lot of it, starting with the hypothesis that she had done it. Not exactly standard operating procedure for an investigation. Usually it goes the other way around on the cases I work, where it's just predators roaming the American Serengeti like lions, ripping into their prey with no prior relationship, moving on to the next as soon as their dark desires were no longer sated from the prior kill.

Obviously, I hadn't needed to see any evidence. I'd finally had my eyes opened. Wide as they'll ever get.

It was like I was just telling Ernie, when Nancy set her mind to something, it was already done.

To say the four months had been difficult was like describing the surface of the sun as a warm place to live. The Bureau had not lifted my suspension. But that was the least of my worries. Aside from my wife leaving me, nobody still working at the Bureau who cared about their career would so much as answer my phone call to tell me to fuck off. Unfortunate, given the fact that I had, by far, the *worst* divorce story of all time. And in the Bureau, divorce stories were something of a popular genre of story to tell.

Add to that fact, I hadn't been allowed to pursue Nancy in any way.

The poison was a whole other story. It should have been lethal in the dosage I'd consumed—at least the best estimate of what that dosage was. By the time anyone found me, it was hard to pinpoint exactly how long I'd been out, how long ago I'd consumed the poison, and how much. It made quantifying the half-life difficult. In the end, I was alive. So whether the quantity I consumed should have been lethal or not didn't really matter.

Except on one point.

Had Nancy made a mistake? Or had she left me simply to suffer but not to die?

I went through all the different scenarios in my head and could never quite settle on one. It would be very unlike her to make a mistake so grave (or in my case, so *not* grave). But the forensic techs tell me that particular poison—some chemical name I can never really remember, hydro-something-something-something-something-something—was a tricky substance to utilize in the way Nancy had been trying to. Notoriously finnicky with dosages, very much dependent on the recipient, what they'd eaten, what other substances coexisted in their system.

They say it might well be that the wine saved me. Tannins, apparently. Ironic, too. Because in our New York City apartment, we had a device about the size of a handheld milk frother that filtered and removed the tannins, which often cause the red flushing people experience when consuming wine—an effect that had always plagued Nancy until she found that particular solution (one which she carried often to restaurants, bars, social events). Even with good wine, she flushed. It was the one thing about her that I could point to that made her an actual, fallible human being.

And then she went all Satan's Evil Spawn on me.

But in our haste out of the city that night, we left the filtration device behind.

Could be that Nancy just forgot it. I wasn't one to flush from wine, even the cheapest crap you could get at your local bodega. So I nearly always forgot it, my head swimming in some investigation as we walked out the door. But Nancy swore by the filtration device. And it was small enough to be easily portable.

Had she forgotten it?

Or had she known the tannins might save me? And in so knowing, was she trying to send some kind of message? Or perhaps leaving my life up to chance?

To make matters worse for me, the fact that the serial killer responsible for so many Bureau murders was my wife brought nothing but scrutiny on me. Proctology-levels of scrutiny. I'd been under enough microscopes and through so many investigations that I was sure the Bureau would know if I was even *thinking* about taking a shit sometime in the next two weeks. They'd repossessed the houses, cars—all the trappings of what Nancy's salary had purchased us. Which was sizable. I was able to get some walking around money out of my accounts once they concluded I had nothing to do with the murders. But only just.

But I didn't really care about any of that. Not anymore.

All I cared about now was the same as I'd always cared about.

Putting bracelets on bad guys. Only now, I'd be putting them on a bad *woman*. One of the worst to ever live, maybe. Because once the tech team ran a few statistical analyses on what we knew about Nancy, about the murders she confessed to, and then her own, actual DNA samples (she had apparently used someone else's DNA when giving elimination samples for cases she'd work on in her capacity as a lawyer), at least ten other cold cases popped up as hits.

High-statistical probability hits. Meaning, Nancy had surely killed before.

Of course, I could have told them that. Few killers display such skill (and I hate using that word for it, but nothing else fits) on their first try. There's usually a dead animal or disaffected family member somewhere on the trail to full-blown serial killer. Often times, more than one.

So if we had ten hits, Nancy had probably been doing this a long time. And given most of the hits were from over a decade before, she had likely gotten far better at concealing her trail, since the only other murders we could pin on her were the recent ones.

Where she killed our—my—friends.

Before my friends, she'd apparently found what we call "disaffected members of society." A clinical term for a horrible deed. People who live on the fringes, not a lot of family. No status to speak of. Nothing that gives law enforcement much incentive to look for them past going through the motions.

Sounds harsh, and it is. But that's the way it works.

Looking through the case files from the likely murders Nancy committed, I had no other way of describing most of those people. But seeing their death, and imagining their pain, I felt the familiar fire that sent me into this line of work in the first place.

Thinking about people like that—maimed, butchered, mangled in their final moments alive—makes my chest heave and tighten. Always has. It's the reason I do this.

Or did. *Officially.*

After I cleared all the FBI investigations—aided by the digital trail of text messages, emails, and phone calls they dug up, not a single one of which mentioned anything about the murders that was out of the ordinary—I followed Nancy's lead and disappeared myself. Went on the road.

Looking for her.

These days, that is no easy feat. Especially not for someone with my, shall we say, notoriety in the media landscape. Luckily the news cycle gets into a fever pitch—and boy, did it ever do that for this case. Bloody Mary, as the media called her, the deadly vixen wife of the hapless and helpless man set to catch her. But that fever pitch always breaks eventually. Then some other nut job goes and shoots up a public space, or a politician pulls his thing out, or someone we know and love and feel partly responsible in propping up to something like a demigod on earth goes and says something or does something that We, the People, deem unsavory and against our Moral Center, and the whole damned thing comes crashing down.

By the time I'd ditched anything electronic that could be traced back to me, I watched as the pundits on 24/7 news talked about the Bloody Mary fiasco like they knew the first thing about it (which, by their commentary, it was clear they did not).

By the time I'd gotten and stayed "underground," my fifteenth motel in as many days, driving an ancient but reliable Honda Civic from three presidential terms ago, the only thing keeping the case alive on the news was the fact that Nancy had not yet been caught.

Now, four months on, there wasn't much mention of it on any sort of news network I could watch in a dumpy motel room or the one-hop-from-jail bars and diners I frequented.

Whether anybody was even looking for me was an open question. Maybe the Bureau was just as happy to have me disappear as I was to do it.

But the searching wasn't totally over.

I was still looking for Nancy.

That was how I ended up at Pete's Watering Hole on the outskirts of Yuma, Arizona.

Because the thing was, Nancy might have been gone. But I specialized in finding sick, twisted fucks just like her. Ones I'd never met before, never knew a single concrete thing about. And now I could direct that considerable skillset toward someone I knew intimately. Someone I shared a bed with for twelve years. My only holdup was that Nancy was clearly a straight-up sociopath. Ice Queen couldn't begin to describe it.

How much of what I knew was real and how much was façade?

Hard to say. But luckily I had nothing like a job or friends holding me back from digging for the truth.

The last thing Brody, my former boss, told me before he put me on permanent suspension from the Bureau—an administrative status that effectively meant I'd never again work for the Bureau but also couldn't work anywhere else they didn't approve—was to just drop it. Do my best to move on.

We'd been friends, once. But he was management and I was just a grunt. One who got too wrapped up in cases and couldn't turn off the investigator's mind without a few too many drinks. Which didn't make me all that much fun to be around after a while.

"For your own sake, Cam," he said that day. He'd come to see me in the one-story motel I moved into after the Bureau repossessed my houses. This was before I'd gone underground and stayed in places far, far worse.

I'd had some to drink that day, but I remember that conversation. "You need to let this whole thing go. Put it behind you."

I just wasn't able to do that.

"So why Yuma, you ask?" I say, turning back to Ernie to finish my story. I'd been on the road about four days, straight driving. Taking actual chances by napping in truck stops, blending in with the invisible people that Nancy had once preyed on. A few times, reclined all the way back in the driver's seat as exhaustion came for me like a hungry wolf on a cold night, I thought about how funny it would be if somehow Nancy and I ended up in the same place. And she preyed on the wrong person.

That was about the state of my sense of humor these days.

Pete's Watering Hole is my first real stop for a bite to eat that didn't come out of a bag (only they didn't have food tonight since the fry cook called out sick). A chance to unwind for an hour or two before getting down to business. Talking to Ernie had helped me clear up a few things in my own head. Put some pieces together.

My wife is an apex predator. And an apex predator needs red meat.

But unlike the lions of the savannah, which hunt to kill only when necessary, a woman like Nancy simply could not rest easy. Outlets for her multivariate energies and abilities had been considerably reduced. No more practicing law, no more swimming with the sharks of New York City society, no more training martial arts or rebuilding car engines.

That left, really, only one place toward which her attention might rush.

Well, two.

Evading capture.

And murder.

Now that she'd tasted the spoils of killing men—powerful, high-profile men—she wouldn't slink back to the streets and start killing hookers or homeless on the fringes of society. Those who taste steak did not go back to eating Hamburger Helper. Nancy now had certain tastes to fulfill. Certain needs, whether she knew it or not.

And Yuma, Arizona represents the best opportunity for her to once again feed her habit.

At least that's my working theory.

"Ernie, you need another beer?" the bartender calls out over the music. Johnny Cash had dissolved into a Dolly Parton song. Something from her bluegrass period, from the sound of it. Just as much reverb when she hit the high notes, so go figure.

Ernie, amazingly, nods his head. Maybe this guy is more awake than I thought. If so, his lack of reaction makes me think this wasn't the craziest story he's ever heard. Given the scenery, and the fact that he seems like a regular, that actually might be true.

He reaches for the bottle in front of him, though, and knocks it over onto the floor. The glass shatters with a light crack that I almost can't make out over Dolly's crooning.

Then again, maybe he's just a drunk. Maybe the nodding is an involuntary reaction to the bartender's voice. Like Pavlov's dogs.

"The National Behavioral Analysis Conference is in town, Ernie. I can't think of a better place for an apex predator to go hunting, can you?"

Ernie's mouth hangs wide open and a long drip of drool lands on his pilled flannel shirt.

I take it as a sign of agreement.

I pull a few bucks out of my wallet and leave them on the pock-marked bar top in front of my seat. I turn to leave. But stop.

I take my wallet out again and pull out a fifty.

"For his tab," I say to the bartender, nodding at Ernie.

The bartender comes over with a fresh Schlitz and sets it down. He has a pudgy face with hair growing out of too many places and going in too many directions. Picks up the fifty, holds it up to the light, as if he'll be able to tell whether it's a fake.

Then he gives me a look and nods. Either he's vetted the bill and is content with its validity or I look like someone who would carry a fifty.

"This is only about half of it," he says, the words coming from somewhere between the pudgy folds that make up his chin.

"That figures," I say and pull out another fifty. Cash isn't exactly falling like I hit three jackpots at the casino, but I've been living on next to nothing for four months.

The bartender takes the second fifty with his left hand, puts it in his right with its twin. Then puts his left hand back out.

The nerve.

I pull out a ten and hand him that, too. I'm in a good mood now. Now that I've got everything off my chest.

I head for the door, the soles of my shoes slurping against the sticky floor, the sound louder than Dolly's singing.

"Hey," the bartender calls after me, holds up the two fifties. "What's this for, man? Never seen you in here before."

"You won't again."

"So what's the deal? You know Ernie or something?"

I shrug. "Just appreciative of someone to talk to, I guess."

The bartender looks at Ernie, sleeping on his feet with his mouth wide open, and shakes his head. Ernie reaches for the Schlitz and takes a nice, big gulp off the thing.

That's my cue. I head out into the dry desert air of Yuma, Arizona.

I've got work to do.

I've got a killer to catch.

DARKLY TWISTED

darkly twisted
[darklee twistud] *noun*

----

good luck shaking these from your brain

WHEN SHEDS TALK

NIZ THOMAS

WHEN SHEDS TALK

A CRIME HORROR SHORT STORY

ONE

There are times in life when something happens to you that makes you question everything that came before—every choice, every decision, every person you ever interacted with and whether you took 'em for a ride or got taken on one yourself.

It was four-thirty in the morning when the police came for me at my home.

That was one of those times for me.

I'd heard about this tactic. Different units liked different times for it—two, four, whatever the hell—but the general concept was the same.

They come when you're dead asleep. Dreaming of a freedom you ain't really got hands on anymore.

I heard them break open the front door, which at my house was made of triple-plated steel and weighs north of two bills. Other than the time, hearing the damn door break open with a metallic groan told me everything I needed to know about these cops.

They weren't here to ask questions. They meant business.

And that business, I had to assume, meant bad things for yours truly. Had no idea what that business might have been, mind (though

I wasn't entirely devoid of reasons the cops might come break down my doors like this), but when that clanging metallic groan of steel separating from steel rings out in the night, you don't stop and ask questions.

I was in bed. *Alone*, mind. Hadn't been the same feeling in my boudoir since my wife left, and as a result I hadn't been sleeping too soundly. From the shriek of the door, even a hibernating bear would have woken up, but I only needed something like a strong wind outside to wrest me from sleep most nights. A heavy steel ram bar against a heavy steel door was mostly just extra.

I threw off the silk covers, the *swish* of the sheets against one another sounding like gunshots in my otherwise quiet house. When you're hiding from cops, every sound you make feels like shooting up a flare into the night sky. Even the damn pounding of my heart against my temples made me wince. While I had something of a plan, it wasn't one that involved a jet pack ride out of this place. If the cops that just busted my door heard me moving around inside the house, there was a chance I didn't get far before they picked me up.

I had a belly full of stuffed shells—homemade pasta, ricotta, and gravy still dancing like sugarplums in my light sleep. *Marone*. What a meal. I wasn't moving too fast or thinking too clear in this state— bleary-eyed, post-meal haze—but my destination was pretty obvious.

The window.

Well, either that or jail.

Three steps across the carpet, I flung open the window like a nun throws the confessional after a weekend away from the convent. I had planned for this exact scenario, though it wasn't always the cops breaking down my door. Wasn't always the front door, either. But just like you needed to know what to do in the event of a grease fire in the kitchen or an electrical fire in the bathroom, I knew what to do now.

Outside, the night air was bracingly cold. Which was unfortunate since I only wore a crisp white t-shirt and my pajama bottoms—slippers be damned. But also good because it shocked me right awake. I needed my wits about me if I had any chance of making it. And my mind—usually focused on the angles—calculated something of a poor outlook for my current situation.

I made the step from my window to the sloped roof over the window eave at the backside of my house that framed my kitchen table and then shuffled my feet like a movie character who finds himself out on a high rise and doesn't want to go splat against the ground. On the far side of the eave, pretty well-hidden from all but the most discerning of surveillance, was a lattice of tangled ivy. Beneath the plants, though, the lattice was made of sturdy metal instead of the thin wood of most latticework.

Like I said, I expected a night like this to come for me eventually.

As I got a few rungs down the lattice, I heard rustling coming from inside my bedroom. I'd just barely gotten out of sight below the roof line in time.

Once on the ground in my backyard, I peeked around the house to see whether anybody was still in the bedroom window. Nobody.

Which probably meant they were searching the rest of the house. Probably headed back downstairs. Depending on how many there were, they might be checking both levels. That's what I'd be doing if I had four guys. Two upstairs (most likely place for someone to be at four-thirty). One guy downstairs (second most likely place for a guy like me at this hour: zonked out in front of the TV in a recliner chair). One guy playing free safety—doing his best to keep an eye on any points where somebody like me would squirt out. Front and back doors. Windows.

I looped around. Careful to stay beneath the big windowsill of my TV room. And had my exit in sight: an eight-inch-wide opening in the shrubs that divided my lawn from my neighbors. It was a tight fit (I mentioned the shells), but it was the best and only real option out of here that didn't involve picking azaleas, Indian Hawthorne, and blue fescue out of my teeth once I got through to the other side. That eight-inch-wide space was once a land of contention when Dan Jones lived behind me. Now a lane of sovereignty that the pushover

Lemieux's lived there. The French. A laissez-faire people. And God bless 'em for it right now.

I edged around the blind spots in my backyard spotlight sensor. Security people would tell you never to have a blind spot. But not too many of them are as knowledgeable in somebody who needs both protection from without and within. You need a way to escape in the night, you better hope you don't get lit up like you're walking the carpet at the Oscars. And anyway, this blind spot was a sidewalk of space along the closest edge of my house, and it stretched the corner of my yard and toward the back part of my property. Careful to stay low beneath the windows. Then shoulder width as the line of pine trees along the left edge of my yard tickled the bare skin of my arms.

That route took me almost all the way to the back third of my yard. Maybe twenty feet from my exit. Almost home free. Just well-manicured grass between me and freedom. And it was all out of range of my sensors.

Just as I was about to make a run for it, I glanced back at my house.

No cops in the upstairs window anymore.

None downstairs either.

Weird.

Not a single sliver of flashlight in the windows. No motion I could see from the bay window, through which was a clear straight view to the dim streetlights that ran along the street out front of my house.

How could that be? Surely they'd be looking for me. Or, having exhausted every place they might look, they wouldn't be lying in wait for me to bust out of a bedroom or something like that.

I didn't much want to wait around to see why. Heck, maybe they got bored. Maybe they were searching the fridge for any left-over stuffed shells (yeah, right, like I'd leave anything behind). Or maybe they thought I wasn't home and wanted to go back outside and wait me out. The thrown sheets and unmade warmth of my bed should have given them a clue that I was just there, but they didn't typically hire the best and brightest for the squad anymore, if they ever had. And they usually didn't send detectives on a night raid, either.

I made a break for the opening, my legs feeling heavier than my stomach (half-full of stuffed shells, mind), and I'm embarrassed to say I was breathing hard before I got there.

"I wouldn't go that way if I were you." A cool, calm, almost melodic voice came out of the dark and startled me so bad I slipped backwards and landed on my back, feet straight up in the air like a cartoon character just turned up dead.

I didn't wait to hear anything else, though. Getting up was all I had on the brain, knowing if I didn't, I was toast. Not many guys like me get picked up in the middle of the night and end up back walking the streets ever after.

I did a slip and slide on the grass but got my footing, half-running, half-crouching like a Neanderthal man before they went upright.

"I know you heard me."

Christ. Whoever it was here had me dead to rights if I didn't get gone soon.

"They're staking out the back, too. You don't really think you're the first con who tried to run out the back door, do you?"

I stopped and stood up straight, searching the darkness for the source of this voice. It was so self-assured and calm in the face of what felt like a frenzied escape for me that I couldn't help but sit up and take notice.

But wasn't nobody there.

"Boo."

It ain't often I jump in the night. A guy like me don't jump much. A guy like me who eats the kind of dinners I do, jumping is mostly a physical impossibility after the six o'clock hour. Laws of physics, and all.

But I might have dunked a Spalding if I'd been holding one. Put my freaking elbow through the rim while I was up there, too.

The voice, the boo, had been closer than I expected. So close, in fact, that it didn't seem possible I could be that blind, that someone could be so close and I didn't even see them.

But that was how it was.

"Over here." The sound came from my shed. "Yeah, genius. It's the shed talking."

I didn't think stuffed shells could go bad, but this trip down Looney Tunes Lane had me figuring otherwise. It was all I could do to keep them inside me, rather than becoming the slippers my now-cold toes wish they had on.

"I'm losing it," I said out loud, mostly to make sure I was still ... me ... and that I hadn't somehow walked through a portal to another world.

"You're about to lose your freedom to walk around out here, if you don't wise up," said my talking shed. "But if you stick with me and do what I tell you, you can at least avoid the bracelets tonight."

"Tell me what to do." (I almost couldn't believe I said it, either, but it was such an outlandish proposition, I figured it was either God reaching down an olive branch on how I'd been living so far in my life or I was already dead and this was one of those fever dreams you hear about on daytime TV when the host interviews a guy who was legally dead for five minutes and came back from the other side).

The shed told me what to do.

Told me that and a whole lot more.

I wish to God I'd just let the cops take me then and there and lock me away for life.

TWO

The shed was right. They had been setup out back of the yard, right past the very spot I'd identified as my exit, that sovereign land between mine and the Lemieux's yards.

I woulda been toast.

Burnt.

As it was, the shed gave me shelter. Ushered me inside its structure and camouflaged me in its womb. It let out its hidden secret suckle of information and lured me along as it spoke of things I didn't know—or if I did, I'd forgotten altogether.

"How did you know they were coming for me?" I asked it as I stood inside of its four wood-paneled walls. The shed was unfinished on the inside, all the boards unpainted, unlacquered, unstained. Not a thing inside my shed, either. I wasn't really a guy who did domestic, around-the-house work. That's what I worked for. Grinding out jobs and putting thumb screws to people who'd borrowed money from people they had no business borrowing from. All so that I wasn't the one had to mow the lawn and get on my hand and knees to pick out weeds.

Outside, a cold wind hissed against the backyard, tickling the greenery hemming in my backyard as it did so. No sign yet of the cops, but I knew they were out there somewhere.

The shed had told me so.

It was at this moment I realized this entire conversation with the shed was happening not out loud, but actually *inside my head*. It was also at this time I had forgone the most obvious question that maybe I should have been asking. Which was: *have you lost your goddamn mind?*

I don't know. Something about the shed talking to me felt so real that it wasn't worth questioning it.

But I bet that was exactly what crazy people told themselves, too.

"I know a lot. Enough that it doesn't pay to talk too much."

"I ... can pay you." Did I seriously just say that?

"You don't know what you're saying. Don't offer up a bounty unless you know what you're getting back in return."

Wise words from the shed.

Words I might've even said myself at some point. Not in so many words, maybe. To some schmuck laundromat who couldn't keep his pony slips fenced off from his quarter slot take until his books were so far stained with red ink even bleach wouldn't help. So the shed made the point: Don't make a sucker's bet inside a sucker's game.

"And anyway, what does it look like I need money for?"

Good point.

"What if they look inside the ... inside you?"

The shed was quiet for a long time. Like I'd asked him a real stumper. Outside, I could hear heavy footsteps padding through the grass now. Typical cop steps, what they sounded like. Whispered voices, talking just barely audible. After a long while, I saw beams of lights coming through tiny spaces where the shed's outer wall had settled over the years, or where the boards hadn't been placed completely flush with one another. Part of me felt bad for the shed. Another part made a mental note that if I got out of this shed without bracelets on, I'd go find the contractor who'd built this thing and give him a piece of my mind.

Maybe even a little more than that.

"Leave that to me."

THREE

It seemed a crazy thing to do. To leave it up to the shed. I mean, this was my life—my freedom—we were talking here.

Outside, the cops were closer. I could practically smell their aftershave and cigarettes and (on one of them, maybe) booze breath. Unbelievable, that these *pissorones* couldn't even come correct to something like this. Maybe they didn't think it was high stakes, but boy, did they have another thing coming.

A few more whispers and I thought it was likelier than not they were getting ready to bang down that door. Anticipatory whispers, what they were.

Nothing else left to do, really, but to leave it up to the shed. My lone, true friend.

Just as I'd accepted this, a *click* sounded somewhere behind me. At first, I wondered again whether somebody got so close to me without knowing. Maybe one of these cops somehow snuck in through the backdoor and pulled his piece out right at the small of my back? That'd be just like them. But no ... it wasn't that kind of sound. It *was* inside the four walls of the shed. But it wasn't no gun.

I hesitated. The sound had come from behind me. But it wasn't wise to turn yourself away from a gun. The cops were on the other side of the shed's front door (and only door, despite my momentary confusion) door. Right in front of me. I wasn't sure I wanted to give up any advantage I had should they pick this instant to bust inside.

But I needed to see what that sound was.

I turned. Slowly. And with some trepidation.

Just behind me, I noticed a space in the floorboards where just before it had been flat. One had risen up higher than its surrounding boards. Just on one edge. Like a hidden door had opened. A trap door.

"It's not a trap," the shed, reading my mind.

"I didn't say it was."

"In you go, then."

Outside, the flashlights seemed to burn brighter. The scant talking I could make out had stopped. I could feel all eyes turning on the shed by all them cops outside.

Normally I wouldn't go through a restaurant door with someone I'd only known for a few minutes, but I'd gone this far in trusting the shed, I figured I might as well go all into the damn thing.

Literally.

I pulled up the trap door, the heavy wood opening silently as I did so. Somebody must've oiled the hinges because they were buttery smooth. The measurements of the thing were just so. You couldn't make out one board from the next until I raised it to about forty-five degrees. Maybe that contractor wasn't so bad after all.

Inside there were two steps down into a crawl space, though I couldn't make out much about it because of the darkness. As if reading my mind, a very spare light turned on, deep enough into the space so that I didn't worry anybody outside could see it. My eyes only. Designed to give me just enough light to see nobody was inside, there didn't appear to be any traps, and I could climb inside without busting my ass. The crawl space was about six feet wide and long, cut starting maybe four feet below the ground and stretching another four feet down. Not the most comfortable hiding spot, but better than nothing.

"Not much time now," said the shed.

I hustled inside, happy to see that the inside was lined with some sort of construction paper beneath the wood boards that framed everything. No sense of bugs or other critters hiding down here. So that was a plus.

"Close it up."

I reached up and pulled shut the crawl space's door.

The light inside the space went out.

It was suddenly middle-of-the-earth quiet.

Followed by an anticipatory pause in the night.

It wouldn't last long.

FOUR

Huddled inside the hidden crawl space, I felt a measure of gratitude that the shed was in my life. But couldn't also help re-visit that pang of a thing I'd felt when the door to my house busted in off its reinforced hinges: a deep questioning of what my life had been about and the decisions I'd made that all led me to here. Underground. Not six feet yet, but already in the damn hole. Maybe I'd made some mistakes after all. Because it was either listen to a telepathic shed to save my bacon, or go with the cops.

Neither option seemed particularly great. But so far, at least, the shed won out by a landslide.

The shed door flung open. Slammed, metal and wood against wood. The door must've spun all the way around on its hinges and knocked into the outer portion of the shed's structure. The hinges whined on the night air, a note that hung resonant like the end of an opera. There was enough force to shake the shed's foundation all the way deep, rattling my bones along with it. Light flooded through the floorboards in blinding arrows. I pulled back, thinking I was somehow found out. As if each of those cop flashlights were pointed directly at me, zeroed in. And when cops point those bad boys on a twilight raid to pick up a perp who's playing games with them, they don't wait too long to pull their trigger fingers, located directly beside the light beam.

For another moment all was quiet.

I could just imagine the cops' faces when they looked inside and found nada, zip, nothing.

But they wouldn't give up so easy. I was sure of that.

The floorboards creaked above me. I was quite literally hidden in the cellar, the lights no longer so blinding as they danced around the shed's interior. The cops no doubt searching out any hiding places.

Would they find me?

I had a strange confidence in the shed's protection.

Dust motes trickled through the tiny spaces of the boards, lit up by the light. I could taste earth, copper, sawdust. I tried my damndest not to sneeze, hiding my nose in the crook of my elbow and trying not to breathe too deep. Or too loud.

"Where the hell did he go?" a gruff voice above said. I could imagine a thick neck full of tattoos. Cops these days barely over the line from their criminal counterparts.

"Tipped off?" A vaguely Hispanic voice said.

"You tell me, Gonzalez." Gruff again. Not so happy. Accusatory, actually.

"The hell you looking at me for? Dingo was the one who uncovered this tip in the first place."

An Australian accent then. "I uncover the tip, then I ruin it. Is that what you're after, Gonzalez?"

Gonzalez didn't say anything. I could imagine a tense scene above where all the cops stared at one another, each taking all the others' measure. I'd been in rooms like that. Never in a shed, mind you, but I'd been in rooms where somebody did something that compromised the group and everybody wondered about everybody else's motivation for doing so. It was all calculations and innuendo until somebody pulled the trigger.

"Do it," I heard the shed whisper.

Do it? Do what?

"C'mon you pansy ass. *Do it.*"

It was only then I realized the shed wasn't talking to me. I don't know how I realized that, but I knew it as clearly as I could hear the shed's words inside my head.

"DO IT!"

"I'm sick of that look, Dingo." This from the cop named Gonzalez.

"This is the look I reserve for the weak and needy. The kids they have to put into special schools." The Aussie accent again.

"Shut up, Dingo."

"Do it," the shed whispered again. I didn't know who he was talking to. But I didn't like where this was going.

Above me, the floorboards creaked. Whereas the air had been earthy and stifled before, there was an acridness to it now. Pungent. Foul. I'd smelled it before. In those same rooms with those same guys in this same situation. Distrust sewn into the seams, hemmed in tight with the feeling of every man for himself, dog-eat-dog competitiveness. The kind that only exists in cops versus robbers. High stakes. Highest there are.

But the smell sprinkling down to me like radioactive rain over Chernobyl wasn't just the smell from the rooms where everybody was looking sideways at the guy next to him.

It was the smell from the rooms where somebody put their finger on the trigger.

"Do. It."

"Easy, Gonzalez. I don't like that look in your—"

"Shit!"

"No!"

My ears popped from the gunshot round that somebody loosened above me, the sound quick and loud and then it was like the old telephone lines that went to a dead ringing after you left the receiver off the hook for too long. With no ear protection inside a confined space, you more *feel* gunshots rather than hear them. And this one had the same kind of inner ear pressure as when you jump in a pool and go down too deep under the water. But instead of just the water knocking and trying to get in, it was a big-fisted metal door ram they use in the military for close quarters combat.

The other gunshots were mercifully less impactful, their effects more like a light tapping along the jaw. Probably because my ear drums got blown from the first one, which maybe happened right above my head.

I wasn't sure who pulled the trigger first, whether it was Gruff, Gonzalez, or Dingo. But I had a sinking feeling that each of them got a pull on the trigger before it was all said and done. Even though I was ostensibly safe, I was still huddled up tight, my hands shaking, my jaw clenched as tight as I could clench it after getting the equivalent of punched in the face with that close quarters explosion of sound. No matter what kind of work you do, there's an abject terror that comes with being in close contact with gunfire. I'd been on both sides—or maybe all three now, given I'd just been *under* a gunfight without ever really being in it.

I don't know how long it took for my hearing to come back, but eventually it did. I didn't hear anything above me, but it was hard to tell. One time I was in a car when somebody pulled the trigger. Three days later another guy in my same line of work came to see me. Practically broke down the door slamming on it—him seeing me sitting at the kitchen table reading the paper while he knocked and knocked and knocked. Think he ended up bruising the hand, was damn near ready to pull his piece at the disrespect. Only after, when I finally noticed him and let him in and didn't seem to catch all but the third word out of his mouth, he understood.

So it was possible I thought I could hear—the wind blew softly, the creaking of old wood settled in as the pressure inside the shed re-normalized—but was missing the wheezing breath of one of the cops who caught a round to the chest and was sucking air above me.

"They're gone." Guess I could still "hear" the shed.

"What the hell happened?" I asked, though I didn't speak the words. And I guess I already knew the answer.

"Don't ask questions you don't want the answer to."

Maybe once I got a little more used to the strangeness of the talking shed, I'd regain my wits about me. But my mind was going to weird places and I was doing and saying things I never would have dreamed of only a few minutes earlier.

"What now?" I asked.

Part of me worried this was another of those questions.

"Go back to sleep."

"You serious? There ain't enough buffalo tranq darts could put me to sleep now." This was, at least, not new. Every time I'd been around a hit, a collection gone wrong, or some other death (accidental or intentional), my body went on a high like I'd just inhaled a whole bag of speed. There'd be a comedown. But not just yet.

The shed kept talking. "Go inside, then. Have a biscotti and coffee. Sun'll be up. Start your day. Maybe take a nap later."

I normally wouldn't take orders like this. But what the *fungool?* I'd come this far.

I reached up for the hidden door. It was already open.

Yeah, I still couldn't hear a thing.

When I climbed up, my eyes were already used to the dark. The inside of the shed was gunpowder and copper put into a cologne and then doused all over the ground like holy water when the Devil was coming. It was too fresh to make me throw up anything, but it wouldn't be for long once the sun came up.

Three bodies lay strewn about the shed's floor. Contorted into shapes that were almost worse than the smell. Bodies aren't supposed to bend like that. And people aren't supposed to see 'em if they do. One of them—almost certainly Gruff—had his neck stretched out long away from his body, his head half-turned away from the front of his body, a smattering of blood where the back right part of his skull shoulda been. He had a tattoo of a long vine with roses on it that stretched from the bloody, gored hole in his skull and around his neck like he'd gotten wrapped up in the plant. It disappeared seemingly a few miles away beneath his shirt.

"Go inside. Have some breakfast."

"Breakfast?" I said, my anger, confusion, and fear rising. "This is the stuff of forty-day fasts. I can see how the Muslims started doing it, what with the Crusades and all that." I did the sign of the cross over my front. "I might lose ten pounds before I have another breakfast. Christ."

It was really getting to me. Maybe the middle-of-the-night wake up or the sudden acts of violence. I didn't know which. I'd seen dead bodies before. Made some of them dead, too. But this ... this was too much.

A thought struck me, though I tried my best to hide it (whatever that could mean, I don't know): had the shed ... *done something* to these bodies?

"I'll take care of it."

I was frankly overwhelmed by everything that had happened so far. So I went back inside, my feet slowly padding across the lawn, producing the only sound of the still-dark night. Nobody's lights were on—no shades at any of the neighbors were drawn, no sirens blaring in the distance. Just me, alone, in my backyard.

Wondering what the hell had just happened.

Inside, turned out the shed was right once again. Once my spiking adrenaline started to plummet back to Earth, I was starving.

And not long after wolfing down a big breakfast, I fell back to sleep.

FIVE

When I woke, it was late in the day. The sun came in crooked between the blinds, which had been pulled back at funny angles by the cops. I had missed them completely in my fatigue when I walked back into my bedroom. I'm usually neat—almost to a compulsion. But my bedroom was like a hair band's hotel room after a two-day stint in town. Dresser drawers open, one of them thrown onto the ground, clothes strewn everywhere.

Had this been a search warrant? No. Not based on what I'd heard in the shed. There was something unprofessional going on. Something shady. If they had been there on official business, there would have been no reason to get all sketchy with one another about tipping somebody off. No reason to turn that shed into the O.K. Corral.

No reason but for the little whispers in their ear.

I shuddered. Tried to keep my head on straight. No sense dwelling on what had happened.

The question remained though: just what the hell were these guys looking for besides me?

Hard to concentrate, to think through options. Because the afternoon sun's odd shadows made me think of the dead, twisted bodies in the shed.

A little knot calcified in my stomach. Luckily it had been long enough since I'd witnessed the dead and since I'd eaten my breakfast, that everything in my stomach stayed right where it was.

For now.

Oh God.

The shed.

I bolted to the window. As I ran through the shadows, my body tightened. As if there was something in those streaks of darkness that could touch me. Something, maybe, I could catch like a cold.

Lord, was I out of sorts.

At the window I had a bout of déjà vu. Reminiscent of last night. The quick bound across the room. Now, though, I was even more confused. Discombobulation of mind and body. The cops had been here, but for what, I still didn't know.

And maybe that wasn't even the thing I should be most worried about, anyway.

Looking out across my backyard, the shed was still there. I didn't know why it wouldn't be. I hadn't imagined the damn thing. Had been sitting unused in my yard for going on fifteen years. But the strangeness of the evening made me question everything I had known about my life and the world I apparently took for granted all these years.

I mean, the shed could freaking talk telepathic. I think I would have noticed that.

Right?

From the outside, nothing seemed different. There was no sign in the surrounding yard or on the exterior walls of the shed that a triple murder had occurred there—if that was even the right term for it. Technically there was no culprit to pin the murder on (though I bet any D.A. or cop would have no trouble trying to pin it on me). But forensic evidence would show these three fools had shot themselves.

The only murderer was ... maybe ...

The shed.

I shuddered again.

Closed the blinds. Retreated back away from the window. Feeling watched. Feeling ... unsettled.

I tried to forget all about it.

SIX

But something wouldn't let me.

Oh, might it have been the fact that three dead bodies were likely piled up in my shed? And for a guy like me to get caught with a thing like that, well, I would have a real difficult time explaining that away. Even if a jury didn't convict me, the D.A. would have no trouble making my life miserable over the next few years. Cops, too. They'd pull me over every chance they got. Stick a knife in my tires. Maybe "find" a half-empty bottle of booze or a bag of drugs.

Yeah, the more I thought about it (despite trying my best not to), the harder it was to see any eventuality that didn't end up in the same place I now felt myself to be.

Completely and utterly *farkakte*.

I walked out to the shed. Did it while the daylight was still with us. I might be a guy in the life, but I ain't no exorcist. Whatever was going on with that shed, I wanted the light on my side of our next encounter.

If the shed was still with us, it didn't say anything.

I opened the door. More gently than the cops had. Easing the thing. Out of respect? Fear? Preservation of my private property?

Who knows. I was focused on steeling myself against the sight of contorted bodies and the smell of newly decaying flesh and blood. No way the shed—without hands or legs or any way to freaking move anything—could have gotten rid of those bodies.

No way.

SEVEN

I didn't go outside for another few days. Just paced around my house like a crazy person. And maybe that was exactly what I was.

I hadn't heard from the ... thing (shed). I was taking great pains not to think of the thing (shed). No conversations with the thing (shed) floating through the waves of my mind. I didn't start any conversations. That was for sure. Wasn't sure I could even "speak" the word of the (ah screw it) *shed* anymore. My mind must've been racing with thoughts, but could the shed hear me? How had it felt when we'd last talked—the shed and me? Like regular talking, right? Had taken me awhile, even, just to realize we *hadn't* been talking out loud. Just inside my own head. It had been just like ... well ... like talking. So now I didn't talk, either.

But I could sense it out there. Stewing. Or scheming. I started to wonder whether it had planned this whole thing. To get to me. Or let me know it knew it *could* get to me. If it wanted. It could call the cops on me (for what, who knows). And it could bring me salvation from said cops. Jury and executioner? Or judge and jury? All three?

I got all paranoid (okay, *more* paranoid) that maybe it was holding a grudge now. Or I had somehow offended it. Like, "Hey, sorry I never called after that time you helped me out of a jam, when those three cops were coming to take me away, or rob me, or maybe kill me. Sorry, I know you were right outside the whole time afterwards. I guess I just got busy. I was slowly losing my mind (but I guess you probably already knew that, didn't you?)"

Had I hurt the shed's feeling?

A few days of this, I couldn't stay in the damn house anymore. After an armed invasion in my home, it was the lingering thought of the shed that had saved me which finally drove me out. Was too close, me and the shed. I didn't know if there was a limit on how far away before it had to be to talk to me. It hadn't spoken to me until I was standing just beside it. Not when I was at the window, the cold air bracing me, stepping out onto the roof. Not when I was tip toeing through the yard so as not to be seen. Heck, not in the fifteen or so years I'd lived in this damn house.

But had I ever really been that close to it? I mean, I enjoyed my lawn. The prospect of it. Looking at it, really. Didn't get my hands dirty in it. Never did much in the way of spending time *in* it. I stuck to the patio, mostly. And these days, me getting older, being crankier, more particular, I guess I hadn't been out there much.

But still. The Border War (my personal version of it) between me and Dan Jones, that ultimately ended with his ass moving away and the Lemieux's moving into the lot behind mine, that had surely had me out there, at the back of my yard, in close proximity to the shed.

Hadn't it?

I could remember days and nights, red in the face, screaming the kind of obscenities through that little eight-inch-wide opening in the shrubs that divided my lawn from Dan's that should've wilted the plants. Killed 'em dead.

And I'd never heard the shed's cool, melodic voice.

Whatever the hell. I was sick of thinking like this, in twisted pretzels of logic and fear.

I hit the road and didn't think I'd ever come back.

EIGHT

But just when I thought I was out, I got pulled right back in.

My wife called, saying she missed me, our life, and wanted to come home.

Well, that got me back. In more ways than one. Bea, was her name. Old time name for a young (for me) wife. She was thirty-eight with Baywatch hair and the body to match. Bea. Always buzzing and bumbling, I used to joke. She broke the shed's spell over my thoughts. Giving me plenty to think about (and to do, if you know what I'm saying) so that the shed loomed no longer at the very forefront of my mind, but rather somewhere near the front third only.

Was another few weeks, though, before I went outside the back of my house. I could barely even look outside the back windows, let alone go out.

Bea had left a glass out there while suntanning and reading a trashy gossip rag during the afternoon (I couldn't come up with any good reason for her not to go out there, even if I wasn't ready to).

She asked me to get the glass.

Couldn't come up with any good reason for me not to do that, either.

None that wouldn't end with her having me committed.

It was nearing dark, the sun having fallen below the tree line between me and the Lemieux's yard as I stepped out back through my kitchen sliders. The shadows were strewn about the grass like my bedroom clothing had been that day after the shed did its murderous work on the cops—over and around the shed, across the perfectly manicured lawn, in tangled knots of light and shadow that snuck through the sovereign land at the back of my property. Fingers reaching for me.

I shuddered. Picked up the glass left beside the lounge chair at the edge of my patio and the grass.

The shed said nothing. Did nothing.

I hustled back inside like something was chasing me.

Wasn't but a few minutes later, back inside, the phone rang.

I answered it.

"Don't think I forgot about you," that familiar voice said. The line was dead. Just dial tone for as far down the line as I could hear.

The shed's voice was inside my head.

It didn't bode well for my ability to determine whether *I* was crazy or whether the shed was the real deal. A strong case could have been made either way.

"What do you want?" I asked. "What did those cops want?"

"What'd we talk about? Not asking questions you don't want answers to."

"I *do* want answers. It's been—" I stopped. Don't say more than was necessary. Not to this evil spirit.

"It's been, what? Eating you up inside? Making you a little cuckoo?" Little birds chirped somewhere in the distance. Inside my head? Or outside in the yard? Somewhere even farther away (maybe, it was hard to tell), I could have sworn I heard a wolf's howl.

"So why'd you call then, if you don't want to say anything?"

"Just to remind you."

"Of what?"

There was a long and drawn out pause on the line. In that

moment, I tried to imagine what this ... this, this *being* ... could want from me. Why now? And toward what end?

For some reason, I still held the phone to my ear like a dimwit.

I hung up.

It never rang again.

Or, at least, not with the shed on the other line.

Over the next few weeks, I avoided the shed pretty good. Until Bea left me once again, citing reasons like anxiety, paranoia, and a short temper. And the real reason—which we both know, me and her, but she mercifully never spoke aloud. But how's a man to please his wife when he's got this kind of thing on the brain? This goddamn shed had aged me a decade over the course of months. And spared no part of me whatsoever. It would have made a killing in my business.

Hell. It *did* a killing.

After a while—no more Bea, no more talking, no more going outside—I decided to sell the house. I just couldn't take the psychic weight any longer.

But the shed didn't let go so easy.

NINE

There were two "accidents" by people who came looking at my house for sale.

The first, thankfully, was just a broken foot. And it was from a guy who didn't want to deal with hospitals and insurance and certainly not lawyers. Not after what he did.

He had been walking out back, taking a little tour around the perimeter of the property. Checking out the vegetation, the mature plants that separated my backyard from the Lemieux's yard. It was a mature yard, the realtor had said when she came for the listing appointment. A Brit lady, this realtor. She pronounced it *ma-toor*. It was a selling point, this *ma-toor* yard. A posh home with such nice landscaping? Pssh. It could practically sell itself.

I couldn't fake a chuckle at that little joke. Even with the added humor of the accent thrown in. I didn't find a lot of humor in a whole lot anymore.

And I wasn't so sure she was right. The accent made her seem smarter than your average realtor. But she wasn't no Einstein, either. In the end I just wanted to get it over with. So I left and told her to call me once it was done.

I checked into a hotel about an hour's drive away.

The hotel room door hadn't even closed behind me when my phone rang.

Thoughts of my own home phone ringing set my teeth to grinding. But no, the shed couldn't reach me from this far away. Right?

It was the realtor. Thank Christ. She said it was the strangest thing. That the prospective buyer was walking in the grass and suddenly, they stepped up to the side of the shed out back and stared at the baseboard, the part of the shed that separated grass and earth from the exterior walls.

"And then, he just started ... kicking it."

"Kicking it?" I was agitated. But not for the reason the realtor probably figured. "What do you mean, kicking it?"

"Like the shed was a football and the buyer was lining up a corner kick."

I knew just enough soccer to understand that. "Uh, okay?" What was I to make of that description though?

"Only ... only he kept doing it. Again and again and again. Working something out, like. A demon. Or proper mad—deep and unresolvable anger. Sort of a surprise, really, that it was only the foot broken. It should have been mangled, the way he was going at things. Strangest showing I've ever done."

I mustered up all the strength in my voice. Told her to find somebody else for the property and hung up.

Then I puked in the nearest trash can.

TEN

The second "accident" happened a few days later.

One of these fucking guys, the realtor said. Well, she didn't say it like that. She said he was a "fellow who liked his motor toys." Had big tires that rose higher than your shoulders. One of those pickup trucks that screamed through the air and hummed like a desert tank.

Like the other of the handful of Brits I ever met, this lady was always telling me information like it was a question. "He was inspecting the shed—measuring it out to see whether it could fit all his equipment, right?"

Something horrible rose up in my stomach. A demon venom that had been hidden there since that fateful night, lurking, its horrible head now emerging from the acid bathwater of my stomach, ready to finally take me forever.

They say that guilt usually gets people. More so than any police work or tips from the crime stoppers or any of that other crap they do to make the John Q. Public think the cops have their best interests at heart. It's the guilt that trips people up. Gets the old clue factory going again. It's what turn the police onto a suspect again, after years or decades of nada, zip zilch, when cases have gone deep-freeze cold, leads have died, and hardly anybody is around still to even remember the crime in the first place.

It's the guilt that takes everything out of that ice box and sets it out on the counter to thaw.

I'd never had that problem. I do something deemed "illegal" by polite society? *Ah fungol.* What, I had any breaks in this life?

But right about now, I sort of got a taste for what that might feel like.

Had they found the bodies the shed iced? Am I suddenly—an hour away from home—an accessory to murder? Or the prime suspect?

"All of a sudden, he pulled a knife from beneath his jumper," the realtor said, her Brit voice getting shaky. "It was massive. Something from those eighties action films you Americans are so fond of. Long and serrated."

I somehow breathed a sigh of relief and tensed with whatever horrible news was coming. It felt good to know this story wouldn't end with the police outside my door ready to take me in.

I didn't figure it would end well for the guy in the story.

And sure enough, I was right.

She didn't fully describe to me what happened, the realtor. Probably because her brain had gotten all scrambled at witnessing something so shocking, like she couldn't quite remember all of it. A protective mechanism inside us. Blur out or cut out altogether the stuff that would leave you lying awake at night wondering whether the window, the belt, or the gun was the best, quickest way out of your waking nightmare. Like those jump cut montages in the eighties action movies us Americans are so fond of. Only the messy bits ended up on the cutting room floor.

There was a police report for that one. Had to be, I suppose, after what had gone done. So I read all the details inside there. Lucky for me, I was out of town. Rock solid alibi. And I'd long ago learned the lesson never to leave incriminating evidence behind in your home.

Never know who might be knocking on your door.

ELEVEN

I might've just left it there. I'd made enough money over the years where I didn't need to sell the house to keep living somewhere else. Not that I'd be able to order top shelf at the Ritz without that house money, but I'd be okay.

It was the shed who wouldn't leave *me* alone. Somehow it found me. In that same hotel room. Ringing me up like a drunken friend in the lobby playing a practical joke. Just hissing breath into my mind when I answered. Hissing a little louder once I hung up. Just to fuck with me.

I didn't know whether it could read my mind or whether it just had a bead into the damn thing.

Or maybe, once we had spilled blood together, we were somehow linked for life.

Since I didn't have any idea about how to fix the former, though, I figured the only thing to do was try my hand at the latter.

TWELVE

If you've come this far, it means one of two things: my attempt failed miserably, or it worked so well that I took the opportunity to bleed into the grey darkness, the one every guy in my line of work dreams of at some point or another.

I wasn't the first to try and rush out the back way when the cops came. And I wouldn't be the first to take advantage of a believed-to-be-dead situation, either.

I never said I was original.

But as I sit and write this—in the here and now (and you, whoever you are, in the future)—I find myself being more introspective than I normally am. This life that I chose—despite being encased in the same sort of window dressing as my neighbors—was not like yours. Most likely. I came and went. Did it my way, as Ol' Blue Eyes said. I took and took and never once thought twice about it. And when those cops kicked in my door, I certainly felt nothing even approaching repentance. It was all self-preservation.

And against all odds, I prevailed. Just like I had so many times before.

Sitting in the kitchen of what was once a home, maybe ... just maybe ... I can admit that I deserve all this. My wife leaving me, dirty cops ransacking my house (and after a long time to think on it, I assume ready to disappear me once they found what they were looking for), and now this ... this ... curse.

It goes against everything I ever thought true, any rule or guideline by which I lived my life.

But such is the nature of self-reflection. Sometimes you don't like the thing looking back at you.

In this state, something else occurs to me, too. Maybe I understand the shed perfectly. Maybe it, too, is feeling guilty. And that guilt is pushing it to act in ways it wouldn't normally act. Pushing me, maybe. Toward the brink of my own sanity as a way to calm the suffering for itself. Or maybe for both of us.

Maybe in the end, we're more intertwined than I even realize.

In the end, maybe, it was the guilt that reigned supreme.

I guess. I don't know. Maybe?

In this life, we make our own meanings.

But on this fine, dry October morning, looking out the kitchen windows toward my sworn nemesis (or secret, long-lost brother?), breathing in the fumes of the gasoline tank beside me, fingering the old Zippo my pa brought back from the war when he could barely speak a lick of English and had to make something of himself in this country, I figure that if the shed is really after me, there's nothing stopping it from having me use these very instruments which I intend to use on it against myself. In that case, nobody will read this letter. It won't be nothing but ash on the wind.

But if the shed is after what I figure—if it's driving me to kill it as a way toward absolution—then this will survive.

It might have been spared the flame. Maybe I will be, too.

Either way, this is the end of my story here.

Whether I rise from the ashes like the phoenix or burn in Hell like the Damned, well, that's for me to know.

And me alone.

RAY RAY'S STOOP

NIZ THOMAS

✝

RAY RAY'S STOOP

AN ORIGINAL CRIME STORY

ONE

Jesus said to turn the other cheek. Unfortunately, he never said it to Ray-Ray Horne.

Before Ray-Ray even came around the corner of Eager Street, he could already tell something was wrong. Course down Baltimore way, something was always wrong--whether it be police raiding corners and breaking skulls or schoolteachers taking self-defense classes before getting re-certified in the curriculum. Something Wrong was practically Charm City's motto. Most days, wrong hardly registered with Ray-Ray, the same way darkness don't register with a blind man.

But today, something was wrong in the streets. Ray-Ray knew that sure as he knew anything. Smelt it in the air, in fact. Heard it in the frequencies, the vibrations of the day. Ray-Ray had a way of doing that. Seventh sense, was how he thought of it. *Fucking batshit, bruh*, was how everyone else talked about it.

Nobody else really got Ray-Ray. Which suited him just fine, since he didn't much get anybody else, either. Wasn't no mutual *getting* required to get out in these streets and hustle.

When he turned the corner he saw what he always saw: twelve

stoops in total stretching over the next two blocks, seven real ones on the left, complete with five stairs and rusted, leaning railings, leading up to buildings that had long ago been abandoned and boarded up. The right side had five lean-tos–random scraps of fabric held up by boxes and sticks, covering a medley of chairs and stools lined up under barred windows of the Latrobe Homes, the windows cracked just enough for an arm to reach in or out of the darkness inside. A darkness that held all number of dead dreams just out of sight from the street.

Nineteen or twenty corner boys stood in their places on either side of the street, some manning the cash, some manning the packs, none manning stoop number four on the left side.

That was Ray-Ray's stoop.

And nobody fucked with Ray-Ray's stoop. Not anybody on this corner, at least. And probably not anybody on any corner in this neighborhood, they knew what was good for them.

But somebody *had* fucked with it, Ray-Ray could see. The first thing he saw, actually, when he finally made the turn. Nobody else seemed to notice what Ray-Ray saw. But that wasn't no thing, really. He always saw shit that other people didn't.

Ray-Ray didn't slow down a beat, taking the corner just as fast as if the coast was clear. Keeping his eyes roaming the block like a guard dog, taking in everything from forty or fifty feet away as he approached.

Kept his ears open, too. Charm City sounded normal–bass bumping nearby as someone rode away in their Accord. Sirens in the distance. Car horns. Laughter. Scheming.

Ray-Ray heard it all and then some.

Other than whatever had happened on his stoop, though, everything else looked and sounded calm and regular. LaQuan and Cook and Bishandre and Tiny Derrick all stationed in their usual places. None of them able to see the treachery that had befallen Ray-Ray's stoop, despite the evidence being out in broad daylight.

But Ray-Ray figured they didn't see it because it was part of his seventh sense. His special visions. He didn't expect those corner boys to put it together. Most of the time, they didn't look in the direction of his stoop anyway.

Like it always did, Ray-Ray's stoop glowed lavender, even in the early afternoon light of day. The color emanated from within the sloppily poured (and long since cracked) concrete steps like it had been mixed up with Day-Glo paint when still wet. Even though for years he'd thought of his stoop's glow as *purple*, he'd come to learn *lavender* one night watching TV.

Who said TV wasn't a good teacher?

Zoned out on the couch, three 211s deep (right when the voices started to quiet down for the day) and trying to find the remote because of what came on the TV: one of those fixer upper shows on that white person network where they fixed up homes (never any homes that needed *real* work, like Ray-Ray's, just some white people places that needed "more better curb appeal," the fuck that means). And some bitch in that show was going on and on and on about painting the new bedroom with lavender paint. Ray-Ray found the remote 'neath three empty containers of China food (but not a single egg roll in sight), was about to change channels, crack into his fourth 211 and maybe hit the pipe and watch Cartoon Network. But something about the word--*la-ven-derrrr*--struck him. Called to him through the TV like one of those small screen preachers. Hypnotic. *La-ven-derrrr.* And he just needed to see for himself what color that was, never knowing much about colors at all, except purple and black like the Ravens, orange for the Orioles, and red like the Jumpman symbol. Colors were for sports and clothes, he figured. But not buildings. Seemed to him that besides his stoop, this whole city was washed in muted colors--grey, tan, and shit brown. Brick was about as bright as it got around here.

And once he seent that finished bedroom--after four, five more commercials for soft-ass toilet paper bears like to use--he knew his stoop was, in fact, glowing lavender. Not purple.

So Ray-Ray walks up to his lavender stoop. Knows something's fucked up with his turf, even if he can't yet figure out what. Feels the heft of his Showstopper, the Desert Eagle tucked into his waistband. And he's just standing there, sniffing at the air like a tracker dog.

Literally sniffing it.

Behind him, Bishandre goes, "Fuck is this crazy fool doing?" Says it quiet-like, almost under his breath. Not under enough, though.

Because Ray-Ray hears everything.

Ray-Ray spins. Quick enough that his Jordan's squeak on the sidewalk. Eyes up Bishandre. African dark. Alternate Sunday black-on-black Ravens jersey hanging down over jeans. Six-two. Coulda been a college wideout if he could read. Scouts told him back in tenth grade they couldn't even fake his SATs if he couldn't fill out the damn Name and Address section himself. No other options (he wasn't becoming no scholar), he came to the corner. Actually, Ray-Ray knew, he'd been on the corner already, part-timing. But once football was out of his life, man's gotta eat.

"Who's been over here today?" Ray-Ray said, addressing the question through Bishandre, but to LaQuan and Cook, too. Tiny Derrick was dealing with a slowed up blue VW Beatle idling in front of his stoop. First sale of the day probably, still early enough that only the dopiest of dope fiends were around.

"Nobody," they all said, practically at the same time. Puppy dogs, all of 'em. Thing was, Ray-Ray was a feared man on this street. The pit bull of the block. Every block, really. But this one in particular. Mainly because it was the street he slung on, so they saw him day-to-day, glaring out at the world around him like the angry black man he was. Saw him intimidating any junkie bitch customer who didn't come correct with the cash. Saw him draw that Showstopper a little too quickly for anybody else's comfort, even around here where gunfights were about as regular as Sunday dinner. Saw him conversating with the voices in his head. Saw him guard this fucking turf like it was the only thing he had.

'Cause it was. Ray-Ray wasn't no team leader. He was a frontline man, a lone wolf.

"Don't make me start some shit outchere, man," Ray-Ray said to everybody within earshot, which was most everyone. Even the corner boys facing away from him had their hood-eye on this here conversation.

"No shit to start, B," Bishandre says, both hands in front of him. Raised up like some bootleg blackjack dealer about to flip over twenty-one. "We ain't even passed by your stoop today."

"Just got here not long before you anyway," LaQuan says, the distant southern lilt to his voice like he just finished a bottle of sizzurp.

"I need to call Big Freak?" Big Freak is the top lieutenant for the Latrobe Housing parcel, the four-square-block piece of city they're standing in. Ray-Ray isn't no kingpin, not like Big Freak. But even though Ray-Ray's out here hustling, rubbing elbows with these corner boys, it don't mean they're on Ray-Ray's level, either. They're young--probably not a single one of them older than twenty-two, except for Didi (but he be slow). Ray-Ray's got some years on him, got some stature in these streets.

Besides, he's so damned loose of a cannon he could start World War III. Loose enough to spray the block right now, in fact. Itching to. That Showstopper needs something to do, begging to come out and play, its thrum and hiss like something out of Highlander. Ready to start stacking bodies in the streets.

Much as he wants to start spraying the block, though, he can tell these little fake soldiers are telling the truth.

"No need for Big Freak," LaQuan says, almost confused at the words coming out of his mouth.

"Yeah fuck you then," Ray-Ray says and turns away, keeping only his hood-eye on the brat pack in case one of them got a funny idea in his head.

Time to find out who fucked with his stoop.

The footprint is clear as day. At least to him. He doesn't bother getting confirmation from anybody else around. Knows they can't see what he sees: someone's sneaker print stamped in the midst of the glowing lavender of the stairs. Same as when a killer leaves behind his boot print in the mud beneath the bedroom window on CSI.

Well I'll be god damned, Ray-Ray thinks. Somebody's been stepping where they don't belong.

"Yo Cray-Cray." A mousy voice calls out from behind him, on the sidewalk. Black Mike, a regular. You can tell by his reluctance to step off the sidewalk and up toward the stoop, especially with Ray-Ray's back turned. Good way to get lead poisoning. Too many eager junkies done found that out the hard way.

"Yo Cray-Cray," Black Mike says again.

"I told you about that name," Ray-Ray says, not bothering to look up. He's got his hood-eye on Black Mike and his neighbor corner boys at the same time.

"Man, you staring at them stairs like they got dinosaur bones in 'em, bruh. And you ain't know why people call you crazy?"

"Fuck outta here, Mike."

"Alright, sorry. *Ray-Ray*, let me holler at you a second."

"Fuck outta here, Mike."

"Yo, Black Mike," Bishandre says. "You trying to cop, come holla 'atcha boy."

"C'mon baby, you know I'm feeling some kinda way about Cray-Cray--I mean Ray-Ray's--product."

Yeah, Ray-Ray knew, not taking his eyes off the stoop, trying to size up the shoe print. All his customers felt some kinda way about what he had, which most of the block referred to as Cray-Cray because that shit made you go bananas. On the outside, your body was stiffer than a three-day-old corpse. But inside, you went on a trip like in them *Lord of the Rings* movies. Far away and full of treachery.

It was the great differentiator. The thing that allowed Ray-Ray to compete on this block, when rival businesses surrounded him on all sides. And the secret sauce was all his.

"C'mon, bruh. No more joking around."

Ray-Ray said nothing. Ignored Black Mike, leaned closer into his stoop. The purple glow grew brighter against the footprint as he got closer, the stoop doing its part to help Ray-Ray.

He saw the waffle pattern of a sneaker but the rest of it looked wrong. Instead of the rounded toe box, the toe box was split in two. Maybe two toes on one side and three on the other. Or one and four. Looked like a ninja shoe or some shit. The rest of it looked regular enough, the long outside curve that led to the heel still rounded like normal. In the middle was a strange symbol—like an upside-down *t*.

"The fuck is this?" he said under his breath.

It wasn't no basketball shoe, he could see that much. Unfortunately, basketball shoes was all he knew.

"Cray-Cray, *c'mon* man. Stop frontin'. It's almost Sunday scary time, yo."

Sunday scary time was when that dope high went bye-bye and the pain of addiction started to creep back on you. Commonly happened on Sunday when newbie junkies first started getting the feeling.

'Course, Black Mike wasn't no newbie junkie.

"It's fucking Tuesday, Mike."

"Man, *whatever*. Let me get that!"

This was one step too far. Ray-Ray unsheathed his Showstopper just like Highlander would, the quick, graceful motion that would make you weep at the sheer beauty of it, were it not for the ten-inch barrel staring right down the center of your face.

"The fuck I tell you?" Ray-Ray said, not needing to even speak the words but appreciating the emotional release they gave him. "I look like I'm open for business right now?"

Bless his little junkie heart but Black Mike started to actually speak. "I need that super duper, yo. You the only one that got that 2020 next level, bruh."

"You make another sound they'll be sweeping your shit-for-brains off the street until 3020."

Black Mike had just enough sense to step back silently and head for one of the corner boys down the street. He didn't even stop at

Bishandre or LaQuan's spot for fear of being heard getting his little junkie hands on the next best pack he could find.

Ray-Ray turned back to the shoe print, trying to get his inner-Matlock on. That crazy white boy always found a clue.

But nothing came to him.

"Hey, yo, Raymond."

Ray-Ray spun back around, hand still gripping the heft of his Showstopper, finger ready to exterminate any motherfucker who dared interrupt him now.

Nobody was there.

From the corner of his eye, Bishandre and LaQuan were eyeing him but Ray-Ray ignored them. They wouldn't get it anyway. Even Ray-Ray didn't get it.

He hadn't recognized the voice immediately but after a second it caught up to him.

"Bitch, you know where I am," the voice said.

It was the good angel on his shoulder (in his head was more like it). She showed her face (or made herself heard) whenever he needed some guidance. She was the only one who called him Raymond.

"Hey Kiki," he said under his breath, suddenly not wanting any of the others to hear him talking to himself.

"See you had a trespasser," she said as Ray-Ray leaned down again, trying to suss out any clues he might have missed while Black Mike was chirping behind him. He didn't see anything else on the glowing stairs–nothing above or below. Just a ninja footprint.

"We sho' did," Ray-Ray said and sat on the stoop, eyes searching the area around the stoop, seeing if the trespasser had maybe left a trail of glowing purple on the street. Nothing there.

He looked down at the print, trying to will *something* from his mind. Some CSI shit, maybe. He put the Showstopper back in his waistband and pulled out a peach cigarillo. Most of the corner boys around him smoked weed all day but he couldn't do that. It made other voices pop up. Voices besides Kiki.

"Well, shit," she said. "Pay that goofy-looking thing no mind. You gon' just hang out your shingle today, Raymond. Ain't worth tripping over some random karate kid stepping on the bottom stair of your stoop. Anybody coulda done that."

Ray-Ray lit the cigarillo and grimaced. As usual, Kiki was right. Turn the other cheek and all that Jesus shit. That was for sure the smart move.

But he wasn't sure he could let something like this slide. Out here, if you let a little indiscretion go, next thing you know someone would be standing on the stoop when he came around the corner. Then they'd be selling their own packs off *his* property. Sooner or later, he'd be irrelevant. Or worse, ten feet deep (because you know no motherfucker around here would ever put Ray-Ray at only six).

Nah. Fuck that. He'd worked hard enough to get this piece of territory. Carved it out with as much guile as he could muster plus plenty of blood and threats. He wasn't about to give no mouse a cookie and let someone else snatch it back.

"Raymond, I know you ain't thinking about doing what I think you're thinking about doing."

He took a deep inhale on the cigarillo, eyes calm, looking around him on the street. He might only have a single stoop in this city but everyone else down here knew who you did not fuck with.

Ray-Ray.

And only Ray-Ray could make sure it stayed that way.

So where the hell was he gonna find a motherfucking trespassing ninja out here in Charm City?

He tossed the cigarillo onto the sidewalk and blew the smoke out in a thick haze like an approaching thunderstorm. He liked the peach taste and the way the smoke calmed his nerves. But right now wasn't no time for calm.

"Heyo, Bish," he called out to Bishandre. The tall former wide receiver turned quick toward Ray-Ray like he was breaking back on a ball from the QB.

Ray-Ray liked it when he made the corner boys jumpy. Knew it meant he was still the one in charge. That he took up real estate inside their heads. At least they'd know how he felt all the time.

"Sup?" Bishandre said.

"Let me get some of that herbal."

"Raymond," Kiki said. "You know you can't be smoking no chronic during the daytime."

"Can't be sitting here like no punk bitch, neither."

Bishandre hustled over to Ray-Ray's stoop but didn't come close enough to hand him anything. He looked both ways up and down the street and took out a Marlboro pack. Inside was a stack of pre-rolled joints.

"Ay, what you want, bruh? Got that Bubba Kush, GG4, and GC."

"GC?"

Bishandre nodded and smiled. "Green Crack. You need some energy, that's the one I'd go with. Just watch yo'self. It can make you see some shit."

Well if that were true, Ray-Ray had been on Green Crack his whole life. "Green Crack it is." He took the joint from him, giving Bishandre a good stare to make sure he knew this wasn't no olive branch.

"Don't do it, Raymond."

"Quiet, Kiki."

Ray-Ray sparked it, puffed two, three, four times quickly, getting it lit and blowing the smoke out in a tight ring that drifted away just like Bishandre.

The effect was immediate. Ray-Ray felt like he could run through a wall.

"Shit, Double R, I got an idea." That was Andre Madcap, the devil on Ray-Ray's shoulder to Kiki's angel. Andre was a wild man and he came out whenever Ray-Ray got to some of the fiendish hoodlum shit he used to get into when he was younger. Have a little sniff? Andre was there to tell you to rob a liquor store. Break out the angel dust? Andre was there to point out that po-lice-man riding by was laughing at your ass and calling you a dumbass capital B, Boy. And oh by the way, wasn't he pointing his gun at you, talking about target practice?

The only time Andre didn't come out was when Ray-Ray was minding his business, smoking the peace pipe on the couch (with some of that low-fi herbal, not like this Green Crack) and sipping on his 211s like a good boy. Like a fucking accountant biding his time 'til he had to punch into work the next day.

But right now, Andre was just what Ray-Ray needed. "Whatchu got, Andre?"

"Get out of here, Andre. Raymond doesn't need your help with this."

"Shut up, Kiki. Double R called me out for a reason. Maybe if your ass was more helpful—"

"Stop arguing, both of you!" Ray-Ray was aware that half the corner boys looked up from what they were doing. He hadn't meant to scream out loud. But they quickly looked away. Always did.

Ray-Ray didn't like it, when he made a scene like that. But he couldn't help it. When the voices inside him started getting loud, Ray-Ray's own voice was the only thing able to drown them out, if even for a moment.

Sometimes he felt bad when he called Andre out. Like he was hurting Kiki's feelings. Then he remembered that Kiki only existed in his mind, which made him feel confused and weird, because she seemed awfully real to him. But he ignored that feeling for now.

"Right, check it, Double R. Them shoes is unique. They probably look dumb as hell in real life. But I bet they expensive."

Ray-Ray took another puff on the joint, nodding along with Andre. He'd seen some shits like that in a magazine once, now that he mentioned it.

"Japanese, maybe," Ray-Ray said out loud. "You know them fuckers are into all sorts of weird shit over there."

"Right, right. Eating eel. Fucking those sex dolls."

Ray-Ray laughed. Nobody else on the corner so much as looked his way. He knew they heard him but right now he didn't care. He was getting lifted onto Cloud Nine.

"So what's the plan, Andre?"

"You gotta find yourself one of them high-end shoe stores. Can't be too many out here. Foot Locker on every corner but who in this city would be caught dead wearing ninja shoes?"

"Preach," Kiki said.

"I know they got that one spot up near that fool George Washington, Double R. Mount Vernon Shoes, or some cracker-ass name like that. Always see some Hons walking out of there with their nose turnt up like they sniffing shit on the streets."

"Probably is," Kiki said.

"Ain't no shit out here," Ray-Ray said, taking one last long drag off the joint, feeling the burn on the tips of his fingers and the hotter smoke burn his lungs. "We got zombies, pushers, and bodies. That's about it. How you even know about this place, Andre?"

"I get around," said Andre.

Ray-Ray didn't bother asking the voice in his head how that was even possible.

TWO

Next thing he knew, Ray-Ray was looking at a high heel in the shape of a leopard that had gold flecks for the spots, wondering what its street value was, when the shoe store manager came over, crossing silently over the red carpeted floor, flanked by a big Russian guy in a suit who could have passed for the villain in a Rocky movie.

"Good afternoon, sir. Is there anything I can assist you with?" The manager wore in a velvet coat over top of a silk shirt and scarf. He had a thin mustache that looked like it had been penciled on his face. Ray-Ray had seen thicker brows on the drag queens coming out of Queenie's Club.

It was clear from his manner (not to mention the security guy) that he wasn't asking to be helpful.

"You got any ninja shoes?"

The Russian flexed beneath his suit and Ray-Ray fought the urge to flex his own bit of muscle, the one tucked into the back of his waistband. But he kept himself in check. Gotta find the motherfucker who stepped on his stoop before word got out that he was soft.

"Sir, we're flattered in your interest in our store but I'm afraid I have to ask you to leave."

Ray-Ray looked around. There were four women in the store besides him, the manager, and the Russian. One was clearly a store clerk—an older white lady, dressed in a fancy pantsuit and her hair done up looking like a beehive. Face was powdered white like George Washington himself. She stood behind a rack in the center of the store like it was bulletproof glass.

Behind her, toward the back of the store stood a young, well-put together sister, rocking parochial chic with a just a hint of a phat ass, maybe waiting on her lawyer daddy to send the car around to get her. Her head hung in shame, burning a hole through the floor, the Uncle Tom look when a colored boy "acted up" in the presence of white folks. Ray-Ray could see her caramel cheeks turning red from here.

The other two were skinny white women, blonde, late thirties. Barefoot. They looked like money, like those housewife hoes from reality TV.

All of them were staring at Ray-Ray.

"Why?" he said, taking in the rest of the store like he would the corner, sweeping his eyes left-to-right. Trying to calm his stoned mind.

The lights inside were bright white, felt like spotlights shining on him. Sweating, he realized even the people outside the store were looking in on him through the storefront window.

The manager scoffed. "Because you're making the other patrons uncomfortable."

Ray-Ray wanted to shove that silk scarf down dude's throat. "Because I'm black?"

"Because you're talking to yourself. Very loudly, sir."

Ray-Ray has never been called *sir* before. But the way this guy said it made it sound like a slur.

"Light this asshole up, Double R," Andre said. The Showstopper seemed to grow warm in anticipation, tucked safely into the back of his pants.

"Terrible idea, Raymond."

Ray-Ray wasn't sure which of them to listen to. Realized he was so stoned that he couldn't even remember getting here or what Kiki and Andre had been saying to him up until right now. Maybe he should have listened to Kiki's ass back on the corner and refrained from smoking.

Still, there was the question of what to do now. He sure wasn't about to sit here and let some old skinny white boy dick-slurper tell him off without any retribution.

"Raymond, you know you can't be causing no drama in here, unless you want to get that karate kid once they let you out of county."

"Time inside ain't nothing, Kiki."

"Jesus," she said. "You won't have a corner at all by then. Let alone have a chance in hell of finding the guy you're after."

Shit. She was right.

"Fucking amateur," she said under her breath.

"Sir?" the manager said, stepping to the side so the Russian had an open lane with which to approach Ray-Ray if necessary. He wondered if maybe he'd been talking to himself again. This chronic was messing with his headspace, making his thoughts and his words mix together until he wasn't entirely sure he could tell the difference between them. He had enough trouble with that as it was.

"Yeah, yeah, alright. I'm leaving."

He could see relief wash over the manager. The Russian looked a bit disappointed. But there was always next time for his ass.

Outside the store, Ray-Ray turned down the first alley he saw that got him off the storefront-lined street. The weed was making him paranoid now. Everybody on the street looked at him like he was some kind of outsider, something he hadn't ever felt before in Charm City. But he'd crossed into a different part of town, one that was lined with glass-fronted apartment buildings and ice cream parlors and shit. He wasn't used to that. More like boarded up shooting galleries and cracked vials.

"Go back to your spot and make that money, Raymond."

"Quiet, Kiki," he said. He leaned against the brick alleyway wall and pulled a peach cigarillo from his back pocket, happy to be away from the lookie-loos back on the street.

The lighter appeared in front of him and he got the cigarillo sparked, taking a big puff on that peach and trying to still his mind.

"So you're looking for...ninja shoes?"

The voice spooked him and he choked on the smoke. Dropped his cigarillo. He reached his hand into his waistband and was about to pull on the Showstopper when he saw caramel and red cheeks, the girl from inside the store. She lit her own cigarette and pocketed the lighter in her purse, leaning against the wall a few feet away.

"The fuck you doing out here?" he said to cute black girl from inside the store.

"I could ask you the same question. At least *I* work here." She reached her hand out and shook his. "I'm Cassie, by the way."

Ray-Ray picked up his cigarillo and took another puff. His nerves were shot now and he felt like he was losing his grip. People sneaking up on him was a good way to get dead. And he wasn't trying to kill no rich girl.

"She alright, Raymond," Kiki said. Somewhere inside his head, Andre gave a grunt in agreement. Weird, because they never agreed on anything.

"Yeah Cassie, I'm looking for some ninja shoes. You know where I can find some?"

Cassie inhaled her cigarette and narrowed her eyes, looking Ray-Ray up and down. "You want to tell me why you're looking for them?"

"No."

"Doesn't seem to fit your style." Cassie pointed the cigarette at him as she said it, as if pointing out the obvious.

"It ain't."

"Well then," she said, taking one last drag and flicking the cigarette across the alley, "I'm not sure I can help you."

She was almost gone back inside before Ray-Ray could tell her to stop. When she turned back to him, the sun glowed off her shiny hair the same way it glowed from his stoop. It was nice, not like the hood rats he was used to seeing. Her almond shaped eyes felt like portals to another world, half of her smooth caramel skin in the light and the other half in the dark of the doorway.

"I'm looking for someone. Wears those shoes."

She came out of the doorway only slightly. "Someone who? A woman?"

He shrugged. "Don't know who. This the only fancy shoe place I know of."

"And this...someone. Why are you looking for them?"

"We gon' merc that fool," Andre said. Ray-Ray could hear the excitement in his voice, could practically see him rubbing his hands together in preparation.

"They did something they shouldn't," was all Ray-Ray said.

"You the police?"

"I look like the fucking po-lice?"

Cassie shook her head no and bit her lip. "So you're gonna hurt them, then. I guess they did something pretty bad."

Ray-Ray couldn't tell exactly, still on the comedown from the weed, but he thought she was kinda digging on him. Like she was the Bonnie to his Clyde.

"Something unforgivable," he said. "And I'm going to set them straight on it."

She gave him a once over. When her eyes met his again, they were no longer portals to another world. They were vacancy signs saying OPEN FOR BUSINESS. She glanced back in through the door, checking the back hallway.

"Well maybe there's something you could help me with in here," she said and pointed to the dark, empty hallway. "And maybe, if you do a good enough job, that will jar my memory loose on if I've seen those shoes before."

Ray-Ray flicked his cigarillo into the alley and nodded his head yes. He knew he should be rushing off to find the motherfucker who stepped on his stoop but he felt like a quick detour couldn't hurt.

THREE

Turns out those shoes were men's shoes. Cassie had seen them before, just not in her store. They were street shoes (literally her words). Ray-Ray wasn't sure what streets those shoes were popular on—maybe the mean streets of Japan—but he sure hadn't ever seen them. Apparently, they were a rare item.

Cassie hadn't seen anyone wearing them but she'd seen them at a pop-up bazaar down near the Inner Harbor waterfront. Another part of town Ray-Ray wasn't too familiar with. *His* Baltimore was a land-locked nation of poor merchants trading pearls for coin. Only their pearls were black and their coins were made of paper and coated with powder and dirt. Down by the water, things were different. There lived a leisure class of lords and nobles content to keep their stinking class of serfs out of sight and out of mind.

The Inner Harbor itself was square shaped, you looked at it on a map. A big brick walking path wrapped around three sides of the square, the fourth side being where the river continued out toward parts unknown to Ray-Ray. He stood right about the middle of the path, across from the side where the river mouth stretched away from land and wondered what it must have been like to come to this country on ships. He knew for some people, descendants of those who lived around this area, the journey had been much nicer than it had for his descendants.

As it was, there was the big ship right in front of him, looming over the corner where he stood. Looked like a pirate ship to Ray-Ray. And standing in its shadow, which crept across the brick in slow increments, he felt a bit like a pirate himself.

Because now that he was down here, he Wished he didn't have to find this ninja who fucked with his trade routes. Because this looked like the land of opportunity to him. A place where his pirate ass could separate a few tourists from their wallets. Then send them back where they came with nothing else but a warning to stay the hell away.

"Maybe you should get a little paper today, Double R. Since you not making any back at the corner spot."

Not a bad point by Andre. Ray-Ray could handle a little temporary hit to his cash flow. But he didn't like the thought of leaving his post unattended for this long. Not that any of those fools were stupid enough to slang their dope on his stoop. But if Ray-Ray didn't wrap this up soon, they might start getting crazy ideas.

"That looks like the bazaar over there," Kiki said, quick to try to quiet Andre's devious influence.

To their right, around the bend in the walkway, was an open field littered with tents and people.

The sneaker bazaar was awash with fresh kicks of all kinds, from the latest Jordan's to the original Chuck Taylors. Ray-Ray made a mental note to come back here at some point in the future when he didn't need to find someone to kill. Plenty kicks here to bring back to his corner and make the rest of the corner boys jealous.

But right now, he focused on the tent of one Usa Takanaki. Asian by birth but Brooklyn by upbringing, Usa wears white denim overalls with a Warn-a-Brother t-shirt--a shirt with a blunt smoking Bugs Bunny and the text of the shirt in the Warner Brothers logo and font type.

"Whatchu need, man," the Asian firecracker says, pronouncing *man* like *main*. He talks almost exclusively with his hands, using the words for emphasis rather than the other way around.

Ray-Ray told him exactly what he needed.

"Yeah, man. I done sold a fly ass pair of 'dem to a guy last week. White boy. Tall, thin, was dressed in all black."

Ray-Ray thinks maybe it's a goth thing, like those high school kids who be shooting up schools. Usa corrects him.

"Not a school age kid, man. Adult. Strait-laced, too."

"Like a cop?"

Usa thinks about this. "No, not like a cop."

"Then like what?"

Usa shrugged. "I sell the shoes, man. I don't check IDs."

"But you remember, don't you?"

"Might do, man. Might do." Usa smiled and crossed his arms mischievously, putting a thumb-and-forefinger-shaped L under his chin.

Ray-Ray played dumb. "So do you or not?"

"Might be that it will cost you."

Yeah, Ray-Ray thought. Everyone's a hustler.

"Shit, this fool better start remembering, Double R."

"Yeah I know that's right."

Usa frowned at Ray-Ray. "You know what's right?"

Shit, Ray-Ray was doing it again, talking to himself out loud. He thought the weed had worn off but Bish hadn't been messing around about its potency. Green Crack was no joke.

So maybe let it be potent, Ray-Ray thinks, let the Crack do its thing. He didn't have to look any farther than Usa's t-shirt.

Time to Warn-a-Brother.

Ray-Ray grabbed Usa, could feel the wind go out of his skinny body. His eyes bulged like they were about to pop and he tried to scream. Ray-Ray put a hand over his mouth, pushed him against the back of the tent. The fabric bent and crumpled against their weight.

Shockingly it didn't fold up and break, though both side fabric walls pushed in closer to them.

Usa struggled but Ray-Ray punched him in the gut, sending a stack of shoeboxes tumbling down around them. The little Asian would probably scream if he could breathe.

Ray-Ray reached behind him, into his waistband for the Showstopper and pulled it out. Let Usa see it first, to get his mind wrapped around what would happen if he didn't deliver to Ray-Ray the answers he was looking for.

Then he put the barrel of the Showstopper against Usa's mouth.

"Open up, bitch."

Usa's eyes really bulged this time. Like a Panic Pete squeeze doll. Started to tear up.

But he opened sesame right quick.

In went the Showstopper.

"When I take this piece out your mouth, I expect the next thing to come out after it to be an answer to my question. If it ain't, I'mma remove this head from your neck."

Snot came out of Usa's nose. More tears rolled down his cheeks.

"You feel me?"

Usa eyed the gun, then Ray-Ray. Not a tough decision.

He nodded yes.

Ray-Ray pushed the gun in a little farther, just to make his point. Then he pulled it out.

"Who did you sell those ninja shoes to?"

It was Ray-Ray's experience that the Showstopper was better than Adderall for improving people's memory.

This time proved no different.

FOUR

Strait-laced like a priest was apparently what Usa had meant. So Ray-Ray was headed to church.

Up Charles Street was Mount Vernon Place, the George Washington park. He didn't like this area of the city. Never had. It wasn't the fact that it was mostly white or that it was mostly on the come-up with new buildings and restaurants that didn't mesh with his idea of what Charm City was all about.

It was the statues he didn't like. He never had liked *any* statues, ever since he was a kid. Always felt like they were watching him, sneering at him. He'd heard them talk before (result: broken hand and a medical bill he never paid). And sometimes, back before Kiki and Andre showed up, the statues even listened, though their guidance was just as questionable as the current cast of characters tucked away upstairs.

But these statues...these motherfuckers loomed *large* in the darkening sky. Larger than everything else around them for miles.

The first was the horse statue. It wasn't of Washington (no, he was up on top of the ozone looking down) but rather Lafayette, some alien-looking motherfucker sitting atop a horse. Ray-Ray never bothered to look into Lafayette—whatever kind of name that was—or how he got himself bronzed out in the center of Baltimore. Mainly because the statue creeped him the fuck out. Something about it reminded him of the Headless Horseman, even though *this* statue had a head.

Not a lot of things that freaked him out worse than the spooky ass Headless Horseman. Ray-Ray had enough problems with his head still attached to his body. He didn't want to imagine a world where he had to carry the damn thing around with him.

As he trudged up through the park, passing the manicured lawn hemmed in by bushes, and the fountain with some gunk-ass homeless guy fishing for coins, he couldn't shake the feeling of being watched. He just tried to keep his mind on finding this priest and putting an end to the man who had the balls to step up on *his* stoop.

He climbed the staircase leading through the center of the park, the setting sun throwing the Lafayette statue into darkness. Ray-Ray shivered, took comfort in the fact that his Showstopper was tucked tight into the waistband of his pants. He'd even made sure to wipe Usa's snot and spit off it before re-holstering.

He just wasn't sure how much good it would do against a statue that had spiritual powers.

At the top of the stairs, he got one long, crystal clear 5k look at the Headless Horseman. And his first peek at the thing that *really* freaked him out: the George Washington monument.

If the Lafayette statue was the Headless Horseman, then the George Washington statue was Freddy Krueger, Jason Voorhees, and that Exorcist bitch all rolled into one.

It loomed large over the park, the city, and Ray-Ray's psyche—a giant white marble column that rose into the sky like some Jack and the Beanstalk shit. From where he stood, it was hard to make out all of Washington's features, which only made things worse for Ray-Ray because his imagination could easily run wild with the few visual clues he could see 178 feet above him, where the actual statue was. He'd always pictured old George looking down on him disapprovingly, his cocaine-colored hair all brushed back, not a single strand out of place. Tonight, the smile on the man best known for having his grill on the dollar had a thousand-watt cocaine smile to match his hair.

And Ray-Ray knew that crazy smile was somehow meant just for him. *I beat the British*, it seemed to say, *so I damned sure can beat your black ass, Ray-Ray.*

"I think he looks kinda handsome," Kiki said.

"Ah nah, girl," Andre said. "That fool was the ultimate trouble-maker. Go tag that statue, Double R. Like him up with aerosol."

"Don't have no paint. Besides, I want to get the hell out of here. I hate this spot."

The church where Usa conveniently remembered his customer-priest worked out of was a few blocks from the park, otherwise Ray-Ray wouldn't be caught dead over here. He kept walking, head low, not glancing backwards at the statues. Trying to keep their devious faces out of his mind. Moving quick but not too quick. Avoiding attention. The neighborhood was on the up-and-up. Gentrification, the news called it. Wasn't nothing to it, really. Just slap up some nice properties and keep the black folks as far away as possible.

"Shit, 'cept when you need some dope," Ray-Ray said under his breath.

A college-age white girl looked up at him and just as quickly looked away, crossing her arms across her chest and quickening her own pace away from him. It wasn't out of the ordinary for a hood to be walking around this part of the city, Ray-Ray knew. But one that was talking to himself might attract some attention. If they confused him for a homeless person, any cop could stop him on the street. And Ray-Ray was still carrying the Showstopper and his unsold pack.

"Keep yourself together," Kiki said. "Better yet, how about you call this stupid game off, head back to your corner, and make that money?"

Ray-Ray appreciated that at least Kiki didn't get on his case about slanging. Not like he had any other opportunity to make a living.

Andre was surprisingly quiet. Ray-Ray gave him a chance to speak up but he said nothing.

Ray-Ray wasn't sure if that was a good or a bad thing.

Before he knew it, he stood in front of the church. It was a five-story brick building with white trim, the whole structure set atop a massive concrete foundation that seemed to grow up and out of the sidewalk. Two white double doors, the right one propped open letting the cooling dusk air in. A tingle ran down his back and touched the Showstopper tucked there like a lightning rod in a storm.

He stayed looking at the door for a long time, not sure why.

"Raymond, you can still go home." Kiki was nothing if not consistent. When it came to making paper, she was ride-or-die. When it came to acting a fool, she always tried to stop him.

She wasn't always effective. But damned if she didn't try.

If he was honest with himself, he didn't really believe her. Didn't see going home right now as a viable option. Ray-Ray had grown up in this city. Hadn't seen shit change. Dope fiends copped and went walking dead on theyselves. Corner boys slang and played cowboys and Indians with both sides losing. Police harassed and stole from all our black asses. Blue got Benzes and beach houses off black.

Always and forever, the cycle keeps going.

"Raymond, please."

The words were desperate, pleading. But Ray-Ray wasn't hearing them.

"Quiet, Kiki."

He went inside the church.

It was cool and quiet. Like walking into a tomb but it smelled like spices. He climbed the short staircase to the main floor and saw the whole inside of the church before him—a five-story cathedral that almost stopped him in his tracks.

It was...beautiful.

Ray-Ray never had much occasion to go to church. No moms to take him. No pops to insist. No aunties and uncles. Shit, even his foster home was one of the few that wasn't hooked up with some kind of church or faith-based organization.

But this place fucking *sparkled.*

Through a wall of glass windows, the nave stretched away from him looking like the yellow brick road, punctuated at the end by a huge dome ceiling over the main altar. The few churches Ray-Ray *had* been in had a Jesus statue looking down over the altar–Ray-Ray remembered that part clearly. But not this one. This one was different. Instead, a giant oil painting of some old white dude kneeling down with angels hovering over him hung above the white marble mantel.

"Shit and I thought I was high," Ray-Ray said under his breath.

None of the voices in his head said anything in response.

On either side of the main altar, toward the front corners of the church, hung a Jesus statue (the one he was used to seeing in the middle of the church) over what appeared to be a prayer area filled with small candles. Strange bits of color dotted those spaces--reds, blues, gold, lavender, green. Ray-Ray wasn't sure if they were real or imagined, or maybe still the -of the Green Crack.

The church itself was empty, about thirty rows of pews on either side of him as he walked farther toward the front.

Orchestral music played from somewhere over the PA system but Ray-Ray didn't see anyone playing. The music was strangely beautiful, tugging at something at the back of his throat as he reached the altar.

Gentle words emerged from his left, from beneath where one of the Jesus statues hung. "Can I help you, son?"

Ray-Ray moved like a stick-up artist hitting a stash house, closing the gap between himself and the voice in an instant. He pulled the Showstopper out from under his shirt and pointed it at the man who'd crept out of the shadows. He was white, tall, and lean. A priest, looking the part, wearing the all-black frock and white collar.

He put his hands up. "We don't have any money here, son."

Ray-Ray didn't believe that for a second. "Not here for your money."

The music continued to play over the speakers—strings and piano like an opera version of a Dr. Dre track.

"Put that down, son. There's no need for it. Let's just talk, huh?"

Fuck that, Ray-Ray thought, I ain't talking about shit after the day I just had. And now that he was thinking about it, maybe he *would* snatch some of that money from the collection basket for all the trouble he'd gone to. He wasn't gonna be reparated for growing up black in this country, he might as well take his own reparations.

The priest didn't say anything else, just kept a level gaze on Ray-Ray, who had to admit that the guy was taking it well. Maybe it wasn't his first stick up.

Something was wrong, though. The priest was too calm. He should have been pissing his pants and saying a prayer or something. Instead he was just standing there, smug. And was he fucking *smirking?*

Or was it all in Ray-Ray's head?

"The fuck is in your hands?" Ray-Ray lunged forward at the priest and knocked something out of his hands. Two books fell onto the floor with a thud, muffled under the rising crescendo of piano and strings.

The priest looked scared now. Maybe realizing it wasn't no ordinary stick-up. He stepped back and away from Ray-Ray.

Ray-Ray felt suddenly felt uncomfortable. He thought Andre would be here for this. Or Kiki. Instead, they hadn't said a damn word since he'd come inside. The voices in his head had gone to sleep.

He was alone.

And he didn't like the feeling.

His hands shook. He felt like he might be sick.

The priest seemed to sense this and asked, "What's your name, son?"

Ray-Ray told him.

"Well, Ray-Ray, there's no need for violence. I can see you're having a hard day. Why don't you tell me what it is you want?"

His hand shook more, the sweat on his palms making the gun's grip feel slippery. Ray-Ray had shot people before, that wasn't no thing for him. But these...feelings. They were new. And he didn't like them.

He gripped the Showstopper harder. Gritted his teeth.

Don't forget why you came here, he thought, trying to get his own internal compass through the storm of confused thought in his head.

"What's that now?" the priest said.

Shit. He was talking to himself out loud again. He hadn't meant to. He shook his head as if to unjumble everything going on inside there, but it was hard. The storm of confusion was gaining strength and velocity. His own internal voice struggled to rise above the hum.

It's your stoop...he done stepped on it...can't let that slide...not after how hard you worked...territory belongs to the man who defends it... 'dem other boys will hear about this...if you don't...do the right thing... they might have lied to your ass...straight up...don't care 'bout you... they want your stoop...might have put this Wonder Bread fool up to it... testing you...see if you still got it...

"Son?" The priest stepped forward slowly, reaching a hand out to steady Ray-Ray, who realized he'd started to wobble on his feet.

"Get the fuck outta my face!" He slapped the priest's hand away with the Showstopper. The priest recoiled, a flash of terror on his face.

Ray-Ray swallowed. Flexed his arms. Sighted the Showstopper. *Time to do this.*

He tried to blink away the doubt.

"Let me see your shoes."

"Huh?"

"Let me see your fucking shoes!" He punched the air in front of him with the barrel of the Showstopper, trying to regain his composure and stop his shaking hand.

The priest put both hands in the air in front of him, showing he wasn't a threat. Then he stuck a foot out from his frock so Ray-Ray could see the shoes.

But Ray-Ray couldn't see shit. He was breathing heavy like an asthmatic running from the cops. The spice-scented air felt hard to breathe. The lights and reflections through the stained-glass windows started to swirl around his vision and mix in with the shadows and thoughts until the priest became a swirl of emotions—colors, shadows, and music.

"Damnit, man," Ray-Ray said, "step into the light!"

The priest stepped slightly forward, his features coming back into Ray-Ray's vision. The shadows subsided but the colors remained, streaming from the stained-glass windows to Ray-Ray's left, the setting Charm City sun almost at rest for the day.

"Is that better, son?"

Ray-Ray blinked a few times until he could see the pasty-faced man clearly. Then he looked down on his shoes.

Ninja shoes.

And not just that.

Ninja shoes awash in purple light.

No, not purple.

Lavender.

Even though he was expecting it, Ray-Ray hardly believed it. Wasn't sure what he believed anymore. Nothing seemed real enough for him to grasp hold of. His own mind least of all.

"Ray-Ray?" the priest said, interrupting the confused tumbling inside his mind. "I said, *is that better?*"

"Huh?"

"Can you see...whatever it is you're looking for? Is that better?"

"Not for you."

"What do you mean? What is it that brought you here?"

"Lavender."

"Lavender?"

"Uh huh."

"I don't follow."

Ray-Ray didn't say anything. Was trying to process everything, which was becoming harder and harder with each passing second. His thoughts were up to Category Five hurricane status.

La-ven-der...Kiki says...Andre says...left you alone...la-ven-der... fixer upper...ninja shoes...Green Crack...reparations...Kiki said...Andre said...

"Ah!" Ray-Ray grabbed the sides of his head, the jumble of thoughts physically hurt.

But it was the lavender glow from the priest's shoes that brought him back to the moment.

Had Ray-Ray's stoop tagged this asshole who dared tread on his territory?

"Do you need shoes, son? I can arrange for some from the rectory office..."

"Shut up." This might be the first time anyone ever offered to help Ray-Ray Horne. And he didn't want that fact to get in the way of what needed to be done.

"Why'd you walk on my turf?"

The priest put his foot down. His face had gone from scared to terrified while Ray-Ray had been lost in his thought-storm. Perhaps realizing that Ray-Ray himself was no longer in control of things.

The priest started to say something but his tongue caught in his mouth.

Ray-Ray kept talking to keep his own thoughts at bay. "My stoop, man. You went and walked on it. And now here you stand, bathed in lavender light. Was only a matter of time before I found you."

The priest tried a smile but he didn't have it in him. His hands were still up and in front of his body. Now *he* was shaking. And sweating.

Ray-Ray's hand steadied as he spoke, his thought-storm beginning to weaken, blow over. Slightly at first, and then more as he continued speaking.

"Sweating like a whore in church, huh?"

He'd always wanted to say that. Never had occasion to.

His target didn't think it was so funny.

"Make yo' peace, man."

"Son, please, no--"

It was as if the priest's rising fear had quieted Ray-Ray's internal mind, if only for a moment.

"Make it. Or don't."

The priest did, crossing himself and mumbling something under his breath.

"I just don't understand why you have to do this."

Ray-Ray sighted the Showstopper center mass on the priest. But he didn't pull the trigger yet.

"Because."

"Because why?"

"Because you're lavender."

The priest started to cry. A muffled one at first. Then a sob.

"I don't understand–"

Ray-Ray shot him.

The gun's roar was deafening. The priest dropped to the ground and was dead in seconds. The Showstopper had that kind of power. Dirty Harry, knock-you-off-your-feet power.

The storm inside Ray-Ray's mind went dormant but for the ringing in his ears. Everything was blissfully quiet for a second. The orchestra music faded away with the thoughts.

Outside the church, the sun had gone down. Nighttime in Charm City.

The lavender glow on the priest dimmed, then disappeared.

Ray-Ray knew this quiet wouldn't last. His whole life, he'd never been able to run from his own mind. It made for a confusing life devoid of what most people thought of as regular.

But Ray-Ray wasn't regular. Was OK with that fact.

He still had his stoop, though. Maybe his most prized accomplishment. And now everyone in the neighborhood would know–again and for always–that if you messed with Ray-Ray's stoop...

He–and the voices in his head–would come for you.

If for no other reason than to find a few more moments of quiet.

THE VOICE OF RAGE
AND RUIN

NIZ THOMAS

THE VOICE OF RAGE AND RUIN

AN ORIGINAL CRIME STORY

ONE

On the day I died, I was sitting at the makeshift dinner table on the back edge of a twenty-six-foot Stingray boat called *Green River*, watching the wake churn and fold in on itself behind us as we glided along the inlet, moving slowly out into the cold purple night.

At least I am pretty sure it was the day I died.

I sometimes am not too good with time. Some passes, and it's less or more than I think. Years disappear. Seconds seem to stretch forever. It's funny like that. Time, I mean.

I had my elbows rested on the plywood tabletop, laid atop two sawhorsies, and they'd even put a white towel over top the plywood like we was in a fancy restaurant. In front of me was my empty plate, a white porcelain dish the size of a frisbee but the weight of a discus, and a plastic knife and fork next to that. No spoon, which was how it was supposed to be done, you're in a fancy restaurant.

I been in one, course. Once. Don Giovanni's, I think it was called. Or Don Pepe's. Or Don GioPepe's. Names were never my thing. Sometimes I even forgot my own.

But the place—whatever the hell it was called—was something else. Tables crowded in on one another like when all your siblings and cousins had to share the same bed on beach vacations. Which I didn't like. I'm not small. And I don't like to be cramped. The little woman sitting at the table next to me got up after a while and left, 'cause she didn't like it so much, being pressed against the wall like I was making her be. Like I was an angry father waiting—*just waiting* —for you to make another sound 'fore I cracked your head open.

The waiters at the place all had white coats on, black buttons down the front of their shirts and immigrant faces that somehow made me feel like I didn't belong. Most of them smelled like sour onions, which I didn't like either. Couldn't help smelling them, though. They had to get close to us, too.

I found out for the first time there about how you did the silver-ware. Even though they seemed determined not to help us, with the low lights and the itty-bitty candle flames on the tables. But anyway, you use the stuff on the outside first and work your way in.

At least I think that was how it was supposed to go. Truth of it is, I never been good at following directions.

When they finally brought food out, I forgot about some of the stuff I didn't like. Until now, I guess. The food, though, made it all A-OK in my book. Smelled like garlic bread and olive oil had a sex baby. The spaghetti looked like a girl's hair after it got smashed in by a hammer or something. But tasted better.

So I knew about how utensils were supposed to work. I had a spoon at Don GioPeppers, or whatever it was called. Had two of them, actually. And when you set down at dinner, you're supposed to get at least one.

Everybody knows that.

They didn't seem to care, here on *Green River*. Or maybe they just didn't know. I guess not everybody gets to go to fancy restaurants. I made a joke to them, before, about how I'd tuck my napkin into my neck collar. That was another thing you saw at a fancy restaurant. Mostly the fat slobs and children did it. But I thought it was funny and did it, too. Nobody had laughed about it when I said it before. At my joke, I mean.

Maybe they didn't laugh, though, 'cause I didn't have no napkin. Or no neck collar. Just my sweatshirt, the one I'd been wearing when they picked me up. They only made me remove the string that pulls the face-opening of the hood closed. Then they didn't have any problem with me wearing it. But before then, sheesh. It was like I peed in their milkshake. They were threatening to make me change into a white strangejacket.

I was happy to keep the sweatshirt, a green one. Hunter green. My favorite color. The fabric was worn through, even had holes in a few places which gave me little flashes of cool air when the wind picked up. Nobody had bothered to ask if I needed a coat out here in this chilly weather. I guess they didn't care but I thought it was rude. Early November down along the Jersey Shore. Most people need a jacket. Especially out on the water.

Luckily, like I said, I'm big. And big means warm. I always got into trouble when I was younger, with my mom. I was big then, too. Not all the way as big, not at first. But big enough where coats didn't help me much to stay warm.

That didn't stop her from tormenting me until I put one on. But I figure moms are meant to torment their kids.

What else use would they be?

Anyway, once I got full big, she didn't bother me so much. Which was good, I guess. Being bothered sucks.

And I didn't always react to well to it.

The gentle hum of the boat and the cool night air was nice. The promise of a candlelit dinner on the water was even nicer.

The rich houses along the water were vacant shadows that seemed to turn away from us as we headed farther out into the water. A few of them still had their deck furniture out atop their decks. Stuff that looked expensive. I couldn't help wondering how hard it would be to take.

One of them came over, a small fella that reminded me of the immigrant waiters at Don GioPepe's. I was supposed to know this guy's name, but I forgot it already. Pointy-face, was how I thought of him. Kind of a bastard.

The light from the moon caught on the tips of his eyeballs and made them look like he had silver puddles moving across. I already didn't trust him but the fact I couldn't see his eyes made me trust him less. He had a thin face, like a raccoon who just smelled something bad, and his tight lips were pulled across his cheeks like piano wire around a neck.

He put a plate atop the frisbee plate, which was close to the first thing they did fancy and right. New plate was the size of an old 7-inch single. I don't know music too good but even I remember the days when I used to sneak records back home from the store.

Jimmy (I forget his last name) had a record player at his house because his dad was a two-bit hustler, according to my mom, and could afford one. The first record I ever listened to on it was "Surfin' Safari" by The Beach Boys, a green disc that always made me feel like going to California would solve all my problems. Problem, though, since it involved leaving the state.

The record was on sale, ten bucks off, because the store was going out of business.

I stole it anyway.

But this record that Pointy-face put down in front of me smelled fantastic. It was probably my mind playing weird tricks, confusing the past with the present like it did sometimes, but I actually heard the beginning guitar riffs and humming chorus of "Surfin' Safari." I just closed my eyes, listening to Brian Wilson crank those tunes out like he stole something (and like I stole his record), and took a nice big whiff of the steaming food courtesy of Pointy-face.

I could smell the warmth, which rose into my nose and felt like it was sweating my brain. The guitar riff led into the doo wop vocals, which all pulsed inside my wet, sweaty brain. Sloshing around inside my skull like a piña colada getting prepared. The buttery crust from whatever they were feeding me started to push away the sounds, squeezing them like toothpaste from the tube.

Mixed into all that was a scent. Something tangy and sweet.

Made me realize I was darn hungry.

When I finally opened my eyes, I was looking down at a cobbler of some sort. Flat, golden crust with wrinkles that reminded me of an old woman's face. In the low light coming from behind me, from the front of the boat, I saw the steam rising from the plate. Same steam like had been inside my skull.

"What's this?" I asked Pointy-face.

He didn't say anything, just glared down at me. Like I said, he was kind of a bastard.

I picked up my plastic knife and slit the cobbler across the bottom third of its face. Quick-like, like I'd did it before. The slit looked like a smile, but not a big one. Not a happy one. More like Pointy-face's lips all tight across his skin.

Maybe that would show him to be nicer to me.

Steam rushed through the slit and overpowered my senses. Almost knocked my head back with its strength. I been punched before, plenty. Only once or twice harder than that.

"What is this?" I said again to Pointy-face, though I already knew. Sometimes I said things I didn't mean to. Mostly I regretted them once they left my mouth, if I ever thought of them again at all. I just stared down at the pie. Glued to the chair.

"Peaches," Pointy-face said.

"Yeah," was all I could say.

TWO

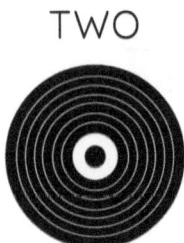

Before they came and picked me up, before we got on *Green River*, I wasn't used to getting fancy meals made for me. I used to go to this diner near my house, a greasy spoon is what they call it, I think. Even though none of my spoons were ever greasy while I was there. I checked them all.

New Jersey has a lot of diners. Some people say the most per square mile. But that is cheating, to me, since it's such a small state and a lot of people live in it. If you ever saw it on a map, you'd think it was like a mini-California, reversed and flipped around kind of.

The Principal Diner was the name of my place. Weird name, you ask me, since nobody likes to be reminded of their school days. Especially not their principal. Who would want to eat in a place named after the guy who spanks you for being out near the jungle gym when you're not supposed to?

Well, I guess me. Since I used to eat there a lot. 'Course, the food was shit. Which in my experience, is hard for a diner to do. Not a lot of other things they can lean on if they have bad food, is the way I see it. And the Principal Diner didn't have any tablecloths and their utensils were so cloudy from use (but not greasy) that you couldn't even see a reflection of yourself, you looked at them. Not even when you held them up to the light.

A few times when I was dining there, people got testy with me. Until they got a look at who they were testing.

But see I got it, why they was all upset. When I ordered coffee, which was always a bad idea 'cause of the sugar and caffeine and how it affected my mood, I had this thing where I needed to swirl my spoon around the edge of the cup. It was one of those things, you know? I couldn't stop until I heard just the right pitch of noise. That particular metal on ceramic that hit just the right spot deep down in the root of my jaw.

So people got upset about it. The manager asked me a bunch of times to stop doing it. But there's that whole thing with directions again. Never did good at following them.

'Course, all that stuff was mostly just my way of avoiding things, the things that drew me to the Principal in the first place.

But the scent of the peach cobbler brought all that back. Because the Principal had an amazing peach cobbler on the menu. One of about three hundred items but about the only thing besides coffee I ever ordered there. Since all the rest of it was borderline inedible.

It was nice, to have something to do there besides just sitting, watching, and dinking and dunking my spoon.

It made stuff less weird sometimes.

Sometimes, too, I would play the jukebox at the diner. Usually if they was out of cobbler or if I already finished mine. They had one of those old ones that lit up neon pink and yellow and blue and green. The top part, where you could see the machine following your orders, using its little arms and fingers to put on the record you wanted, was curved so it kind of looked like the juke was smirking at you.

Come to think of it, it kind of reminded me of Pointy-face and his tight lips. Except less of a bastard.

Once, the lights went off inside the diner, after hours. You could see the jukebox glowing from the parking lot off to the side of the building, especially once the parking lot lights went off, too.

Then the thing inside came alive like some kind of sleeping dragon, awakened.

Another thing I did that I think annoyed people: I played the same CCR song again and again on the jukebox until I was out of quarters. I had a lot of them, on account of me knowing when the manager at the laundromat around the corner took his smoke break.

And sometimes I got confused. The song played so much that I wasn't always sure if it was playing in real life or just in my head. But that night, with the jukebox lit up, "Bad Moon Rising" was playing in both places, I think. 'Cause when I came to, I was inside the diner and those prickly fingers of John Fogerty were creeping up and down the neck of the guitar, plucking out the joyful opening chords.

Just like my fingers were creeping around the neck of the waitress.

I didn't mean anything by it. Was just in a trance, like. Sometimes that happened to me, when I got confused about past and present and future. When the things in my head and in real life mixed all together like how I mixed my coffee at the diner. Except sometimes they got murkier instead of lighter like coffee did when the cream got mixed into it.

She got all upset. The waitress, I mean. Really got out of control, to be honest. I didn't like to see her like that. Not at all. And I wondered what it was had made her like that.

Sometimes I think it might have been me.

I'm not sure how long we went on like that, her screaming and me doing, well, what I was doing. But the tears running down her face got mixed with the snot running down her nose and after a while, I simply couldn't take it anymore. The sight of it made me feel all weird.

By the second or third time "Bad Moon Rising" spun back around, she'd gotten hold of the tiered glass pie dish.

Boy did that hurt. When she stuck me with it, the sounds on the record got all distorted, like.

Time slowed down, I think.

Honestly, it's a little hard to keep it all straight.

THREE

The exhaust smell of our slow-moving boat pulled me back into the present. Choking me with its thick, tasty fragrance. I always liked the smell of gasoline. I just never felt guilty about it like most people.

I looked down at my cobbler and saw that I'd basically smashed it around on the plate. Like I beat it up, pressed my hand down into it or something. The pulpy remains of it were all over my hand and the sleeve of my sweatshirt.

Like it got out of hand and I tried to quiet it down.

I shuddered. Once again confused about what I'd done. What I was capable of doing without even knowing.

Pointy-face was still looking at me. Bastard look. I gave him the same look back.

Behind him, another one of them emerged from the darkness out front of the boat. A chubby guy, Irish features. Potato nose and a red hue to his face. But dirty, dangerous eyes that I could see clearly in the darkness. Eyes that meant me harm, no doubt.

Thing was, they were both looking disgusted with me. Like maybe they just watched me do something they didn't approve of. I knew something about that look. Saw it on plenty of faces over the years.

I couldn't help but be overwhelmed again with the smell of peaches from the cobbler. There was cinnamon buried somewhere deep inside, the smell of it now coating my hands, sweatshirt, and especially the white (now speckled) towel laid down to make this a fancy dinner. Especially now with the wind changed direction, which blew away the smell of the boat's exhaust.

I blinked my eyes, trying to get away from the yammering jaws of memory biting at my ankles.

Potato-nose snarled at me. The same look he'd given me the whole time since him and the others had come and picked me up. When I really thought about it for a second, I had to say maybe it wasn't just Pointy-nose was the bastard.

Might have been the whole lot of them.

Green River edged past the last house along the bay. A mansion lit up with lights from the inside like it was impersonating a lighthouse. Every other house on the block was still dark and cold, it being the off-season. But this last house grabbed my attention, like. Mainly 'cause it looked so empty. And its emptiness was highlighted by the fact it was blasting light out into the bay like the sun had been born there.

Something about the house made me turn away from it. Too cheerful.

There wasn't nowhere else to look except down, at my plate. And that was when I realized I had only picked up the knife. So I'd made this whole mess with only the one utensil. And they still hadn't given me a spoon.

Potato-nose had a nasty looking face on when he sidled up next to me. The boat was moving out into more open water now but we were still in the no-wake zone, so it wasn't too unruly just yet. A slight bob up and down.

"The hell you doing with that pie, you sick fuck?" he said to me. He looked angrier than he was 'cause his face was already so red. But he might've actually been pretty angry, given the whole reason we were here.

I didn't say anything to him, mainly because I wasn't sure *what* had happened with the cobbler. I thought about correcting him about what it was called but decided not to. It happened like that, sometimes. The cobbler, I mean, not correcting people. It's that thing where different times all blur together. I just sort of come to, right in the middle of something. Like waking up from a dream. No memory of what happened before or after.

But he got in my face like I just blitzed his quarterback and spiked his head harder than the pigskin.

"You prick bastard, we should've killed your freakshow ass back at the station." His breath smelled like a hungry caveman ready to hunt. Or my father when he came home from work.

Maybe the bastard award wouldn't go to Pointy-face after all.

I stared down at the demolished peach cobbler in front of me. It's bitch flesh and flaking, crusty skin all mashed together in a dirty, disgusting mess. Someone would need to clean this up.

"He hasn't said a damn thing yet," Potato-nose said to Pointy-face. "That shrink said it'd be instant. The pie would trigger the memories and we'd find out about Lisa."

"Yeah, I know."

"I don't like being out here with this freak. Don't like him living any longer than he has to."

"Me either."

I was looking down at the cobbler, scent of the peaches dominating my nostrils. The name Lisa triggered something else inside me. Names aren't my thing but that one stuck out. Was wrapped inside the peach scent like a body you were trying to get rid of. Where had I heard it before?

When I looked up, Pointy-face swallowed and looked over at Potato-nose.

"What'd you do with her, you sonofabitch?" It was Potato-nose talking now with more desperation than I ever would have imagined. But then again, I never had any kids myself.

I was pretty sure he was the guy with the kids. Couldn't remember everything they said at the beginning. Too many punches and kicks, screaming voices. And that was all before they put the hood over my head.

Potato-nose took another drink, his eyes clear under the moonlight. It was brighter out here as the boat started to settle down its rocking 'cause we were picking up speed now. His eyes were wet, like two pieces of cotton dipped in a glass of water.

There was a wild anger in his eyes, something I'd only ever seen in the mirror before.

Something told me he *was* the one with the kids.

And I guess he was all pissed 'cause one of them he wouldn't ever see again.

FOUR

My memory gets patchy there and here, 'cause of all the stuff I already said. About getting confused with time. The blackouts. Not following directions doesn't help none, since a lot of times it ends up with me getting hit in the head. I'm no doctor but getting hit in the head probably isn't good for memory.

My old man could never remember a thing, though. And so far as I know, he only ever hit me in the head. Never saw him get hit once.

Like I said, I'm not a doctor.

Pointy-face pulled a cardboard box with letters markered along the side out of a cabinet beneath the steering wheel and onto the captain's chair. I kinda turned to him, wondering what the box was for. I'd sort of lost my appetite, since the orange-pink of the peaches and the brown of the crust started to look like a bloody mess to me. And I'm not one of those sickos that like that sort of thing.

Pointy-face pulled the top off the box. I saw the letters on the side again. They read LISA SIMMONS. It was written neat-like, better than I could do. He pulled out a manila folder, the same kind all the cops use.

Oh, duh. That was right, I only just realized. If Potato-nose had the kids, Pointy-face was the cop. That was one of the things he said at the beginning, through the punching and kicking.

I seen plenty of cops in my life. They never left me alone. So Pointy-face the cop took out a square piece of paper about the size of a peanut butter and jelly sandwich from the folder and handed it to Potato-nose.

Then Potato-nose came over to me, holding the paper against his chest like he was saving it from blowing away. I guess it was windy, but I didn't think it would go anywhere. He looked at the paper, his hand shaking. His other hand had a grip on the metal flask he'd been drinking from.

He snorted, a little snot coming from his nose. Just like the wait-ress had done. Then he buried his face in the sleeve of his jacket and cried for a second. It made me feel weird, watching him do that. Like maybe he didn't have it all together.

He stopped crying fast. So fast it shocked me. Like maybe he had been faking it. Except his eyes, which were still wet like cotton balls, told me he really had been crying. I thought about laughing at him, pointing out to him about being a sissy. But I didn't do it quick enough.

He took another swig from the flask and then bent down next to me. It stunk. His breath, I mean. Smelled like my father coming home from work.

He held out the piece of paper and I saw it was a picture. Like one of those pictures you snap and it develops in a few seconds, right in your hands. I'd heard about those before. Someone told me how it worked but I forgot all that now.

It wasn't a great picture, let me just say. It needed more light, I guess. More something. I'm no photographer but I seen plenty of pictures in magazines. Even sometimes they have them on the adver-tising placemats in the diner. Lawyers do pictures like that, I think.

But anyway, I saw it was a nice pretty girl in the picture. Blonde, which I like sometimes. Especially like when it's all around a cute face like this hair was.

I looked away from the picture. Back to the peach cobbler, which wasn't steaming no more. I guess the cold got to it.

"Look at it, you bastard," Potato-nose whispered, his stinking breath mixing in with the sweet scent of the peaches. "Do you remember her now?"

That was one of the things that brought the memory back a little more clear. The acid smell of stomach bile and peaches mixed together. Melded into some new scent. Peaches gone rotten. Left out in the sun. Fermented like grapes. *Yeck.*

I didn't want to look back at the photo but Potato-nose kind of shoved it in my face. I couldn't bear to look at the girl but I saw the familiar green uniform with the pink trim. I couldn't see the back but knew it would have said PRINCIPAL DINER in pink letters. I'd seen it plenty over the years. And I guess sometimes there's things that even I can't forget.

The name tag was there, too. LISA, it said. Spelled just like on the cop's cardboard box.

"Tell me where you buried her," Potato-nose was almost kissing the edge of my ear. It made me feel weird. Like a little excited but also gross and funny. Like a tickle from someone who you know isn't supposed to touch you.

The whole night came back to me. A jolt like my brain reached out and touched the electrical socket. That's how it goes sometimes with how my memory works. Things get mushed together until finally they get clear. If they get clear. But it happens fast and intense. Weird, I know.

I looked at Potato-nose, his whole face a blur since he was so close to me.

And I told him where I buried her. Told him I wouldn't have had to but I didn't want anyone to know what I did. And mainly I only did what I did on account of her getting so upset inside the diner. I was the only one around to help. Everyone else had already left for the night.

Potato-nose didn't cry anymore. Pointy-face stood behind him, his hand on the cardboard box. His eyes still swimming beneath those shimmering silver discs.

"Turn around," Potato-nose finally said after I finished talking. He sort of stumbled when he said it, which was weird because we weren't bouncing along the top of the water. The roar of the boat's engines died down and we slowed in the water, only floating now. The engine roar still hummed in my ears and the wind whipped a little harder out here at sea.

I turned back to the dinner table where the pulpy mess of the peach cobbler was everywhere. All over the white towel, the floor beneath me. Even on my sweatshirt. Too bad. Because I was getting hungry again.

The wake behind the boat flattened. It didn't remind me of anything now.

Potato-nose said something to Pointy-face. I didn't hear what it was, but Pointy-face said, "You know this goes to the grave. But are you sure you want to do this?"

Sloshing liquid against metal. Probably another drink. "Just give me the fucking gun."

I looked down at the black water, wondering how cold it was. About how bad the pie would taste once the water got onto it. About how fast someone would disappear from view, you dropped them in right now.

"You don't even deserve something this good," Potato-nose said. I guess he was talking to me but I wasn't sure, really.

But I just stayed quiet. I didn't really like him.

There was a click right behind my head. Another slosh of liquid. This guy better be careful. If you drink a lot, bad things can happen. Worse than just stumbling around on the boat. I'd been in plenty of bars to know that for a fact.

"You have anything to say for yourself?" Pointy-face, this time. From the sound of his voice, he was closer to me now.

I thought about it.

I wasn't sure.

Then it came to me.

"How come you didn't give me a spoon?"

ELDER HUNGER

NIZ THOMAS

ELDER HUNGER

*On trial for his life
Mob fixer Jimmy Hanson
bears witness to a secret
born from the dark intersection
of science and man ...*

A CRIME HORROR SHORT STORY

ONE

"Please state your name for the court."

My right hand instinctively reached for the collar of my shirt--a move my lawyer had explicitly told me not to make, saying it was associated in everybody's mind with guilt. Hot under the collar, and all that.

I couldn't much help my instincts, though. They had long ago abandoned me--first cowering in fear against something they could not hope to understand. Then putting up the same kind of token resistance that medieval villages did when faced with an overwhelming army emerging from the forests of their home. Finally, my instincts had retreated to some far-off land, a place they thought they'd be safe from the invaders. Cowardly, of course. But in the end, the invading berserkers stormed the hills of my subconscious, rooting my instincts out and razing the land they had come to call home.

It was hot and humid inside the courtroom--a South Florida afternoon of the soggiest kind. The collar of my shirt was uncomfortable. This particular discomfort was almost welcome to me now--certainly it was nothing compared to the torturous conditions I'd been forced to endure in the months leading up to my trial. Chains.

Straitjackets. Even a god-awful mask to cover my face. A ridiculous precaution that, if my lawyer had his way, would have been introduced at some point during this trial. Arguing for biased treatment of the defendant or cruel and unusual punishment. I'd overruled that piece of intrigue, much to his confusion. It was irrelevant to my purpose here.

To tell it plain, I was just happy to have a moment of mild discomfort now that I was wearing a suit and tie. It was the shirt, really, that did it. Not itchy--itchy would have been a godsend--but not exactly painful, either. Every fiber of the shirt against the smooth, baby-like skin that I'm still getting used to. It hadn't started to tingle just yet, but I knew it would be coming. My tie felt like one of those cowboy ties wrapped around my neck--the ones that look like they're only a tall tree away from being a noose.

I averted my eyes from the prosecutor. Another thing I'd been told not to do. "It makes you look guilty," my lawyer, Greg Flake, had said. Apparently liars didn't have the spine to look someone in the eye as they fabricated the truth.

Whoever had come up with that tidbit of information hadn't dealt with some of the liars I had.

"Sir?" the clerk said. "Your name?".

I suppose he wasn't looking to hear all the names the court might know me by now.

The Senior Slayer.

The Aged Assassin.

Grandpa with Guns.

Alliteration had done me no favor in the press.

Four hundred eyes bore into me as I sat on the stand, realizing that I'd already broken two unspoken rules that would make me look guilty before I even opened my mouth. Not that I had much chance of a not guilty verdict--the newspapers had all convinced everyone of that. So much so, in fact, that the trial had proceeded without a jury, despite the truly heinous nature of the crimes I stood accused of. I had to agree to such a trial, despite the vehement pleas from Greg that I not consider such a foolish and ridiculous move. I had no choice but to agree to it, however.

I needed this. And I needed it now.

Two hundred people--a max capacity crowd, I'd been told. My eyesight wasn't what it used to be, and the faces of the fellow elderly stared back at me in a blurry mass behind the defense and prosecution tables. The courtroom was kept at a balmy temperature--seventy-four degrees, I would guess. And I had no doubt it was because of the age of just about everybody whose opinion mattered around here.

Well, except maybe one.

"Sir," the clerk said, face scrunched into something like a frown.

I hesitated, hand held somewhere between my collar and my lap, which undoubtedly just made me look worse, maybe like I was a little slow. Or as if I was having a stroke. Wouldn't that be a riot.

"James Hanson," I said by way of introduction, finally getting my right hand down and into my lap where it belonged. To make sure I didn't screw it up again, I wrapped my fingers around the glossy scarred flesh representing what remained of my left hand.

The prosecutor stood up at his table after we all exchanged pleasantries. He was a dark Hispanic looking fella straight out of a daytime soap opera: slicked back black hair, angular cheekbones, and a shave so close it made his cheeks look spit shined. Nice looking man. Probably worked out more days than not. Ate his salads and did whatever else the health nuts were about these days. Colonoscopy vacations, maybe.

Even if he wasn't the youngest person in the courtroom by three decades, he would have stood out in any crowd of average citizens.

"Good afternoon, Mr. Hanson. Can you please tell—"

"Jimmy," I said.

"Sorry?" the prosecutor said.

"Call me Jimmy." I'm not *that* old, I wanted to add.

"OK, Jimmy," he said, pausing to look down at his notes in front of him. He seemed momentarily taken aback and adjusted the knot of his Armani (I'm guessing) tie while he collected his thoughts. My lawyer hadn't said anything about trying to throw off the questioning attorney, though to be fair, he didn't need to. Messing with people was kind of my go-to mode. Or it had been, until I got myself caught in this mess. Besides, Greg Flake wasn't running the show here. I was.

"OK, Jimmy," the prosecutor said. "Can you tell the court your occupation?"

I kept my right hand gripped tight around my left and in my lap, despite my sudden desire to touch my collar again. It was chafing now, I could tell. The courtroom felt hotter still, each of the two hundred people inside leaning forward slightly, awaiting the words that were about to come out of my mouth--the mouth of some kind of Devil if the papers could be believed. Two hundred mouths breathing heavily, fogging up the already balmy Southwestern Florida air.

It was like a swamp in the court.

Sorry. Couldn't help myself.

"I settle disputes," I said, trying to keep my gaze fixed on the prosecutor's Windsor knot.

"What kind of disputes?"

"Disputes that can't be settled via the normal channels."

"Such as through the courts?"

"Such as through the courts."

"Could you give us an example?"

"I'd rather not."

"Please answer the question, Mr. Hanson," the judge snapped. I guess I didn't have a friend on the bench, which was too bad, given that it was a bench trial.

"An example of a dispute I might settle? Let's say someone owes somebody else money but can't hire a lawyer to sue. They hire me to reconcile their loss, so to speak."

I heard a murmur of confusion spread across the courtroom. Maybe even some laughter. I had forgotten for a moment about what that must sound like to everybody in the room.

The prosecutor was able to keep a straight face, not a single line etched into the young man's skin yet. I could tell from the intensity of his gaze on me that he was taking this trial very seriously. It was a chance for him to move up in the world, maybe to the brighter lights and more dazzling crimes of Miami.

"So you were an enforcer, then?"

Was. "Correct."

"And have you ever settled a dispute with violence, Jimmy?"

Now it was my turn to laugh. It took a lot for me to keep my face as straight as the prosecutor's, though maybe with a few extra lines etched into it than the *All My Children* wannabe. Luckily Greg Flake was awake and doing his job today. His objection, however, was over-ruled by the judge.

"I have," I said. Normally someone on trial would not make this kind of admission--self-incrimination and the Fifth Amendment and all of that. But we were way past all that.

"And could you give us an example of a time when you used violence to settle a dispute?"

I felt the gallery lean closer to me and take in a collective breath of expectation. This was probably like when they asked Ted Bundy if he ever accidentally crossed the line when making it with a woman.

"Why don't we cut to the chase, counselor?" I said. "You want to ask me about what happened out there on The JUNGle, don't you?"

My eyes were still on the prosecutor's Windsor knot, but I could make out face-shaped blurs turn to their right and left out in the gallery. The JUNGle had been all over the news recently, almost as much as me, so this morsel was like throwing chum to a gator. They thought they were going to hear lurid details about what I'd done in my past. Instead, they were about to get a taste of what they all *really* wanted to hear.

Mr. Soap Opera looked down at his notes for a moment and flipped a few pages on his legal pad. "In fact, I do, Jimmy. In fact, I do."

"Well, ask away."

He did. And I started talking.

TWO

The Research Institute of Social Gerontology, or as it was known colloquially (or maybe jokingly), The JUNGle, was part-psychological research facility and part-sociolibertarian lab experiment. It was a floating research barge that had docked itself somewhere off the coast between the Ten Thousand Islands chain and Chokoloskee Island. Gulf Coast of Florida, though not exactly your parents' retirement community. That was located inland, on actual, honest to goodness contiguous U.S. of A. Most of the island chain was wildlife preserves and swampland. It just wasn't a place anybody in their right mind wanted to *be*, let alone live.

All in, the population of the Ten Thousand Islands was nowhere near as majestic as the name, estimated as somewhere south of a thousand souls, even if you counted the criminals, refugees, and poachers that used the dense, remote area as a haven to escape the persecutions of society. Part of me had to laugh at that, given the situation I was in. I'd actually *started* my journey toward societal persecution there and now found myself answering for sins, real and imagined, in a much different place: Naples. Home to everybody who ever retired with enough money and health to get on an airplane.

And it seemed every single one of them was in the courtroom today.

How The JUNGle got docked in the Ten Thousand Islands, I can't say for sure, though I imagine it wasn't a legal arrangement, given the type of activity I witnessed going on there. Not to mention the fact I got involved with the place at all.

Either way, I was contacted by a former client of mine, a Mr. Conrad. That's the only name I ever knew of the man and no, I will not divulge any additional details about him--I'm already screwed enough being on trial. He told me about a financial stake he'd put into the Institute which had not produced a sufficient return. It had come to Mr. Conrad's attention, and then he brought it to mine, that the founder and head of The JUNGle, a Dr. William Invictus had been holed up aboard the vessel for some number of months returning none of Mr. Conrad's repeated outreach attempts.

And I would like to clarify that Mr. Conrad is not exactly a subtle man. Nor a patient one. The terms of the investment he told me--an investment, mind you, in medical research--were frankly ridiculous, unrealistic. The lovechild of Albert Einstein and Marie Curie could not have produced the results Mr. Conrad was looking for, and certainly not in the timetable he'd been looking for them.

"How you want me to handle this?" I asked Mr. Conrad as we sat for a café leche as thick as pudding at a bright Cuban restaurant on nearby Marco Island.

Mr. Conrad waved the waiter over and handed him fifty dollars. When the waiter was making change, he said, "Handle it the way you handled the last thing for me," by which he meant: I'm tired of this shit, get my money no matter what you have to do.

I finished my café leche and was gone before the waiter came back. Though it was still early morning, there was still a lot to be done.

Four hours later I was aboard a cigarette boat Mr. Conrad had hired for me to use on this job. An associate of his named Nitro (his legal name, I believe) was manning the boat's controls, and I was catching some shut eye as we jetted south down the coast through the few gallons of the Gulf that hadn't yet turned slick with oil.

It was still light out when Nitro nudged me awake, indicating we were close to The JUNGle. With the sun at my back, the unrelenting wall of trees ahead of me ignited an instinctual fear unlike anything I've experienced before. It was the primal fear of overwhelming, foreboding nature. Pilgrims felt this fear when they looked toward the uncut forests of the New World.

And they didn't have to worry about gators.

I kept my eyes focused on the single inlet of water that was to be my entry point into the dense aliveness that was the swamp looming before me.

"Out you go," Nitro said as he plopped the one-man canoe, stored in the cabin beneath the foredeck, into the water with a gentle splash. With the specter of the vegetation, I'd almost forgotten we were on water. It grew increasingly dark with each passing minute as the sun descended toward the horizon behind me. The cigarette boat was nice--top of the line, honestly--but it was too bulky to get into the narrow crevices of the inlet, the lone break in the otherwise irrepressible vegetation. And I could only imagine the waterways grew narrower upon entry.

Hell, I could only imagine that to be the least of my worries.

Nitro was nice enough to hold the canoe steady as I tossed in my pack and got in. He handed me first a GPS unit with The JUNGle's location programmed in, which I stowed in my bag, and then a paddle. He used his foot to push me off away from the cigarette boat, the water still rocking gently from the boat's intrusion.

I took one last look at him when I was about twenty yards from the boat, but could only make out his black silhouette against the top edge of the sun's corona. He didn't bother to wave.

I turned back toward shore, if you could call it that, and paddled my way into the dark mouth of the swamp.

THREE

"Was this an unusual, uh ... assignment for you, Jimmy?"

"Depends on how you define unusual."

"Let's say I'm defining it the normal way. As in, *not* usual. Out of the ordinary."

Smart ass. "Sure, it was a little unusual. My clientele is typically more land based."

The gallery laughed until the judge knocked his hammer-thing and gave everybody a stern look, including me.

"But there was something else unusual about this job, wasn't there, Jimmy?"

A cold hunger spread forth from my core. It was subdued in its intensity, though not for lack of malevolence. Starved but not dead. This hunger was simply dormant, conserving, smart.

Learned. Evolving.

An inferno of blue light dances somewhere behind my eyes, taunting. Shadowy figures twist and turn in abnormal, sickening ways. Oh, *Young and the Restless*, you have no idea how unusual this job was. I long to spit it out, exclaim it for all the court to hear. But the hunger stops me. The hunger can sense nourishment.

"Well, sure. There was something else unusual about it."

"What was it?"

"I knew Dr. Invictus. In fact, he was also one of my clients."

A collective gasp from the gallery elicits another stern look from the judge, though this time he spares me the bullshit.

"And you don't typically work with a client who is attempting to settle a dispute with another client?"

"Not typically. I would consider it *unusual*."

Rico Suave gave me a tight smile but it didn't touch his eyes. In fact, I don't think it even creased the skin of his face, so youthful was his complexion. He flipped over the top page of his legal pad and fixed his incisive gaze back on me.

"Can you tell us a bit about Dr. Invictus, Jimmy? Hopefully more than you could tell us about Mr. Conrad?"

I squeezed my right hand tighter around my left to steady myself. The heat in the courtroom was making my right hand sweat, and it slipped along the smooth, scarred patches of skin on my left. The patches around my hands and wrist were the most sensitive. The patches in all the other places felt normal to me, though I could never forget what they truly were. But my hand was different. It was awake. Pins and needles.

The skin itself looked scarred, burned. As if it had been covered in three inches of candle wax and smoothed down by a sculptor's knife. Five weeks ago, when all this started, I'd been disgusted by the look of it. My hand and wrist, splotches on my back. But I'd been clamped down enough as the mass-murdering grandpa, committer of heinous acts against mankind, requiring manacles, straitjackets, and all the other restraints man had conceived over the years, that I'd not been able to look at my own skin much. Thank God for small favors.

Somehow, somewhere inside of me, I knew a truth that gave me hope while bringing a dark sense of despair. I had no idea how I knew this. Perhaps it was simply *part of me* now, the way a young lion cub knows to kill the runt of the antelope. But knew it I did. Once the tingle started--once the hunger came back--it would not leave without nourishment.

"Unfortunately, I *can* tell you more about Dr. Invictus."

"Please do."

"Dr. Invictus was a lot of things, I guess you could say. Inventor. Psychologist. Researcher. Adventurer. He held patents in twelve countries, studied the minds of killers and the souls of monks--or maybe I have that backwards. He once even recreated Stanley's trek through the Congo, though with far less cruelty toward the natives. An explorer in every sense of the word.

"He'd hired me a few times over the years to collect on bets he'd made with other rapscallions like himself. Having swum in a lot of different circles in his lifetime, Dr. Invictus sometimes dealt with people that didn't abide by the same rules as the good people of this courtroom..."

I watched as every citizen in attendance practically gave themselves a congratulatory pat on their own back. At least those of them still limber enough to reach that far.

"...but for the most part, Dr. Invictus was on the up-and-up."

And that was the first lie I told in the courtroom.

"As it pertains to our case here, over the past decade or so, he started The JUNGle as a way to study the social effects of aging, which he had said, 'Was finally coming for me.' The field is called social gerontology. I'm not much of a scientist, but as I understand it, the field itself is a widely developed and diverse field of thought. Dr. Invictus certainly wasn't the first guy to consider what the mind and the environment contribute to how quickly people age, why, and the deterioration that occurs in the process.

"But like most things about Dr. Invictus, the manner in which he applied himself to this field was eccentric. Including his choice of location for his lab, though it might have had something to do with his methods."

The prosecutor steepled his hands in front of his body and took several steps right and left in the courtroom. The sheen from his alligator shoes almost blinded me as they click-clacked along the linoleum floor.

"I see. And before we go any further, I'd like to come back to your relationship with Dr. Invictus--a client of yours, as you mentioned."

"That's right."

"And was there anything else about your relationship that might be relevant to this case?"

"Sure," I said, seeing where this was going.

"Can you share that with the court, please?"

I looked over at Greg Flake--another thing he had told me not to do under any circumstance. "A guilty witness always looks to be coached," he'd said. But I couldn't help myself. He had told me (what must have been a thousand times) to never, under any circumstances, reveal the answer to the question that the prosecutor had just asked. One of many questions I'd already ignored his counsel on. Under different circumstances, I think Greg would have been highly capable of winning this case.

But now he avoided my gaze, studying the contour of leather on his briefcase as if it were a centerfold, and he a twelve-year-old boy. I supposed he knew what was coming. Or perhaps was hoping against hope that he was wrong.

"Dr. Invictus wasn't just my client. I was also an investor in his venture. In The JUNGle."

The courtroom took a collective gasp, but the judge quieted them with a quick frown. It wasn't every day you saw the accused provide the man trying to put him in jail with motive.

"I see," our polished prosecutor said, pausing long enough-- longer, really--to let the information sink into for everybody in the room. I wondered about that pause, if he'd done it as an acknowledge- ment that an old mind is not as nimble as a young one. Perhaps because he'd instantly grasped the import of what I'd said. But then, he'd always been quicker than those around him, regardless of age, hadn't he?

"Thank you, Jimmy. Please continue with your story."
And so I did.

FOUR

It didn't take long once I'd passed through the wall of prehistoric swamp foliage for me to start losing my nerve inside that waterway. The plants and trees only grew thicker and taller and more imposing as I slowly made my way deeper. In a few places, I was basically floating my canoe over less water than I'd use to brush my teeth in the morning. I was surprised I didn't have to get out and pull the thing. Thick mangrove roots jostled for position against one another, as if the tips of their tree branches were just itching to get their hands on anybody or anything too stupid to come close enough.

The constant chirp and chatter of the swamp was enough to lull a man to sleep if he wasn't careful. And I had no doubt once it did, the swamp would take no time at all before devouring him.

Once the waterway opened up enough so that I was certain I wouldn't get snatched by a pissed off tree, I reached into the pack and removed the GPS tracker Nitro had given me. It had a green LED screen covered in black dots that indicated land--or whatever passed for it around here. Mostly it was just mangroves grouped together in unpassable masses, though I suppose I could have walked out on the mangroves if I broke out the machete in my bag. It was too thick to go far, but on the GPS, it looked like land. Dead ahead, farther than I could see in the dim light of dusk, there was a dot showing my destination. The JUNGle.

I paddled the canoe closer, eager to get The JUNGle into my vision with a clear line of sight before it got too dark to see. I ducked beneath a looming mangrove, almost needing to touch my nose to the canoe's bottom to avoid its tentacled branches. When I raised my head, I saw the facility's outline in the dark.

The JUNGle was a flat-bottomed barge with several building-shaped structures built atop it. It was about half as long as a football field, and maybe three-quarters as wide. It was low--no single structure on deck was taller than two stories. From the highest point to the surface of the water looked like a fun distance to jump from. Dim light streamed out every window but hardly penetrated the darkness enough to light the water below. The light was helpful, however, to illuminate any mangrove branches silhouetted along my route to The JUNGle's entrance. And to point me in the direction I needed to go.

I had no idea how such a strange, massive, floating facility found its way to this spot, especially not through the thick swamp that my miniature canoe was having trouble navigating. The parts of the vessel that I could see were old, rusted. Other than the rust, it was non-descript to the point of obscurity--it could have been made up of anything. Had it been here for centuries, the relic of some seafaring conquistador who realized he hadn't quite hit the mainland yet? Or perhaps some floating debris that had floated in on a high tide? The forgotten husk of metal from a cruise ship? Had it been brought in piece by piece? Or perhaps designed specifically for the purpose of being hidden in an otherwise inaccessible place--something made to look like scraps, no different than any of the other infinite slow-moldering detritus left to rot in our oceans.

Whatever its origin story, the barge's deck was covered along the perimeter with structures of varying heights--no higher than two-stories. The exterior sides facing me were newer than the lower part of the boat, but even they had begun to show wear and tear. Below them, barnacles and grime and rust prevailed. The entire thing had a real New-Age-meets-Garbage-Dump décor about it.

I floated toward it and pulled my paddle from the water, following the course I had set toward the vessel and using the slow movement of the boat to take in the surroundings and compose myself. No two assignments for me were ever the same. The type of disputes I typically presided over brought out strange things in people and I never knew what I was walking into. But something about the location, the darkness, and the hum of unseen (but not unheard) wildlife activity around me told me that this particular job would be the strangest one I ever went on.

Strangest and last.

A deep sense of dread sat in the pit of my stomach--the last of the sun's light disintegrating into darkness doing precious fuck all to ease it. The thick vegetation closed in on The JUNGle, slowly pulling it farther into the wilds of nature in the same way abandoned houses eventually vanish into the undergrowth. As the canoe drew me closer, I couldn't help but feel as if I was being pulled along with it toward some elemental danger.

Little did I know how accurate that description was.

About ten yards from the stern, a figure passed by one of the lit windows. What was it? More man than woman, though something intensely disturbing about the shape. I both wanted to see more and run away at the same time. Whatever it was, it was there one instant and gone just as quickly.

But my first instinct screamed: inhuman.

That was how I knew the darkness and the isolation of the spot was getting to me. I was already seeing things.

The only trouble was, my instincts were right.

FIVE

"*Inhuman*, Jimmy?"

I squeezed the scarred flesh of my left hand, hoping the pressure would postpone what I knew was coming. Maybe if I simply squeezed harder, it would keep the skin numb. Perhaps if I could just keep the pressure on forever, it might never tingle again.

I know that as a witness, I'm not supposed to lie. But I wondered if that included lying to myself.

The prosecutor lifted his hands to either side, shrugging, as his head turned toward the gallery and then toward the judge. The look on his unblemished face was one of mock incredulity.

"Yes."

"And you expect us to believe that?"

"I don't expect anything from you."

Greg Flake sat at the defense table, eyes in his lap, probably wondering how much of a hit to his bank account this defense strategy would be once word gets out. And get out it surely would. This trial wasn't something that could easily be swept under the rug. The charges of which I stand accused, mixed with the incongruity between them and my appearance, guarantee this trial will be discussed for a long time. Putting the defendant on the stand would normally be a controversial move. Putting one on the stand who was practically making the case for the prosecutor was a downright disbarrable offense. But Greg wasn't running the show around here. I told him about what most of my testimony was going to be, just not the parts that I figured would be coming out soon, if our prosecutor was as slick as he looked.

Nor did I divulge my overall aim in stepping up to the stand in the first place. Telling him would only have put the kibosh on this. Not that Greg had much of a way out. Sure, he didn't like my decision to testify. Threatened to quit, actually. But I'd been involved in a few settled scores for him in the past, things he hadn't realized at the time I'd been involved in. So he owed me. Word getting out about an off-books association with me would really do a number on his reputation--especially now that I was the Monster of Metamucil, or whatever crazy name the press had coined for me this week.

That was the reason I'd chosen Greg Flake to represent me. I needed putty. And Greg provided just soft enough in the right places for me to mold.

The prosecutor flips pages around in his legal pad, though I don't expect he'll find any line of questioning related to the supernatural. I can't say I fault him--before this whole mess I would have laughed a guy like myself right out of the courtroom. But I can see people's faces in the gallery, faces that aren't as skeptical as the pretty boy prosecutor is (or is pretending to be). They've all heard the stories, drummed up by a rabid press frenzy. The local reporters all smell blood in the water and see promotions just offshore. They want to peddle rumors and conspiracy and the people want to believe them.

This is Florida, after all. If something crazy was going to happen, it would happen here.

"Before we get back to your *riveting* story, Jimmy, I'd like to take a second to discuss your investment in The JUNGle."

Like any good prosecutor, he's revisiting a point that could easily send me to prison for a long, long time. By coming back to the fact that I was an investor, he's pounding the motive drum like he's trying out for freshman year marching band.

"How is it that you came to be an investor in The JUNGle?"

"Dr. Invictus asked me."

"Why you?"

I glance over at Greg Flake, who is still looking at his lap. Apparently, he doesn't feel this question warrants an objection. This doesn't surprise me, nor does it concern me. He's only here to ensure everything goes according to plan. Only he doesn't know it.

"You'd have to ask him."

"I don't suppose we can do that, can we?"

"No, I suppose not. Maybe he asked me because he thought I had money."

The gallery gives a low chuckle, though not one large enough to elicit a reaction from the judge.

"Do you know the reason behind the Institute's nickname?"

"The JUNGle? Yeah, it's a play on words. Since part of Dr. Invictus' method was psychological, a good deal of it rooted in the Jungian camp, that's where the name comes from."

"And might you explain to us what the Jungian camp is?"

A glance over at Greg Flake surprises me. He is *actually* twiddling his thumbs. He might not even be listening. He'll happily collect a check for his services, I'm sure.

"I'm no psychologist, counselor. Don't know much about Jung." I wish I knew even less than I already do.

"Well certainly as an investor, you must know something. There had to be some pitch to get you to buy in. Just tell us what you do know."

Our prosecutor is certainly slick, agile. I don't think Greg Flake would have held up against him, even in a more traditional trial. "As it pertains to Dr. Invictus, I know he was very much interested in the concept of the shadow self. The unconscious part of a person's personality. The dark side."

A sense of unease descends over the courtroom and the air grows hotter, stiller. Even the hot shot prosecutor adjusts his tie, though he doesn't look out of sorts at all. He's not even sweating. Me, on the other hand, I can feel the starch of my shirt scratching against the tender skin of my chest and back.

"And to your understanding, how did this concept fit in with the overall research that Dr. Invictus was conducting? You mentioned he was doing something related to aging?"

"Gerontology. The study of aging. I can't explain it the way he could—"

"Yes, you seem to have made certain of that fact."

"Objection." Greg Flake, from the cheap seats.

"Sustained."

"Please explain it as best you can, Jimmy."

I paused and looked like I was composing my thoughts. In reality, I was thinking about the prosecutor. He wasn't easily riled. Calm seemed to be very much his M.O. I'd noticed this during the preceding days of the trial. With not much to do but sit chained to the defense table like a dog, due to the fact there was no jury (and therefore no one to influence, the judge being of such impeccable and immovable moral character), I'd studied this man. Now that I was up on the stand, I needed to figure a way to get under his skin.

"Dr. Invictus believed that when people deny themselves access to their shadow selves--the parts of them that want to be bad--the primal parts--they lose the ability to counter the aging process. Basically, society, family, cultural norms? They strip away the evolutional desires to fight, frolic, feast, and..."

"And?" The prosecutor smiles at me and this time the smile does touch his eyes. It reminds me of a Cheshire cat, waiting to eat the canary. He is almost daring me to say it.

"... And fornicate," I said, enjoying the momentary satisfaction of his smile turning to a frown.

"I see," he said and steepled his fingers. The perfectly smooth skin around his eyes housed perfectly white eyeballs and distinctive green irises. Those green irises burned with a quiet intensity, calculating the best next course of questioning. Clear eyes, clear conscience. That's what the judge would see, the court's crowd, too. He was a man of great conviction. A charger. A stud, young and full of himself. I could imagine him as a young boy--eighteen--applying that intense gaze toward his college boards. I could imagine him as a college student, smoldering in a campus rec center, considering whether it would be the law or medicine. I could imagine him last night, applying his intensity toward his legal pad, considering all the options and contingencies this testimony might lead him down.

For several moments he looked off into the middle distance, seemingly deep in thought. Maybe he was full of it, just pausing for effect. But I decided this moment was an opportunity for me to wrestle back control of the questioning. A charger like this prosecutor could only be thrown off if he wasn't in control. There were a few things I needed to say, and I needed to make sure they got said before the prosecutor tendered me into the care of Greg Flake.

"Do you want to talk scientific theory, counselor? Or would you prefer to hear what happened once I went aboard?"

The question seemed to startle him. His face and eyes twisted up, momentarily confused. The closest thing to a wrinkle I'd seen today. Quiet intensity broken, his green eyes now stared at me, stark in contrast to his dark, caramel colored skin. But one thing about prosecutors--or any lawyer who is questioning a witness: they are storytellers. They have to be. And one rule about storytellers is that you can never hide something from your audience. A good lawyer can't make it seem like *they* are the ones hiding things from the court, though it is one of the most powerful tactics if you can make it seem like your witness is doing so.

And because of this, when a witness pipes up and asks if everybody wants to hear the lurid details of the crime in question, they have no choice but to surrender the floor.

"We were going to get there sooner or later, Jimmy. Might as well be now."

"Very well," I said. As I rubbed my thumb against the tingling in my left hand, I prepared myself to relive the story.

SIX

As soon as I got onboard, I could tell something was wrong. The hair on the back of my neck tingled and every nerve inside of me told me to cut bait and head back to the cigarette boat. But I knew Nitro would never bring me back with him if I didn't have some answers for what was going on here. Answers, of course, and cash.

The only issue was, both of those things would mean that something would have to break right for me in The JUNGle. Because *something* wasn't wrong here.

Everything was.

Nothing about the deck screamed research vessel. It was more like a rundown courtyard–wide-open space with faded stone walkways and small clusters of dead shrubs covering what would have otherwise been empty space on deck. The low structures I'd seen from the canoe provided a perimeter around the edge of the barge. They were made of corrugated metal with cheap, trailer park doors on them--every single one of which was flung open as if there was some stink inside that needed to be aired out. The whole courtyard reminded me more of a shanty town than a place of science. Part of me wondered if that meant I might actually find the money I came for--that perhaps Dr. Invictus had not yet spent any of it. But one more look around told me that whatever I might find here, the money was the least of my concerns right now. Still, Mr. Conrad would accept nothing less than a thorough explanation of what happened here. I could leave now, maybe, and come up with some story that might placate him. But he could just as easily send in someone else like me to corroborate it. There were plenty of men out there willing to do far worse than I have for less pay.

Besides, I had a stake in this myself.

From the water, I'd only been able to see light through all the windows that faced out. Now, standing inside the courtyard, several sodium floodlights threw patches of dim yellow at strange angles. They only partially lit the deck, casting murky shadows into the far corners of the buildings. At least half of them were dark--busted out completely, glass shattered below them on the deck. The entire scene reminded me in some ways of a small community park in a lower-middle-class section of a city. Something a two-bit politician would have schemed and clawed and backstabbed his way to get pushed through some pathetic Ways and Means committee made up of busy single mothers and penny pincher divorced dads deluding themselves into thinking they were making a difference.

But just like those parks out in the real world, this one sat empty aside from a few benches that dotted the space.

Ten feet in front of me was a legal pad, its yellow paper crinkled and mustard colored from the moisture. Several of the pages were folded or ripped, but I picked up the mushy cardboard back and tried to make sense of it.

I flipped through the pages, at least the ones that weren't stuck together from the moisture. They didn't help me to understand what was going on here. But they were evidence that whatever was going on, it had become twisted in some perverse, unstable way.

Each page was filled, from top to bottom, side to side--even in the margins and the backs of pages--with scrawled handwriting in blue, red, and black ink. The writing itself was hardly legible--chicken scratch mixed with Parkinson's. With the use of the flashlight from my pack, I could just barely make out what was written there. At least, after I could get my hand to stop shaking. The pad was completely covered with a single phrase, written repeatedly--probably at least ten thousand times.

It simply said: WHAT'S OLD IS DEAD AND WHAT'S YOUNG IS BLUE

I had no idea the meaning of this phrase, but the way the words were scrawled did not suggest they were some clever limerick. I flipped the pad over. The phrase was scrawled on the cardboard back of the notepad as well, though the words were written backwards.

A primal scream emanated from somewhere inside one of the structures, the open doors to each room boosting the decibel level to hair-band-stadium levels. I dropped the legal pad and fumbled in my pack for my handgun. I couldn't pinpoint which structure the scream came from and the volume and depth of it made me wonder if it had come from some unseen cabin below, echoing up through the structures and out into the night air like some jury-rigged speaker system.

The scream stopped, though not so sudden to make me think the sourced had ceased to exist. In its wake, the scream left behind a quiet unlike anything I'd ever experienced. Perhaps it was the intensity of it that created in its absence a sort of volume-vacuum. Perhaps it was the scream itself that temporarily scared the swamp's critters and wildlife into silence, to assess whatever potential threat was in their vicinity. I knew it hadn't made me go temporarily deaf because I could still hear the water lapping against the edge of The JUNGle and the metallic groans of its hull bobbing atop the water.

I swung my pack over one shoulder and steadied my gun, moving slowly across the open space of the deck's courtyard, past one of the benches, until I reached one of the single-story structures along the outer edge of the barge. The new position opened up an area of the deck I hadn't previously been able to see--a smaller courtyard framed on three sides by taller buildings, which I took to be some kind of headquarters.

Inside the smaller courtyard, three bodies--all men--lay splayed out, face down. Not dead of natural causes. The bullet wounds in their backs made that pretty clear.

Out of instinct, I pressed myself back against the wall of the structure behind me, wishing I could press myself straight through it and back home. Five feet away from me, one of the doors hung open lazily like all the others, swinging almost imperceptibly with the barge's movements. I tried to collect myself as I stood there, tried to find a breath in the thick humidity of the swamp. But no amount of composure could help me escape what I already knew to be true.

I was up shit's creek. And my canoe paddle wouldn't help me.

This was a crime scene--a triple homicide, at least--and who knew what other legal complications might be thrown in, given the fact that we were on the water (and surely this entire operation was illegal).

I looked around once again, a deep sense of foreboding growing inside of me. A sign maybe that my troubles, as they presently stood, were really only the beginning of things. I looked around at all the open doors on deck, the dark vortexes beckoning me toward their untold (and unimaginable) terrors. The remnants of that shrill pitch, that inhuman, bestial scream still tingled the invisible hairs inside my ear. That scream, still imprinted on my psyche, kept my pulse racing and my back slightly arched like a frightened cat's.

Any man who went on, who didn't just cut bait and run, was nothing short of mad--certifiably, unquestionably, *Here's Johnny!* mad. I used my left hand to wipe the sweat streaming down my face with my shirt and gripped my handgun in the right, letting these faint reminders of reality ground me in some kind of normal.

And, like the lunatic I was, I continued on.

It only became clear to me afterward how little I knew of madness.

SEVEN

"So you are testifying--and may I remind you that you are under oath--to the fact that three of the seven dead aboard the research barge were dead prior to your arrival?"

I love it when a prosecutor reminds me not to lie. "Not that three of the seven were dead, counselor. All seven were. I didn't kill anybody."

The audacity of this statement stuns the room. It had never occurred to anyone that I might be innocent of the crimes we are here to discuss. I'm sure there wasn't anybody around who wanted it to be true, either.

"Despite the fact that your handgun fired seven rounds of 9mm ammunition, all seven of which were recovered inside bodies found aboard the research vessel. All seven of which were matched to your handgun. And that's the story you're sticking with? That you, what, fired your weapon into dead bodies?"

The physical evidence in this case had already been on display. I'd be the first to admit, it didn't look good. I *had* fired those rounds.

"That's not it, exactly."

The prosecutor waved his right hand up and around him, showcasing the courtroom to me like a television presenter showcasing the next grand prize. "Well, sir, please tell us *exactly*. No better place to get your story on the record than here in this courtroom."

I looked down into my lap where my right hand struggled to keep the scarred skin of my left hand covered. I was shaking now, imperceptible to anyone else in the court. But I could tell. A ripple inside of me which would soon grow to something far greater.

The tingle had started already, slowly at first. Like pinpricks deep inside the flesh, pressing against arteries, perhaps, or the underbelly of thick, nerveless muscle. Echoes of pinpricks, really. But with each passing moment, the dial on the knob turns by fractions of a degree--one decibel increase at a time--until some point very soon where the intensity will be like standing beside a rocket ship taking flight from earth.

My hands are clammy from the damp air inside the courtroom and from my nerves, reacting to the sensation, which will continue unbidden. But I'd calmed myself just enough now. Resigned myself to what was coming. We were heading into the home stretch here. Soon it would all be over.

I removed my right hand from my left and looked at the smooth, scarred skin. It was glossy, slick with an electric blue sheen. Even despite the impression my right hand had left, the sheen was the most distinct part of the skin. And with the tingle would come the cold. The kind of cold you can only experience touching your hand to a flame--the instant your body reacts. That is what I know lies ahead of me. Colder than ice. Colder than death.

It was beginning. Soon I would be cold everywhere.

And soon, this would all be over.

"Very well," I said and launched into the rest of my testimony.

EIGHT

Considering I'd come for answers, I needed to check out the three dead bodies inside the smaller courtyard. Standing over them, I could see they were fresh. In the heat of the swamp--not to mention with all the critters and wildlife around--these things wouldn't have lasted more than a few days, tops. If they'd been left anywhere else but the barge's deck, they might not have lasted more than a few hours.

Why they'd been shot in the back, I hadn't the faintest idea.

I flipped one of the bodies over with my foot. An eighty-year-old man with liver spots and thick white hair stared up at me--icy blue eyes that were open wide as if trying to take in as much of the scenery around him at his time of death as possible. The expression on his face, what I imagine to be his last emotive act, was one of carnal lust--eyebrows twisted into a deep V, mouth open, teeth bared. Like a vampire ready to suck the proffered bare neck of a succulent teen virgin. I'd seen dead bodies but none like this, as if the life had been snatched from him in a final moment of terrifying ecstasy. He wore hospital whites, which made it quite clear that in addition to the bullet wounds in his back, he had two more in his gut.

I quickly checked the other two men, both similar in age and very similarly dead. They too seemed to have been ushered across the River Styx with lust coursing through their still warm bodies. I found something unsettling about these three bodies. Certainly, the circumstances and what was looking to be a very serious legal situation were troubling. I'm sure the specter of Nitro and Mr. Conrad were holding court somewhere in the back of my mind, as well. But my sense of unease lay somewhere beyond those considerations. It wasn't just the chronology of things, though they had certainly died recently. Most dead bodies I'd encountered seemed to lose something--a certain exuberance or vim--once the blood stopped flowing. A dead body ceased to look real in almost no time at all. And something about these ones still did, though there was no question that they were very much dead.

It wasn't until one of the lights in the small courtyard burned out that I saw what I believed to be the source of the strangeness.

The first man I'd examined was now half-covered in a new darkness, the light that had gone out having been almost perfectly trained on him before. I could still see fine otherwise--the burned-out light being an isolated incident, not power failure. Everything else in the courtyard was still dimly lit with the same muted yellow hues as the rest of the deck.

But in this new spot of darkness was a faint blue glow that peeked through the man's white shirt.

I knelt beside him, used my gun to push the fabric away from his torso for a closer look.

Patches of the man's skin looked smooth, almost shiny, like a burn that had healed itself but lost all texture of the skin from before. Beneath this sheen was a blue glow ... coming from ... *inside* him.

I had never seen anything like this. The man looked as if he'd been stuffed with Christmas lights and left on deck to light the way. After several moments, I checked the other men and found they, too had the blue glow in various patches of shiny skin.

But what in the hell did it mean?

I glanced around me, having almost forgotten that something

horrible still lurked on this barge--something much more immediately concerning. Something *alive*. And from the sounds of it, something very unhappy. But a quick glance told me that I stood alone.

The swamp at large had once again resumed its chorus, having apparently determined the horrible scream I'd heard earlier was not an immediate danger.

I myself had doubts.

The building directly in front of me—what passed for the main building in this courtyard — stood stock still despite the slight list of the barge, lording its size over me like a giant standing before mere mortals. It was two stories, one of the taller buildings aboard, sided with corrugated metal but feeling somehow sturdier than everything else around it. There were two dark windows on the second floor that, when taken in with the blackness of the open doorway, reminded me of a jack-o'-lantern. Almost as if the building had spat out the three dead men like the scooped-out pulp of its insides.

Another guttural scream erupted from somewhere inside and I almost dropped the handgun, so urgent was this cry. The building seemed perfectly suited to magnify the sound, built up and towering above like a grand megaphone. The scream itself seemed to invert on itself, bursting forth from the high windows, pounding down upon me like a massive wave on the shore, then being sucked into its own powerful tide back into the open doorway and up again.

Now, at least, I was certain of where the scream was coming from. I just wished I wasn't standing directly in front of it.

Holding my gun as steady as possible, I went inside.

The interior was surprisingly modern compared to the outside. The room was divided into two main areas, separated by a frosted glass wall, though the layout was otherwise open. In the room to my right, four empty metal lab tables stood in a row, one next to the other. They were bolted to the floor. Along one wall sat three computers, their monitors dim but giving off a blue glow from the screensavers, a hue that looked almost identical to the skin of the men outside. The blue light of the screensavers reflected off the tops of the tables and the frosted glass, sending odd reflections all around the space. Lab equipment dotted the far wall, arranged neatly on a long metal desk that had been built there. This was the only part of the room that looked like a watercraft, as each piece of equipment was fitted into its own space and tied down. The entire space looked clean, sterile.

The contrast of the lab and the outside of the building — research-modern compared to swamp-shanty-contemporary — was startling. It made me feel like whatever I was going to find would be even more horrific, by design. The worst things in life have been created in the most sterile and unassuming places.

The left side of the space was different. Seeing nothing troublesome on the right, I crossed around the frosted glass divide, which was awash in the same hue of blue light, but more subdued in its intensity because it was farther from the computer screens. The larger space on the left was broken into three ten-foot square cubbies which, also made of frosted glass. Inside each cubby was a metal stool without wheels parked next to an examination table like the kind you'd find in a doctor's office, complete with a sheet of white paper pulled down to keep from spreading germs from one patient to the next.

Aside from the fact that I was on a barge in the middle of the swamp, this could have been any examination room in any doctor's office in the world.

Oh, except for the twin blood stains on each table. They were positioned in about the same spot on each table, gut-high, and had since dried from their slick red wetness into more of a rust color. Beneath the spots were various smears, where the blood no doubt had pooled and been rubbed in from tormented writhing. They looked, in some perverse way, like smiley faces set against the blue-lit exam table paper.

I had no doubt the three dead men in the courtyard had each been shot here. But I had no idea why. And more curiously, I had no idea what the blue glow emanating from inside of them was.

I passed the cubby entrances, my gun still raised about chest high. The gun felt heavy in my sweaty hands, all confidence in the weapon seeming to leech out of my body with each passing moment. I just hoped the gun wouldn't slip out of my hand if I needed to use it.

Past the three exam rooms, almost completely in shadow because it was the farthest point from the blue light of the computer monitors, was a doorway. The door, just like every other one on this barge that I'd seen, was swung wide open. As far as I could tell, this door was the only point of entry or exit from the first level.

I willed one foot in front of the other and went toward it.

NINE

"Ladies and gentlemen, in all my years in a courtroom, I've encountered any number of people. Good Samaritans. Thieves. Rich, poor. Killers and rapists. Liars and conmen. Good people who were stuck in a bad situation. All manner of folks. But in all my years as an attorney, I have never heard a story as preposterous as Jimmy's here."

Greg Flake objected to this soliloquy from our handsome prosecutor, who apparently had given up on questioning and decided editorializing would be a more effective strategy.

The judge sustained, though I could tell from the lack of enthusiasm in his response that he was still trying to make sense of my story. I couldn't blame him. I was still trying to make sense of it, too.

It wasn't the trauma that got to me. As I said, the three dead bodies I'd found on that barge weren't the first I'd ever seen. I'd been in hairier situations, to tell the truth. Like the good prosecutor, I'd encountered all manner of folks in my work. None of them were Good Samaritans nor good people caught in a bad situation, but the rest of his list sounded about right.

I kept a straight face on the stand, my eyes fixed now on the prosecutor as he stood at his table. I found it amazing that in the heat of the courtroom, the man didn't have a thread out of place. Not a single hair had shifted on his head, not even to frizz in the moist midafternoon air. His suit looked like it was getting pressed as he wore it, each movement of his arm smoothing the fabric out beneath it before a wrinkle could even form. He looked about as calm and collected as a man on vacation, reading lazily as he sipped Piña Coladas poolside.

Me, on the other hand? I was getting mighty uncomfortable in the box. Not from the testimony, though all the talking and the heat were combining to make me sweaty. I was getting--hell, I was *already--uncomfortable* because the tingle I'd been experiencing in tiny pinpricks all over had graduated to something more akin to jackhammering, demolishing my already fraying nerves. The cold sensation had gone from numbness to dull pain, something I knew would continue to get worse, much worse, the longer it went unabated. I didn't bother to look down now, though I knew the blue glow would be there, its pulsing blue beneath the smooth, glassy surface that had replaced my skin. It would be hidden beneath my clothing. And to make sure I didn't give anything away, I put my left hand in my pants pocket.

"Do you expect us to believe your story, Jimmy?" the prosecutor finally said, contempt edging itself into his voice.

I didn't. Not really, anyway. If I were in their shoes, I wouldn't have believed it. I still hardly could.

"I guess your fancy boarding school and law degree didn't prepare you for this type of thing, did it, counselor?"

The prosecutor acted as if I'd reached across the courtroom and slapped him. He raised a single hand to his chest like an old-time movie dame, insulted and not afraid to show you.

"Excuse me?" he said. The words were polite, but the tone beneath them wasn't. It was the look of faux outrage, masked in contempt, and hidden beneath a veneer of manners. An elite look. A how-dare-your-kind-does-or-says-that look.

He looked to the judge for recrimination, though I didn't want him to get it from there. I was getting cold up on the bench now. And the cold was yearning for something.

"Don't look at him," I said. "Your beef is with me."

The prosecutor stepped around the table but seemed to catch himself after a moment. He was, after all, still going toe-to-toe with an old man in front of a crowd of old people. Even the judge was old enough to be the prosecutor's grandfather. No matter how guilty I may have looked, no lawyer worth his salt would want to come off as domineering toward me in this environment. It wouldn't help his case any. And every single person in the court would identify with me, the apparent victim of the domineered.

Anyway, it was clear he felt he'd won the round, having thoroughly reviewed the entire case against me, confirming all the most incriminating aspects with my own story. I had done nothing to stop this, nor had Greg. I'd even contributed in some ways to helping this poster boy make an air-tight case into one that even the most skeptical person would have no trouble believing.

But that wasn't important to me anymore. It never had been. A veil of cold darkness had enveloped me and provided a screen for every thought, sensation, and feeling to pass through. There was nothing now that mattered more to me than to quiet the yearning flaring up all around me.

The prosecutor went back to his legal pad, flipped a page. There were no more notes. It was empty.

"Your Honor, I'd like to–"

"Not so fast," I said, the words tumbling fast out of me, desperate. I couldn't let him get away so easily. "I'm not finished."

The prosecutor looked to the judge but neither of them said anything.

I took that as my sign to keep going.

TEN

The roof. I had followed another primal scream up the stairwell, led by the metallic clank of footsteps echoing down from the top.

I stepped through the stairwell's doorway, gun ready. I saw no one.

Behind me, though, I heard another scream, this one more muted than the others.

I spun and almost fired my weapon at the strange old man standing there at the edge of the roof. His hair was a shock of white against otherwise tan skin. He was almost naked, wearing only white underwear, having apparently ripped off his shirt, lab coat, and pants, which lay in strewn tatters along the rooftop like a lovers' bread-crumb trail.

Only there wasn't any love here. Not even close.

Standing so much higher above deck, each shift and lilt of the barge was that much more magnified. Less fun up here than it had looked from the canoe. No water to jump into up here, only hard deck stretched beneath us.

The man was hunched over but not from age. From scoliosis, maybe? No. Something else was happening here. Muscles taut, like he was fighting against some powerful full-body spasm. His back bent enough that it seemed close to snapping in half. Arms reaching around to his back, wrapped tight like he was administering a strait-jacket to himself. The entire sight was grotesque. Stretch Armstrong in the hands of a budding sociopath.

It took me several seconds to recognize him. It made no sense at first--the age was wrong, the graying of the hair. About the only thing about him that seemed right was the eyes. They still held the intensity, the vivacity of the man I knew, though even that had been largely extinguished.

Or perhaps because it was being strangled from him.

It was Invictus.

"Doctor?" I started toward him but kept my gun up, unsure even after recognizing him that I could trust my own perception. Though I could see now that this was the man I knew, the man who I'd invested in--someone who I actually believed in--my own sense of survival could not get over the sheer *other*ness of him. He looked so different, so old.

I stopped when I was about ten paces from him.

"What's happening to you?"

He went to a knee and the rest of his body seemed to tighten around him like a vise. His back hunched further forward, face flung toward his bent knee as if pushed by some unseen hand on his neck. Arms wrapped tighter around himself, looking close to snapping out of their sockets from the force. I worried he might suffocate himself to death. Or possibly break apart from the sheer force of whatever was going on.

I lowered my gun and moved closer.

"No," he muttered before I could touch him. Weak words that clearly took a great deal of strain to get out.

"Let me help you," I said, though I had no idea how I might do that.

"Can't," was all he said.

Another crank of his muscles sent him down on both knees in

front of me. Something was exerting itself on his body, crushing Invictus into a man capable of fitting inside carry-on luggage. I couldn't get over how old he looked now. He'd aged decades since I'd last seen him, perhaps only months earlier.

The barge swayed beneath me and it took me several steps to one side to catch myself. As I did, I saw what I thought was the source of his problem. In the middle of his back, mere inches from the outstretched tips of his fingers, was a black-handled knife. It appeared to have been stuck there, almost perfectly in the middle, though I assumed from his ability to move at all that it had missed his spine. It glowed blue, same as the skin of the dead men two stories below us. Had it been stuck there by the same person who'd killed the three men below?

I gripped my pistol tighter to remind myself I didn't yet know what was going on here. But there was nobody else on the roof. Nobody moving around below me on deck, either.

"What is that?" I asked.

Invictus grunted against the strain his body was under. His back cranked tighter and he was now practically folded in half, his nose and face almost touching the ground in front of him now. He let out another grunt of pain from the stretching and compressing of his muscles. No man, however old, could withstand stretching like this.

I took another step toward him. The pressure in his body seemed to relax momentarily, a few of the muscles around his arms going slack. He panted, trying to catch his breath.

"The knife," I said and reached for it.

He slumped forward, seemingly even less tense. "Don't," he said between labored breath.

"What's happened here, Doctor?"

"I figured it out, Jimmy. The whole damned thing. Youth, aging. Imagine that--a bum like me figured it out."

A smile crept across his face between deep, heaving breaths. Skin creased the leathered skin on his neck and around his eyes. Tears trickled out.

I didn't know what he was talking about, though whatever was happening here didn't appear to me to be "figured out."

"Let me help you," I said, again reaching for the knife. Dr. Invictus' body lost all tension then and he fell forward slightly, over the bend in his knees. He was almost flat on the rooftop now, though still breathing heavily.

"You can't, Jimmy. It's too late for me."

"But I'm here. I can help. Let me take this thing out of your back."

"No. If you touch it, you'll have it, too."

"*Have* it? Have what?"

For the first time, Invictus turned his head toward me. It clearly took him a great effort. Quiet determination simmered in his eyes. He'd always had a certain bravado about him. It was the thing that drew others to him during his exploits all over the world. It was what drew investors to this venture. It was why, despite all signs pointing to Get The Fuck Away, I was still here trying to help him.

"It doesn't have a name, Jimmy. But you don't want it."

The barge shifted beneath us and I stepped back from the edge, trying to steady myself without falling over. Invictus spasmed at the edge, whatever force acting upon him seeming to have only been resting a moment before slamming back into him like a tidal wave. He lurched forward, head splitting open against the rooftop. Blood replaced tears streaming down his face.

I almost lost my stomach when his back broke. The crunch is something I still hear, always will. Heaven--if such a place exists-- would be a place without the memory of that sound.

As Invictus' limp body fell, the weight of it rolled him off the side of the roof.

Dr. Invictus, a man who lived life like the roar of a lion, died with little more than a splat against the deck of the barge.

ELEVEN

"Surely you can appreciate the court's skepticism, Jimmy." The prosecutor's words were spoken with gentle care, as if he didn't want to break the hushed reverie of the room.

My own body was now starting to fail me, mirroring the downfall I'd just recounted. I had no idea how I looked to the court, but inside I was being tossed between the heat of the room and the kind of cold, punishing pain that I imagine Invictus must have felt in those last few moments on the roof.

For whatever reason, my body wasn't thrashing around, though I had my guess about that. Invictus had been clever. His creation, ingenious. But there were things about it he didn't understand. In his research, he had only taken into account the dark side of his subjects-- of mankind in general.

But his creation had become something else entirely. Something Other.

And he had never factored that into the equation.

That was my theory, at least. And I was in a very unique position to have one. But whatever the reason, the pain welling up inside me was making it hard to concentrate on anything the prosecutor was saying now.

"Your Honor, permission to treat the witness as hostile."

My mind came back for a moment, like I'd just woken up here. I had obviously missed something because everyone was looking at me--even Greg Flake. I couldn't quite read his face, but I sensed something akin to concern.

Whatever I'd missed, the judge granted the prosecutor's request.

As he stepped around the table, the cold chill inside of me steeled itself. Anticipating. Mad with expectation. Kids staying quiet on Christmas morning.

The prosecutor dropped his legal pad onto the table with a smack that echoed around the room. The gaggle of faces behind him went dim, like the house lights in a theater before the curtains went up.

"The fact of the matter is, Jimmy, you shot those men on board. Single shots into the backs of the three men found on deck. Two into Invictus, both point blank in the back of the head. Cowardly. You might have dropped him from the roof to try and cover your tracks, but we've already heard the M.E.'s testimony."

He was right. I had shot them. But not the way he'd said.

"And don't even get me started on all the pieces of your story you left out. What about the three other men? The ones we found below deck, chained like rabid dogs in the dark."

The prosecutor takes two big steps closer toward me, hand outstretched in front of him like a gun, aimed waist high. He mimes pulling the trigger three times. Theatrical intensity on his face. Clearly on a roll now. He's fired up with indignation against this man who sits before him, Guilty. Just like the good little prosecutor he is. Star on the rise, ready to shoot across the sky into bigger and better and younger markets.

I shot those other men, too. I hadn't gotten there in my story yet. Didn't much want to, honestly.

Inside me, I can feel the frigid, pounding winds of hunger--the new feeling I've come to associate with my story. A story I felt ready to let go into the wild, my part in it no longer necessary.

The winds were gusting inside me now, demonstrating I was no longer anything but a passing season. Swirling. Rustling like autumn leaves. Whispering. Anticipation like a summer romance at the Fourth of July fair. Hushed excitement.

Just not my excitement.

"So why can't you just admit it? Admit what you did to the court so the families of the men you killed can get closure. And you can rot in hell."

I smile at this, something big and flashy and cocky. The opposite of how I feel. But I am no longer in control. I'm merely a servant now. A pawn.

"You think you're so smart?" the words tumble from my mouth faster than I can think them. If I'm thinking them at all. "You haven't gotten a single fact right in this entire case. I've been cut down at the knees over at the defense table, keeping my mouth shut. And I came up here to tell you what's what, since you're too stupid to figure it out on your own."

The words ding off his pageant armor, the air about him that told me what kind of man I was dealing with. Always good at reading people. That was something I had going for me. Now, though, that skill only has one use.

And it would serve its purpose--this cold intensity raging inside me would make sure of it.

The prosecutor steps closer, now hardly out of arm's reach.

"You disgust me, Jimmy. I bet if we had more time with you--ya know, before putting you in the electric chair--I could dig up every-body you've ever buried. Because nobody in this courtroom believes these seven were your first."

"You're pathetic." My last effort to wrest control from what Invictus unleashed. I tried to spit the words, like they might release me from the death grip of the cold.

He steps closer, clear, intense eyes blazing with contempt.

Nobody talks like that to him in this courtroom. Or any courtroom. He seems so sure of that fact. And that he'll be around long enough to see to it that fact it shall stay.

Only he's wrong.

"Let you in on a secret, counselor. You might think my story was bogus but after Invictus fell, I did the one thing he'd asked me not to do. The *one thing* he practically died trying to prevent. I've no idea why--loyalty, pity, compassion, maybe. But I've never been one to let something go."

The prosecutor straightens up, his expensive suit still immaculately pressed. Up close, I can make out the micro pattern of his tie and the fashionable pin stuck through it, pierced into the fabric. I almost laugh when I see that it's blue topaz, glowing in the light of the courtroom. It seems fitting enough.

I can smell him now, his youth like the invisible spores of a pollinating flower. Vitality.

The opposite of me.

At least now.

"I may look old, but there was some information you omitted early on in this case. Easily overlooked, not relevant to your case. Any competent defense attorney would have brought it up a million times already, never let a judge, jury, or newspaperman forget it.

"You were never really able to identify me, were you? I had no identification on me when you picked me up. Couldn't match me in your databases. Could you?"

When they'd picked me up, I was practically naked, just like Invictus had been. And my DNA was no longer mine. Not to mention I'd already aged some thirty-odd years in a day. One blink of the eye and my life was practically over.

The prosecutor says nothing to me, though I can see this outburst has thrown him for a loop. He looks to the judge, but I'm not through just yet.

"Turns out that Invictus *had* figured out the whole thing. Just what he'd set out to do. Aging, its causes, its processes. And he'd set out to stop it or reverse it. But *that* was where he went wrong."

My insides feel about ready to leap from my body, so punishing is the frigid hunger of Invictus' creation. There is an intensity inside of me that I'd long ago lost control over. Being up against it, experiencing it, has muddied my understanding of things. Part of me wonders if the entire concept of control had been anything more than an illusion, a lie I'd been telling myself over the years. Like if you go to school, get a job, raise a family, you'll be alright. But such a quaint story--such a happy ending--is nothing more than a fragile tower of cards, one wrinkle in the uncaring universe from being revealed for the shell game that it is.

But that no longer matters.

The prosecutor turns slightly, half to the judge and half to the crowd. Looking for sympathy, or to make a face to indicate I'm off my rocker.

Instead, I'm out of my seat, leaping over the railing and wrapping the prosecutor in a bear hug. I move fast, swift. No longer in control of my aging body, possessed by an otherworldly spirit, I'm amazed it's able to move like this. Conquering warrior. Savage beast. Hungry, desperate.

Once upon a time I could move like this.

The cold winds swirl through me, roiling up a hunger that could never hope to be satiated. The blue patches of my skin gravitate to the prosecutor, infecting him. Leeching onto him, running their course through his blood and guts and soul. The youngest person, probably for miles. Maybe in the whole county. A man who could provide more sustenance for this hunger, this *elder hunger*, than I ever could.

Already I could see how much the hunger had evolved since it robbed me of my years. There was no seizure. No loss of consciousness. No rabid dog symptoms. All around us, I could hear gasps and groans, the smacking of the judge's hammer thing. I felt hands grabbing me--hands that under other circumstances would be the victims of the hunger. But today, they proved old enough to be spared. Besides, the hunger was already dining, looking for the exact type of person who could give it what it truly wanted.

A man who could expose it to the wider world, release it from this Sahara of youth. Release it into the clubs of South Beach or the avenues of New York. Places it could run wild and free.

Four arms grabbed me--two beneath the armpits and two around my legs. I had no fight left in me.

As the last of the hunger released me from its grasp, I felt tired and sore and empty. Sad, even, that the only way for it to live on was to evolve, to soften itself. To lure instead of conquer.

As the bailiff dragged me away, I watched the prosecutor's face-- confusion, fear, anger like any man would feel by being physically attacked. Beneath it all, though, I saw an almost imperceptible stoop of his shoulders, a loosening of the skin around his cheeks. It had set it. It had taken everything from me in a matter of days. The savage shooting spree, my pathetic attempt at *really* killing this hunger, so much as it lingered on, glowing beneath the skin of the corpses. How long might it take this time? Weeks? Months? It would need more youth to feed on.

I locked eyes with the prosecutor, trying to impart all that I'd learned from the experience to him. Not to save him, for that was no longer possible. But to prepare him, maybe.

I'll never know if that look was enough. But I doubt it.

SERIES STARTERS

series starters
[sireez starterz] *noun*

----

stories with characters you'll want to spend more time with

THE OMEGA DINER

A LEDGERMAN STORY

THE OMEGA DINER

NIZ

AUTHOR OF THE *TRUE NAME* SERIES

THOMAS

ONE

Ledgerman takes a long pull from his diner coffee, the scalding liquid and heavy, bitter aromas waking him up like a sparring match against Mike Tyson. He didn't much believe in heaven, but if he did, this would be his idea of it:

A nice table (nice as you could get anyway) at the Omega Diner—your typical New Jersey greasy spoon.

Big windows displaying an icy thoroughfare of hard-pack snow, rock salt, concrete, and passing cars going too fast on a road that wasn't quite a highway but not a municipal street, either.

A mouth-watering aroma of strong coffee, sumptuous, creamy eggs, and the silky sweet hint of pancakes and syrup. But mostly, enough bacon to keep cardiologists in business for the rest of eternity.

In front of him, paper placemats with Omega Diner written right in the middle—the symbol for omega in place of the letter O—so it reads Ωmega Diner. Not that clever or original, but it shows some effort at differentiation. It contains advertisements for everyone from the local newspaper delivery to a video rental store to a shady lawyer to help you when you fell down on an icy sidewalk and weren't already trying to con somebody (else you would have called the lawyer first). It seemed the diner placemat was the last holdout from the internet's encroachment on modern life. For crying out loud, how could a video rental store still be in business, if not for something *just a little bit off* going on there?

And then of course, there was the feel of the diner.

It was a place of refuge for Ledgerman. A safe, calm place where the world's problems didn't dare creep in past the big windows.

A place where time seemed to stop. Welcome relief.

Not just this one, either, as it was almost indistinguishable in so many ways from the multitude of others he had spent time in. More, the genre of diners appealed to him. He read a magazine article a while back (in another diner somewhere) about how children often created strong emotional connections to foods and places their mother visited when they were forming in the womb. Ledgerman knew nothing about his mother, but based on his own feelings about diners, he would have put a tenner down on her sitting in a booth like this one, Disco Fries and a nice greasy burger on its way while *he* was getting cooked to the right temperature. *Ding, ding, order up.*

Place like this, you could sip coffee, read a magazine, the paper (or just the ads on the placemat). Ruminate. All without time rushing in on him.

In this case, he was reading a local paper, taken from a pile by the hostess stand. It was an area paper (not confined to just this town, but not covering the entire state, either).

He'd been flipping through, mostly scanning the articles: the measure to increase property taxes had failed (of course it had); the approval to cut art and music classes had been given the go ahead (who needed culture); the mayor of the next town over would break ground on a new, state-of-the-art police station (despite crime being down, he boasted); the boy's soccer team would host their end of season dinner, celebrating their county championship (good on them); Bethanny Ebbells, aged 94, died in the loving arms of her family after a long battle with old age.

Not exactly the Watergate scandal, but this was what you got. He wasn't complaining. The news had become a rough, nasty thing these days. Reading a paper like this heartened him somewhat.

And he wasn't a man who could be easily heartened.

Aimless reading, of course, wasn't the only thing he liked about diners.

This one, especially, allowed him to watch as cars sped by outside (being Jersey, that was all of them). Wonder what destinations lay ahead for them and their occupants. What winding roads and dark pasts lay behind. You could watch people of all sorts and play the same mind games.

Games Ledgerman didn't get to play, really. The rest of his life was situated a lot differently than that. More rigid in its construction.

The diner allowed for him to sit and bask in the temporary facade of a man with nothing much to do.

Mostly, let it be said, you could eat. And diner food suited Ledgerman just fine.

"What'll it be, hon?" A teenage waitress stands next to him at the table. Pad in one hand. Pencil in the other. Ostensibly attending to Ledgerman but not looking at him—eyes on table twelve, the one with four kids in letterman jackets playing a game where they put every ingredient within reach in a glass of water, make the loser drink it. And this was a diner not short of available condiments.

Ledgerman watches the waitress watching them. Wondering if she does so longingly or in anticipation of a problem. Are they classmates, maybe? No, she looks older—by a hair, not by much. Former classmates, maybe. They don't seem like bad kids. But in today's day and age, can you ever be sure?

She has shoulder-length blonde hair pulled back in a ponytail that reveals one side of her head shaved short, perhaps with a number one buzzer blade. Punk rock, maybe. If kids still were into that sort of thing.

Already speaks like she's a veteran in the service industry. *Hon.* She has sad eyes.

"Three eggs, scrambled with cheese. Extra-large side of bacon. An order of French toast. Orange juice. And," he holds up his mug, "more coffee, please."

"Toast?"

"Heaps. You have Texas toast?"

"Afraid not. You want, I could scrounge up some challah in the back. They're using it for the lunch special today."

"What is it?"

"What is what?"

"The special, for lunch."

"Oh. Right. Fried chicken club sandwich."

"How's that work?"

Mandy—according to her nametag—gives him a winner's smile that almost reaches up to those sad eyes. "Big, beer-battered fried chicken pieces—boneless thigh, not any of that lean breast stuff," she rolls her eyes as if to say, because who would want to live half-assed when you can live hardcore, to which Ledgerman would simply nod in agreement, "—and let me just say, the head cook knows how to fry a mean chicken. Top those honkers with a thick slice of melted cheddar cheese, add our thick, applewood smoked bacon on top. One —and only one—piece of iceberg lettuce atop that, a slice of tomato, and a nice heap of fresh avocado. Stuck between two pieces of untoasted challah."

Ledgerman makes a mental note to come back for lunch if he can.

"You had it?"

"Last week, first time we made it. Been dreaming about it ever since."

Describing that sandwich was the first time Mandy's eyes almost turned up. She wasn't a heifer, was actually skinny. Long, too-young legs. Might have been a middle-distance runner. Eight hundred meters, maybe. No less than that. But nothing more than a miler, either.

"Tell you what, have the cook use the challah in the French toast and we'll call it even."

She smiles, making him believe she means it this time. "I like your style, Mister."

Without hardly more than a glance, Mandy makes the appropriate notations on her pad (though Ledgerman feels maybe she was just doodling, 'cause it ain't too hard to remember a breakfast order) and makes the pencil and pad disappear into the front of her apron like a magician performing a long-practiced trick. "Coming right up."

She disappears for a second, not even enough time for the letterman jacket boys to pour three dabs of tabasco into the cup, and gives Ledgerman another steaming pour of the coffee.

He thanks her, though she's already gone to fill someone else's coffee, and he watches the steam rise up from the cup, twisting and twirling in on itself. Creating shapes akin to watching the clouds roll by on a sunny day. Each one a puffy white Rorschach test of the viewer, though he doesn't see anything much in them.

One of the letterman boys is half-standing, half-squatting now, feet up on the patent red leather of his booth, squeaking up a storm. Taunting one of the other kids as he pours a packet of one of those fake sugars into the cup.

Ledgerman turns away from them, content to just watch the cars fly by and disappear into their distant, imaginary nowheres while he sips on his go-go fuel.

His watch vibrates on his wrist, stopping him as he lifts the mug to his lips. He could almost taste the brown elixir. Has a moment of sheer panic that he won't ever taste it again.

But when his watch vibrates, it means it's time for him to do what he was put on this earth to do.

It's a smartwatch—which is about the most ridiculous notion he ever heard. But he's gotta admit, it *is* pretty damn smart.

For a watch.

The screen lights up with the time when he looks at it (but never when he doesn't). Tells him how many steps he took (none since he sat for breakfast), how long he sat down for today (all the minutes between sitting for breakfast and now).

But perhaps most consequently, when the watch vibrates, it tells him he needs to do one of two things to somebody:

Save them.

Or kill them.

TWO

Ledgerman has an insane notion that he should ignore the watch.

It only vibrates the one time, so far as he knows. He never really ignored it before, though. So maybe it would vibrate again, in a minute. Or five. Ten at the outside. Enough time, anyway, to finish his breakfast.

He could probably just ignore it, go about enjoying this moment inside. Sip his coffee. Fill his belly. Mind his business.

Of course, there's always the chance that ignoring it would mark him for some unknown fate, the same way it does to others.

He wonders these things in the split second it takes to place his steaming cup down atop the paper placemat, the brown coffee ring forming already where he sets it down. Right on the symbol. The omega. In place of the O.

It seems fitting, now that the watch has vibrated. Omega. Last letter of the Greek alphabet.

The end of the line.

Ledgerman raises his wrist, his black wool button-down shirt lifting helpfully enough so he can see the face.

He knows he won't ignore the vibration, silly as it is to imagine he would.

As it always does, the watch lights up with three pieces of information:

A name.

A picture.

A time.

Ledgerman sees all three pop up in order, just like always.

Mandy Beaudreau.

A picture that looks like it was taken thirty seconds ago, when Mandy the waitress was ringing his order into the ordering system.

10:05 a.m.

In the upper corner of the watch, rendered in tiny font because of the notification, Ledgerman sees that it is now 9:55 a.m. That leaves ten minutes before he needs to either kill Mandy or save her.

Sometimes he wonders why the watch doesn't tell him the fourth piece of information he needs: which of the two options it is (kill or save). Seems like it would be more likely to result in the correct outcome. Though of course, *correct* is in the eye of the sender.

And Ledgerman has no idea who that might be.

No idea how any of this fits into the larger puzzle that is his life. Not even sure why he knows—knows on a cellular, *molecular* level—what he must do with the information provided to him. There simply is no thought to ignoring it.

And while it might be simpler for him to know which choice—death or salvation—the person in question has been ordained to receive, that would take all the fun out of it. Somewhere deep down inside him, Ledgerman enjoys the challenge of figuring out right from wrong. Putting the scales of justice back into alignment.

Nobody dies without a reason. And nobody gets saved without one, either. At least not when he's involved.

Mandy Beaudreau places down three steaming plates (one of which she holds with a toweled hand). One plate of scrambled eggs with cheese. One with a heaping helping of freshly cooked bacon (he can tell because it doesn't have that re-heated sheen to it that so many diners fall back on). One with fluffy challah French toast, doused in butter and powdered sugar that looks like freshly fallen snow. That's the hot plate.

The time is 9:56 a.m.

"How you fixed?" Mandy says, doing her best octopus impression —somehow topping off his coffee, despite having just set down three plates.

Ledgerman looks at his food, the aromas rising up, grabbing hold of the primitive areas of his body and soul, the way they probably had back when he was in the womb.

"I'd be fixed just fine if you sat down and joined me for a cup of coffee."

Mandy freezes, obviously not expecting that. "Sorry, Mister, but I got a ... like ... a man. A boyfriend, I mean."

Ledgerman smiles. "I'm sure you do. And I didn't mean it like that. No offense."

"None taken."

"Just was hoping for some company. I'm just passing through. Sometimes it's nice to talk with a friendly face."

Mandy let out a little laugh. "First person to ever say I was a friendly face."

Ledgerman notes the time. 9:57 a.m. He picks up his fork and knife and nods across from him. "How about it? Not many tables left in here."

Mandy looks around, gives one last look at the letterman jacket table (who have found a squirt bottle of yellow mustard for their concoction), and seems to agree.

"Coffee?" Ledgerman reaches across the aisle to an empty table and grabs an upturned coffee cup. He takes the pot from Mandy's hand and pours her a cup.

"Thanks." Her eyes are half-here and half-looking around the restaurant. Maybe for her manager. Maybe for an abusive boyfriend. Ledgerman isn't a sentimental fella, but he sure hopes she isn't looking around for a partner who's looting the register or getting ready to rob the place blind.

Ledgerman starts in on the eggs, knowing they will get cold the quickest. Bacon isn't bad if it's cold. Neither is French toast, especially with warm syrup (which this definitely was). But cold eggs could ruin a meal before it started.

As it was, they're heavenly. Cooked to perfection. Fluffy without being dry.

"So what do you want to talk about?" Mandy says.

Ledgerman sips his coffee. "How long you been working here?"

Mandy reluctantly sips her own coffee, having put no cream or sugar in it. "Three years."

"Three? You barely look eighteen as it is."

"Nineteen. You can start waiting tables about sixteen, usually. Gotta be older if you're at a place that serves booze."

"That what you want to do?" She has a look on her face like she's a minor league baller talking about the show.

She nods. "Bigger bills, better tips."

Ledgerman studies her. In his experience, there are people you could see had a rough upbringing. Whether it was the way they talked, the way they walked, or the things they did—tiny mannerisms that mostly go unnoticed—he had a sixth sense about that sort of thing.

"Why do you need money so bad?" Seemingly a dumb question. Directed at some people Ledgerman has come across in his work, it would be akin to asking what you needed oxygen for.

Something about Mandy tells him it wouldn't seem quite so strange to her.

"Everybody needs money. What kind of question is that?"

"Sure, people need some," he says in between forkfuls of eggs, him having to lift the fork damn near above his head to break the stretching cheese, "You're working here three years already. But you don't like it. Why not find something else?"

As he says this, he checks his watch.

9:59 a.m.

Six more minutes until something must be done.

Mandy takes another sip of coffee, not taking her eyes off him now. Squinting at him as she sips. Curious. Or annoyed about this intrusion on her personal life.

"You think I grew up pretty easy, huh? Like why's a girl my age not in college?"

"College is for thinkers. Pontificators. You're a doer, clearly."

"Meaning I'm stupid?"

"You know I don't mean that. You're dancing around it now." Ledgerman stabs his knife and fork at the French toast, careful not to drip any syrup onto his eggs. Even though lukewarm French toast isn't terrible, no sense letting it get too cold.

"Dancing around what?"

"Whatever it is you need three years' worth of off-the-books cash to pay for." He nods to the shaved spot along the side of her head. "Clearly it's not for trips to the salon."

That was probably either the thing that would make her split or get her to open up like Hoover Dam.

Ledgerman watches her reaction, slipping a piece of thick, fatty bacon into his mouth to mix with the ecstasy that was challah French toast. No matter what happened here, he would always remember Mandy Beaudreau for introducing him to this wondrous creation.

The thing about his line of work—if work was what you wanted to name it; *calling* might be a better word for it, but damned if he even really knew why or how he got into this in the first place—was that the *calling* involved a certain measure of violence. Violence was, by its nature, unpredictable.

So each time his watch buzzed, Ledgerman never lost sight of the fact it could be the last time. One day there was bound to be a person he flat couldn't kill, because that person would kill him dead first.

That's why he always enjoys a meal. Each and every one.

24/7/365, his watch could vibrate, giving him minutes, hours, days until he was supposed to step in and settle some score. One he never saw the bigger picture for, nor did he learn the final score at the end of regulation. Probably he never would. And maybe that was for the best.

To someone or something, Ledgerman was simply a pawn with which the score could be manipulated.

"Mandy!" A voice from somewhere behind Ledgerman. Back toward the hostess stand, which also doubles as a cash register. Three cameras were perched in view around it, all of them pointed straight at the cash machine. Ledgerman notices two others, better hidden, pointed at the same place.

They didn't, apparently, trust the waitresses with cash.

Mandy shot up straight like she'd just been stuck with a cattle prod. Before Ledgerman could blink, she was gone, back toward the kitchen like a dog who just pissed on the rug.

Ledgerman scoops up another fluffy serving of eggs, tops it with a piece of bacon, and washes it down with a thick pull from his steaming mug of coffee.

The time is 10:00 a.m.

He wonders if he is going to have to kill Mandy Beaudreau.

THREE

Ledgerman stands up from the table, walks himself around to the seat Mandy had just been sitting in. The patent leather is warm, the way leather gets when someone's been sitting on it. It squeaks as he slides into the booth, his back to the group in the letterman jackets (who have finally found the Tabasco, though you'd think they would have started with that). As he sits, Ledgerman sees the cup is a putrid brown color.

The loser will have his work cut out for him.

Ledgerman's new seat has two distinct advantages from his previous one:

First, he can now better see Mandy—where she went, her interactions with the rest of the Omega's staff. If she needs to be saved, the threat it more likely to come from someone she knows, rather than a stranger. And he hasn't flagged anybody seated in the diner as a threat. Meaning any threat would come from the back of the house.

Second, his new seat affords him a better angle to eat his challah French toast, having now finished the eggs. He can do so with less fear of burning his hands on the plate, which has somehow kept its heat despite being out of the kitchen now for almost six minutes.

He puts another piece of the sumptuously sweet and cinnamon-y French toast into his mouth, this time adding a sprig of bacon so he may enjoy the flavors together, and he thinks about what he knows so far.

Mandy does not appear to be a criminal. The first obvious tell is that criminals typically cannot hold jobs long term. They also typically do crime for one of two reasons: for the rush or for the money.

If Mandy *was* a criminal and she did it for the rush, working at a diner would seem an odd choice. You get about as much rush working here as from returning a book to your local library.

If Mandy did crime for the money, the diner represents an even weirder choice. Not much to be made here. Probably not even enough to cover basic expenses without another job. And when do you do crime if you have to hold down *two* jobs?

So probably criminality is out.

Meaning Mandy must be saved.

Saved ... but from whom?

Ledgerman ponders this as he hears one of the letterman jacket kids (now behind him) say, "OK, last one. This milk."

"Dude, no," another one says, "that smells gnarly!"

"Shut up, Pirchman. Don't be a bitch."

"Yeah, bitch," another chimes in helpfully.

Ledgerman takes a honker of a bite from his French toast and stands up. Wherever Mandy has gone—and he assumes it was the kitchen—she has not reappeared since.

He steps to the table of the four letterman jacket boys. Immediately spots Pirchman, a slim kid swimming in his jacket. Face clear of freckles but pockmarked with pimples. Glasses, light skin, and hair that could best be described as sand-esque in color. As sad as it was to say it, being called *bitch* might have been the best-case scenario for Pirchman. He was smiling, though Ledgerman could see that behind that smile lay multitudes of quiet, agonizing pain.

Kids can be cruel to one another.

And he knew cruelty. Had been cruel to many people, though none of them children. And every one of them deserving.

Another boy, the biggest and most muscular of the group (this clear from the industrial bucket of a neck protruding out from the jacket's collar), was pouring the milk into the glass. It turned the putrid brown into something resembling coffee with milk splashed in it. If Ledgerman drank his coffee with milk, this sight would surely have convinced him to stop.

He said nothing. Not at first. Mainly because he still chewed on the French toast, his bite having been taken with the understanding that once he stood up, anything could happen. So it had been large, enough to remember this breakfast by, should one of these kids be carrying a gun or something (unlikely, but unfortunately these days, not outside the realm of possibility).

After a moment, a third kid at the table, sitting on the far inside seat away from Ledgerman—a kid who could simply be described as forgettable—said, "C ... c ... can we help you, sir?"

At least he was polite.

Ledgerman finished chewing as Big Neck put the glass of milk down.

"Actually," Ledgerman said, "I think I can help you."

Four confused looks (though one mixed with that deep emotional pain) stare back at him.

"How do you plan to choose who is going to drink it?"

Bless their hearts, the answer to this question had clearly not occurred to them yet. They all look at Big Neck, obviously the leader of the group. But nobody says anything. Despite their somewhat rambunctious behavior, they were quite obedient. Perhaps they were good kids after all.

"I have an idea," Ledgerman says. "I'll choose."

"How would you do that?" Forgettable asks, finding some confidence.

"Three simple questions. I ask them, you answer. The loser is the one left at the end."

Open mouths. Confused, short-circuited looks.

"Each of you put your pointer finger on the table. Go on, now. This won't hurt."

They each comply, slowly, the commands registering in some part of their adolescent brains that hasn't yet formed to completion. It is the one that adults access to control children as much as they can, before said children start to realize they don't have to listen.

Ledgerman checks his watch.

It is 10:01 a.m.

Four minutes until something needs to happen.

The last few minutes are always a jolt of energy and action. This time, amplified by the helpful aid of about five different kinds of sugar and several cups of coffee.

"Each question I ask, if your answer is yes, you remove your finger. You are safe. If your answer is no, you leave your finger on. You are still in the game. Got it?"

Three heads shake yes.

"This is on the honor code," Ledgerman says, giving them the same look he's used to quell fighting instincts in stronger men than these. "Don't lie. You won't like the consequences."

They all nod like good boys.

"Good. Question one: Do you know the waitress? Mandy?"

All four of the letterman boys look at each other, clearly confused at this seemingly random question.

Pirchman, however, removes his finger. Big Neck glares at him. Pirchman says, "What? She used to babysit my neighbor."

Perfect.

"Question two: Have you ever won a county championship game?"

This, of course, is a cheat. The fourth kid at the table, the one who had yet to say anything, wore a letterman jacket with a giant soccer ball patch on it. He smiled, pumped a fist, and removed his finger like he just won the World Cup. Apparently the track and field team (Pirchman) and the lacrosse team (Big Neck and Forgettable) weren't quite as accomplished programs.

"Two of you left." Lederman looks at Big Neck, looks at Forgettable. He honestly doesn't care who wins, doesn't know enough about either of them to goose the results.

But he can make an educated guess.

"Question three: Are you still a virgin?"

Pirchman giggles, the word virgin itself striking some comedic chord that runs even deeper than his pain, breaking through it like a fat boy standing on thin ice.

Big Neck removes his finger and pounds the table. He points at Forgettable. "Ha! You're still a virgin, Freddy! Probably always will be. Pussy."

Ledgerman puts a firm hand on Big Neck's shoulder. This would feel good. "I think you've misunderstood the rules. If Freddy over here is still a virgin, he answers *yes* to my question. Meaning he removes his finger."

Big Neck looks up at Ledgerman, uncomprehending.

"Meaning you lose."

Big Neck does not take this well, some color draining from his face. Ledgerman imagines that Big Neck had perhaps been the one to dream up this game. That he might lord the notion of drinking this disgusting concoction over his tablemates for as long as possible, asserting his dominance over the group (who would never expect that he be the one to ultimately drink it).

Not that Ledgerman cares much, but this intervention over the small-scale terrorism of bullies might very well make a nice feature story in the paper tomorrow.

"Haha, drink it!" Freddy says, relishing the fact that he has yet to score with any of the ladies. Probably once the concoction is gone, he will come back down to earth about this particular boast.

Ledgerman is now done here, with the exception of one other thing.

He points at Pirchman. "Tell me about Mandy. She's in trouble."

He blinks, glasses bouncing around on the bridge of his nose as he does so. "Trouble?"

"Someone wants to hurt her. Who might that be?"

Ledgerman knows he is taking a long shot here. There are perhaps three, three and a half minutes left until he needs to do something. If he cannot determine for sure that Mandy must be saved, he must kill her.

But this town seems small enough that Pirchman the bitch will know any possible suspects.

"Um ... uh, I mean,"

"She has a boyfriend."

"Brent?"

"Sure. What's his deal?"

"Good dude, man. Used to run track, too. Two years older than me. But we hung a little bit." Pirchman says this with neither disdain nor pride.

"What else? Where can I find him?"

"Well, I mean, I guess if you knew what dorm he was in ..."

"He's in college?"

"Yeah. VCU, down in Richmond. Hear it's a pretty cool party school."

Ledgerman clenches a fist. The boyfriend is most likely out as his target.

"He's not around much?"

Pirchman shakes his head.

Ledgerman nods, thinks. Turns back toward the kitchen.

The time is 10:02 a.m.

Three minutes left.

And he doesn't have answers yet.

FOUR

As Ledgerman passes his table, he picks the largest piece of bacon off the top of the pile, folds it, and pops it into his mouth.

Goddamn. That's good.

He marches toward the back of the diner, passing an elderly couple being shown to their table by a presentable hostess of about thirty (one who is not fooling Ledgerman, though).

Despite being presentable, Ledgerman can see within her what he could not see within Mandy. A hard life, etched into her like a someone writing their name in wet concrete. If you really thought about it, that was pretty much what a hard life was.

Behind her and the old couple, another elderly group of four wait. Three others, all moving like glaciers, are behind them coming through the diner's entryway.

The lunch time rush.

In front of Ledgerman is a long bar top counter with fixed stools in groups of two, each covered with the same patent leather as the booths. All empty at this time of day. Condiment caddies containing salt, pepper, ketchup, mustard, and napkins dot the counter—one between every two-top that the barstools create. A soda machine and several glass dishes showcase various pies, cakes, cookies, and muffins. The Omega Diner does not serve liquor, but with a little sprucing up, this wouldn't be a bad place for a beer.

There are two doors fixed into the wall that runs behind the countertop. One that leads you out from behind the bar and into the restaurant. Another that goes back into the kitchen.

Ledgerman puts a hand on the bar top and hoists himself over. His boots touch down on the squishy non-slip floor mat behind every bar and kitchen in America, a nice brace against the weight of his frame. His knees were once flexible, spry things. They are less so now.

Ledgerman imagines himself working here, what that might feel like. He turns away from the door to the kitchen and looks over the restaurant. Sees himself picking up the damp towel hidden just out of sight on a shelf under the bar. Wiping down the counter after a spilled milkshake. Big smile. "That's alright, Champ," he's saying to a kid who isn't far away from tears. "How about a refill, huh?" The kid nods.

Ledgerman, with the order coming up.

He slides it halfway across the counter, connects right with the palm of the kid's hand. Smiles all around now, as the kid gets back to slurping his shake, the sprinkles and whipped cream getting slowly sucked down into the vortex created by the straw.

Another happy customer.

As this reverie fades away, Ledgerman notices the elderly woman staring at him as the hostess puts serious distance between them. Practically already to their table—the corner booth that sits seven (which they presumably requested). Desperate to avoid congestion at the door, she is. Probably needs this job, maybe is even already on thin ice from being late or flaking out early before. Today, though, it's the letter of the law. Get 'em in, get 'em out. Diners make their nut on volume, not a fine dining experience.

The old woman seems confused by Ledgerman jumping over the counter like he owns the place.

He gives her a thumbs up and turns away, confident that if she does tell anyone about what she saw, he'll already be long gone.

Behind the doors, the kitchen air is humid enough to swim through. It has a musk, one that can be either pleasant (bacon, pancakes, eggs) or off-putting (unwashed dishes, food scraps) depending which whiff you get. The humidity carries scent further and more intense than dry air, so that doesn't necessarily help much either. Otherwise, though, the place is clean.

Two chef looking guys are working in the back of the area to Ledgerman's left, behind a few shelves and racks of kitchenware. One is scrambling up a storm—using a whisk the size of a baseball bat on a bowl of eggs that could fill a moon crater. The other is knifing strips of chicken like they killed JFK or something. He can't see either one besides the outline of their figures.

Or, like the lunch special today was the fried chicken club sandwich.

The kitchen is bigger than Ledgerman expected. Most he'd been inside were the opposite. It's separated into four quadrants.

Back left is a prep area, where Scramble and Chop are doing their thing.

Front left is all the hot stuff—ovens, stovetops, and a flat top grill that has a sheen like a glazed donut. A window out to the diner sits empty, save for the completed tickets pierced through the center of an upright metal pin like shrike food. Twin heating lamps, directed at nothing but the metal surface where finished orders are placed.

This placed really died down during this time of day.

The two right quadrants are for storage—jars, spices, extras, all went in front on wire shelves. In back is the walk-in freezer.

The door isn't fully closed.

Ledgerman checks his watch. 10:03 a.m.

Two minutes left.

FIVE

Before Ledgerman opens the walk-in freezer door, someone comes out. He can't actually see who. They are hidden behind five frosty boxes labeled PAPAS FRITAS. To avoid a confrontation, Ledgerman steps out of the way.

Just not in time.

The man tumbles. The PAPAS FRITAS tumble. Luckily none get free from their captivity. Would be a shame to lose good fries.

"Hey, which one of you dipshi—"

The man stops mid-cuss. Ledgerman is not whoever this man was expecting to see. "Who the hell are you?"

Sizing him up immediately: wrinkled, slightly frumpy collared button-down shirt, collars curled in on themselves.

Khakis not made by Dickie's or Carhartt.

An externally jangling key chain with plain white swipe cards for voided mis-orders or 86'ing an unsatisfactory meal.

This was the manager of the diner.

And his first reaction after anger (then confusion) was fear.

"Hey Freddy!" he says over his shoulder. Then to Ledgerman, "You can't be back here, man. Right, Freddy?"

Chops (apparent real name: Freddy) steps out from his prep station. He's a bad looking man—dirty bandana wrapped around his hair, low on his face so his eyes are draped in shadows. At least three fuzzy dark blue tattoos poke out from beneath his kitchen jacket collar.

The massive chef's knife in his hands doesn't help much, either.

"Who are you?" Freddy says, voice instantly dropping any pretense of politeness. Dropping into the clipped tone of a guy who'd done time.

Ledgerman thought back to the extra cameras around the register. The fact the waitresses weren't allowed to handle money. The reaction from these guys made him think that maybe this place had been a robbery target recently. Maybe more than once. Was close enough to enough feeder roads, leading to everything from major highways to smaller three-lane county roads that led you in pretty much any direction you wanted to go. Not easy to throw a police blockade around, that many methods of egress. Made sense as a target, you were desperate enough to risk arrest for what was probably only a couple thousand bucks, max.

All these things coalesced into a single, flashing red neon sign inside Ledgerman's mind:

PROBLEM.

PROBLEM.

PROBLEM.

Freddy steps fully away from around his station now, standing in the middle of the four quadrants so it wouldn't be easy for Ledgerman to get out in any particular direction.

The knife catches the glint of the bright fluorescent overhead lights like it's being lit for its movie closeup.

"Easy now, Freddy," Ledgerman says. Puts both hands up to show the guy he isn't any threat. Freddy takes another step closer as the manager slides a body length back away from Ledgerman across the floor, knocking PAPAS FRITAS boxes out of the way as he goes.

Freddy smiles. Is unusually chipper for someone who is about to get into a knife fight. But then again, if you are getting into a knife fight, always better to be the guy with the knife.

Probably that was the reason that Freddy Neck Tattoos got this job in the first place. Enjoyment of violent confrontations. Saved from having to pay for a security guard.

"C'mon now," Ledgerman says, flashing his winningest smile. "Surely you don't think I'm here to rob you." As he said it, he saw that the back exit from the kitchen—probably leading to an alleyway of dumpsters and maybe an employee parking lot, or the back of another small business backed up against this one—was unlatched.

"Last three guys who robbed us said the same thing right before they pulled their pistols," Freddy says, taking another step closer. Relishing this moment.

"If I had a pistol, wouldn't I have pulled it by now?"

Freddy takes a half-step forward but hesitates, this question leading to something a guy like Freddy—who *definitely* looked like he grew up hard—hasn't come into much contact in his life:

Logic.

"Uh—"

Ledgerman takes this moment of confused hesitation for the opportunity that it is.

In less time than it takes to blink, synapses inside his consciousness fire, pushing unseen levers and connecting electronic currents that even the most modern of science did not yet understand. Millions of years of evolution all merge into one single, glorious moment of savage violence.

Ledgerman's left foot plants, his boot finding purchase against the squishy non-slip floor mat on the floor of every bar and kitchen in America. His weight shifts there, slightly to the outside of his left foot, about equally spread between the ball and the heel. Slight bend in the left knee.

From this position, Ledgerman could punch, jump, balance, or tap dance.

Instead he unleashes a hellacious roundhouse kick, letting his right leg fly like Cristiano Ronaldo letting loose a corner kick.

He likes a kick for this situation for many reasons:

A prison brawler like Freddy is used to fighting a certain way. Hands-centric. Punches, elbows, grappling. That's prison fighting, mostly, if you include stabbing. Holding a knife makes Freddy even more likely to focus on the hands, a smart move when that is the likeliest source of death you might be facing.

No one in prison ever got a shank from someone's foot.

Not to mention, I'd you're going to throw body parts around in space, there is precious little on the body that weighs as much as the leg. Couple that with the sheer size of the muscles in the lower body, and a kick is impossible to beat when trying to generate maximum force.

To say Freddy's jaw was unprepared for the impact it received would be like saying a toddler was unprepared to get blind side sacked by Lawrence Taylor.

Freddy was undoubtedly a tough guy, in the sense that he'd probably been in plenty of scrapes and he never walked away from a fight. But even tough guys get knocked stone cold on their feet every now and again.

This was the now for Freddy. He does one of those zombie shimmies that you see every now and then in the NFL—the one where it seems you might have just witnessed a death on the field.

The knife lands silently on the rubber flooring. Approximately five seconds later, Freddy lands there, too, though with a considerable thud that will reverberate around his body for some time still.

The manager has hardly had the chance to back up another body length away from his fallen bodyguard.

Scramble has since put the whisk down, his eyes bulging from his head like a cartoon character.

If Ledgerman were a vindictive person, these remaining two members of the (apparently) dangerous Omega staff would be in trouble. They might end up in worse shape than their buddy Freddy.

They might even find themselves at the end of the line.

But Ledgerman is not that sort of man.

And even if he were, he is now running out of time.

It is 10:04 a.m.

"Where is Mandy?" he says to the manager, not bothering to soften his words.

He needs to know this information.

And he needs it now.

The manager's face twists into confusion. Then something else comes over it, something Ledgerman can't yet identify.

Never a hint of defiance, though.

He simply points toward the unlatched back exit.

One minute left.

SIX

Ledgerman rips open the door and storms through, a gust of late winter cold wind as sharp as knives pushes back against him with all the might of Mother Nature. He stands and takes it.

Eyes scan the immediate vicinity outside the door.

There is a small alleyway to his left, one narrow enough so that no car could travel down it. Littered with trash bins, puke-inducing puddles filled with liquid that looks like the letterman jacket boys' concoction, and the random, rusted appliances that was too often forgotten and discarded in out-of-sight places like these.

To his right is a collection of green industrial dumpsters. Black plastics lids closed, not overflowing.

Straight ahead is a five-car parking lot, partially blocked off from the street by a fence which now stood open just enough for a single person to slip through.

He is basically in the parking lot now, the exit not having much to it besides the door and a single step down to the pavement.

Beyond the fence is a red Oldsmobile about ten years older than it should have been, brown rust spreading out from the edges of the tire wells like gangrene. Black exhaust spews from the back pipe like it's giving the EPA the middle finger.

Inside the car were two people. From this distance, Ledgerman can't make them out exactly because the passenger side window is fogged up.

But he sees the outline of a girl that just has to be Mandy. How the hell could she have gotten farther than that in the last few minutes?

He wasn't about to fail this mission. He never failed before. And given the swift and exacting justice he meted out—the omnipotent watch on his wrist choosing targets, deserving or not—Ledgerman did not want to find out what would happen *should* he fail.

He sprints across the lot, not bothering to slither through the fence. Scaling over it instead. Uses two smooth movements:

One—left hand grabs the top of the fence, right foot plants about waist high.

Two—left foot explodes off the wet, salty sidewalk. The momentum from the run and jump makes him weightless as he clears his hips and chest over top.

He lands with something between grace and a thud on the other side of the fence.

Give him a 7.2 on the dismount.

He is at the passenger car door in a second. Rips it open.

Mandy's startled face meets him, cheeks red from the car's heat, which blasts out of the open doorway like he just got to the mouth of hell.

Based on what he saw, that wasn't too far off.

Mandy's face looks like a kid just got caught sneaking in the house at night.

Two men sit in the car—one in the driver's seat and one in the back, directly behind Mandy.

Two-on-one. Bad odds for such a young girl. And one more than he saw from the doorway.

The man in the driver's seat has a thick, hairy hand out, touching

Mandy's lithe upper thigh where her uniform rides up. Not touching in a good way. Clearly making her uncomfortable. His dark skin and the forest of hair on the back of his hand and wrist are a stark contrast to Mandy's innocence.

The other guy in back is squirrelly, slits for eyes, face cast in shadow from the dome light. His hand is also out, though it's small and feminine. It has a stack of wadded up bills in it. Mandy's tips. Ledgerman can tell because Mr. Squirrel dropped one as he reached for it inside the pouch of Mandy's apron.

Whatever's going on here, Mandy isn't making out on top.

"Who the hell are you?" the hairy man in the front seat says.

Ledgerman says nothing. Knows it's time. Or just about. Not official yet.

One second later, his watch beeps, punctuating the quiet that has befallen all four of them. The quiet before the storm, or the calm before the boom. However you wanted to say it.

Either way, the beeping meant only one thing.

10:05 a.m.

Time to finish the job.

SEVEN

There are a million ways to play this scenario. None of them involve kicking, though, so Ledgerman uses his fist.

He levels a left roundhouse punch through the back window, careful to punch toward the top so no shattered pieces of glass fall down on top of his arm.

Most people couldn't punch through a car window. But this is an older car, not yet using the improved shatterproof technology created in the past two plus decades.

Also, Ledgerman punches damned hard.

Besides, this plan of attack carries the element of surprise with it. And takes Mr. Squirrel off the board almost immediately.

Ledgerman isn't sure how, but he knows Mr. Squirrel carries a gun. Not a conscious thought, simply the intuition in the heat of the moment. Maybe because Mr. Squirrel is the one grabbing the money. Or because he's the one in back, where bosses usually sit (or at least guys who want other people to think they are bosses).

His punch has an additional agenda item embedded within it, other than simply surprise.

It flies through the shattered windshield and connects directly with Mr. Squirrel's right temple. Ledgerman doesn't even bother to go for the gun that scatters across the backseat. Mr. Squirrel won't be able to grab for it again soon. His time in this fight is ended.

Ledgerman removes his fist from the back window, careful not to catch his forearm against any of the jagged glass, and centers his attention on the hairy man in the front seat.

The man's hand is still settled atop Mandy's thigh. This guy didn't move too fast, though he was beefy. A punch or a slap from him would certainly intimidate a girl like Mandy.

Just not a guy like Ledgerman.

The next half-second is a poetry of movement. More impactful than Shakespeare. More elegant than Henry James.

Ledgerman pulls Mandy out from the passenger seat. So fast that her body doesn't slacken or tighten. It simply goes. Effectively, he replaces her body with his own. This requires both a violent efficiency of movement and a graceful touch, so as not to send her staggering down onto the sidewalk where she might hurt herself.

So there he is, in the passenger seat of the Oldsmobile, the interior a funky combination of stale chips, cigar smoke, and one of those cheap gas station air "fresheners," which Ledgerman always thought should have been called air stranglers, since their scent didn't so much freshen the air as it suffocated anything else that lingered.

This switch happened so quickly that the hairy hand of his next target was still stretched out in the same place. Now touching Ledgerman's decidedly not-innocent thigh.

Easy place to start.

Ledgerman uses both of his own hands to take hold of the thick, hairy one. With a violent wrench, he pulls the pointer and pinky fingers in opposite directions, both away from the center of the hand.

There are two crunches as bones and tendons shatter into mere memories of working parts. But it would be easy to miss both crunches, as they occur with the sort of timeless precision you only see on high end wristwatches.

Before the hairy man can scream—or frankly, react—Ledgerman

reaches across the ash covered center dash, his left hand placed behind the head, his right against the temple.

He slams the head forward onto the steering wheel at first, the janky ass car's horn not even blaring at the impact. As the head bounces back, Ledgerman catches it, slams it again. Not necessarily aiming for the steering wheel this time (without the beeps, it hardly seems necessary, or fun). Content to make impact with his new bouncing ball on anything hard inside the car. The radio serves as an acceptable target. And the dash above it. And the stick shift, too.

It is over quickly, at least for the men on the receiving end.

For Ledgerman, each movement is part of a fluid symphony of pain and violence that comes so naturally to him that he does not even question its source.

To do so would be like someone questioning their desire to drink water.

The time is 10:06 a.m.

Ledgerman has once again completed his task.

EIGHT

Ledgerman needs maybe two seconds to catch his breath. His heart rate returns to normal almost immediately, a fact that the watch will confirm for him later when he checks it.

The scent of burgers, bacon, and grilled cheese permeates the fresh air pouring in from outside, the scent wafting out from the massive industrial vent on the back side of the diner. However, in its toe-to-toe battle with the stench of the inside of the Oldsmobile, it is losing.

He checks unnecessarily on Mr. Squirrel sprawled out cold in the backseat. Ledgerman reaches for the gun on the floor and places it inside the glove compartment, turns off the car, removes the key from the ignition and locks the gun inside the glove compartment.

He steps out of the passenger seat and stands above Mandy, who has not even moved in the second or two since he placed her there.

Then he winds up like Orel Hershiser and launches the keys onto the roof of the building across the alley.

Mandy reacts unconsciously by putting her hands in front of her face, nearly immediately realizing Ledgerman intends her no harm.

She lowers them, eyes darting toward Mr. Squirrel, then to the hairy man and back again in a crazed loop.

Having experience in this situation, Ledgerman allows her to retrieve her wits, not pressuring her to do so on any timeline.

This way, actually, always ends up being fastest. It is not even 10:07 a.m. when Mandy finally speaks.

"You're bleeding," she says first, her eyes breaking the loop of knocked out scum bags and catching on the red mess all over Ledgerman's hand and sleeve. There is also blood on the shoulder of his shirt, the moisture from it clinging to his skin. Mandy doesn't see that, though, because the black of the shirt masks it.

She reaches for his hand, her eyes glazed over, still in the dreamlike state that so often follows violent action—at least for those who are not experienced in it.

"It's alright," he says, meaning it. He's had plenty worse before, undoubtedly far, far worse still on the horizon. He doesn't need Mandy's help to mend this wound.

She squeezes his good wrist and forearm, though. Her mind clings to the opportunity to help this man—this stranger—in any way she can. A concrete, tangible task that can be done before wrestling with the far more vague and obscure arithmetic that Ledgerman has just done, irrevocably changing her future life.

"You're bleeding," she says again. This is, Ledgerman knows, a common symptom of what was once called shell-shocked, but is today called PTSD. It is perhaps too soon for Mandy to be experiencing the true dangers of the disease. But in the moments immediately following, those in its wake often present themselves as people on a loop. Repeating themselves, stuttering, unable to focus on the reality that is present in front of them. Their brains not moving as quickly as the real world around them, trying once again to anchor itself onto some stable shore.

In the movies he might smack Mandy across the face to get her attention, center it on the present moment.

In real life, he simply allows her to gaze at his hands, her soft and innocent fingers holding him like a buoy in a dark and churning ocean.

When the fast-forward button in her mind is finally pressed OFF, Ledgerman sees coherence return behind her sad eyes.

"Oh, no ... God-G-G-God," she stutters. "What's happened?"

Ledgerman puts a hand on either shoulder, a gesture intended to both center Mandy's attention and put her at ease that she is now safe.

"The scale has been set back to equilibrium, Mandy."

"W-w-what?"

They never got it on the first try.

"Ours is a world of disparity. Differences exist between the haves and have-nots. Inequality abounds. The scale, such as it is, is not evenly distributed."

Mandy looks at him, blinks those sad eyes once, twice. Still not quite getting it.

"I am an agent of change. A counterweight, as it were. I'm an instrument by which the ledger can be balanced. You understand?"

Mandy stares.

"What happened here, Mandy. The scales have been—if not balanced—adjusted closer to an equilibrium. These animals won't hurt you anymore. You can go on with your life, free and clear of this monkey on your back."

Mandy nods, though her eyes don't belie understanding.

Snow starts to fall atop them, the back alley and street behind the diner completely silent now that the Oldsmobile is turned off. Seems to Ledgerman like a hidden, private place where only Mandy and he share this moment.

He lets go of her shoulders. Goosebumps crop up on the skin of her forearms. She is a picture of innocence, though one that has been tainted by the corrosive air of the outside world.

But Ledgerman thinks she'll be alright. Mandy is a fighter, a tough girl in a world that mostly just got a bit easier for her. He's not a sentimental fella, but this particular outcome suits him just fine.

"Here," he says, and turns back toward the Oldsmobile.

"No!" Mandy shrieks, the words careening off the brick and stone and concrete all around them like a SuperBall.

She grabs his forearm, sending a temporary shock of pain up into Ledgerman's armpit and shoulder. He'll have to take care of the cuts from the broken window. Could maybe have gone about that better. But the pain is little compared to the aura of relief that Mandy now exudes.

"It's alright," he says, extracting himself from her grip.

He turns to the car, reaches through the broken window, and manually unlocks the back passenger side door. He leans in the doorframe, putting his hand on the headrest of the driver's seat to hold his weight (to avoid the broken glass strewn about), and uses his other hand to grab the cash fallen from Mr. Squirrel's grip onto the floor.

Before he gets back up, Ledgerman rifles through Mr. Squirrel's pockets, finding a wad three times as thick (and ten times as valuable) stuffed into the back pocket of his dirty jeans.

He hands the cash to Mandy. "This doesn't fix everything, but I hope it at least goes towards making things right."

Mandy stares at the cash now resting in her palm. She hardly reacts, just blinks at this newfound revenue.

Because he isn't sure if she'll do it, Ledgerman uses his good hand to fold her hand around the wad, hammering home the thought that it's now hers.

"Thank you." The words still ethereal. The actions all around her not yet real. Ledgerman knows this, but it doesn't much matter. Perhaps there are other factors that will come into play later. Maybe this isn't Mandy's only experience with the Ledger, as he's come to call it. The entity (whether it is man, woman, computer technology, or deity) that delivers to his wrist the information upon which he is compelled to act. To save or end a life, without hesitation or remorse.

Ledgerman is not privy to other entities acting toward the same aims as he—the rebalancing of the moral fiber of society. Probably he is not the only instrument, he thinks. Probably there must be others—social workers, bankers, information gatherers, technical people.

At least he hopes he isn't the only one. What a depressing notion that would be.

But those are thoughts for another time. Right now, Mandy requires his undivided attention.

"Listen here, now," he says, using the same quiet yet firm tone he so often deploys once he gets to the end of things. "There shouldn't be any blowback on you from this. These guys, far as I can see, won't have people snooping around, looking for them."

"What about Aidy?" Mandy says.

"Who?"

"Uh ... Devillo's girl."

Now he gets it. "Front seat or back?"

Mandy doesn't look back to the car. But a shiver runs through her body, raising a fresh round of goosebumps. "Front."

Ledgerman nods. "I'll take care of Aidy. Don't fret another thing about her." He can put potential collateral damage in a report, something required of him after each of these missions. They'll be looked after.

Mandy seems to accept this.

"What happens when the police find them?"

"No reason they'll think you're involved, is there? No cameras back here. No witnesses. I'm certainly not telling anyone. Neither are they. As long as you don't answer any questions that you—an employee, and *only* an employee, of the restaurant—shouldn't know, they won't have reason to suspect your involvement. Then they'll move on. They won't be pounding the pavement too hard looking for suspects. Anybody could see these two don't deserve more than a cursory glance at the facts, if that."

Ledgerman feels, but ignores, the strong desire to ask Mandy just what in the hell was going on in that car. The answer to that question is almost entirely meaningless right now.

Instead, he simply says, "My advice to you is to treat this like what it is: a bad dream. One that you're now awake from. But rather than continuing on your day, forgetting the darkness the moment your eyes open, keep this entrenched somewhere so deep yet so far away in your mind that you both never think of it directly, yet also cannot ever truly forget it, either. That way, you'll carry forward in your days appreciating this gift you've been given. And you'll pay it forward. Not tomorrow, nor on any particular day. Just in drips and drabs along the way."

Mandy nodded but Ledgerman sees she doesn't understand. Not yet, anyway. How could she? He just needs to make sure she hears him. It would all settle in later.

Mandy lets out a cry, then another. Tried unsuccessfully to hold a third one in. Ledgerman pulled her close to his chest, warm tears and hot breath soaking into the front of his shirt. He didn't mind.

"They just took and took, you know?" she says, holding the sobs back after a bit. "And they acted like they were doing me a favor."

"Plenty people like that out there. Just because you escaped these ones doesn't mean you won't ever encounter others."

"I just ... it was like I couldn't get out."

Ledgerman didn't need an active imagination to understand the dark times Mandy Beaudreau had gone through with those men.

"Well, now you are. Watch yourself, sometimes these things come and go in cycles."

She squeezes in harder against him.

"You hungry?" she asked after they stood there together in silence —Mandy coming down from her haze, Ledgerman basking in the after-effects of adrenaline, which had so come to color the glow of a job well done.

Ledgerman was, having not entirely finished all of his breakfast, having to rush through the end to take care of business. Hard to believe all that was merely minutes ago.

"Fried chicken club sandwich, right?"

Mandy nodded, the familiarity of talking about the Omega menu probably feeling like divine comfort right now.

Somewhere not too far away, sirens scream out into the cold winter air.

"That's alright, I should be going. Much as that sandwich sounds incredible, I'd rather not have to finish it up from inside a jail cell."

"B-but I can tell them that you helped me. You won't have to be arrested or anything."

Ledgerman thinks about Freddy inside, still passed out cold on the kitchen anti-slip mat. Thinks about the manager, so quick to sic the dogs on Ledgerman.

"No, you won't. Remember what I said, about not saying anything other than what any normal employee might know about two guys getting beat up in a back alley. You didn't know them. You never saw me."

Mandy nods into his chest.

He gives her one last squeeze and then puts some space between them.

This is always the hard part. Ledgerman's protection, by design, ends here and now.

"One last thing. You should get out of here, this job. While these guys shouldn't bother you anymore," he points to the Oldsmobile, "they ever get a little crazy idea, they'll know where to find you. Besides, this place doesn't deserve you. Go find one of those high-end places, one that serves booze."

Mandy sniffs and wipes the tears away from her eyes.

"Ok."

"Promise me, kid." Last thing he needs to hear about is some young thing found in the dumpsters behind the Omega Diner, some violent ex-con brought too much booze in his flask and let out his aggression in the wrong place. It didn't happen often, but occasionally he helped someone who didn't take advantage of their second chance.

For whatever reason, he felt strongly that he didn't want to see the same thing happen to Mandy.

He didn't want this place to be her end of the line.

Another burst of sirens screeches through the air like an attacking band of birds.

"I promise," she says, and Ledgerman can tell she means it.

"Alright," he says. And then, because he's unable to come up with anything else, he says, "Now get back inside, it's cold out here."

Maybe it's the daze, but Mandy nods and listens.

She's gone in an instant, just like she appeared before him at his table.

He checks his watch: 10:12 a.m. Like so many of his other missions, it seems like it went by in an instant. His smartwatch has once again guided him to a target that must either be saved or killed. Typically, he has no preference. This time, however, he was happy that target required saving.

But now, his strange arithmetic completed, it's time to go.

He ducks into the wind as it gusts down the alleyway, stuffing both hands into his pockets.

Tomorrow, who knew where he'd be.

For right now, he needs to find some place far enough away to eat lunch.

THIN AIR

A LEDGERMAN STORY

A
LEDGERMAN
ASSIGNMENT

THIN AIR

A SUSPSENSE THRILLER

NIZ

AUTHOR OF THE *TRUE NAME* SERIES

THOMAS

ONE

Ledgerman's heart rate spikes, the adrenaline that always hits when he first reads the watch's notification—the time when the countdown begins, where the effectiveness of his next six, or twenty-three, or sixty-seven minutes takes on the utmost importance.

Ledgerman stands, forgetting to duck his tall, thick frame. Smashing his head on the luggage compartment (which these days inexplicably can hardly hold any actual pieces of luggage) in the process. A new pain shooting through the base of his brain, joining the more profuse but widespread neck pain he experienced from sleeping crack-necked for the first five hours of the flight.

In his haste to stand, Ledgerman knocks the overhead light on above his seat. An accident, one that temporarily blinds him, leaving a residue of lighted spots floating around his eyes. He fumbles back to turn the lights off. Something much easier said than done.

"Excuse me," someone says from the row of seats in front of him, cringing and pulling away from Ledgerman's general direction. He knows himself to be an intimidating figure at times—often one look can be all it takes to convince a person their sudden concern is no longer relevant.

"Sorry ma'am," he says back, holding up a hand in a small show of peace.

She turns away from him with a look of either bitter disdain or quiet disgust. Either one perfectly fine with Ledgerman, so long as he doesn't have to deal with her anymore. He doesn't mind fraternizing with the general public, as he calls them. But once his watch vibrates, it becomes an operational hazard for him to do so.

Ledgerman is not a clumsy man. He is actually frighteningly precise with his physical movements. A fact that many who have been caught in his preordained path came to find out the hard way.

But there is something about the past few minutes that's turned him into one, apparently. And he's pretty sure he isn't going senile yet.

Was it his unremembered dream, the afterimage of which is imprinted onto the inside of his eyelids? The fading vision of it only visible for a fleeting second when he closes them? He can't be sure. Can't even remember the damn thing to evaluate whether it was the cause or not.

He closes his eyes for a second, inhaling in a deep breath through his nose to center himself. He hears the laughter of ten, twelve people as if they are still sitting next to him. Warmth in their hearts. They are close, though he can't see them. The laughter is there. So, so close.

The laughter rises, falls, crescendos. It's ten, twelve different laughs all come together as one.

Until it's gone.

Not faded away.

Muted.

He opens his eyes, the laughter echoing in his memory.

What the hell was that?

Ledgerman feels off today—tonight, whenever the hell it is—on this plane.

Which is very unfortunate for his current state.

Because the main thing Ledgerman's watch does not tell him

about the person it identifies is which decision he must make regarding that individual's future.

To kill them or save them.

Those are the only two options. And it's up to him to figure out the right one for this situation.

TWO

The trick is how to find Kylie Rudd on an airplane in six minutes or less.

Step one. The most direct, but not always the easiest. Ledgerman sometimes looks up from his watch into the smiling face of his subject. Sometimes he needs to smoke them out of a hiding spot.

Looking around the dark cabin, with exactly three lights turned on above random seats between him and the back of the plane, Ledgerman thinks finding Kylie might be a difficult task. He sees people zipped up in hoodies, beneath blankets, even wearing eye masks. He can't make out many faces.

Not going to be easy at all to find Kylie Rudd. Much less determine which of the two conclusions she deserves.

Ledgerman doesn't have much of an issue being judge, jury, and executioner (or exonerator) in these situations. He isn't sure exactly how long he's been doing this work, for he can't remember a time before doing it. There *was* a time before, however. Of this he is certain. His memory only stretches back so far. He doesn't remember school, parents, his first job. All of that is as dark and distant as the world he falls into as he dreams each night.

Though he still can't get past the feeling that he's missing something from that time earlier—something big, the feeling sitting in his chest and stomach like dread embodied.

He isn't a jittery man. He detests unsteadiness in people and would never tolerate it in himself. Yet the weight of unfulfilled dismay hangs heavy around his neck. He can't understand this feeling, simply has no mechanism even for comparison.

Ledgerman believes, deep down, that he wears the watch because of his reliability and steadfastness at completing the tasks that come to him. He is a man capable of improvisation. Of calm amidst the chaos.

He can't stand the fact that the inner chaos of a dream has gotten to him. That some unremembered darkness has got him shook.

He shakes himself free of the thoughts. Or tries to, at least. With only five minutes left, Ledgerman doesn't have the luxury of time anymore. He needs to get moving now.

He starts off for the back of the plane, having already gotten a sense from his earlier bathroom trip that Kylie wasn't in the first twelve rows of the plane. As a matter of habit, he scanned through those passengers already. He would have noticed her, even if she was zipped up tight in one of those hoodies that, for some reason, can be closed over your face.

"Sir," a stewardess asks, placing a small hand on Ledgerman's considerable shoulder.

He spins, quick and precise. The type of movement that most people who sneak up on him see just before drifting into their own land of darkness and dreams.

As quickly as he engages, though, he can slam the brakes, avoiding what would have been a horrific mistake. Thus far, Ledgerman has avoided the long arm of law enforcement when completing his missions. No matter how skilled or tough he is, getting off this plane in anything but handcuffs seems unlikely if you get violent with the staff.

Laying a hand on a flight attendant would surely land him in federal prison.

Knocking her out cold on her feet for placing a gentle hand on his shoulder would have put him there for quite some time.

She senses something, though it's clear she can't quite fathom what that is. He can relate, his own sense of some foreboding event on the horizon making him uncomfortable. She leans back, eyes focusing first on his chest and shoulders and then on his hands.

The human mind is a terrific judge of danger. Often, with people who find themselves injured or in need of saving from some horrible event, they can point back to a thought or feeling in their mind that should have clued them in to reassess the situation. A gut instinct, a smell, a *vision*. All ways the human mind strips away the infinite kaleidoscope of sensory inputs around us when a certain few of them need to be focused on.

It's only when people talk themselves out of the need to listen that they wind up in the wrong place at the wrong time.

The flight attendant takes several seconds assessing Ledgerman's chest, arms, and shoulder for danger, which is smart. Those are the places most likely to do her harm. But, seeing a lack of danger and harm, her eyes rise up to greet his face.

When they do, Ledgerman feels a sweat forming on his lower back. The haze in his mind dissipates, if only slightly. His eyes open wider, as if they could somehow take in more of the beauty in front of him.

These days, it wasn't common to see an attractive woman as a flight attendant. A thing which he figures shouldn't be voiced aloud, like so many of his thoughts. He can't actually remember a time when it was common, though a not-so-careful rewatching of *Catch Me If You Can* tells him that, at some point, this custom was an honored part of airline travel.

Now, of course, the honor seemed to be found in how miserable a particular airline could make its customers.

This attendant, however, was something out of the vintage catalog.

Brunette, flowing hair cut stylishly to her shoulders. Big, almond-shaped eyes with flecks of blue sky mixed in with the green.

Thick, pouty lips.

A uniform that fit in all the right places.

Ledgerman notices all of these things immediately, pleasure centers bombarded with information-carrying neurons like Iraqi air force bases back in '91.

Under normal circumstances, this flood of hormonal and evolutionary information might signal to him that it was his lucky day—that he might be pressing the call button a few extra times to get the chance to talk to her a bit more.

Instead, Ledgerman tries to wrestle his dry tongue from the back of his mouth, the dry air leaching every last bit of its moisture.

The flight attendant standing in front of him is an exact replica of the woman in the picture on his watch. Her green eyes beam out at him, the same color as a field of clovers.

Kylie Rudd.

"Sir?"

Ledgerman's pulse slows down to its normal resting rate of fifty-two beats per minute. He knows the watch tracks this (he even will check it on occasion), one of the few useful things he actually does with the watch besides taking its messages and plying his craft on those it says for him to.

His eyes dart down to the flight attendant's name tag, which reads: KYLIE RUDD.

This confirms it.

"Sir, is there anything I can help you with?"

Ledgerman thinks, takes what seems like forever to acknowledge her and form a cogent response through the surprise of stumbling on her like this.

It takes him an extra second to actually produce this cogent response from his dry mouth, an internal warning sign that does not go unnoticed by Ledgerman.

A master of improvisation, he is not today.

"I think maybe there is, actually."

THREE

Kylie's beautiful green eyes open expectantly, waiting for Ledgerman to reveal whatever it is he needs from her. In the dark and cramped aisle, with only the faint light from around the cabin and peeking in from two lowered window shades, she looks like a sultry dream.

Now that she doesn't fear for her safety, she takes him in, her eyes drawing a circuitous path from his broad shoulders, down the front of his wool button-down shirt, and then back up to his face.

Maybe she likes him.

Maybe he likes her, too.

She opens the angle of her body to him, her perfume enveloping him in a mix of sandalwood and cool lavender, replacing the stale, filtered plane air in his nostrils.

No one around them stirs, everyone either asleep in the darkness or hunched over phones or glowing tablets that light up rapt faces. Such concentration tells Ledgerman they are effectively alone. Most of these people are so deep into a binge, they might not even notice if the plane started to go down.

Beyond Kylie, in the forward area where the first class attendants prepare fancy beverages for their fancier passengers, no one looms.

Kylie, it seems, might be the attendant responsible for the front of the plane.

"I think we might know someone in common," Ledgerman says, the words tumbling out of his dry mouth faster than he can consider them, or the overarching plan they may or may not suggest. One thing about having your back against the wall that has always worked for Ledgerman, though, is to get your conscious mind out of the way and let your instincts simply go to work.

The human soul has an amazing penchant for surviving and thriving in uncertain situations, one that predates any single living organism today by hundreds of thousands of years of evolution.

He watches Kylie's face as the words register over the constant hum of the plane's engines. What might, on some people, read as a straightforward mixture of surprise and delight at this news instead reads as concern—or maybe fear?—masked with the veneer of delight. What could the reason be for that?

It seems Kylie is hiding something.

"Oh? And who is that?"

Good question, Ledgerman thinks. "I fear that telling you outright might ruin the surprise." He says this with a coy, flirty smile.

Kylie is familiar with this game. Male passenger, above a certain age. Alone on a cross-country flight, unable to get his mind off what all men have on their minds 24/7. And she, the perfect embodiment of it.

She smiles, one that touches the edges of her eyes. Almost looks genuine. Probably a thousand guys before him have gotten this same one.

"I see. So it's a game, then?"

Ledgerman nods. "I suppose it is."

Kylie giggles, more nerves than actual enjoyment. She looks back over the cabin behind her, confirming there isn't anything pressing that requires her attention.

This is part of the game. The naughty feeling of doing something you shouldn't in a place you shouldn't, and (for her) during a time you definitely shouldn't.

Satisfied that no one requires her attention, she turns back to Ledgerman and nestles in closer to him. Once again, her perfume overpowers him, its warmth and sweet lavender wrapping him in the warmth and luxury of femininity. Say what you will about women. They smell damn good to a man.

Ledgerman fights to keep his composure. The scent itself isn't familiar to him. But the *feeling* of it is. Finding himself tied up in it like bedsheets on a lazy morning. The warmth of another right next to you.

Kylie's hand brushes against his.

Skin-to-skin contact.

How long has it been for Ledgerman since he's felt that? Too long.

He uses his other hand to steady himself against the seat, the feeling of having a beautiful woman so intimately close with him going to his head like a few glasses of gulped-down champagne.

His face reddens, not with excitement or nerves, but with the enshrouding fog of the forgotten dream that he experienced earlier.

His mind reels, sliding toward the cliff-edge of confusion. Is this sensation a memory? And if so, a memory of what? And when? He perfectly remembers everything that's happened to him since he started on his calling, this unholy alliance between himself and whatever entity delivers him messages through the smartwatch.

He remembers nothing from the time before. If there even was one (though, there must have been, right?).

"You from New York or L.A.?" Kylie asks, flipping her hair over her shoulder.

"I'm not really from anywhere," he says, catching himself from tumbling over the cliff of confusion. Holding on for dear life as he tries to navigate through the fog suddenly enshrouding him. She has no idea how difficult of a question it is for him to answer.

Kylie smiles mischievously. "How mysterious. A real man of the road, huh?"

"I guess you could say that. Where are you based out of? L.A., I'll bet."

"How'd you guess?"

Ledgerman has no idea. "You're tan. Hard to do in New York in mid-winter."

Kylie laughs. "A regular Sherlock Holmes, this one."

Were Ledgerman trying to pick Kylie up, this conversation would be well on its way to promising. He has, however, only four more minutes to determine if Kylie is going to live or die. And if she is to live, he must determine how he's supposed to save her when the time comes. There is no clear threat present. He wishes it was as simple as just shadowing her, though that, even by itself, is difficult to pull off without being a total creep. Especially on an airplane.

Besides, if killing is the way it has to go down, it has to be done at the appointed time.

And saving her life needs to be done before he can rule out murder.

It's just then she gives him an idea.

The same hand that brushed against his hand before now reaches up, squeezes his bicep. "And not the book version, neither. I'd say you're at least the Robert Downey, Jr. one." After another squeeze, Kylie says, "Maybe even in better shape than that."

Ledgerman gives her his best half-aw-shucks, half-devious smile.

"Say, I'm thirsty. Got anything to drink in the back there?"

Kylie smiles, licking her pouty upper lip as she does so.

"I thought you'd never ask."

FOUR

Kylie expertly opens a drawer about the size of a shoebox and slips a manicured hand inside. Out come two airplane bottles of vodka—Tito's, Ledgerman is pleased to see. She grabs two plastic cups and loads them with a scoop of ice from another drawer.

"Straight?" she asks.

"Yes, I am."

She hoots with laughter, putting a hand over her mouth to keep herself quiet, but unable to stop the giggles. She peers around the corner, looking to see if she woke anybody. Then she slaps him playfully on the arm.

"You're bad."

"Can't help myself," he says, surprised this flirty strategy is actually working. He makes a mental note to try this more often, especially when the woman he's flirting with might *not* be dead three minutes from now (by his hand, no less).

Kylie pops both caps off as if by magic and pours the vodka into each glass at the same time. She sticks her chest out a little as she does so, which Ledgerman pretends—rather poorly—not to notice.

They tap cups and both take a swig. The ice does very little to soothe the burn of vodka, though on balance, Tito's isn't bad. Of course, a little time spent with ice in a shaker would be a huge improvement. But they were throttling through the air twenty-five thousand feet above the earth, after all. So beggars can't be choosers.

He must have winced after taking a sip because she says, "I thought you could handle the burn, baby. What's a matter? You don't like it too hot?"

Ledgerman takes another sip, careful not to wince at all this time.

He grabs Kylie's ass and pulls her closer. "I like it hot just fine. How about you?"

Her neck arches back, her weight held up by his arm, which he's still got wrapped around her. She doesn't know that this move, aside from being generally pleasurable for him and totally in character for the situation, is also designed to find anything on her that might be pointy or stab-y, if it comes down to him needing to kill her.

Luckily for him (in more ways than one), it's all flesh and bones. Plenty taut, for sure. But that never hurt anybody.

Not too bad, at least.

Her scent rises up, chokes him (in a good way). The movement pulls her undershirt beneath her blazer down just enough to give him a peek at the top of her breasts.

A fine, fine peek.

Then she snaps back up like a stripper at the end of her song. Leans into him, all soft hair and warmth.

"Let me freshen up, Mr. Wanderer."

She slips into the front bathroom behind her, the same one he used earlier.

Ledgerman finishes his vodka, the third sip going down easier than the first. His face is flushed, the remnants of his unremembered dream and brain fog still stubbornly clinging to his skull like an early afternoon fog in San Francisco. But the burn clears his head a bit.

Probably the increased blood flow helps, too.

He checks his watch. 5:00 p.m. on the dot.

Three minutes left until he needs to decide if Kylie deserves to live or die.

FIVE

Ledgerman looks around the kitchen area. It's nothing but plug-and-play drawers and cabinets. Like those houses of people obsessed with keeping all their possessions hidden away in secret compartments, as if they don't really live there.

Not interesting, really. Except for the drawer with the booze in it.

But also not useful.

Behind him is the plane's emergency exit door. In front of him is the other one, the exit door that they would also deplane from. To the right of that is the bathroom Kylie is in. And farther right of that is the cockpit.

Not a lot of space to find answers here. Which doesn't bode well for Kylie's chances of walking off this flight.

Ledgerman doesn't fly much, but he remembers seeing something that might be worth checking out when he entered the plane. The short bald man in front of him had a head like Mr. Clean and a body like Mr. Magoo. Carried himself the same way, wore a big heavy coat with a fur shawl collar that looked as expensive as it was ostentatious, especially on a plane to California. This was a man who hadn't a care in the world. He strutted down the jet bridge like he was in slow motion.

Upon entering, one of the stewardesses (not Kylie) took his coat and placed it in a closet right inside the emergency exit doorway in front of him. Ledgerman never saw the guy's face, but he was sure it had a look of smug satisfaction on it the entire time.

Now, he would never allow someone to take his coat (in this case, Ledgerman wasn't wearing one) but the person behind him tried to give their coat to the same stewardess. They were denied. Only first class passengers can use the closet, apparently.

Ledgerman crosses the kitchen area. A glance into the first class section tells him that everyone is either asleep or has their head down. No sign of struts-with-the-shawl-collar, but the darkness throughout the cabin makes it hard to see anyone.

At least, if Ledgerman needs to end Kylie, nobody seems to be paying much attention.

He opens the closet—like everything else, about one-fifth the size of normal, human size and tucked away like the hidden piece required to finish a damn puzzle. Inside, three coats hang on hangers, one of which is Mr. Magoo's. Seven additional hangers—all empty—remind Ledgerman that air travel is perhaps the last bastion in modern life where it is acceptable to blatantly discriminate against people because of how much less they have.

Well, that and the lines to get into sporting events.

Everywhere else it's considered bad taste. The airlines seem to have made it their business model.

Aside from the coats, Ledgerman has to squint to see what he's really looking for. Another factor of planes he didn't even realize he hated. They're too dark when trying to investigate someone.

A purse about the size of a binder. And not just any purse—this one is faux cheetah fur lined with black lace and fringe.

A purse he immediately pegs as Kylie's taste.

He unzips the top, has to practically cover his nose to lessen the heavy perfume scent pouring out the top. Holding his breath, crouched down in the tight space inside the kitchen, he flicks through the contents of the purse: a thin brown leather wallet (cheap), a thicker alligator skin wallet (expensive), and two books—*The Divine Secrets of the Ya-Ya Sisterhood* and a battered copy of *Pride and Prejudice* (if you can square those two). Beneath that is a one-quart plastic bag full of an astonishing amount of over-the-counter medications—Tylenol, Advil, Tums, etc.—band aids, tampons, an inhaler, and at least three kinds of cough drops of various colors. Ledgerman's fingers unearth a keychain with keys from three different kinds of cars, various unmarked house keys, and an electronic fob that might open a garage or the front door to an apartment building.

The rest of the items aren't much—makeup, a travel-sized hair spray.

Nothing at all to suggest foul play is afoot.

Ledgerman checks his watch. 5:01 p.m.

Unsure what to do next, Ledgerman almost puts down the purse before another flight attendant emerges from the aisle and sees that he's got it in his hand.

"What are you doing?" he says, startled by the man hidden in the shadows of the dark plane.

Ledgerman is wondering the same thing.

SIX

Ledgerman is never tongue tied.

Mainly because when he doesn't know what to say, he just shuts the hell up. Too many times he's been on the other end of a person trying to make something up on the fly. Usually, you practically have to duck out of the way of their verbal diarrhea. But he gets it—people get nervous (especially around him). They babble.

The flight attendant doesn't say anything either, just steps back, instinctively putting distance between himself and Ledgerman. Sensing—much like Kylie did before—that danger lies here in the dark.

Ledgerman means him no harm, of course. But his instincts aren't wrong. Harm may very well come to him if he interferes with Ledgerman's task here.

The entity who provides Ledgerman guidance has never explicitly told him this (or anything, really), but he *knows* it to be true: there can be no failure to perform the task in question, no matter the collateral damage.

Ledgerman tries to keep this damage to a minimum, never using more force than is absolutely necessary.

But he isn't afraid to use it, either.

It comes as very little surprise to Ledgerman (who must often stereotype in split-second moments of indecision) that the attendant is not a physically imposing man. He's never seen one who was. He stands a lean (not mean) five foot ten, buck sixty-five at the most (maybe on a day when he's bloated *and* soaking wet). White-blonde hair, almost albino. Chalky skin to match. His shoulders are straight, the posture of a dancer or equestrian. Not someone, though, who is going to physically harm Ledgerman.

But harm can come in many different ways.

"Excuse me, sir. I said, 'what are you doing?'" The attendant's (do they call them stewards?) voice rises an octave, discomfort creeping in like Jack Torrance entering a locked bedroom. His eyes dart between Ledgerman, the closet, and the rest of the airplane like a pinball.

There isn't much time for Ledgerman to explain. Not that he could. Why, I'm *snooping through a stranger's purse, hoping to find incriminating evidence that can be used as the justification to kill her,* doesn't seem like a response that would go over well here. Oh, what's that? *Yes, I understand killing is wrong. Sometimes. But you see, I have this special smartwatch that says it's all ok...*

Yeah, Ledgerman isn't sure that will fly at all.

On the other hand, he doesn't want this pipsqueak making too much noise in the next ninety seconds before doing what needs to be done.

Whether Kylie lives or dies, Ledgerman doesn't yet know (though if he can't find any reason for her to live...).

"Sir, please answer me."

The shrill tone of voice tells Ledgerman that this is close to the breaking point. A point that normal people reach once they are truly pushed to the limits of their comfort. While this might not seem an extreme example of being made uncomfortable, Ledgerman can appreciate that a flight attendant—a *steward*, he's decided, is the appropriate term—carries additional emotional baggage in their place of work. People are already dumb and rude enough before they get on a plane. Combine their nature with the third-world confines of "Economy" travel and you have a recipe for disaster. Add in all the associated security concerns, and the fact that perhaps the first priority of a flight attendant is to keep everyone on board as docile as possible (lest they think about the reality of the situation—shooting through the sky at hundreds of miles per hour, thousands of feet above the ground)?

Being a steward was damn near miracle work.

This steward—nametag reads: Alex—though, seems intent on causing trouble for Ledgerman (not that he has any hard feelings about it, hard to blame the guy for doing his job).

Unfortunately, trouble for Ledgerman also means trouble for Alex. Much more trouble than his pasty little body can handle.

Alex grabs the white plastic phone next to him but doesn't put it to his ear.

"Sir, please put the purse down and your hands in the air where I can see them."

This is not good. Ledgerman must put an end to this.

"Listen," he says, trying to keep his voice calm and non-threatening, which is tough to do when you need to yell over the hum of the jet engines.

Alex puts a hand up to stop him. "Sir, please do as I say."

"Just put the phone down, Alex. Let me explain. It's not what you think."

Alex hesitates.

"Just getting something for Kylie. No nefarious activity. Promise." Ledgerman gives Alex a big wide smile. Knows the name drop probably buys him a few extra seconds.

"Where is Kylie?" Alex asks.

That's a good question, Ledgerman thinks.

SEVEN

Alex says, "Something's not right here."

And he's right.

Ledgerman needs him to put down the phone, though. Even through the hum from the plane, he hears someone's voice on the line.

Ledgerman senses the tension returning to the man's actions and mannerisms. He's falling prey to the tight quarters of the kitchen area, the increased pressure on his ears as the plane lowers in altitude, the relative smallness of himself compared to the strange, dangerous man standing across from him.

"She's in the bathroom," Ledgerman says. No sense lying about it.

She'll be back out in a second. He checks his watch.

Been in there ninety seconds already. And now he's up against time.

Ninety seconds left before he needs to do something.

And all signs point to her dying once that time limit is up. Which is going to prove tricky, now with Alex in the mix.

Would be tricky anyway, though, on a damn plane.

He never questions the watch. It pings him with information as it sees fit. And he knows deep down that it can somehow see all things. Trusts deep in his gut that when it identifies an instance where he needs to get involved—whether by killing or saving—that it does so from some all-knowing source of fairness and equanimity.

Alex holds the phone in limbo.

If he doesn't put it down, Ledgerman will have to kick it out of his hand.

Or just kick him in general.

That would get ugly.

Luckily, he doesn't have to make that determination.

A thud against the bathroom door. Unmistakable, even over the thrum of the engines:

Dead weight.

EIGHT

Ledgerman doesn't hesitate, slams a right fist against the bathroom door to his left.

Doesn't budge. Not even a little.

He could probably hit it harder, but based on his first try he doesn't think that will do anything different. Airplane bathroom doors don't operate like normal ones. Normal ones, he has no problem knocking off the hinges.

He's never had to do that with an airplane bathroom.

Isn't even sure it's possible. After all, they fold by design.

"What was that?" Alex asks, a little slow on the uptake.

Ledgerman steps away from the door, into Alex's circle of trust. He pulls the steward close to him, so their noses almost touch. He smells the residue of Wrigley's Double Mint Gum—which tells Ledgerman the man he is dealing with might very well be mentally unstable. Only a psychopath would chew that gum, which loses its flavor within ten chews. Alex's cologne is of indeterminate brand, and Ledgerman has been standing here long enough to know that at least it lasts longer than the steward's choice of gum.

Alex tries to back up. Ledgerman's hold on his arm ensures he doesn't go anywhere.

"Hey! What the heck?"

"Quiet. Don't move."

Alex obeys, as if Ledgerman just deployed a magic spell.

Ledgerman grabs the phone from his hand and hangs it up. Then he stares Alex in the eye for a long moment, making sure the steward feels something of the gravity of what's going on, even if he doesn't actually know what that is.

Eighty seconds left before the deadline.

Content that Alex will not cause him anymore trouble, Ledgerman turns back to the bathroom door.

NINE

"Kylie?" Ledgerman says, speaking loud enough for his voice to penetrate through the folding door.

No answer.

Ledgerman presses against the door, which should fold up and in when pressed from the outside. But the indicator is turned red, meaning it's locked. And he can feel from his hand against it that the dead weight on the other end of things is too much of a counter-weight to make any progress.

At least not without crushing Kylie in the process.

"Do you have any sort of special key for this thing?" Ledgerman asks Alex.

The steward shakes his head. "There isn't even a keyhole."

He's got a point there. The locking mechanism is all on the inside of the door. Outside is just the wheel that spins to tell you not to try to enter. Someone else is already doing their business in there.

Sixty seconds left.

And Ledgerman doesn't have the faintest idea how he's going to complete his mission.

TEN

Behind them, a few passengers are leaning out of their seats and into the aisle. It's clear—probably from Alex's body language—that something is wrong up here.

And these days, that gets people's attention on an airplane.

"I need to call up to the pilot," Alex says.

"Don't. I might need your help. He's got better things to do anyway, like make sure we don't crash."

Alex seems to take this into consideration. Nods in agreement.

"There's no key to open this thing..." Ledgerman says, hoping his words will lead his mind toward the conclusion. The fog he experienced earlier hasn't fully lifted, but the adrenaline of the last two minutes is doing its best to push it offshore upstairs, "...so let's open it ourselves, shall we?"

"How are you going to do that?"

Ledgerman pokes a finger at the spinning indicator on the door, which shows red for OCCUPIED. It moves a little.

He punches it twice, the hard metal pieces sending shooting pains up through his knuckles and into his elbows. Probably there is cut skin, blood. But there will be time for that later. Probably. He's never failed a mission before. Isn't sure what the penalty is, or even if there is one. He has seen the justice the watch metes out, though, and doesn't want to find out.

Reaching two fingers into the space that he just punched loose on the lock's outer indicator, Ledgerman finds a hard and sharp metal environment that doesn't seem willing to budge. It bites him, leaving behind a small trail of blood.

Luckily, he isn't dissuaded so easily.

Thirty seconds left.

Ledgerman turns around, scanning the LEGO block structure of the kitchen. So little metal, airlines afraid of too much opportunity for stab-y behavior.

The closet.

He pushed past Alex, reaches into the closet, and grabs one of the empty hangers. Silently thanks the stewardess earlier who turned away the first plebe requesting his jacket be hung up. It would have triggered others to want their own. And that would have made for a bunch of hangers full of coats.

Ledgerman moves with an economy of motion that scares Alex. Probably it scares anyone leaning out of their seats and looking toward the kitchen, too.

He rips the hanger apart with his hands, removing the wood from the wire frame. Straightens the wire hook as if it were a pipe cleaner, then takes this newly developed shank and jams it into the loose locking mechanism he's punched some daylight into.

Three, four violent jerks of this jerry-rigged lock pick and the mechanism breaks free from the door, bouncing off the floor.

Nothing happens. The door doesn't open, doesn't loosen. Kylie doesn't stumble out of the bathroom.

"Shit."

Twenty seconds left.

"Oh gosh, you broke the door," Alex says helpfully.

Ledgerman ignores him, doesn't have the time to deal with him right now.

Ledgerman pushes against the door, finds it much more amenable to moving than it was before. Pushes a little further, gets daylight.

Kylie's dead weight still pushes back against the door, a surprisingly strong counterweight to Ledgerman's efforts. Physics can be a real bitch sometimes.

But he has daylight.

He reaches his arm through the opening he's created in the doorway. Holds the opening with his other arm, making sure not to let go, lest he crush his arm with the door in the process.

With the free hand, he open-palms Kylie on the shoulder and pushes her back away from the door. Toward the back of the bathroom.

The rest of the door opens, Ledgerman first catching himself from falling into the bathroom.

Then, catching Kylie as he tumbles out through the space where the door had just been closed.

He lays her slowly to the ground. It becomes clear to him, now with less than fifteen seconds left until he needs to complete his task, that Kylie doesn't need to be killed.

She needs to be saved. Only not from someone else. She needs to be saved from Death himself.

Her face is white and blue, like how Alex's would look if Ledgerman needed to knock him around a bit. She feels cold—scary, since it's only been seventy seconds since she went dead weight against the door.

"Oh, gosh, oh, golly, what in the world is wrong with her?" Alex says. He's got his hands up on his face like an old maid who just found out Aunt Maude died.

And how should Ledgerman know what's wrong with her? Despite the flirt show he put on, it isn't exactly like she opened up about all the ways she'd be susceptible to an early death today.

Ledgerman looks at her, practically feels the seconds ticking off his watch (though it doesn't tick, it's a digital), and doesn't know how he's going to pull this one off.

Ten seconds left.

Nine, eight, seven...

ELEVEN

Ledgerman turns around. Lunges across the small kitchen space.

Grabs for Kylie's purse inside the closet.

Rifles through her things, pulls out the big plastic bag full of random medicine.

Thanks to whatever force allows him to remember things.

Finds the inhaler. The one he'd glossed over before.

Turns back around, puts it to her blue, Rigor mortis lips like the elixir of life.

Five seconds left.

Depresses the inhaler's button.

Holds his own breath.

TWELVE

Ledgerman's watch beeps, the shrill alarm sound cutting through the kitchen area, through the thrum of the engines.

Alex is horrified, his eyes hardly moving, some unknown movie playing behind his eyes acting as his only true interface with the outside world. Shadowed faces behind him in the dark part of the plane emerge from their strange slumbers like wraiths in the aether.

The darkness of the plane's cabin seems to expand, inky blackness diffusing, leaking out and blurring the edges of Ledgerman's vision like a broken film projector.

Did he fail his task?

Kylie coughs. Once, twice. Launches into a full-bodied cough that emanates from her stomach, the muscles in her neck contracting tight against the effort.

But she develops a hue of rouge around the neck and cheeks. Color returns to her lips slowly.

Ledgerman feels a massive sense of relief, knowing that he has once again completed his task, that the smartwatch he so slavishly obeys has put him in the right place and time to positively affect the world again. He has, just in the nick of time, fulfilled his responsibility to the universe.

And avoided the unknown fate that exists were he to fail.

Kylie regains her breathing. Slowly, though Ledgerman is in no rush now. Her eyes open, wide and thirsty for the kaleidoscope of colors that life offers. True understanding now of what was so close to being lost fills her green eyes, which shine through, even despite the fear.

The emerald orbs find him, though they don't yet recognize him as the flirtatious man who shared a drink with her a few minutes earlier. Instead, they see him as the beacon upon which her new life can count its blessings—the lighthouse that guided her back to shore through stormy seas.

For his part, Ledgerman feels a constriction in his chest. Kylie isn't a bad looking woman, even after being medically choked-out for a minute and a half.

As he always does, Ledgerman never tries to steer the person he saves in the minutes after he saves them. Often, they have seen him inflict mortal damage upon others. He's happy that wasn't the case here, that Alex didn't become collateral damage. That overall, this experience was one that only had good outcomes.

That isn't always the case.

Watching people in these moments, though, gives Ledgerman an interesting glimpse into the human psyche. Into how people process the traumas of their lives. Despite being human himself, he often feels a step or two removed from truly *belonging* to the greater community of mankind. While he can sit in a restaurant and conduct a conversation, something about his unique journey also sets him apart from the crowd. He supposes this is mainly due to his own unique focus, one not shared by many. Probably not shared by any. He has no attachments, no true home, none of the obligations that make up a *normal* life, like family or friends. No real memories to speak of. No idea what may have come *before*.

He has only the calling. And it often puts him at odds with people.

Though in times like these, it also brings him closer. Within arm's reach, at least.

Two minutes after he saves her life, Kylie speaks.

"What happened?"

Ledgerman looks at the inhaler in his hands. "Whatever you need this for seems to have caught up with you. I'm guessing you fainted in there before you knew what hit you, couldn't get out."

Kylie puts a hand to her collarbone, similar to the damsel in distress in an old-timey movie.

"Gosh...that's never happened to me before. My asthma is usually under control."

Ledgerman says nothing.

"But I guess you just never know when your time might be up, huh?"

THIRTEEN

Three minutes after he saves her life, Ledgerman helps Kylie up to a seated position. Alex the steward and a number of people in the first few rows watch stunned, their journeys in the sky momentarily interrupted. Their eyes make him uncomfortable, but he's unconcerned. If he needed to kill Kylie, eyes on him would be an issue.

As it stands, he can just take whatever credit and attention from his act of heroism, minimize it as much as possible, and then disappear back into the anonymity of life and continue on his journey.

But there is still one thing left to do.

Now Kylie is ready for it.

He puts a hand on her shoulder. "Listen to me," soft at first to get her attention. Then with more gusto. "You've been given a second chance, have received a gift of sorts."

"I don't understand," she says.

They never do.

"You don't have to. Not yet. I just need you to understand that you've been given a unique gift. An extension of life that otherwise would never be available to you. And now that it *has* been made available, I want you to keep it in the back of your mind for the rest of your days. To never think of it directly, but never let it flit away too far from your mind, either."

Kylie stares at him blankly, emerald eyes wide and uncomprehending.

"Live your life. But don't hesitate to pay this back when you think you can. Little here, little there. Pass it along, huh?"

Kylie nods agreeably. Alex does too, though nobody expects him to make a damn difference in the world after this.

Ledgerman leaves Kylie with that message in the quiet and the two sit next to each other in the dark of the front kitchen area as the rest of the flight proceeds normally.

Several minutes later, the pilot comes on the intercom and says, "OK, folks, we had a bit of a medical scare up here in the front of the plane, but everything is handled now. Sorry for any confusion or fear we caused. But we are getting ready to settle in for landing. So thank you again for flying with us and hope to see you again."

"Thank *you*," Kylie says to him. "Seriously, thank you so much for saving me."

"It's nothing. Same thing anybody in this situation would have done."

Not exactly true, of course. Nobody else would be in this situation.

"What you did..." she says again, still replaying whatever memory of it she has.

"...was nothing. Seriously." Nothing she would understand, at least.

Kylie goes quiet then and leans a head against his shoulder. They sit like that as the air pressure grows and the jet engines scream out in preparation for landing.

FOURTEEN

As the plane's door opens, Ledgerman steps back and away from the medical team who comes in to take Kylie's vitals. By now the passengers are up, reaching overhead in the miniature luggage bins, ready to move about with their day.

Kylie is talking to the first EMT on the scene, a thirty-something guy with muscles like an ex-linebacker. Hopefully she can continue some of their flirty banter with him—Ledgerman will sure miss the feeling. He's grateful for the reminder of how fun it can be to enjoy the company of another. Especially another of the opposite sex.

He just knows it won't be something he gets *too* familiar with. His calling will take him away from here, a wandering divining rod of extrajudicial equilibrium.

This brings him neither joy nor self-pity. Not exactly. Instead, he finds himself...longing, perhaps, is the right word for it. A deep and depressed sense of gnawing inside. A new emotion, certainly, in a man who hasn't a need for that side of himself.

All in all, it's been a strange day, he must admit.

As the passengers start to deplane, Ledgerman slips into their exiting stream like a ghost. No goodbye. No fanfare. Simply blows away on the back of the wind.

The narrow, cramped jet bridge feels like it's a million-mile pilgrimage, him just a single pilgrim trying to make his way to the end of it.

The air is hot but not humid. Smooth Southern California charm. He notices—quite late given his usual vigilance, the last sleepy wisps of fog still stubbornly clinging to the shores of him mind—the man in front of him. The same one who'd hung his heavy, shawl-collared coat in the front closet when he got on the plane. A strange coincidence, seeing him again. And not the first Ledgerman ever experienced during his time "in the field," so to speak.

As they emerge from the jet bridge the man turns his head, as if he's forgotten something on the plane and just remembered.

Ledgerman freezes.

In profile, this man's face sends a lightning bolt of vague premonition through Ledgerman. He's never seen the man before today, he's sure. Even seeing him earlier on the plane hadn't given him any strange notions like this one.

So, what is this?

Ledgerman isn't sure, wracks his mind and condensed memories to place the man. But simply can't.

Though he occasionally experiences the odd coincidences like seeing a man who factored into the task he's called upon to perform, Ledgerman does not believe in any higher power—at least not like most people do. Instead, he believes in an ideal—a disembodied sentient communications device that he wears on his wrist.

As strange as it sounds, he knows this constant companion to be the only thing he believes in that can't be explained by science.

But he wonders now if perhaps something has shifted. If his perspective changed—or if it needs to.

Outside of the plane, in the open spaces of the terminal, the fog of his earlier dream has finally cleared. With it, Ledgerman feels like the man's image in profile has floated away with it. Turned to atmosphere. He doesn't know exactly why he associates the two with one another, but he does nonetheless.

The man turns back away from Ledgerman. Continues walking. If he has forgotten something on the plane, he just decided it wasn't worth the trouble to go back for.

Ledgerman keeps walking, deliberately and at a slower pace, to stay behind the man, his eyes following him, hoping for an epiphany as to why he looks so oddly familiar.

None comes.

Instead, the man peels off into the airport men's room.

Ledgerman, eager to put this whole strangeness behind him, decides not to wait. To simply continue on his way, waiting for the next moment that his watch vibrates.

In the meantime, he would get something to eat.

He is starving.

CALL ME BETSY

A TRUE NAME STORY

AUTHOR OF THE NOVEL *FAMILY TREE*

NIZ THOMAS

CALL ME
Betsy
xo

A
TRUE NAME
STORY

ONE

If you boiled her down to two distinct elements—the core of what she was—they would be these:

First, the steady, slapping patter of keyboard iron springs against platen on her daddy's Hermès Rocket typewriter. The sounds of fiction being created out of thin air like an alchemist turning common metals into gold. Daddy had gone another route—turning thoughts into stories. Gold always seemed to elude him.

But the typewriter's percussive action was woven into her like hidden seams on a dress.

Second, the steady, ferocious tumult of the Hudson River—known to the Native Americans as the river that flows both ways. Able to drag anybody wading in unsuspecting off into the Atlantic. They'd be halfway over to Africa before they knew what hit 'em.

There'd been a cabin upstate, just beside the banks, where the Hudson got choppy and white-capped. Where Daddy could get some peace and quiet for his writing. A place he could afford, since keeping it warm meant mostly keeping logs in the wood stove and ignoring the soot seeping into the air.

The closest thing she ever had to call home. The mix of warm milk, a rocking chair, and the open window of their one-room cabin—her only companions in sleep for those first few years.

She knew all this because her daddy had said it was so. And because she could still feel the ink-laced family yearning for myth and scrapping and danger running through her veins.

Right now, she almost had to laugh at herself for embodying all of that at once. The walking cliché that she was. Or sitting cliché, since that's what she'd been doing for the past sixty hours.

She was tucked in tight to a tin-rattling boxcar she hopped the day before yesterday. Seated directly between two crates of potatoes the size of hog pens. Surrounded by maybe a hundred more of them (though she was waiting for hour eighty before deciding she was bored enough to count). Her once-lithe body fitted in a space big enough for only a dog's crate and probably half as comfortable. It was approaching rigor mortis.

The entire boxcar smelled like raw spuds ready for slicing, dicing, and hot oil baths. The only salve was the constant rush of air as the train cut down the eastern artery of the country. The slatted sliding door off to her right provided just enough air flow to eliminate the possibility that the men unloading the car wouldn't turn up a dead body along with their delivery of potatoes. And *just* enough morning light so she could see the few feet in front of her if she needed to. Once the sun got over the horizon, the whole car would be lit up with long, strange moving shadows like a low-budget burlesque show.

Not the most luxurious mode of transportation she'd ever taken, but a free ride out of a hot and sticky situation up north wasn't something she would complain about. Not today anyway.

A steamy summer morning that only the south could produce leaked in through every crack and crevice in this slow-moving tin can. Even with the wind, it wasn't approaching cool. And the ride itself wasn't exactly a hot shot, making more stops than she cared for—and at half the speed. Beggars and choosers, though, and all that. If the freight train went any farther south, which a southern-facing train was bound to do, she'd have to figure a way of cooling herself down. At least she could gorge herself on self-combusting french fries.

By the salt on her tongue and the sticky balm in the air, she figured she was somewhere near Norfolk. Maybe headed down the coast. Or bucking inland toward the Research Triangle before hitting all points that passed for cosmopolitan in the Tighten Your (Bible) Belt. If the train banked that way, she might be able to slide into a nice fried chicken joint somewhere near Nashville. Get into some hot chicken upon arrival, extra mayo, brioche bun, extra pickles. Nothing like taking down an artery bomb your first night in a new town.

'Course it didn't matter much where she was headed. She had plenty of practice spooling up a story—hell, a whole fictional life— like a spider weaving her web. And whether she was a daddy long-legs or black widow had everything to do with her own mood, the whims of the day, and the situation she found herself in when she arrived.

Right now she was feeling just fine and alright, baby. She had that Good Vibration going—something she procured from an acquaintance back up north right before skipping town. She smoked the last of it only thirty minutes ago. The mushy mellow set in— though she never got stupid on the stuff. Not that she was doing anything on this gravy boat that a little mental distraction would have prevented.

But that wasn't how it worked for her. She just got relaxed. Zoned. A way to break a little farther into that fourth dimension. But never twice baked.

Luckily, she'd been able to slink another old school treat before crisscrossing the industrial tracks double-quick and hitching onto this slow, methodical beast. It was the sort of thing that anybody else would have looked at as trash. But it was the perfect pairing with her current state.

Get this: a cassette player. Sony Walkman. Junked, but still in working condition—white paint splattered on it like Jackson Pollock had owned the thing. A few scratches and dents, too.

Cosmetic stuff. Tossed away because to somebody else, it was obsolete trash, baby. Today it was all on-demand, gimme-gimme-now. It was all *in the cloud*. Which was fine, except it took away the serendipity of the world. Put you in the vortex of information of your own choosing. Because from her perspective—chemically altered as it was—there wasn't a red cent of problem with this here Walkman.

In fact, it punched above its weight, sweeping her away to the feet up, windows down, radio blasting feeling of high school and a semester of college and all the slow-riding *drift* that came after.

All rolled into one little obsolete gadget.

Maybe that Vibration she caught back up north was a little greener pastures than she thought. Which was far out enough for her. There wasn't much else to do until they hit a place that wouldn't look twice toward the spud train riding through town, so she could hop off and spin up her new story.

Her throwback present came with an even better consolation prize: an actual cassette inside. And not just any old juked-up mix tape ripped from radio tracks, with bleeding edges where your song melded into the high-pitched-cool-dude talk of the DJ—your friend one minute and the next, he's ready to hawk you women's undies or sugar smacks or cancer sticks just to keep his gravy boat rolling.

No, no, no. This cassette was the real deal, you feel?

Unfortunately, it was only a single.

Fortunately, it was a good one.

And something about the high, the heat, the spud-tinted fresh air wafting downstream through the rattling boxcar slats up ahead of her felt like the universe designed this moment just for her. Conspired to give her precisely everything she required to fully appreciate it.

And appreciate she did.

The slow-drip crooning that opened the song was like a date's coat opening up against a cold, bleak night. It ushered her in. As natural as accepting a gentleman's hand and a crook inside his coat during a time of frosty discomfort. And sure, there might have been an ulterior motive—a little grabbing here, a little groping there. But she'd worry about that later.

For now, she closed her eyes and let the harmony bring her into the mix.

Once the sweet-molasses drip of the guitar kicked in, followed immediately by the polite-and-sincere baseline and drum parts, she was already halfway into bed with the cut—a smooth, slow jam of Americana that took her halfway around the world in the blink of an eye. But it always brought her back to the good ole U-S-A of her early days. At least her early days in spirit. She wasn't old (though she wasn't about to put a number on it for you). This song was ancient compared to her—having been conceived maybe thirty years before her. But Daddy always played records like these when she was coming up. So it made her feel like she grew up in that era, too.

This song made her feel like she sidled up to a cherry red leather stool at the milkshake counter with a nickel and a dream of chocolate vanilla swirl. Like she just put money in the jukebox and was waiting for the prom king to finish football practice and come around to ask her for a date.

It was wholesome as all get out. Not exactly her bag. But right now, for whatever reason, it was *just fine.*

All the while, the crooning continued and she leaned back against her extra-extra-large side of almost-fries in their wooden crate and bobbed her head to the beat.

The song was "Ballad of Ole' Betsy" by The Beach Boys. She didn't know the words or the meaning or the history behind the song, but she didn't care. It was just her, the Walkman, and the subtle whine and shake of the cassette tape telling her that everything was going to be A-OK, even though there wasn't a damn thing in her life to back it up.

Nothing other than this moment right here, which, despite every hardship that had preceded it, was peaches and cream, baby.

Just as the cut wound down to the end of the tape—a momentary lapse in the all-out jelly-jam she was immersed in — the player whined and shrieked on her like a guinea pig with too much sugar in its water bottle. The tone touched a nerve deep inside her ear—totally harshing her high. She spasmed, pressed pause, unable to allow herself to hear that sound for one more second. If she had, it might have been the last thing she ever heard. And wouldn't that be a damn shame?

When she paused the music, she heard two things.

Strange, since she hadn't heard hardly anything since she hopped this joyride. Though loud trains and pumped-up music in your headphones tended to drown out other noises.

The first sound: the intermittent low-power mode of trains across the country. Switching tracks, taking a catnap. Whatever you wanted to call it. They were like half the men she'd been with—if you don't count the other half. All bold-faced youthful exuberance until you asked them to change course. *Then* they hit the pillow like a thousand pounds of bricks just got read a bedtime story. Only thing they ever did faster was head for the door—though they only tended to do that much later on, when things got the way she liked them.

Complicated.

The second sound—which was only possible because of the quiet provided by the slowdown: the rumbling scrape of metal-on-metal. An industrial metal rocker's dream, maybe. But not the sort of thing a freight hopper wants to hear. It meant either the train was ready to head off the rails or there was somebody coming. Maybe somebody already here. A maintenance man, maybe. Or a coal-shoveler. Looking for a place to lay his head.

Or worse: there was a 'bo-rustler afoot.

If the train went off the rails, there wasn't much she could do. C'est la vie.

If it was someone who worked on the train, it wouldn't be an issue. Probably they wouldn't see her, even. She was tucked away behind and between crates big enough to hold a full-grown tiger. Most people milling about the train were either people like herself or workers looking for a spot to lie down. Preferably one that wouldn't end with a massive crate to the forehead.

The rustler, though. Kind of a wildcard. They didn't always work on the train, proper. Sometimes they were independent contractors, paid direct by the train company's owners. Men (always men) that had a vested interest in keeping things neat and orderly on their precious metal prize ponies. And they didn't care if that meant a few hobos or down-on-their-luck hustlers needed to pay the price to keep them that way.

So a rustler...that could be trouble.

Which meant it could be interesting.

Rustlers these days—much like herself—were a throwback to an older, simpler time. Back when hobos were a "scourge" on the American train world. Daddy had written a few pulp stories about the hobo life way back when, after trying and failing to sell the same stories to the slicks—which branded him everything from a communist to Satan's red-headed stepchild. Those fated attempts all but ensured he never made a single cent off the glossies. That was how she got so enamored with the lifestyle.

Unlike so much of the modern world (certainly the world of music, as the dilapidated guinea pig screamer in her hand so aptly proved), a rustler's job hadn't changed all that much. It was still: find hobos, get rid of them. Not rocket science. And none of these big venture capital funds that dominated headlines were particularly interested in introducing cutting-edge tech in the space.

Something creeping up the back of her spine told her that being able to hear what was coming would be important. And she was pretty sure it wasn't just her butt having gone to sleep.

She pulled off the headphones. Eager to assess the situation. Only the left headphone had a pad on it, so the tip of her right inner ear still ached from where the bare plastic dug into place. But it would be easier to hear her surroundings without them in. And until she could get a fix for the demented squealing, they weren't doing her any good.

Her eyes immediately darted to the single closest point of entry to her: the open grate sliding door off to her right. Luckily, it was easy to see if anybody was coming from that direction. Their outline would be visible against the silhouette of the morning light. If she were playing the odds, someone coming at her from that angle wouldn't be a friendly. Conductors and coal-shovelers and maintenance grease monkeys were more likely to use the simpler and safer option of stepping between cars. Less likely to end up a pile of mush and crunched bones, stopping up the rail wheels because of an overhanging tree branch.

Rustlers could come at you from any angle. And they didn't always have the same penchant for mundane safety considerations.

But she detected no movement from the side sliders. Just the ever-present *whoosh* of the wind, the constant flowing companion when you were just letting yourself fly free as a bird. It was the sound she'd been jonesing on recently, before lighting up and putting on the headphones. And a strong case could be made it was the sound she'd been jonesing on her life entire—in one way or another. Because she always found a way back to the road.

Or, more often than not, the tracks.

The road and the tracks had their problems, sure. But they always provided the *whoosh* of movement and adventure. Sometimes it was so loud, you didn't even notice your whole life fly by with it.

She closed her eyes and listened closer.

The lazy-bones train was drifting through its dead zone. High-stepping, like. Keeping an eye out for land mines, like she witnessed during a strange period overseas where she traveled through Laos. Methodical men with marbles for eyes and no more than eight and a half fingers. Looking for historical artifacts that just happened to go boom.

Didn't they all?

Here, the train's hundred-plus tons shifted on four-inch thick slabs of steel. The slightest problem with either one spelling little else but doom and gloom for her. Her, and America's proverbial blood supply of groceries and grain and cattle and who knows what all else this beast carried. If the feeling creeping up her back was a derailment, there wasn't much could be done about it now. But how would the supermarkets sell their sugar-bombs tomorrow?

Somewhere far off was a whistle—either feeding time or another cargo heading back up north, doing the dance the way this one would be doing pretty soon.

Nearer, there were seagulls screaming out. Probably circling the train line as it rolled down the coast, hoping it might drop off some scraps they could swoop on down and scavenge. There wouldn't be anyone rooting for derailment more than the damn gulls.

It wasn't the gulls that worried her, though.

A second crank of metal told her she hadn't just been imagining things. That her wacky tobacky wasn't in control of her.

This time, the sound became clear: doors sliding around on the other end of the boxcar. Got her back tightened up against the spud crate. Telling her which muscles could use a stretching. Which ones had plumb given up already. Up in a hackle, like a cat being sprayed with water. She'd ridden a lot of trains in her day. And that sound wasn't a normal part of business.

It was the part that made things interesting.

Somebody was here alright. The real question was: who?

She didn't get nervous. Didn't ball up and start sweating. In fact, she took a deep breath and closed her eyes again. For a brief moment, she wished for the chance to go back to only minutes ago, when she was enjoying a mellow moment alone.

Only then she remembered who she was. And that mellow moments—while nice—didn't quite do it for her. Otherwise she'd be holed up in a suburban enclave somewhere, sipping down her first dirty martini of the day and locking the kids in the basement (*with toys*, Alma, don't go calling protective services).

Yet her whole life had been an avoidance of that in one way or another. So it seemed that something deep down inside her was telling her that wasn't the life for her.

The door she just heard was near the other end of the car, anyway. Nothing else around her to indicate trouble. No reason to get all riled up just yet. That would only make the situation worse. This wasn't an ambush—if it was even anything at all.

So this rustler, if that's who it was, would have to rustle a fair bit to find her squished into the back like she was. If it was a coal-shoveler, he'd shove off and get to napping. And if it was a conductor who was back here, well, it was as likely he had a lady friend with him as that he, too, would be looking for a nap. Possibly his lady friend was even some other hobo picked out from on up the line. And this might be his lunch break. And they might just be doing what grown folks who find themselves with a little too much time and a little mischievous bug in them do.

And she certainly didn't have any issue with that. So long as they didn't tread on the road she was bumping on. Just two horny, lonely folks trying to find some closer connection with the universe. She could dig that. Could *grok* it, as she might have said if she'd gone down a different path in life. One that had been more in touch with nature, *man*.

But she hadn't. She'd hoed her own road—and never had to hoe in the process. And her road, if it could be defined by anything, was defined by what she did next.

Like a cat, she gracefully went from seated to crouched. Like she flipped a switch. She arched her back and stayed low beneath the top crate of Idaho golds to her front, somehow staying clear of the opening between boxes on her left. She ducked to her right beneath a cantilevered crate that served to block anybody passing through the car from seeing her, bending and swooping around like she was Catherine Zeta Jones breaking into the laser vault.

Despite the safe play of simply not moving—just going statue-still and riding out whatever was coming—she couldn't help herself.

That was the thing about her—she liked the danger. Got a little dirty. Just like these spuds had been, before they were scrubbed clean and made presentable the way society expected of them.

She crossed behind an extra sturdy stack of boxes, stopped, then peered out around the left edge. Looking on down the somewhat open vantage point of the boxcar now. Not open enough for a full-on panoramic view of the place. But enough to see who it was coming in to disturb her blissful one-ness with the ole Universe.

It was a man, of course. It was *always* a man.

His back was to her, knees bent, both arms up in front of him as he slid the boxcar door into place with a grating *thunk*, keeping his arms on the iron door handles, bracing against the inevitable back-bounce of the door. These trains were made before the days of hydraulic lifts and pin dampeners. These were the roll-up-your-sleeves, grease-up-the-wheels doors. The coal-on-your-face-when-you-crack-open-a-punch-can-of-beer-after-the-day's-done doors. This wasn't no Amtrak, baby.

And this man—dressed in a long, brown leather duster, tanned, and worn in like he'd had it on since taking it from a Native American a hundred years ago—he knew how to operate in this sort of environment.

Outside, the train must have been going around a long bend because as the door bucked back, she got a glimpse of longleaf pines and thick, mosquito-infested hovels taken root amongst the shrubbery. Beyond that was a hazy morning, obscuring the lazy waves slapping against the seashore with as much enthusiasm as a trick at her last appointment for the night.

The light against the enclosed darkness of the boxcar blinded as the train ambled along its loping bend without any power. For a moment, it was serene and peaceful.

The rustler handled the bucking door with ease. What she imagined were big strong muscles beneath his duster. They absorbed the shock of the door without so much as a jitterbug backwards. Strong hands for that. Strong back and legs, too. Not muscles, even. Just live wire sinew and repetitive stresses—probably a lifetime of them. This was a hard man. Like steel and iron melted down into a single bullet, loaded in and fired off straight through your heart. Before he even turned away from the door, she knew she was in for more than she'd bargained for a few minutes ago, laced-up and face out to the meandering wild wind of the road.

It might be a fun adventure, anyway.

Or it might be the last one.

The rustler got the door corralled in his easy, strong way. Then he turned away from it and back toward the boxcar. He had a thick chin and nose like a boxer who never learned to duck out of a punch. Cauliflower ears that suggested his love for getting punched in the face was maybe only outshined by his passion for getting choked-out in street brawls. She couldn't see a lick of definition through the duster but knew for certain now that his shoulders, arms, and hands were as thick and sturdy as an unused catcher's mitt.

His beard was easily the least surprising thing about him. And despite the fact she couldn't see below his waist, it was obvious that he wore decade-old shit kickers who had seen their fair share of action out on the road. Maybe he'd even replaced the soles with something like rubber. Better for traction when he patrolled the cars. Never a great place to fall, especially when rolling through humid country so close to sea.

But all that went in and out and through, not more than a half-second. Three quarters, tops.

What she was really watching after were his eyes. Those two soul-windows that would tell her more about this fella than if he were wearing a pair of ballerina slippers and a pink tutu around his waist.

Only she couldn't make out his eyes from this far away. Bad light in here, now that the door was closed again. She squinted, sure. But his face was part-blocked, given the angle and the boxes stacked haphazardly between the two of them, obscuring her view. The part of his face she *could* see was all shadow beneath his Stetson hat brim.

Did she need to see his eyes, though? Instinct said no. That this man was exactly what he appeared to be: trouble for someone like her.

Still, the eyes would tell her for certain. Seeing them would determine her next move. Seeing them would get the measure of him. She'd seen killers and thieves, priests and saints. And everything in between, all colors of that morality rainbow. She always knew where they fell from one long glance into their eyes. She needed to see this man's before figuring what to do next. Only she didn't want to give up her location. She might have danced on the edge of safety, but she wasn't a chump. It was possible he didn't suspect a thing. No telling what he was doing here. Maybe he *was* just coming in for a nap.

Only that tingling sensation up her back told her otherwise. This fella being here for a nap didn't feel right. Not now that she'd seen him.

He probably didn't even nap as a baby.

She watched him a moment. He didn't move—not his head or his hands or his chest. Like he wasn't breathing. Until he made a strange clicking sound with his tongue, the way someone does when they just realized they left something behind, like their keys or their wallet.

She spun around, moving silently behind another stack of boxes farther toward the outer edge of the boxcar to her right. Careful not to silhouette herself against the slatted doors. But there were two nice stacks of spud crates that she nestled between where she could watch this man in the relative security of being hidden.

Not that there was any real security here. Not anymore. Only a fool in her position would see a man like this and think security still existed.

Not to mention the fact that getting found out by a rustler could mean all sorts of bad things.

For one, there was the trouble with the law. That wouldn't be *so* much trouble to her, since she didn't plan to stick around long enough in whatever state this was to see the judge. Plenty of bad eggs in the basket once you tangled with the boys in blue, though. Or in black, depending on which branch—federal or state or county—you ran across. Any single one of them could spoil your omelet. Getting caught and finding yourself in the hands of Johnny Law could be bad *before* you ever saw the inside of a courtroom.

But then there were the other troubles. The nitty-gritty, as one of her marks back up north might have said. It was poor-person for "fine print," only—bless their heart—they never had enough money to even be fine-printed themselves. There wasn't any profit in hoodwinking those without anything to take.

Nitty-gritty in this case meant the bad stuff that could happen to you that wouldn't occur to most people.

Rustlers, by their nature, were tyrannical. Their train, their rules. Their kingdom. The potential troubles for matching wits with a fella like that were legion. And very much contingent on the particular rustling bastard. It was just as easy to get taken into the railroad company's equivalent of the school principal for a slap on the wrist as it was to find you were in the hands of the wrong rustler. One who determined justice in an altogether different way.

One road led to a slap on the wrist (or the bum) by a bespectacled ivory-tower-sitting-cross-legged man who was more concerned with pinching pennies than he was with justice.

And the other—well, that led you down an altogether different road. That led you into the private throes of some sick, deranged, and often very specific childhood fantasy gone horribly wrong.

That was a place that even someone as addicted to the thrill and the burn as she was simply didn't want to be.

Of the bad men that rustled boxcars, some were out for cash. Fiendishly stealing anything and everything a hobo might have on them. Not the best target to rob—banks, for one, would be more lucrative. But what banks had in spades—namely: security, institutionalized federal protection, guns, and big buildings with locked cages to keep you out or keep you in—hobos tended to lack.

Some were out for bruises. Wouldn't be the first profession that attracted that certain kind of man. A pugilist. A flesh pounder. Someone who liked to work on their glove game—only they usually left the gloves behind. Fellas that too often got too rough. Schoolyard bullies who never really left the schoolyard.

And who knows the reason? Maybe it was too much to drink.

Maybe it was too much anger. Or maybe he was just a sadistic sono-fabitch. But either way, rustlers like that just lived to find conflict and mete out justice against the relatively weak and powerless in such a way that bruises and blood were assured. They just wanted the chance to inflict and witness.

'Cause that's exactly what they liked. And why they got into this racquet in the first place.

Then there were the ones who were out for something else. Clothes. As in, they'd make you take yours off, hold them out 'til they caught a breeze coming off the coast. Let go, watch them whip away on the air like Canada geese come wintertime.

As soon as the clothes were out of sight, of course, the game changed. The appetizer course was finished.

For dinner: pain and humiliation.

Not so different from the bruising rustlers. There would still be blood. It just came as a byproduct. Because this sort of rustler was out for the squeal. The breathless plea of a choking throat. A spanking that veers off from disciplinary and deep into the Core Inferiority Range, where the sick and the sadistic play.

These, of course, were the rustlers she needed to be most wary of. That any woman alone did. The kind of predator who wanted nothing more than an easy, vulnerable, and voiceless lay. The lay, frankly, was probably the least important part. They took it one step farther than the bruisers. And some liked to take a leisurely stroll beyond even that.

These were men that needed to feel *power*—total, unbridled. To exert it. To dominate. And nowhere better to hunt and take your rightful tribute than within the untamed wild confines of the boxcar train.

The main question she needed to ask her: which one was this fella?

The train kicked back into gear. Scraping wheels and creaking metal swaying this way and that, all picking up steam and moving as one multi-thousand-pound unit. Power was back, meaning the wind would be whipping away the smell of potatoes, now thick in the air from a reduction in airflow. Soon, the boxcar would turn into an orchestra complete with a screaming industrial string section and the guttural, heavy baseline of side rods, crank pins, and pistons *chug-a-lug-lugging* their way down the track. Pretty soon, she wouldn't have a guess as to the rustler's location if she lost sight of him.

And if he caught her—and he was one of the bad ones—nobody would be able to hear her scream.

She peered around a beat-up stack of boxes filled with earthy red potatoes. The rustler was right where she last saw him. Didn't appear to have moved an inch. From here, she still had trouble seeing his eyes. If they were open, the whites weren't visible beneath his hat. His whole face was shrouded in shadow. Like a demon ready to start wielding his power in the new dark.

He swayed with the train. His only movements. Like he was part of it. Comfortable. It really picked up steam now, the sounds of the passing wilderness now mere afterthoughts. The mellow Beach Boys cassette hardly more than a distant dream.

On the precipice of turning into a nightmare.

She didn't want to act all damsel in distress. She'd been in bad situations with bad adversaries—both men and women, and sometimes the women were worse.

But this man seemed different. Not in a good way. She didn't yet quite know who he was, other than the fact that he could handle himself and looked to have a particular penchant for fighting.

The train screamed along a bend in the tracks, enough so she almost lost her footing and had to place a hand against the stack of spud boxes beside her. The box shifted, teetering in the direction of the turn.

For a breathless second, she watched as the box tumbled over and slammed onto the ground with a thud that might as well have been a GPS ping. Spuds spilled all over the floor, making some McDonald's franchise manager in Bowling Green or Biloxi or Knoxville supremely unhappy. She wondered if he'd keep her awake until she cried, or if whatever he was here to do would be quick and final so he could move along. And hopefully she could, too.

But the box didn't topple over. It shifted just enough to scare her. Not enough to alert him to her presence, the scraping wood drowned out by the sounds of train on track, steel on steel.

The train righted itself and kept on going.

Crisis averted.

She thought.

That was, until he said, "I can *smell* you in here."

She froze like the train just plummeted into the Arctic Circle.

Mainly, she wondered: do I smell?

"And it ain't because you stink. This here car is one hundred percent starchy Murphy's. You smell like a nice lady. So why don't you come on out and we can do this thing the easy way."

The way this man operated titillated and confused. But mostly, it scared.

Still, she wasn't sure saying anything was a good idea. Her mind raced through all the available possibilities, jumping from one eventuality to the next and back again. The only other sound in the whole damn car was the regular *tit-tat-tit-tat* of the train cruising south.

Finally, she got her head back about her. Too much Good Vibration, maybe. She wasn't one for long-term plans or processing through every eventuality. That just wasn't her at all.

"Easy compared to what?" she said, loud enough so he could hear it over the train. She didn't dare move from her spot. His small sample size of communication didn't tell her much, but it definitely didn't rule out danger. It could have ruled out any other eventuality. But not danger. Anyway, from where she stood hidden against the side of the boxcar, she could watch his reaction.

It was something that could have been a smirk or grimace. Pain or pleasure, baby.

She still couldn't see his eyes, though.

"So this isn't the first time you've played this game." This through either the smirk or the grimace. His voice didn't give away either emotion.

"I don't know *what* you're talking about."

"So it's the hard way, then?"

He still hadn't moved from just inside the boxcar door. She got a strange feeling in her gut—in her everywhere, really. Something was off here. No rustler she ever tussled with had ever been so slow to act. So...methodical.

He said, "It's alright, you know. If you want to do it that way. Seems like you may not know any different."

"And what do you know?" she felt a bit bolder now. Like this whole train was riding straight off the rails. And she was fixing to go down with it. Better to lean forward and put your arms out like a bird.

Enjoy the ride on down.

The train jerked right. She was lucky. Had the rusted steel of the slatted door to lean into, stop her from getting tossed. She hit the side without any parachute, though. The slatted siding would leave a mark. Maybe draw blood. But she was lucky not to have made any noise.

The rustler, though...he didn't move at all. And he had nothing to hold on to or lean against. He just stood stock-still. Like he had magnets in his feet or something.

The train righted itself and he said, "I know about what I'm doing right now. Know all about it, in fact."

"And that's it?"

"That's about it. Yeah. No need to know much else."

"So you're ignorant, then."

"Never claimed anything else, did I?"

"Never claimed that, either."

"Say, I never met a lawyer hobo before. What's your name, counselor?"

She thought about this, how he was a smartass. What did that tell her about him? She couldn't be sure. Right now, he was just a witty rustler who seemed awful confident in himself. Either he was experienced, good, and a sporting fellow, or he was downright sick in the head and liked a complicated situation as much as she did.

He liked the chase, maybe. She could dig that.

But did he like the kill, too?

He still hadn't moved a single step from his position near the door. Like he took up roots.

She figured to hell with it. He wants to be a smartass, two can play that game.

"Call me Betsy."

"Obliged to meet you, Betsy. But I didn't ask what I should call you. I asked for your name."

How could he have known it wasn't the real thing? A shiver that defied the odds ran up and down her spine like the Tasmanian Devil after a long night down in a Colombian whorehouse.

"What's your name then, hoss?"

Another smirk. Or a grimace. Pleasure or pain.

"You can call me Genghis Khan, Betsy. Because no matter if you're running, hiding, or fighting, the full force of my epic dominance is coming straight for you. And there ain't nothing you can do about it."

Pain, then. Though for this guy, was there even any difference between the two?

"A history buff, I see. So much for ignorance."

"Objection. Asked and answered."

Betsy's heart crept up into her throat. Sweat pooled around her lower back. The breeze seemed impotent against the heat. The car had only gotten hotter since this fella rolled in. And not hotter in a good way. More like it was reaching a broil. The sun baking the outside of this, the last of the tin cans she might ever see. The smell of uncooked potatoes was overwhelming, just a hint of ocean air mixed in. It got any hotter in here, there was a good chance this car would at its destination full of enough boiled potatoes to keep all of Ireland fed for the next year or so.

Betsy pictured the rising sun outside burning an orange hole through the ozone like a blowtorch against an igloo. Pictured Genghis Khan throwing her body off this train. Her bones'd be bleached inside of a month with heat like this. Maybe less.

"Big talk for a man who roams trains all by his lonesome."

"I like being alone. Something about it that tests a man's mind. Either it hardens or it softens."

"Isn't that how it always is with men? Most men, it's the latter."

Genghis Khan laughed. A baritone chord that punctured the boxcar like a gunshot.

"Well, Betsy, I sure am glad to make your introduction. Sounds like you need some exposure to a real man."

"When you find one, send him my way."

That same strange expression passed over the lower portion of his face. He turned his head slightly, nose toward the ceiling.

"Never mind about the name. Betsy will be fine for today, I guess. Won't do you much good, anyway."

"Why's that?" she asked.

The rustler clicked his tongue again—a primal animal sound that made her feel gross.

"'Cause I got you right where I want you. And your name could be Jesus Christ Cometh and it wouldn't do you no good now."

Betsy's blood ran cold as the rustler's head turned—sudden and with an alien precision.

It turned directly toward her.

She pulled back behind the crate, though she knew it wasn't quick enough. Toward the front of the car, she heard heavy, thudding footsteps—rubber-bottomed shitkickers with either metal spurs or metal toe caps jangling against the corrugated steel floor of the car.

Her heart rate had gone from Good Vibrations and a Beach Boys croon to a heavy metal encore performance. A guitar opening like Satan's bargain. A confident, naughty thing that would have pulled a girl like her—at a younger and more naïve time in her life—onto the road less traveled. The hippie-dippie weirdo bus, Day-Glo in her eyes and on her clothes and inside her heart. Instead, her heart was filled with the detritus of a life lived on the edge and on the move. And right now, a hummingbird at a Megadeth show would be gasping for air. The first bass riff punched through the floorboards like she was the dark horse at Indy 500, waiting for the last second nut punch to propel her straight up the side wall until the checkered flag sparkled the whites of her eyes.

The drums rumbled like approaching summer rain. She felt faint, like her chest might explode.

And all the while she couldn't stop herself from sweating.

"Nothing in this world can help you now, Betsy."

She almost believed him. But she never truly believed anybody who said something like that. And there'd been plenty of bums over the years who'd tried to get one over on her and pull her down into the depressing muck that so many people got stuck in.

They always left one thing out, though.

Her.

"You ever wonder, maybe, if going looking for the sort of woman who rides the rails is a wise idea?" She said this to try to buy some time. Maybe to cause him to stop walking, consider his response.

She leaned forward to peek around the crate she hid behind.

The rustler did stop to consider his response.

But he was still looking directly at her.

Only looking wasn't the right word for what he was doing.

Maybe it was the distance, which he'd closed to about fifteen feet. Or the brightness from the rising sun streaming through the open slats of the boxcar, situated at her back. Or maybe he'd tipped his Stetson up and farther back on his head.

But she got a good look at his eyes.

Or, where his eyes used to be.

From getting a look at the whole thing now, his face wasn't marked by the cauliflower ears or the beard or the grin-grimace (and would he just make up his damn mind about it, anyway?).

It was marked by the callused pits where his eyes used to be.

He was blind.

And yet he seemed able to see her just fine.

He gave her a grin that turned her stomach inside out.

"Smile, Betsy. You're on doomsday camera."

Without thinking, she pulled back and slammed into the slatted doors behind her, then slid down until her bum found the floor. There was a single three-stack of crates in front of her.

She slinked down, head between her knees. Desperate to avoid his non-gaze. Wanting to shrink away from existence.

His footsteps continued. *Thud-thud*. Getting louder. Closer.

The same preternatural click she'd heard before followed his footsteps. Then again. *Click-click*. Quick. Rapid succession. She had no idea what it was. Maybe some weird tick he had. Like Tourette's.

"Come out, come out, wherever you are." The words rattled around this tin can car like sharpened jacks being thrown against the wall. There was something about the acoustics in here that seemed to echo the sound. And all she wanted was for it to be quiet—to leave her alone. She pressed down tighter into a ball, her whole body contracting as she did. The cassette player in her hand jammed into her palms. She was white-knuckling it. "On second thought, you might as well keep trying to hide. Maybe I *won't* find. Besides, you already forfeited your chance at the easy way out of this."

For once in her life, she didn't know what to do. Sat frozen in place. The only reason he hadn't found her just yet was the haphazard nature of the boxes, strewn about the boxcar in seemingly no order. It was the same reason she'd chosen this car to hide out in. Easy to take a nap and tuck herself away, out of sight.

Of course, she didn't account for someone looking for her who didn't have any damn eyes.

The callused pits flashed in her mind's eye again, sending a slice of sharp fear, served cold, up the back of her neck.

Wood scraped against metal. Him moving crates out of his way. How in the hell did he even see them? And how did he know which direction to move them?

Another clicking sound. Maybe twelve feet away now. Approaching from the same direction. Dead ahead. Her legs wouldn't move. She couldn't get up.

"I guess I was wrong about you, Betsy."

The words grabbed her. Shook her. But still, she couldn't get up.

"How's that?"

Another scrape of a crate somewhere behind the ones in front of her. They were now the only thing standing between her and him.

"I thought you had a little more *oomph* to you."

Hell, she used to, didn't she?

She stood up on shaky legs, using the metal siding of the boxcar to steady herself. The wind whipped behind her, just inches from the door. She didn't want to die here. Didn't want her bones to get bleached. Not here. Hell—not ever, anywhere.

If she had any tricks up her sleeve, now would be the time to use them.

The top crate on the stack in front of her disappeared and slammed down onto the ground somewhere on the other side of the boxcar.

In its place was the rustler. Only feet away now.

The crate must have weighed a few hundred pounds. He made it disappear like an empty cardboard box.

She could see him now, in all his hideous glory. Confident. Not a question in his mind he'd catch his quarry. Probably already thinking about what he was going to do with her.

She shuddered, visions of squids, spiders, worms, bats, and all other creepy-crawly things flashing across the front of her eyelids. Giving her the creeps. Sending shivers not just up her spine, but out to her fingers and toes and back again.

He was about four feet away now. Two crates—one stacked on top of the other—stood in his way. Almost close enough he could reach out and grab her. Up close, he was far bigger than she thought. Six-seven, probably. Ringing the register near three hundred pounds of solid slab. Like if someone took a steer from the refrigerated car and brought it back to life, mad and ugly as all hell. He smelled like spices—cinnamon and paprika. And up close he was even more beat-up and worn in than she could tell from afar.

But the eye pits were by far the most frightening part of him.

And he still somehow stared right at her.

She took a step left. His head tracked with her.

She went back right. Same thing.

A slow simmer of a smile crossed his face. This time, no doubt that it was all pleasure. No grimace here.

"I guess I was wrong about you, too, Genghis."

He stood up. Not quite straight. More like a bear might stand up before attacking an intruder to their territory.

"How so?"

"I thought you'd be more interesting. I'm already bored."

She backed herself up against the slatted door. Taking one last look at this pit-eyed freak, she expertly unlatched the door with one hand and slid it open.

The rush of wind burst through the door's opening like a river breaking a dam. Had she not been holding on to the handle with her free hand, it might have knocked her back into the car. Into him.

The steep drop into the deep gorge below her almost pulled her out of the vertigo.

They must have veered over a section of track that cut back inland because the ocean was a few miles away. An escape that might as well have been on another planet. Directly beneath them was a deep and raging river that stretched out east away from her, toward the sea.

All up along the edges of the river were two vertical stone faces that looked slick as glass and high as half the buildings in New York City.

The tracks seemed made of toothpicks. They were laid atop a bridge that looked outmatched compared to the weight of the train. Hardly anything beneath her to stop a fall.

Not until you hit water, anyway.

"Thinking about jumping to avoid your fate?" He said this with a smug tone to his voice.

She thought she felt his breath on the back of her neck. Spinning around, he wasn't quite that close. But he was staring directly at her like a just-returned G.I. looked at his wife.

If the G.I. hated her, that is. And meant her all sorts of unnamable harm.

"Guess not," he said. A big wicked grin cut across his ugly face.

She wasn't sure what to do. Jumping was probably a death sentence.

But at least it would be quick.

"End of line, Betsy."

"Looks like it."

He took another step closer. Paused. Clicked his tongue several times—fast and with enough *oomph* behind it that some deep and repressed memory inside Betsy's mind jarred itself loose.

It wasn't a nervous tick.

"I sure hope you don't jump."

"Why not? Ain't you planning to do me a load of harm?"

"I sure am. But it's better if I do it. Better for you, too."

"*Oh really?* Bowl me over. What luck."

He shrugged. "My way, you at least walk away." He paused a beat. "Well, you'd live, anyway."

He clicked again, pointing his mouth past Betsy and out the door. His head jerked side-to-side. Quick, almost imperceptible motions.

"That way?" he shook his head. "I'm not so sure you could say the same."

He was probably right about that. Betsy could see the gorge out of the corner of her eye.

It looked like Death personified.

"Right. Guess you're not jumping." He stretched his fingers out in front of him. "You want to say anything before we get started?"

She furrowed her brow, edging herself backwards. The wind

once again whipped about, this time almost sucking her out of the speeding train car.

"You're so sure I'm going with you, are you?"

He shrugged and opened his hands wide. As if to show her that his way would be better.

"I sure hope so. Would love to hear you squeal before you start sobbing."

What a bastard. Betsy wondered how many others he'd done this to.

He pressed forward, using one arm to knock aside the top crate between them. It tumbled over, falling to the floor with a thud. Sending spuds rolling in all directions. One fell over the side.

Betsy watched it for a brief moment. It splattered into the wind once it careened off the bridge, like a bug against a windshield.

The rustler slammed both hands down on top of the lone crate left between them. Clicked his mouth again.

His empty, callused eye-pits bore directly into Betsy.

He reached for her across the crate. She could almost feel his vice grip hands. Capable of manhandling a thousand-pound door or a few hundred pounds of these crates.

What might they be able to do to her?

And for how long?

He stood up straight. Clearly ready to get on with it. He clicked his tongue one last time.

And this time, it all finally came into focus for Betsy.

In the back of her mind, she'd been trying to access the memory. The one he jarred loose a moment ago.

Before it even came rushing back to her, though, she reacted.

It was either that or jump.

Betsy pressed play on the cassette player in her hand and heard the guinea pig whine and squeal as the cassette tape rolled forward. She cranked the volume knob up to maximum.

The rustler jittered like she just zapped him with a cattle prod. His head went backward and forward. Left and right. He stepped back, uneasy on his feet. Like all that muscle and strength just got shredded up into a trash can and lit on fire.

Just to check, Betsy pressed pause. The rustler shook away the cobwebs and seemed to steady himself.

Clicked his tongue again. Five, six, seven times. Fast as all get out.

There was a time in Betsy's life—after Daddy got run out of the cabin on the Hudson—that they headed out west. Daddy looked for work in a number of menial jobs. All stuff that today they claim is done by migrant workers and immigrants. But it was the same people doing it back then. Backbreaking work. Stuff that puts you in an early grave or a late wheelchair (if you can even afford that much).

Betsy wasn't sure exactly where they ended up. She was only just old enough to remember. Young enough not to care or ask.

Daddy was picking blueberries and cherries. Somewhere in the Midwest. It was Ozarks hot and humid—like the southern morning outside the boxcar, but with less wind and more mosquito bites along your legs and arms. Coming to the end of the picking season. Mid-August dusk, with the setting sun making the sky look like a whole packet of blueberries and cherries got smushed together in a bowl and spread out across the sky.

Daddy had a mason jar with clear liquid in it. He was talking funny. Drunk, slurred. Having trouble twisting the words around his tongue, or vice versa. Whenever he got to drinking, he always spoke with a deep southern drawl that belonged more to a moonshiner than a writer. Half the words Daddy said when drunk weren't even real—you'd be hard pressed to find them in any dictionary. Even those strange almanacs that circulated the south once that newfangled War of Northern Aggression finally died down. Even the words he spoke that *were* real, honest-to-goodness dictionary members were often in the wrong order, or carried a twang so thick it might as well have been molasses.

They were sitting (or *setting*, as Daddy would have said that night) on what would have been the porch of their home. It was made of three cinder blocks, procured from somewhere, undoubtedly either illegally or at least without letting the true owners know they were getting borrowed. Atop the cinder blocks, Daddy laid a single piece of plywood. Because he only took three of them, the plywood was crooked and slunk into the mud patches all around their little shanty.

Through the purple and red darkening sky, birds flitted around. Making strange noises and flying in odd patterns.

Betsy—whose name was something different then—pointed this out to her daddy and asked about the strange noises.

"Them's ain't birds, puddin'." He paused to look up, as if to confirm a suspicion. He elaborated no further, just took another sip of his mason jar and wiped his chin with a dirty handkerchief he seemed to always carry in those days.

She watched him for a second. Perhaps realizing even at that young of an age that this man didn't know everything there was to know—the way most girls expected their daddy to. But he wasn't short of ideas about how things worked.

"Them's bats, pudding."

When she asked why they were making such strange noises—*click-click-click*—Daddy simply said, "Reckon it's their ech-o-lo-ca-t-i-on." His words slowed to the point even a geezer in the old folks' home would have told him to hurry up with it.

"Ech-no-lo-ca-t-i-on?" She could remember trying to mimic his words, just like he said them. The syllables rolled off her tongue like raindrops in a summer storm.

"Ech-*o*, pudding popper. No, no, not ech-*no*. Double, triple—*No!* Quad-negative—throw up some extra points on the home board." Daddy held his hands up as if signaling for a touchdown.

He took one heaping sip from the jar and made a face that even an alcoholic would've been disgusted with. The veins in Daddy's forehead and neck popped and went red, as if he'd somehow had his air cut off.

"What does it mean?"

When he spoke again, his voice came out in a hoarse whisper. Like the fire-liquor he was drinking scorched the inside of his throat.

"It means he can't see, pudding. Blind as a bat. *Blind as a bat.* They *see* with their ears. Sounds is what they see."

At the time, this made no sense to her.

Later on, she'd learn about echolocation. How bats use it, sending sound waves out from their bodies. The sound waves bounce off objects and travel back, creating a map of everything around them.

It was one thing her daddy had told her that might actually come in handy.

The rustler stood back up straight, having passed whatever ailed him like a kidney stone. He pulled down the front of his leather duster and made another series of *click-click-click* with his mouth, the sound emanating out of his bearded face just like those bats back on that night on the porch.

He was using echolocation.

He turned back to her, obviously having found her form again in the confines of the boxcar. She didn't know how it worked. But it did.

He moved faster than she did, reaching over the crate between them with his tree branch arms and grabbing her by the back of the head before she could duck. His grip was what it felt like to get caught in the back of a garbage truck just before they pressed the hydraulic lever down to crush its contents.

She tried to fall backwards, willing to take her chances with the gorge.

But his grip was too strong.

"Betsy, so nice to finally met you." He ran a hand along the front of her face, using his fingers like tentacles. Gliding them over every contour and crevice like God himself brushing the last motes of dust off his latest sculpted creation.

Her feet were half over the edge of the train car. But she couldn't get free.

His eye pits were deep chasms, as if whatever had happened to his eyes had extended beyond that. Scooped farther into his face like it was the Saturday night special at the neighborhood ice cream parlor.

He pulled her even closer and clicked with his mouth. It vibrated his lips when he did it. His tongue clucked and slapped against the inside of his mouth to produce the sound.

One last buck of her body told her that breaking free from his grasp wasn't going to happen.

"You smell like a good time, Betsy." It made her squirm and want to throw up just looking at his face. The mouth moving to talk, but no eyes. Really threw things off. Down into the uncanny valley. "Most of the time, when I get to this part, the smell needs to be overcome." He took another long sniff, pulling her so close his beard tickled her neck. "But you, Betsy. *Mm mm good.*"

He lifted her off her feet. By the back of the neck. Like a puppy straight from the litter. A move so jarring it stole her breath. She kicked her feet, but he easily swatted them away with his free hand, knocking them out over the threshold of the boxcar so that the wind whipped them around.

She lifted up her arm, desperate to hit this sonofabitch in the face, the way she'd done to so many men in the past who overstepped their bounds. Most men never stood a chance in a fistfight with her, though.

This one didn't seem like he'd much care—or even notice—if she started hitting him.

Only she didn't need to hit him at all.

She pressed the play button again on the cassette player. She'd almost forgotten it was even in her hand.

"Ah!" He stumbled backward again. "Ahhh!"

He reached his free hand to his ears. The vice grip on her neck opened, his other hand rushing to the other ear.

The rustler fell completely backward, screaming the entire time.

She landed awkwardly on the spud crate with a thud that almost knocked out her wind. She rolled off and hit the boxcar floor, not exactly sticking that landing, either.

The cassette player rolled away from her.

Her neck stung. His insane grip had left her with an Indian burn. She desperately wanted to rub it—hell, to put a cold compress on it.

But she didn't have time for that.

His screaming stopped.

Betsy rolled to her side, searching the ground frantically for it. She knew it was the only hope she had to stop him.

She couldn't see him now. Both of them were below the level of the crates. Her on hands and knees looking for the cassette.

She didn't know what he was doing.

A series of clicks emanated from the direction he'd fallen.

Oh God, oh God, oh God.

"That isn't very nice, Betsy." His voice was even keeled. The way one might speak to a toddler who just took a toy from another one.

His hulking form stood up, looking like an unfolding skyscraper to her on the floor.

Her hand brushed against plastic. The cassette player. Thank God.

She grabbed it.

"Come and get me, you bastard," Betsy said, standing back up in front of the doorway.

He was still twisting his neck, raising his nose up to the air. Getting his bearings.

Her voice seemed to jar him back to the present. He turned toward her, eye pits finding her in front of the open boxcar door. Nostrils flaring out as he sniffed the air between them.

He bent his knees. Ready to lunge at her.

As quick as he'd moved before.

This time, she was quicker.

She pressed the play button on the cassette player just as his feet left the ground.

He arced through the air like a torpedo arcing around the curve of the earth.

Betsy half-ducked, half-slid her aching body out of the way.

Feeling like she got about half her flexibility back after sitting in this boxcar for sixty plus hours.

Adrenaline tended to help with that.

Instead of his quickness and strength being an asset to him, it proved his downfall. He couldn't adjust himself. An object in motion, and all that.

The last thing Betsy saw before she slammed into the corner just inside the boxcar door were his pitted eyes passing by her.

His agonized screams were only perceptible for a second or two before the gusting winds took over.

Or until he hit water below.

TWO

She wasn't sure how long after he went out and over into the void that she sat there, staring at the cassette player in her hand, or listening to the train rumble on down the tracks. At some point, she stood up and closed the slatted door, dampening the wind that seemed so intent to suck her out behind the rustler's path. It all felt like she was someone else, watching a movie projected on a screen far away from her.

Eventually, she slept.

She didn't dream.

Slowed movement finally woke her.

The train was stopping. It hadn't made any more stops until hitting the port city of Charleston, South Carolina. Chucktown. The Holy City. Home of Palmetto bugs, sweet tea vodka, and shrimp and grits.

As the train slowed its speed, approaching its final destination, Betsy once again opened the boxcar's side door. If she thought the air had been hot and humid before, she was in for another lesson in the depravity of Mother Nature. The open door poured in on her. Air awash with thick humidity, as if the entire city was stuck inside a hot-air balloon.

She stood in the open doorway looking for an open spot on the passing ground that she could jump out. Sand or grass was preferable, though she'd take woodchips or tiny pebbles. Even concrete, if she could see it was flat enough and without anything she might accidentally roll into.

She thought about the rustler. About how he'd come *that* close to getting everything he wanted. About how she'd come *that* close to getting everything she didn't. About how this was one more crazy story from a life lived on the run.

But mostly about the fact that she was in a brand new city, on a brand new day. Not a dollar in her pocket or a single possession rolling in with her.

And it was about time she became a brand new person with a brand new story.

Born again and facing forward, just like Daddy would have done.

CALL ME GERTRUDE

A TRUE NAME STORY

NIZ THOMAS

A
TRUE NAME
STORY

CALL ME
Gertrude
xo

ONE

The dual scents of peaty swamp bog and sprayed skunk told her she was finally, totally, and *at last* lost out here in the wilderness area of the Francis Marion National Park.

Hallelujah.

As if to drive the point home, she stood before a tangled under-growth of hair-clump ferns, cypress knees, and waist-high pine bushes thick enough to be a hedgerow befitting Buckingham Palace. About as impenetrable as the little soldier boys dressed up in their red coats, too. Impossible to see beyond it. Could be anything on the other side. A traveling carnival, maybe. Or even more lush, abundant vegetation. Hell, even the Queen herself sunbathing her pasty crumpets.

All Gertrude—as she was calling herself now—knew was that the natural barrier before her blocked any clear trail forward.

The first indication, in fact, that she hadn't actually seen a *trail* in quite some time.

It took her a while to realize it, she supposed. How long ago had the familiar indications of civilization recessed? Had to have been hours on foot since the tar-paved roads and car exhaust at the park's entrance gave way to thicker and thicker vegetation—what a man she once dated for a week out in Wyoming might have called *country*, using the word with so many definitions in the only true way that called to mind some menace.

That was how she thought of it now, with the *country* closing in around her and choking out any semblance of fresh, breezy air.

Charred burgers and boiled hot dogs no longer hung on the heavy air, either. They'd been her steady companion on the hour drive up from Charleston—first along the highway as she passed Cookout and McDonald's and all the rest of the bulging, rotund Meccas of the South. There were no shortage of fast-food joints dotting the major arterial roads leading away from the city, all waiting expectantly like vultures lining up to watch the roadkill finally expire. No question about if. Just of when.

Off the highway, past the fast-food joints, it was the campgrounds inside the park itself that exuded the same smells. Charcoal-finished beef, mixed with easy conversation, and cold beer, all of which had long-ago fallen away behind her with each step deeper into the wilderness.

All of it now gone.

Gertrude turned back around. No way she could continue forward without a team of strapping, machete-wielding ruffians. Perhaps a pack of donkeys or pack horses, too—just to keep her ankles free of annoying critters and snake bites. And if she were going to start making wishes, Genie, she wouldn't mind a litter carried by a few more of those strapping ruffians. And a fan to keep her cool, too.

But wasn't that sort of daydream that got her out here, lost in the first place? She'd been so much in her own head that she'd walked right on through a surprisingly sparse clearing of longleaf pines that stretched up overhead like multiple-story tenement buildings. Unlike the hedgerow, she could actually see daylight. But along with the change in perspective came an intense rush of loneliness that told her three things:

One—there had been a lot of steps between the food and people at the campgrounds and here. She'd been deep inside her mind for what seemed like hours (and her legs confirmed that as fact). Given the shift of the sun, now on its descent down toward its summer nap, she'd put her best guess at four hours.

Two—she was once again free. Facing toward the unknown winds of The Road—her only true companion in this life. Sometimes The Road took shape as a freight train, or a beater car with one hand air-gliding out along the breeze. One bare-and-black-bottomed foot up on the dash. Windows down (using the manual knob, of course), wind blowing through her unwashed curly brown hair like Tom Petty lyrics come to life.

In this case, The Road was the dense South Carolina wilderness. Far enough away from Charleston to lose any heat that might have been following her. Far enough to lose just about anything, other than a rogue hunter or forest ranger. Not a thing in her pockets. Not a packed bag to accompany her. Only the Holy City (her personal favorite of Charleston's nicknames) and the vapor of myth and memories she'd spun up at her back, a fleeting cloud left behind as she journeyed forth to a new start.

And the third thing?

That she was truly and utterly alone out here.

Dark-side-of-the-moon alone. Deep-voids-of-*outer*-outer-space alone.

Well, there she went with Daddy's hyperbole again. Maybe not *totally* alone.

The longleaf pines stood awkwardly with her like dweebs at the school dance, hoping someone—*anyone*—will come talk to them. Not even a breeze to sway their thin trunks, still as bald and unblemished as young skin. Not so much as a sneeze of the wind to ruffle their bushy, leafy tops.

Just a thick, unrelenting Southern soup of humidity and scorching heat. A little dash of ozone-free sun mixed in, too.

On second thought, maybe she was actually baking-on-the-sun alone.

'Course the lack of breeze was evident to her in other ways, things she might have noticed if she hadn't been so lost inside her own mind. Namely that her once-white silk going-out blouse was now stuck to her, suctioned at her low back like an industrial plunger. Silk and moisture and rough hiking didn't mix all that well. Go figure.

Swamps in the South tended to have that sort of effect. Wring the water right out of you like laundry fresh out of the washing bucket. Maybe that was why so many of the women she'd encountered back in the dance clubs of Charleston looked like all the moisture in their bodies had been sucked out with one of those vacuum sealers used for keeping your food freezer-burn free in the freezer, or for keeping your camping gear nice and compact until you needed it next.

Well, that and all the forty-dollar-a-pop workout classes. And the plastic surgery. A new phenomenon in the South, from Gertrude's experience—and she'd been around to see plenty. Perhaps beauty-for-all had finally become cheap enough that even the middle-class housewives had got them some.

But none of that followed her here, to the isolated wilderness. An area that was remarkable for not only its isolation but also its resilience. A placard near the entrance said that a hurricane came shredding through here about five years ago, ripping out most of the old growth. So most everything left was new. Which maybe explained the fact that this clearing—the one she'd just walked through before reaching the hedgerow—wasn't too thick to turn her back. And why these pines were tall and skinny, not yet having reached puberty where they filled out and put some meat on their wallflower bones.

She bit her lip at the thought. *Have mercy.* A couple more years' growth would make it so she wouldn't even be able to walk through this spot. And the hedgerow. Forget it. No chance for her to mind-lessly wander in like she had. Probably no chance to even get within a mile of it.

All the untamed wild around her carried a certain *weight* to it. She couldn't help but feel the ground's ancient roots underneath, stretching down into the center of the earth, leaching up the nutrients from this soil. Something Gertrude herself felt a certain amount of kinship to.

Maybe because it was sort of how she'd lived her life up 'til now.

She walked further into the longleaf pines, letting her hands dance along the tops of a row of tall grass as she did so. The willowy tops tickled her palms.

What was she doing out here, anyway? And why hadn't she bothered to change her top?

Most importantly, why was she drawn to this place? Never been here before, never even heard about it. Until she read the placard near the trailhead she'd started this journey on, she'd never even heard of Francis Marion at all. Though now that she read a little about him, she had to admit feeling a kinship to him as well. A lone soldier in the Revolutionary War. One who scrapped and clawed his way into the nightmares of those dirty Brits (probably the Queen's great-great-great-cousins) using irregular tactics and guerilla fighting to make an outsized impact on their tea-loving fannies.

So far as she could tell, Francis could only claim ownership of the park because he often disappeared into these swamplands, eventually earning himself the nickname The Swamp Fox.

Gertrude shuddered with delight thinking of a scruffy Southern man with enough dog in the fight to become a fox himself.

Alas, she was a few hundred years too late to make that love connection now.

One could make an argument that finding any sort of love connection was a task best put on ice for a while, given the situation she left behind back in the Holy City. She'd only spent six days there, rolling into town on a freight train with another crazy story propelling her forward. Different name, different identity. Both dumped in the proverbial trash once they no longer suited her. She had to say, though, her six days in Charleston had been awfully busy.

And productive. So much so that she'd acquired a car, a husband, and an old-time Southern plantation—and not necessarily in that order.

Of course, she couldn't take any of that stuff with her, for various reasons which no longer meant much of anything.

She had no rituals, except for maybe this one:

Each time she shed one identity, it was like experiencing death. A nice reminder that time on this earth was both long and short at the same time. If you lived it right, you lived your days like it was all going to end, but you tacked enough of them together to pile up the years. But at the end—no matter when it came for you—you couldn't bring a damn thing with you.

The car she left town with wasn't even the one in her possession. Her own plates would be too easily spotted around here, and she had no desire for anybody to spot her until she emerged outside the immediate radius around Charleston. And even then, Gertrude would be long-gone behind her in the rearview. And so anybody who *did* spot her would be trouble.

The plantation, for all its charms, didn't travel well. Even if it had, she thought she might head north. Get out of the sticky Southern summer. And plantations *really* didn't fly up there.

The husband was portable. But she was already tired of him, anyway.

So each sticky situation was a reminder of what was ultimately coming for her. Just not today.

And just like she'd always done, all that was behind her. Part of a book already closed.

Only The Road lay ahead.

Unlike most people, though, after death, she got to experience rebirth.

And today—for now—rebirth meant she was Gertrude. An odd name, surely. Old-timey, folks might say. Formal. Wholesome and a little strange. Out of fashion. But whoever might say something like that was missing the point.

Gertrude was a fascinating name. The classically misunderstood character. Shakespeare thought so, at least. Though, of course, anybody who had an ill word to say about the name wouldn't know *that*. People today wouldn't know Shakespeare unless directed the next comic book adaptation.

Too many were so quick to judge Gertrude. Hamlet's mother. Woman of a thousand rumors, innuendos, and ascribed motives. Her husband, King Hamlet, was poisoned. She took up with the King's brother, Claudius.

For centuries, Gertrude was labeled a sinner. The reasons were as varied as those who proposed them (so often men, eager to flex their intellectual muscle in some vain and pathetic attempt to impress a woman, blind to the fact that their frenetic first-order thinking might actually say more about themselves than those who they cast aspersions unto).

Gertrude was an adulteress, it was said. Having an affair with Claudius even before he murdered King Hamlet, it's been suggested. Or perhaps she was complicit in the murder? Aware of the plot, but too cowardly to stop it? Many even believe she was the murderer herself (and most of these theories, praised by other men as capital-E *Empowering* during the Feminine Awakening—*insert eye roll here*).

Even still, the aspersions cast do not end there. One must consider the second-order effects.

Did her guilt over her alleged actions negatively impact her son? Perhaps fostering a helicopter-parent bubble of protection which drove her son to madness? Or, depending on the interpretation, drove him to become an indecisive wimp. Or some devious plotter himself, feigning madness in order to let others do his dirty work for him?

That all is to say nothing of the undercurrent of Freudian sexual tension—again, more theories by little boys with too little to do but wind themselves up into sweaty-palmed balls of twine.

But Gertrude was none of these things.

She was simply a woman put in a tough situation, trying to do her best to survive. Add to that, she had a grieving son. Was perhaps even grieving herself (though, maybe not—even in death, her first husband was a bit of a tattletale). And yet, stones were cast on her. Did her worry for Prince Hamlet not come honestly? Did mothers ever stopped worrying after their brood?

Gertrude, the character, was in a position envied by none. A job no woman would ever want. And yet, over the course of history, it was the job so many of them were stuck with. Just trying to pick up the pieces and do the best they could.

So Gertrude was the name today.

It had a long and proud tradition.

And that was only part of it.

She couldn't explain what brought her here. Aside from a need to get gone immediately from Charleston, there was nothing about this particular spot that drew her to this place, even as she found that the energy suited her fine.

Except that in her haste to get gone—to just go ahead and *get away*—she'd gone ahead and got herself lost. Lost in the middle of the woods without even half-a-clue as to which way was which, nor any skills or tools with which to leave.

It seemed she might have gone and overcompensated.

Disappearing, good.

Dying out in the wilderness, bad.

Gertrude turned back around, taking in her full surroundings. Not just the way she'd come and the way she couldn't go, but the rest of it, too. Looking for anything resembling a landmark. Seeing only the land part of that word. Finding that it was almost identical to the view in front of her. In fact, looking in all four directions showed her a lot of the same things—skinny, full-barked longleaf pines stretching overhead, short grass in varying shades of green, everything from lime margarita to Ben Franklin greenbacks. A bunch of insects buzzing around the space. And thick, lose-the-British brush that seemed impossible to Gertrude, for she had to have walked through some of that on her way to where she was standing right now.

So which way to go? Other than airlifted out of here, what in the hell had her plan been on the way in? Perhaps she'd stumble upon a white rabbit who could lead her to the way out of here.

No rabbits materialized. And the scent of peaty swamp bog some-where nearby told her that any rabbits who might have lived here would more likely be alligator snacks than tucking a pocket watch into his waistcoat.

So she asked herself again. What the hell had she been thinking?

Nothing, it seemed to her now. Upon reflection. Her mind had been as blank as a turned-off television. A million possibilities going on behind the screen, but not a single thing you could see or remember.

And maybe now she'd finally taken her last joyride out on The Road. Because here in about a few hours, darkness would fall over this place.

And that wouldn't be a good turn of events at all.

The caw of a crow woke her back into the present. She'd been too much in her head. Part of it simply a way to clear out the last place, the stint in Chucktown (her least favorite Charleston nickname—mainly because she'd only known three Chucks in her life, and they'd all been bona fide diddleteasers).

And hadn't she wanted to get lost? Come right on out into this wilderness area for that very purpose?

Well, if she were being honest, the answer was no. Or not exactly, to be precise. No point in being honest if you're not precise.

She hadn't come out here to get lost, per se. Just to disappear.

Which she felt she'd done well enough. Disappeared practically back to the Stone Age.

The cawing crow got her hackles up. Out here in the woods, her thoughts went all primitive. She could see why humanity had been pagan for so long, worshipping the gods of the Earth. Scared of the forests. Slaves beneath the sun. There was power here. And it stemmed from the solitary menace of the place. Each shadow a potentially unseen danger. Each stick or branch or blade of long grass sharp enough to cut.

The crow watched her from a branch about ten feet off the ground. Gertrude couldn't be sure whether it had been there all along or if it just landed there. She hadn't noticed it, but she'd been enough in her head it could have snuck past her. Now she looked at it closely. It was the size of one of those big bottles of wine you only see on display at real Italian restaurants. Head turned away from her, so that only one marbly eye was visible. It was pitch-pure black—a black so deep even the Lord himself would be impressed with the fidelity and chilled at its commitment to the dark arts.

A particularly sinister organ.

Gertrude had done some things in her life. Things that she wasn't ashamed of, necessarily. But things that most of society wouldn't classify as nice and proper. All of society, actually. Anybody who condoned at least some of her past actions wasn't a part of society at all. They might shop in the same grocery store as the next Joe Schmo from Alamo, but they were on the fringes, baby. They were the dregs. Just like her.

'Course, she blended in just fine with society. Always had, if you only got a peek at the surface. Which is all she ever allowed. She blended in better than fine, actually.

Young women looked. Old men needed immediate chiropractic help, their necks cranked so much. Old women scowled. Come to think of it, young women did, too—even more so recently, as Gertrude got a little older but still kept that smoldering taste for the weird, dangerous, and, most of all, *complicated*.

And young men? The ones in their prime? They clawed, fought, and schemed. They started wars. Sold state secrets. Cried out to their mothers.

They were nothing but putty. And she, like Swayze and Moore in *Ghost*, the master craftsman who could vanish into thin air.

But all that in her past made her a little jumpy at times, if not ashamed. Not so much because she thought anybody was out to get her. More so because, despite her being nobody's fool, she knew that deep down inside of her, at the bottom of a dark and dank well with no ladder or rope or purchase on the slick rocks, with only slivers of sunshine seeping down from the very top of the opening, with little Timmy down near the bottom, broken legged and hope-dashed, whispering in a quiet and ashamed voice that not a single soul could hear —not even the ones that Timmy found himself sitting amongst, those skeleton souls that had once (long ago, from the looks of it) been in the same place as he—even in these most private and isolated of places, Gertrude harbored a secret.

She believed in the supernatural.

Now, didn't she have good reason to? Well, that depended on who you asked, she supposed. Plenty of strange experiences. Things and feelings and circumstances that were just a little too suspicious. Too woo-woo. Things that maybe some highfalutin scientist might prove were legit and not just the existence of a spiritual entity, or some rip in the time-fabric of this dimension. No, no, Gertrude didn't care what any study said.

There were some spooky shenanigans out there in the world. She'd bet the farm on that, daddy.

She wasn't sure exactly where her belief had come from. Knew nothing about her mother—not a name, not a picture. Not even a story of why she never came around. No peep from her daddy about the subject, and that was a man who knew how to talk, able to spin a yarn that'd catch just about anybody from changing the channel for minutes. A storyteller, natural born and Lord-blessed. He never much developed his craft beyond engaging conversation, though. He wrote up stories from time-to-time, but his engaging nature combined with a bit of charm, good—if rugged—looks, and enough rapscallion to never stick in one place too long had been more a recipe for wasted potential than it had for the chair and the page and the typewriter ding. Suffice it to say, Daddy never hit the big time the way some of the other pulp-era fellas did.

Daddy just never could slither in through the cracks. A damn shame, too. Because Gertrude wouldn't have minded a little extra coin in her pocket. And because Daddy'd been able to slither into almost any other position he wanted, though very few worth anything enticed him. She knew that the writing life was one game he desperately wanted to break into—one that could actually put some distance between the old man and the hard labor of the fields. He just never quite made the inroads.

Which was to say, in the longest possible sense, that she didn't come by this voodoo outlook from her momma, whoever that may be. Women over the centuries—at least the ones who believed in that sort of occult stuff—typically learned it from family. Mothers, of course. Or aunts. Same way that women over the centuries learned what to do when a man got frisky. Or worse. Same way as how women learned to control and manipulate a man in the first place. To make sure he *didn't* get frisky. Or worse.

It was a safety thing.

Mothers cared about their daughters. And aunts about their nieces. No point in going through hell yourself if you don't teach the lessons unto the next generation. It might as well be the Eleventh Commandment. Thou Shall Not Keep Knowledge to Thyself.

And one thing that mothers and daughters and aunts and nieces had to face over the years was the sudden panic and hysteria that not only did witches exists, but they could be here and now (and *here* could be anywhere, while *now* was only confined to the times between the Pleistocene and today's date).

So the normal way for Gertrude to learn about the occult was never once on the table. Daddy didn't have no sisters, and no in-laws that she ever knew.

So where did all this spooky crap come from, then?

Hell if she knew. It had been there before the incidents—the ones that went a little funny and a lot freaky. Where blue-lipped little girls trapped in the aether were desperate for one last shot to get into the afterlife. Or when she went toe-to-toe with a man on a boxcar who wasn't quite what he seemed to be.

And right now, this crow was giving her the same sort of vibe. She'd be the first to admit that having such a thought run through her might have been indication that she'd gone off the Looney Tunes train somewhere after the last of the camping grounds. To the best of her knowledge, she hadn't picked any magical forest treats along the walk, so she hadn't knowingly ingested anything that might be considered consciousness-expanding.

But still, this crow gave her the creeps.

As if it knew this to be the case, the crow cawed once again. This time, loud and reverberating around the forest. Like it just cranked up the amp for the curtain call at a Black Sabbath concert.

The branches and leaves rattled. The tall grasses swayed. A breeze blew through the area, one that felt like almighty Heaven to Gertrude—though in reality, it probably only made the temperature go from eighty-nine with ninety-nine percent humidity to eight-six with ninety-nine percent humidity.

The crow raised its head up to the skies like Zeus himself was descending into the forest.

Then it flapped two thick, oily wings and took off.

The wind brought on its back a most foul smell. Worse than peat moss and skunk. Something rotten.

No. Something rotting.

Gertrude raised her arm up to her face out of instinct, but there was nothing could be done about it. The smell kept coming, creeping up at first like a sly forest predator. But a moment or two later it leapt at her with the same kind of ferocity as a pissed-off, hungry mama lion finding an antelope sniffing around near her cubs.

The stench wrapped itself around Gertrude, bypassing her clothes and skin and hair and seeping right down into her nasal cavity. Expanding itself. Coming for her olfactory like the robber barons of the Gilded Age.

Making her wretch.

She didn't even have time to move her arm. It was an involuntary movement. The body purging itself of something vile and vicious and dangerous.

The smell of death.

Gertrude anchored both hands on her sweat-slicked knees, open to the air through the frayed-knees of her black jeans. They were skintight, as was appropriate for the occasion to which she'd worn them. But now they chafed, had even sagged and loosened a bit with the heat and the activity.

She tried to catch her breath, spitting the last of the liquid her stomach had just ejected.

Her right arm was covered in sick. So were her sneakers—the lone out-of-place item she wore, having found a pair in the car she'd procured on her flight out of the situation she'd left behind. The shoes she'd been wearing were hot, engineered to raise men's temperatures above boiling, to somewhere on the Kelvin scale. They'd done that, for certain—part of the reason she had to skip town. But they were about as comfortable as a root canal, so she'd had to ditch them before being able to walk anywhere.

Good thing, too. She'd have been pretty pissed if she threw up all over them.

She was staring at the stolen sneakers when the crow came back.

The caw caught her attention. It was closer than before. And something about it told her it was coming even closer still.

And right at her.

Gertrude looked up just in time. Saw a matte-black beak aimed straight at her like a murdered-out missile dropped right on target. Two eyes bore down on her, neither of them catching the glint of the sun.

She ducked, feeling a tickle of feathers against the lower portion on the back of her neck. A narrow miss. She knew the wilderness could be dangerous, but did it always follow that animals went after humans with such aggressive posturing?

Staying low, Gertrude tried to find the crow. Like Quasimodo, she tried to both look skyward and at where she was going. Her eyes danced across the canopy of leaves and pine needles above her, trying to detect jet black amongst the varying colors. Despite it seeming to most that deep swamp, without any flowering plants or exotic reptiles, had almost no color variation at all, Gertrude found that not to be the case. Not even a little.

Instead, everywhere her eyes fixed was a medley of shades—clover-green, gator-green, frog-green, camo green, leafy green, swamp water green. Brown: bark, dirt, mud. It was as if a painter had done a study of how many minute variations he could make with just the few colors he had left in his palette—the colors too drab to never be used for anything else.

But the crow wasn't anywhere to be found.

The breeze blew again, this time harder. Brought forth that horrific scent again. Coming from the thick hedgerow of impenetrability. It was to her right now, after all the twisting around looking for the crow. This time, she was almost ready for it, able to keep from taking in a deep breath through her nose.

But this scent didn't much care for her precautions. It wasn't the sort of thing easily dissuaded from its assault.

Gertrude wretched again. Hardly anything this time. A reminder of how long it had been without food or water.

A wing-flap over her right shoulder drew her attention again. The crow, coming on the back of the mephitic odor.

As she turned, the crow was already practically on top of her. Wings extended out like a solar eclipse. Talons first, sharp as a blade and blacker than Gertrude's soul. The sight of the beast's belly—so different from what she ever would have associated with an animal of the sky—would have made her wretch, had she anything else to give.

And then, as quickly as it appeared, the beast was suddenly gone.

Only the dying light of the afternoon stood in its place, still visible through the trees.

But not for much longer.

The gunshot only registered for her afterwards. What felt like two interminable seconds, but was probably less than the snap of a finger. Speed of sound, and all that.

The crackle of the spent round both scared her and made her ears ring like she'd just gotten married and divorce at the same time.

Gertrude's reaction was to cover her ears. But wouldn't have done a damn thing had the bullet been aimed at her.

She supposed that much was self-evident.

Anyway, it wasn't.

The hand that eventually touched her on the shoulder proved it to her. Until she felt it, she wasn't entirely sure that she wasn't already dead.

The unlucky owner of said hand was also the unlucky recipient of one of Gertrude's go-to self-defense moves.

A punch right into where the sun don't shine.

This fella was quick, able to slightly deflect the attack from Gertrude with a raised knee and a push of her shoulder with his right hand, knocking her off-trajectory and balance.

Sending her teetering over a cypress knee and onto an open patch of dirt that was soft enough of a landing, though it wouldn't do any favors for her once-white blouse.

"Easy there, Missy," the fella said. He seemed as tall as a house from her ant's-eye perspective. Not as tall as the pines, though, which framed him in the middle of her vision. But not so far off, either. He wore a curved-brim trucker cap, which was tucked down low over his eyes. Wild golden hair spilled out from beneath, curling over itself behind the ears, creating those wings that preppy college lacrosse players kept. But this here was a *man*, with a thick, flaxen beard that added an inch-and-a-half to his chin and neck, both of which were sturdy.

In his right hand was nothing. Lucky for her, since he'd used it to put some space between the two of them. A blade would have cut her deep, surely. And with the heebie jeebies going around this part of the forest, she didn't want to think about what spilled blood might attract.

He did have a blade, though. It was a machete, of all things. Not something out of the Lord's Resistance Army, but big enough to strike a chord of fear inside her like an expert guitar player picking away at his favorite ballad. It measured about the length of her forearm, sheathed on a utility belt. Slung off his right hip for easy access, she supposed.

In his left hand was the rifle he used to shoot down the crow, which she now saw was about five feet behind him. Dead as anything created by Satan could ever be.

"Could be dinner," he said when he noticed what she was looking at.

"Not for me, it couldn't."

"Vegetarian?"

"Jerk."

He smiled, though between the low hat and the beard, she couldn't quite read past the gesture.

"Dressed awful fancy for these parts. Lot of fancy-types like you don't believe in eating flesh."

"I believe in it just fine. But I ain't some backwoods hillbilly who eats scavengers. It's nasty. Those things eat garbage. What you think it's going to do to your insides?" She didn't bother to mention about the dark spirits so often tangled up inside of the creatures.

"Sounds like fancy talk to me. It's meat, don't matter much where it's from. You know what a turkey eats?"

She didn't.

"I thought not. Human beings eat all sorts of weird stuff, Missy... whether they know it or not."

Gertrude felt a shudder tickle the back of her neck. Where the crow had grazed her. In this heat, a shudder was like an Eskimo starting to sweat.

Human beings do all sorts of weird stuff, Missy...

She sat up, making sure everything attached to her still worked. Especially her legs, in case she had to get to running.

"Speaking of doing weird stuff," he said. "What are you doing out here? Long way away from any sort of party you'd go to dressed like that."

He wasn't wrong. But he made it sound as if she was dressed up like a hooker hustling tips on the corner. There was something about her—something innate—that hated when someone talked to her like that. Like they knew better. Or like they knew anything at all. And through her life, there was only one commonality she could point to when someone acted like that.

"You ain't never been to a party with anybody dressed like this. Not even in your dreams."

She just couldn't help herself.

Probably not the sort of thing you're supposed to say to someone with a gun. Especially not a gun with which they've shown such pinpoint precision. And all the way out here, in the middle of absolutely nowhere at all...

"I prefer a more intimate affair. Dinner party. Not...well, gee, I don't even know what you'd do in clothes like them. Dancing?"

"Something like that."

"I guess tastes...differ," he said, the words trailing off, like he was somehow distracted. She decided not to press any further on this point. Perhaps a sign of maturity. Perhaps an instinct for self-preservation.

She decided to change tack. "And anyway, I could ask you the same question."

He was at least dressed a bit more for the occasion of being lost in the woods, though she wasn't quite sure he *was* lost, at least not directionally. Maybe a little spacey upstairs, but who was she to judge?

He seemed comfortable enough in these surroundings. He wore a camouflage fishing shirt, olive green cargo pants, and boots that looked like they could take a licking. Even the machete sheath was military-green, almost invisible against the backdrop of vegetation all around them both.

"We're a long way from a lot. And I'm not positive, but I think you can get into a whole mess of trouble using firearms in a National Park."

"You part of the Ranger Service now?"

She shrugged and pushed herself up off her butt with her hands, then to her feet. Standing, she was spotting him about a foot and a hundred pounds.

Oh yeah. And a gun and a machete.

He put up his hands in mock surrender. "You got me. I'm out here for the peace and quiet. Like I said, *an intimate affair*. Always carry this here with me, though. Never know what you're going to run into. Gators, bear. Snakes, even—ones bigger than you could ever imagine. Like that movie *Anaconda*. But nastier. And sometimes, that's just the start of the sort of trouble you can run into."

Gertrude made a whole life out of reading people and situations. If she weren't so addicted to The Road, she could have hustled along with the best of them. Be living in a big house with a big, gated entrance and fountain out front. Two ferocious marble lion statues situated at the gates. A few servants waiting on her beck and call. Maybe keep a few of the strapping ruffians around, the ones who would hack their way through brush and carry her on their backs across the shredded remains. She'd hustled used car dealers in Frisco and card sharks in New Orleans. Played with loaded dice in the Keys and grifted bankers on Wall Street. She just needed a good gaze into the double-bay windows that revealed man's soul. That was enough for her to know the core of a person—their faults, weaknesses, and everything in their heart. Maybe it was simply the *woo-woo-juju* she believed in that had her playing all Miss Cleo. But when Gertrude looked into anybody's eyes, she saw their aura in all its technicolor glory.

But with this man's eyes, she saw only one color.

Black. Big, inky marks. Rorschach in their twirling complexity. As vast as the Exxon Valdez oil slicks. The sort of aura that put even her own dark past actions to shame.

She didn't believe the tale this fella was spinning up. And she would have told him so.

Except for that gun.

His eyes went off somewhere. Not looking at anything in particular. Just...spaced-out.

"Rangers don't get out here too often," he said.

Time to distance herself from this cat and his *intimate affairs*. Whatever he was doing here, made no difference to her. So long as he left her out of it.

So instead she offered up, "Makes sense to me. Better safe than sorry, bub."

"Alan."

"Better safe than sorry, Alan."

"Pleased to make your acquaintance."

She couldn't say the same about him. Some of the dark venom was gone from his eyes. But that was like saying they got a few dozen gallons of oil cleaned up once the spill finally got sealed.

Only about eleven million more to go before the waters were sparkling clear.

"What's your name, then?"

"Call me Gertrude."

Another confusing smile stretched out across his bearded face. It obscured his dark eyes—for which she was grateful. But his teeth weren't what she figured. Rather than the fugly, jacked-up wildebeest mug she expected, instead she saw Alan had teeth that belonged in the *Dental Hygienist Monthly* Hall of Fame. They sparkled, even against the dying afternoon sun. Each one perfectly shaped, perfectly proportioned to the one beside it and below or above. Maybe a bit sharper on the canines than your average fella. But not by much.

It confused her, due to its incongruity to their surroundings. It was the megawatt smile of celebrity. And it looked so much farther out of place here than it would have anywhere else in the world she encountered it.

"That's an odd name."

"I'll bring it up at the next committee meeting. You'll be there?"

"What meeting is that now?" Alan asked.

"Meeting for people with weird names."

He scratched as his beard absentmindedly. Two fingers practically disappeared in that forest of growth.

"Funny."

Gertrude sighed. He seemed to be setting her up. "I'll be here all week."

Alan didn't laugh. Maybe he'd heard that one before. Or maybe whatever was going on inside his head was distracting him. Instead, "So what is it, then?"

"What is what?"

"What is it that you're doing out here?"

How in the world could she answer that question?

Before she could say anything, a voice came from behind Alan. In all the twisting and turning and ground-rolling, Gertrude was now looking straight at him. At his back was the hedgerow. Beyond it was anybody's guess.

The voice came from beyond it.

It was quick. A snippet only. Like someone pressing play on a cassette tape and then pause right after. But she heard it clear as anything for that one moment.

"*Help.*"

A woman's voice.

Alan twitched at the sound. Just a split-second. Like he was reacting to interference on the other end of the telephone. His neck twitched momentarily, then returned back to normal as if nothing happened.

Every fiber in Gertrude's body screamed out not to do anything. To pretend like she hadn't heard a thing. *Hey Alan, beautiful day out here, nice to meet you, and thanks again, old pal, for killing that dastardly kamikaze crow for me. I sure do appreciate your aim, your timeliness, and most importantly, your decision to let me leave this area without another moment's notice—thank you and goodbye, sir.*

Instead, her eyes darted past him, toward whatever it was lay behind the wall of vegetation.

He might have been trying to play it off, but Alan just smiled that megawatt smile. Which for a moment seemed *all good* to Gertrude.

Only then he said, "Nothing wrong with running away,

Gertrude. Some might think it's a cowardly act. But not me. I think it shows real courage, to drop everything and start up again."

Gertrude's heart threatened to exit her body the same way the contents of her stomach had. It was like he'd just read her mind.

"Oh, I'm sorry, I didn't mean you running away from this specific spot. Sometimes I jumble my words, you know? Like you said, I ain't never been to no fancy dancing clubs where the women dress up in tight pre-ripped jeans and silky shirts. So my words don't come out all slick and polished like yours. Heck, all my pants got rips in 'em from wear-and-tear."

Gertrude couldn't move.

"What I meant was, nothing wrong with running away from the city. Things get a little hot back there, you just pick up and go. Like Robert *De*-Niro himself in that bank robber movie. What was it called again?" He furrowed his brow, wiped a bead of sweat on the sliver of weathered cheek between his beard and his eyes. "Ah, right. *Heat*. An apt name for our current predicament, don't you think?"

He wasn't reading her mind. He was reading into something deeper—her past.

"How...did...you..."

"...Know that?" Those opaque, black, oil-spill eyes gazed at her, reflecting back nothing. "I see things, Gertrude. Not with these here," he pointed his right pointer finger to his eyes, "though, of course, they work just fine. No, I see things up here." He pointed instead to the middle of his forehead.

His proverbial third eye.

"And I know you been awfully bad back in town. A real blasphemer amidst the *Holy City*. But then, you been awfully bad in a lot of different places, ain't you?"

For once in her life, she didn't have a word to say edgewise in response. She felt as if someone had forced open her throat and poured concrete down it.

"Only, now that I get to thinking on it, I see one major drawback to this lifestyle of yours. All the running away. Especially the way you been doing it. Scorched earth behind you, only kerosene and ashes blowing on the wind. And doing it again and again. For so long, too. Always looking for *The Road...*"

He knew about The Road. Gertrude's knees went slack, almost giving out from under her. Like the end of a night at a real good dive bar, blowing off steam, shots and beers and whatever else managed to make it down the ol' gullet.

If he knew about The Road...

Her brain stuttered on itself. A car engine that wouldn't start. The afternoon light speckled her vision. Dusk approached. Soon it'd be dark.

And if she didn't already think she was in trouble here, the idea of darkness on top of all of this was too much for her to take.

"You're not curious?" he asked.

Her throat caught the words. She tried to shake her head but it didn't obey her command. Like they were being delivered in another tongue.

Finally, she simply said, "No."

"Oh, come on, Gertrude. You've considered this before. You must have. Somewhere deep down, maybe?"

Gertrude's brain felt like a tire stuck in loose snow. It couldn't get any purchase.

"That's alright. I'll go ahead and spoil the secret."

She didn't want him to, but it was clear he was having too much fun with all this.

"Nobody is bound to be looking for you. Are they?"

The words hit her with the same sort of speed and finesse of runaway freight trains or angry bulls right before the bucking chute opens wide.

If she didn't do something, she was going to die here. And with the creep-factor boiling up over the edge of the pot, however it went down, it was sure to be unpleasant.

All her life, she knew the ride along The Road would come to an end. She'd been having all the fun in the world up to this point.

Knew how to work people, how to get by with everything or nothing at all.

She took a moment to collect herself, realizing that of all the places she'd ever been caught in a jam—and she'd been in *plenty* of dives and flophouses—this was by far the least comfortable and lowest class.

"Oh, Ger-*trude*," Alan said in a sing-song voice. It didn't suit him, though she was beginning to think that the creepy-crawly vibe she'd been getting from the crow was actually coming from Alan himself, who—for an extra creep factor—had obviously been here already.

Watching her.

"Ger-*truuuuuuuuuuuuude*?"

But the name...

...It was the ignition switch. Brought something else to mind. Not Shakespeare this time. Older. More powerful...

There is a legend, ascribed to untold numbers of ancient civilizations. One of those things believed to be a "universal truth." It's said the first human names were little else than handprints on a wall. One came in, blew red or brown dust over the back of their hand, leaving behind a print of only the natural stone color where their hand had been. The ancient precursor to fingerprints and DNA scanners, maybe. Or those Thanksgiving turkey drawings that kindergarteners make.

But as time went on, and language grew more complex, names took on more power. Many great societies believed that a name's meaning bestowed certain qualities upon you. Naming was important, a sacred ritual. Athena meant you would be wise. Fleda meant you would be fast. Ballari meant you would walk softly.

Gertrude had always believed in this great truth. In the True Name of things.

Alan stood across from her amidst the chorus of insects. Grinning like a lion with his prey cornered. She wondered, did he know what she was thinking now? Did his third eye have *that* precise of foresight?

She didn't know exactly what he had planned for her. Whatever it was, the smell behind the hedgerow told her there had been others. Their end hadn't come pleasantly.

She wouldn't be the first to die out here.

But she had something else on her side. Spontaneity. One of her constant companions over the years. The ability to take things as they came to her—whether in the physical world or the metaphysical.

In this case, it was her chosen name. Even though she never really knew which name might suit a particular situation, she always trusted her intuition.

It once again proved to be far more all-knowing than she could ever be.

When she chose Gertrude, it was not simply because of the misunderstood character from *Hamlet*.

It was because of the meaning of the name.

Spear of strength.

And Gertrude, as she was calling herself now, sure as hell wasn't prepared to go down here. Or today.

"Yeah..." she said, clearing out the cobwebs and concrete in her throat.

Alan took a step closer to her. Closing the distance. Removing possible avenues of egress.

"...I know what you're talking about, Alan. Only there's one thing that I don't think *you've* considered."

"And what's that?"

"That when I leave a place behind, everybody there gets down on hands and knees—day and night and all the time in between—praying that *I don't come back.*"

This put a dimmer switch on that megawatt smile of his. But just for a second.

"Good one, Gertrude. I can tell you mean it, too. Only issue with it—in terms of it being a threat? When I'm through with you, ain't going to be no question about if you're coming back. Where I'm about to take you, it's a one-way ticket, Missy."

The wind picked up again, rustling the leaves and branches so hard that the sound even cut through the drum line going on in her skull. She talked a good game here, but she couldn't act like fear wasn't on the menu this evening.

Only this menu had something else horrid on it.

Something rotting.

The smell poured over the hedgerow like water over a levy.

She'd had enough. Gertrude turned to run.

Only Alan was faster and stronger than he looked (and he looked plenty of both). He reached an arm as thick and solid as steel pipe and quick as one of those killer snakes he mentioned, wrapped it around the top portion of her arm. This time, he was too far away to get her preferred return shot in. In boxing, they call that a reach advantage.

Alan wrapped one arm completely around her upper body, pinning her arms against her side. He had her subdued and off her feet, holding her like he was dragging a new carpet into his living room to try it out with the furniture.

Then he stopped. Leaned in close to her, his beard tickling the area under her chin.

He waited until she opened her eyes. Looked into his. Once again taking in the wicked aura of the Stygian orbs.

Her own eyes watered at the smell. As rotten and dead as anything she could have ever imagined.

He took a long, deep whiff in through expanding nostrils.

This sick bastard actually *enjoyed* this rancid stench.

"Smells like—"

Gertrude head-butted him.

She didn't much give a damn what he thought it smelled like.

She thought it smelled like shit.

The head-butt knocked him back on his haunches. A one-two step stumble. He was strong, though, so he didn't let go of her.

But his grip loosened.

Gertrude wriggled an arm free. Reached up and out.

For the machete.

She got it halfway out of its sheath. Struggled to keep a grip on it. The way her body was contorted and the pressure of Alan's grip around her made it difficult to get a strong hold. The handle was wrapped in some kind of rubbery material. Grippy.

But Alan tensed his arm around her like he was hog-tying a baby steer.

His face was bleeding by now, sheets of blood raining down from where she'd made impact. The crimson liquid spattered around his face—cheeks and forehead, all mixed up into his beard hairs.

But his eyes were wide open, blinking through the red elixir of life that didn't seem possible to staunch. His neck was flexed. Mouth open. Almost a smile. Sick, sadistic. If she'd been wrong about his aura, it had been to the downside. This was one sick puppy.

Except he was more like a bloodhound.

His expression reminded her of Jack Nicholson in *The Shining*. *Heeeeeeere's Alan!*

He bared his white teeth. A stark contrast against the rivers of blood.

Opened his mouth even farther as it continued to stream down like a crimson stigmata.

And was he...drinking it?

FUUUUUUCK that....

Gertrude head-butted him again. Just reared back her head, channeled her True Name, and used the hard portion of her skull as her spear of strength. Absolutely dive-bombed Alan's nasal cavity.

She'd had enough of this creep.

This time, the impact sent shockwaves through her head, neck, and jaw. Something snapped and crackled beneath impact. Like the old cereal commercials. All that was missing was a pop.

Alan gasped. Stunned, but not taken out.

Gertrude felt him give a little slack again and tried to wrestle free his machete.

She couldn't. He was still ready for the move, reaching his vise grip of a right hand—the one not holding onto her—to try and sheath the sharp tool.

Only Alan miscalculated. Instead of grabbing the machete's handle, he grabbed its blade.

That was enough pain for him to lose his grip on Gertrude. She wriggled free of Alan's galvanized steel grip. Hit the ground, but this time she was ready.

She rolled away from him, made sure to get far enough away that he wouldn't just be able to scoop her back up again.

All she could hear through the thump of her heart inside her head was his grunting. The sound was muffled. Probably due to most of his sound-making parts being bashed to bits and drenched in blood.

Disoriented, she saw dueling images in her mind, fading in and out of one another.

One—the image of him pointing a finger toward his third eye before. Smiling, as if at a joke that only he knew. Telling her things about herself that nobody could know. As if to put to rest any internal waffling inside her regarding whether the supernatural was real.

Two—him sniffing at the open wound in his hand, which now dripped blood at an even faster rate than his face. Alan was holding it close to his face. Using his other finger to inspect the flayed skin...

Both images suggested that Gertrude needed to get as far away from Alan as she could. As quickly as possible.

As if she needed any more reasons to do so.

She rose off the ground. Her black jeans felt two pounds heavier with all the moisture they retained. Her shirt was probably half-ripped, like some janky, clubbing Amazon woman of the jungle. But none of that mattered now.

Gertrude ran.

Only she didn't get far.

She tripped over the crow.

It didn't take her all the way to the ground. The crow slipped out from under her footing, shooting out ahead of her somehow. Sending her off-balance. Toward a tumble.

She tried to stop her momentum.

It proved unstoppable.

Her foot caught on something hard, wooden, and deep-rooted into the ground. Like it had been there for hundreds of years.

A cypress knot. Probably one of the few things not taken out by the storm a few years back.

She tried instead to brace for a fall. A fall that, given the speed and unexpected nature of how it happened, wouldn't be pleasant.

Only she didn't hit ground.

Instead, she fell only about half as far as she expected. And her landing was—if not pleasant—at least softer than what she was braced for.

Stray branches and sharp grass nipped at her skin. Like falling into a vat of paper, each thin piece taking its pulpy revenge by taking a teensy-tiny bite out of anything exposed.

She was suddenly...somewhere else.

It took her a moment to realize where. The first thing she noticed was the smell. Like the rancid breeze coming over the hedgerows on steroids. She wretched again. Awkward, on account of her position, caught as she was in the bushes. Fruitless, too. Just a dry heave that pressed down on her upper chest and diaphragm like getting crushed under a boulder. An involuntary movement, like someone else had taken control of her body.

Through tear-soaked eyes, she surveyed the scene.

There was a well-trampled, circular clearing. About forty feet in diameter. Around the outside of the clearing were five wooden posts stuck into the ground in a semi-circle pattern. Like telephone poles, but only twelve feet high instead of twenty-five. Around the clearing was thick, impenetrable Southern forest. A tangled mess of plants and vines and grasses that not only provided a natural fence for the perimeter of the clearing, but also, as the sky turned from oranges and reds into deep purple, grew increasingly haunted.

Of course, the haunting of the forest paled compared to the rest of it.

In the center of the circle were two things. The first was a fire pit with no flame in it. Bonfire pit, was actually the more appropriate term. It was dug into the ground, maybe two feet deep. Inside was a charred and raveled black superstructure of melted-together organic material that made her inner Geiger counter spike off the charts.

Something bad was in there. Many bad somethings, probably.

The second thing, about ten feet away from the bonfire, was a cheap TV dinner folding table and chair. A place setting for one—a metal camping dinner plate and a spork and knife—were placed atop the table. The table and chair were setup to face outward, toward the five posts.

Gertrude blinked. Several times. The last thing she noticed was perhaps the most obvious. Her eyes must have glossed over it. It had to be some sort of mistake. An apparition, maybe. An evil spirit of the forest.

Some seriously, grade-A level, bad-to-the-bone juju.

But no amount of blinking made it go away.

It was real as can be.

Each of the five posts of the semi-circle at the edge of the clearing had a woman chained up to it. Each in the standing position, backs against the posts themselves. Chained tight. Each with a bandana tied and duct-taped around the bottom half of their face. They were all equally dirty, though their clothes seemed to be in varying degrees of threadbare. The woman in the center had clothes that were much like Gertrude's—some rips and tears and plenty of grime, but every-thing was still mostly held together.

The other four women weren't so lucky.

All of them looked starved—skin and bones. And even the skin was starting to wither away.

Gertrude's eyes took all of this in. Instantly, though, she wished like hell it was possible to go all Men in Black on the images.

One woman looked like a trap for mosquitos, with bites covering all the exposed skin (and there wasn't much coverage for her, clothes having long ago disintegrated to see-through).

Another had lost clumps of her hair. Whether by lice or stress or what, Gertrude couldn't say. Didn't much want to know, frankly.

Another had...

Gertrude dry heaved again.

...been...

...*gnawed on* by some sort of forest critter. Gertrude hated herself for thinking: *smaller than a wolf, but bigger than a swamp rat.*

"Help!" This from that woman, the one who'd been something's snack. Her bandana was loose around the front of her face, the duct tape having ripped, probably pulling the skin with it as she'd struggled to wriggle her face and cheeks out of the bind. Or been chewed through. And not the only thing that had been. Her left leg no longer had skin from the knee down. Where something smaller than a wolf but bigger than a swamp rat had gotten at her. It reminded Gertrude of those cat towers, covered in carpet, where the cat could just *scrape* and *scrape* and...

Suddenly, these women disappeared.

Alan was somewhere near Gertrude's feet, pulling her back through the hedgerow she'd fallen into.

Out of his horrific nightmare.

He lost his grip on her, stumbling backward. Her head hit the ground like a basketball dropped on the court.

Alan was laughing. At least she thought that's what he was doing. The sounds going in and out of him wheezed and whistled like wind through cracks in a cabin.

"Very good, Gertrude," he said. "I never saw that coming."

She rolled to her side, trying to get to a position from which she could stand up. Feeling the new throbbing on the back of her head. The dizziness kicked in and drowned her mind in two feet of water.

She finally got to her back, pushed herself up with her elbows. Had a spot of déjà vu from before, when he'd blocked her punch to his groin. Back when things had only *seemed* on the precipice of danger. Before they rocketed on down the roller coaster of this freak's madness.

Alan rocked unsteadily side to side, raising his sliced right hand up to his face—blood meeting blood. Muscle and tendon were showing through the cut on his hands. They looked like brains. his face looked more like bloody mashed potatoes.

"Help!" The snack-woman's voice from the other side of the hedgerow was louder. More desperate. She'd seen a light, far away, down the other end of a very, very bleak and dark tunnel.

"Quiet!" Alan said, putting both hands to his ears. Like a child trying not to hear his mother tell him to go to bed. "Just *BE QUIET!*"

Gertrude recoiled away from Alan, but she couldn't move back very far. The hedgerow was right at her back now. It would take a running start to get back through it. Not that she wanted to.

Whatever he was doing over there, he had five victims in tow. She hated herself for thinking: and how many more in the forest?

She crab-walked backward, despite not having anywhere else to go.

Behind her head: the tickle of hairy reeds from the hedgerow.

Beneath her hand: the crow's oily feathers.

Luckily, she'd already gotten everything out of her stomach. Her stomach muscles ached from the previous efforts, but she couldn't stop herself from dry heaving again.

Alan lifted his red right hand, opened it out from him, as if show-casing the space around them—his little psychotic playpen of a world. It dripped an arc of blood as he did so, dotting the surrounding leaves and tall grasses. Almost catching blood on her shoes.

"As you can tell, my guests are anxious for me to return."

"I doubt that very much."

"They're well taken care of. Water's important in this heat. Even food, from time-to-time."

"You're a real Martha Stewart, aren't you, Alan?"

He didn't seem to get the reference. Maybe they didn't get her station out here.

"I admit, you're a real interesting guest to run into all the way out here. Most of them?" he motioned toward the direction of the hedgerows. "I gotta bring 'em on out here. Just to get some privacy. So we can drown out all the noise, you know? It's a noisy, noisy world out there, Gertrude..."

She didn't say anything.

"And then one fine day, you just show up out of the blue. No advanced notice. No chance for me to put out a table setting for you." He paused, as if this caused him great consternation. "But luckily, I'm prepared for more guests."

She shuddered. Saw him digging out a sixth hole, inserting a sixth pole into it. Saw herself chained to said post, her skin and bones melding into one day-after-day-after-day. Withering away like the rest of them.

Fumbling for something to keep him at bay, she said, "I thought you could *see* things. And yet you didn't know I was coming?"

He nodded. A whistle and an air bubble of blood came out of the jumble of mashed face where his nose used to be.

"I see fine. I guess you're just a little too unpredictable for me to see everything. Makes for interesting company."

"Help!" This time, a different voice. No less scared. No less desperate. Not the snack-woman, though. Somebody different.

Alan tried to smile, but something about the women yelling was clearly grating to him. Gertrude didn't figure it to be a guilty conscious coming into play.

She watched his face. The little twitching muscles. The subtle spasm of his neck. Almost like he was a robot and somebody was messing around with his controls.

Alan tried to collect himself with a half-hearted smile. "Must have got free of her handkerchief." The smile dimmed. "That *ungrateful little*..."

"Help us! Please!"

He twitched again. Collected himself again. But with more difficulty. Their screams were getting to him.

Through clenched teeth: "You should know, Gertrude, I don't allow any talking during dinner."

"Some dinner party."

"I don't need to hear all the babbling. Understand? I hear it all just fine up here." He touched his fingers to the tip of his ball cap, leaving a smear of blood. "All without anybody ever opening their *stupid* mouths."

"Help!" A third voice now. The women must have been able to better evade their handkerchiefs than Alan thought. Probably waited until he left and screamed their bloody heads off in hopes of someone out here being able to hear them.

Alan took the rifle off his shoulder and fired a round into the air.

"Quiet down, all of you!"

The air around them went silent. Even the chattering of bugs ceased for a second.

Alan slung the rifle back on his shoulder and shook his head like he was trying to pool water out of his ears.

"I treat all my guests real nice, Gertrude. You'll see."

He bared his red-speckled teeth. Not a smile this time. A grimace, cutting across the thick beard like someone ripping two pieces of paper apart.

He came toward her then. Not fast like before.

Just like he was inviting her in for dinner.

In the only way he knew how.

He put a hand out into the space between them. "Come now. Can't make the rest of our guests wait."

She didn't want him to get any closer. And anyway, she thought she had figured something out.

"Listen to me!" Gertrude screamed the words, hoping they'd be clear on the other side of the hedgerow. "Keep talking. It's...hurting him. Somehow. Just keep going."

Alan scowled at her. Then he used his good left hand to pull the machete out of its sheath. It *zinged* as he did so, the sharpness of the blade accentuated by the sound effect.

He was ten feet away from her. His reach was probably three feet. The machete, two-and-a-half feet long.

It wouldn't take much for her to be in range of that blade.

"Help us, please, anybody." This from the snack-woman. She sounded desperate but exhausted now.

Another twitch from Alan.

"Please, please, please," said a fourth voice. One Gertrude hadn't heard yet. It was hoarse, like a smoker's.

Or, like someone left out in the woods for too long.

"*Help.*"

"Help!"

Soon, a chorus of voices leapt from over the hedgerow. Each one individually seemed to upset Alan.

Together, they sent him twitching and his muscles jerking around like he kept putting his finger into the electrical socket.

He spasmed, dropped the machete onto the ground. His face still leaked blood, though the flow had subsided a little bit. Wounds cauterized, but his speech was still garbled.

"S-stop..."

But the women's voices kept coming.

Alan put his hands over his ears. Even resorted to using his fingers to plug them up.

Neither seemed to help him. He kept jerking around.

Finally, Gertrude said, "Admit it, Alan. You're no damn good at hosting *any* sort of dinner party."

This seemed to take him over the top. His cold-aura eyes bulged in his head. His mouth twisted into a snarled scream, but no words came out.

"Q-q...q-q-quiet..." the impotent words trickled out of his face hole.

"Keep going!" Gertrude shouted to the women.

They kept going. Their shouts became energized. A single ray of hope lay ahead, amidst a horrible corridor of darkness.

More shouting. More energy.

Finally, their voices rose to a crescendo.

Gertrude watched Alan become even twitchier. Muscles contracting in different directions. Flailing. He screamed in apparent psychic agony. His eyes screwed up inside his head. His neck muscles beneath his beard flexed until they seemed likely to burst.

Finally, apparently unable to overcome whatever it was about all of this that ailed him, he gave up.

He unshouldered the rifle, put it under his chin, and pulled the trigger.

TWO

It took Gertrude almost an hour to chop through all the wooden poles with the machete. Luckily—and unlike the rest of this camp, or whatever you wanted to call it—it was kept in good condition. The blade was sharp and stayed that way as she slowly but surely hacked away.

The women all reacted differently. Some were quite gracious. Others quiet.

Everyone seemed relieved to lie down on the dirt, though.

By the time she was finished, a colorless darkness had fallen on the forest. The peaty smell of the swamp receded a little bit, since the temperature and humidity dropped.

Gertrude eventually got used to the odor, the horrifically rancid one the breeze carried with it. It hadn't emanated from the clearing where the women were kept. She knew this because it only really got into the air when the breeze crept in. As night rode in, the breeze seemed to ride out. So it was rancid, but bearable.

Whatever it was causing the smell, it was coming from the dark and tangled forest beyond.

And Gertrude was happy to let it stay there.

She had plenty to worry about as it was.

As much as she wanted to *really* get out of Dodge from this situation, the women weren't in any sort of physical condition to move themselves to safety.

And as sinful as she'd been in the past—as much as she had left plenty of folks in a lurch—most of them had it coming. She didn't know much about these women, but ain't nobody alive who deserved this.

Except maybe Alan.

Overhead, a gaggle of clouds passed by. The moon came out. Full and bright. Casting the forest in a tint of white light. Just enough so Gertrude could pick her way through the open spots, trying as best she could to find her way back toward civilization.

It took her another hour before she found a trailhead.

Another thirty minutes before she found a Ranger station.

She first saw the light on in the window, before she could even see the building. As she approached the one-story building from the trail she'd picked up, she pushed away feelings that she was walking into a trap—something she quickly reminded herself was less important than helping the five women she'd left out in the forest. Alone and injured.

Despite her typical distrust of authority, she forged ahead. The sign out front was shaped almost like a guitar pick. It was half-brown and half-canary yellow. Playful, almost.

She sure hoped they had someone serious and competent on duty tonight.

Gertrude walked through the front door.

She gave a description of what she'd left behind. A general sense of where. The Ranger taking her statement—dressed in clothes that (*shudder*) reminded her of Alan's—asked her questions about how long she'd been walking. About how she ended up so deep in the wilderness area in the first place. Showed her maps of different areas, trying to get a sense of any geographical milestones she might recognize. She played dumb about the beginning of the story (which wasn't hard, she hadn't known where she was or where she was doing in the first place). And nodded about a few areas she was certain she recognized.

He seemed suspicious. Especially given how she was dressed. Not a woman who just went out for a hike and got lost.

But he also had five people to coordinate a search and rescue mission for. They would take priority.

He got up from his chair to make a few calls on the radio. Pushed his cap back on his forehead, gave her a once-over.

"Sit tight here, Miss. Going to need to ask you some additional questions after we get the rescue mission started."

"Yes, sir," Gertrude said.

"Can I offer you anything?"

Gertrude nodded yes. "I'm awfully thirsty. Maybe some water? Or do you have Gatorade?"

"How about one of both? You'll need the fluids, after what you been through."

Gertrude flashed her warmest smile. "Bless your heart, sir."

"It's Fred, ma'am."

"Thank you, Fred."

Fred was almost out the door when he turned around. He was a pleasant-looking man. Gentle. The way so many park rangers were. They were good stock, mostly. Committed to nature. Being out in it. Preserving it. Fred smiled, almost as if he didn't want to bother her any further but needed to ask anyway.

"And, my apologies, but I don't think I ever got your name, ma'am."

"Call me Gertrude."

"Gertrude. Nice name. You don't hear it enough these days."

"No, sir—I mean, Fred. No, you don't."

Fred nodded and was out the door without another word.

He was right. It wasn't a name you heard much about these days.

And as she slipped unseen out of the building, back into the moonlit darkness, toward the never-ending allure of The Road, she knew it wasn't a name he'd hear about again.

At least not from her.

AFTERWORD

Okay so another word on structure ...

(Just kidding).

If you are reading this, I am humbled. You just uploaded some-where in the neighborhood of a few years' worth of my work into your brain. I sure hope you enjoyed it.

If you didn't, well, I apologize for letting you down. I do hope you'll give me another chance (I mean, there must be *something* you liked here, right?! You're still reading!).

If you enjoyed this collection, there is a lot more for you–both now and far into the future (one hopes, though, of course, tomorrows are only a device of the imagination). But this book was created with the accumulation of many yesterdays. And depending on when you read this, I expect those yesterdays will continue to stack (time waits for no man, and all that, hopefully Death waits for this one, though).

What I mean is, there will be many more of my books in your hands (or your device, or your ears, or straight into your mind) should you want there to be.

The best way to find out more–both about new releases, free releases, and news about upcoming releases–is to join my newsletter, which you can find at nizthomas.com/newsletter. It's free, it's semi-regular, and it requires nothing from you. I don't just hawk my own wares there, either. Often enough, I'm recommending books and articles and movies that I have nothing to do with, but that are worth your time. So if you liked my stuff, you will probably get a kick out of the newsletter, too.

Mostly, I wrote this afterword to say thank you for taking a chance on this collection of short fiction. It means the world to me that you did. I know it's a time commitment, so if you made it all the way through, I don't take for granted just *how much* time you spent. Drop me a line any time at niz@nizthomas.com where I occasionally pop in to procrastinate what I am really supposed to be doing (writing).

See you on down the road, I hope.

Niz Thomas
March, 2024

EXCLUSIVE SNEAK PEEK

Keep reading for a look at the forthcoming crime suspense novel from
Niz Thomas.

For more exclusive content, sign up for Niz's newsletter at:
nizthomas.com/newsletter

FAMILY TREE

A SUSPENSE NOVEL

WRITERS OF THE FUTURE AWARD FINALIST

NIZ THOMAS

FAMILY TREE

A NOVEL

by Niz Thomas

ONE

Joe Parry woke up with a jolt, like he'd just been struck with a cattle prod. His eyes shot open but it took him a second to register where he was. His heart was pounding against his chest like it was trying to escape. Or explode. For a brief second he wasn't sure it had a preference, though his would have been for whichever did the job faster.

He saw a single salmon-pink splotch of paint on the bedroom wall, peeking out from under what was otherwise a complete cover-up job. His daughter, Samantha, must have missed the spot last month when she sponge-painted the entire wall charcoal grey, part of a number of recent changes that Joe wasn't completely comfortable with. He didn't need another look at the nude art posters she'd hung above the eave of her desk for a reminder of that fact.

Joe tried to catch his breath. He'd been dreaming of something dark and ambiguous, a heavy weight of a feeling, like impending doom. Or an anvil on his chest. Unfortunately, he knew the feeling well. He'd had plenty of nights like it in recent years, though this one felt somehow different for him. Worse, sure, but also like the end of something that he hadn't known had started yet.

Turning his neck — which he realized, with some discomfort,

hadn't managed to find a pillow in the night — and he felt his heart rate slow a bit, knowing he was at least in his own house. He took a long, deep breath to reacquaint himself with the land of the living and inhaled the orange and lavender scent from the candle he'd bought Samantha two months earlier, and given to her last week for her eighteenth birthday. He felt ashamed now that he'd bought it so far in advance and upon giving it to her, it couldn't have seemed any stranger of a gift.

Even unlit, the smell was so potent it crept through his nostrils and settled deep in his throat, constricting his windpipe just enough to make him cough. Like a feminine version of chloroform.

That scent, and the thought of every moment since he'd first smelled it at the mall, hurt him more than any cattle prod could have. He could see now that two months could move mountains in a teenager's world. Even the two weeks since Samantha had turned eighteen had felt to him more like wrangling cattle than being one. Things started happening much faster and he felt like they needed to be contained.

He could never quite get his hands around the situation though.

Joe put his feet on the floor and slowly pulled himself up. His neck cried out something fierce at the effort and he felt a few muscles down his back and ribcage light up with their own protests, too. He let himself sit there, on his daughter's empty bed, the realization of her not coming home another night made it feel like he just woke up from a car wreck.

Five nights. Five of the longest nights he'd ever had — and that was saying a lot. He wondered if Samantha had ever sat up at night as a kid, waiting in vain for him to come home. He put that thought aside as quickly as he could muster in the cold of the empty room and the darkness of a fall morning. Talk about the shoe being on the other foot.

Sitting there, he picked up the cordless phone next to Samantha's bed. He'd brought it in from his room, just in case she called. It was the only phone in the house and he'd thought about getting rid of it for the last few years but never cared enough to do so. He checked the caller ID but saw there had been no missed calls. He put the phone back on the side table.

He became aware of the tick, tick, tick of his wristwatch. The rest of the house was silent. A far cry from the city sounds he'd spent most of his life cocooned in. There wasn't a single car horn or emergency siren to be heard. The sticks — as he referred to them, but in reality, what most people would call the suburbs — were far too quiet for him. It gave all the thoughts inside him more amplification than he liked.

He always could have used more of a chance to think before he acted. But sitting in silence, thinking about the worst? Well, that just wouldn't do for him.

Even after two years living in the sticks — a northern New Jersey town called Mendham — he didn't feel adjusted to the quiet. The town wasn't far from where he grew up in Newark, but it might as well have been in another country. The biggest commonality was that people breathed oxygen in both places. Most of Newark was rundown now, but it hadn't been so bad when he grew up there. It was a city of immigrants back then — Italians, mostly. By contrast, the houses in Mendham consisted of a few historic sites built by militia men during the Revolutionary War surrounded by lawyers' and bankers' mansions built sometime after the last bull market. The legacy was still alive, Joe supposed, but the reality was that, despite the fact that just a few miles away George Washington and his army camped during the winter of 1779, the only thing that still remained from that era was the quiet.

And sitting alone in the house his then-wife convinced him would be the salve on half-a-lifetime of putting the badge first, the silence of this place felt personal. Like it was made specifically to torture him. He wondered if any of those militia men had felt that, too.

He got up and smoothed out the bed's comforter, wanting the room to feel exactly how Samantha left it whenever she decided to come back home. Then he went to the threshold of the doorway and turned once more back to the room, wondering if he was being too naïve. If the thought of her coming back to him and this house wasn't more than a pipe dream.

The room looked so different now. Grey and black color had replaced the pinks and pastels from only a few months ago. But that felt like another lifetime at this point. Samantha's closet, neater than any kid's he ever knew, was more of the same color palette. Black and grey jeans and long tees replaced the rainbow colors of dresses and blouses. And a growing collection of nude art posters.

He closed the door and went downstairs.

In the kitchen, he set up the coffee. Samantha had taught him how to use the thing when she bought it for him a year earlier. It was one of those machines with more levers than it seemed to need — like Rube Goldberg's idea of a coffee maker. At the time, Samantha had been going through a "coffee phase" and he was pretty sure the gift had been more for her than for him. Either way, he had to agree with her. It tasted better than the watered-down version his old drip machine produced.

Joe opened the cabinet above the machine and reached past the decaf and lighter roasts for a brand called Unleaded Java. It was that type of morning. After loading the beans into the dispenser, he switched the machine on and it went to work grinding them up. It couldn't finish the cup fast enough for him.

He reached for the stereo remote and hit play, not sure what would come on. It had sat silent for the past five days. Since his wife left them, Samantha had always worked the stereo for him. While her taste in music didn't really match his, he felt it was something that brought them together. Especially before she decided coffee wasn't for her anymore, due to the injustices involved with making the beans, or whatever the issue of the day was.

The song that started up was faint at first, almost mechanical in its introduction. There was no singing or words yet, just a low humming sound mixed with the timbre of a factory — grinding metal and power tools. Definitely not the type of music that Samantha would have played six months earlier, but he guessed those days were long gone. At the moment, he didn't care about the music. He just wanted the noise. The song had an eerie quality mixed with the grinding of the coffee machine. It hearkened back to the days when people like him would have been working the factory floor, not much more to worry about than what the wife was making for dinner that night. But then, he guessed those days were long gone now, too.

Joe stood there, eyes closed, letting the sounds wash over him. For a moment, he fell into a trance, thankful for the brief respite from his own mind.

Once the machine was done, Joe took a big sip of the coffee, the bitter smell and taste bringing back the closed throat feel from the candle in Samantha's room. He hardly noticed, though, desperate to wake up. The song kept playing, growing in intensity, leading him toward something dark and mysterious. He felt like he was moving toward the end of a hallway in a horror movie.

His phone buzzed on his hip, making him jump and almost spill, and pulling him up and out of the trance-like state the music created. He lifted the remote and turned it off.

"Parry."

"Joe, it's Shea," the voice said. Shea Walters. With the music and the fog from a shit night of sleep on his mind, he'd forgotten she said she'd get back to him today. She was a private investigator who used to work undercover with him. A good, reliable cop, though she'd had a bit of a fall from grace in recent months, from his understanding of things. He knew the feeling well enough — his move out to the sticks wasn't *exactly* a self-less move — and he also knew a cop like Shea wouldn't let it get to her. He'd asked her to pull in a favor with a contact she had.

"Hey Shea, you got something for me?"

"Yeah, I'm doing great, Joe. Happy to help a friend in need."

"Sorry. My mind's a little fucked right now. She hasn't come home in five days. I'm just worried."

"Yeah, well, when kids turn legal, sometimes they rebel. My parents would have killed for me to just slip out of the house for a week. They still, to this day, don't believe I was a cop. I didn't have the heart to show them the newspaper clippings after I got canned, just to prove it to them. Try not to take it personal, Joe. It's probably more about her own thing than anything you did."

Joe wished that were true. He took another sip of the coffee, finally feeling it working on his cobwebbed brain, and went over to the sliding glass doors off the kitchen. Growing up, Joe could never have pictured himself living in a place like this. It was too green, too wholesome. He'd worked narcotics and then homicide for a bit in his hometown. The only green he saw was the money they took off the dope dealers when they popped them. The setting out here was more like something out of a Stepford brochure. Not even the dealers wanted to score big and live like this. He doubted they even had the imagination. And these were the same sort of people who started sculpting fake toys made out of cocaine to avoid detection.

He took another swig of the coffee, having a sudden hankering for a shot of Jameson in it. He stared out at his manicured backyard, the showcase piece of which was a twenty-five-foot tall chestnut tree that sprawled at least as wide, canopying the flowers and hedges planted in mulch on the back end of the property. A single rope swing hung from the tree's thickest branch, an addition he'd made on Samantha's fifteenth birthday. He could practically hear her laughter from that afternoon echoing through the quiet of the house.

It was thought to be one of the last surviving chestnut trees in the whole northeast. It was basically the reason they chose the house in the first place.

"You there, Joe?" Shea asked.

"Yeah, sorry. Just trying to stay positive, that she took off with a friend or something."

"I'm sure that's what it is, bud. I wish I had something to help ease your mind. Unfortunately, my contact came up empty. The phone's been off since Tuesday night."

An icy fear rose up in the pit of his stomach. That was the last night he'd seen Samantha. The night of her birthday. He wasn't all that surprised that she hadn't turned it back on yet — other than being a teenager and have the phone practically be a third appendage.

"I figured as much."

"How's that?"

"The night she left. We had a fight. It got kind of ugly, the mudslinging back and forth. I would have left it at that, but she decided to fling the phone, too. It got busted up, though I thought they made those things out of titanium these days, so I was hoping it didn't break all the way. Or that she'd gotten it fixed if it had. I know she took it with her because it wasn't on the floor when I came back downstairs. She's got pretty good aim, Shea. If I hadn't ducked, that trace would have led you straight between my eyes."

He could hear Shea laugh on the other end. "A girl that takes after my own heart," she said. "Or my dad's, at least. You think he didn't want a son with a golden left arm, you'd be dead wrong."

Joe watched a squirrel bounding through the grass, into the mulch, and up the front of the tree. It worked itself around to the backside and disappeared from his view. He had a sudden urge to tell Shea the rest of what happened that night with Samantha.

"Well, the Amazin's sure could use one right now," he said, ignoring the urge.

"Yeah, every day since '76."

"So what do you think I should do, Shea? I figured she might replace the thing, turn it back on. Your search would have caught that?"

"Yeah. Even if she used a different SIM card or a new phone. My guy is at the company. He checked it all. And what should you do? Shit, it's hard to say. You call around to her friends?"

He had, though Samantha had recently changed more about herself than just her favorite colors and taste for coffee. A few months back, she started hanging out with a different crowd at school. Artists, mostly. At least that's what she'd told Joe they were. He hadn't pressed her because, well, he didn't think she was preparing to run out on him. And because after so many years working the streets of Newark, the kids out here wouldn't have alarmed him unless they started leaving IEDs along the side of the town's lone main road.

He'd need to do a better job digging them up.

"Listen, Joe, I've got another call. One other thing you might try? Her phone is listed under your account. Check who she'd been talking to recently, see if any patterns emerge or any numbers that might clue you in. Gotta run, though. Let me know if you need anything else, alright?"

"Sure. Thanks, Shea. And let me know how I can pay back the favor."

They hung up.

Joe finished his coffee, but by now it was lukewarm and the bitterness tasted like stomach acid fighting its way up into his throat. He'd spent a few days assuming Samantha was just blowing off steam. Then a few days telling himself not to overreact. But now he felt the cold instinct that something was wrong creeping up the base of his spine.

Outside, a gust of wind blew through the backyard, swaying the rope swing as if a ghost were sitting in the seat.

His little girl was missing.

And maybe not of her own volition.

JOIN THE MAILING LIST

Did you like this story? How about another one for FREE?

Join Niz Thomas' mailing list for a FREE copy of the short story *The Omega Diner*, which placed Honorable Mention in the prestigious *Writers of the Future* Contest.

Join now to also get:
MEMBER DEALS & DISCOUNTS
FIRST LOOK ACCESS
AUTHOR INTERVIEWS
LIMITED EDITIONS
AND MORE

Join the newsletter here: nizthomas.com/newsletter

ALSO BY NIZ THOMAS

For a full list and links to purchase, visit: nizthomas. com/books

Nizpatches

Volume One: Crime Stories

Volume Two: Twisted Crime

---

the Ledgerman series

The Omega Diner: A Ledgerman Story

Razor's Edge: A Ledgerman Novel

Thin Air: A Ledgerman Story

Last Ride: A Ledgerman Novel

---

the True Name series

Call Me Betsy

Call Me Gertrude

Call Me Aileen

Novels

Family Tree

Door Number Five at the Memory Motel

And The Moon Is Full And Bright

Election Day

SHORT STORIES

A Refraction of Kind Light

A Void of Ascendant Light

Becalm This Mighty Sea

Burn Off

Burn Together

Cheers

Elder Hunger

Fiona's Mercy

First Light of Every Morning

How to Commune with a Futurist

Lady Death

Lane Change

My Bleeding Kansas

No Control

Paint It Thrice

Rail Music

Ray-Ray's Stoop

Recidivist History

Red Tempest

Ships in the Night

Songbird

The Bad Guy

The Climb and The Glory

The Forever-ish Flame War

The Imminent Fire

The Impassable Way

The Light Alone

The Two O'Clock Killer

The Voice of Rage and Ruin

Upon Your Dreams They Prey: A Lullaby

Vanguard

Vida's Sixth Trip Around the Sun

When Sheds Talk

ABOUT THE AUTHOR

Join the mailing list for a FREE short story
website: nizthomas.com/newsletter
email: niz@nizthomas.com

Niz Thomas grew up a fan of *The Silence of the Lambs,* heist movies, and 007. Not surprisingly, as a kid he wanted to be an FBI agent, a cat burglar, and a spy. He decided to go to college instead and has regretted it every day since.

Niz is an eleven-time honoree in the *Writers of the Future* contest, receiving a Finalist designation for his short story *Vida's Sixth Trip Around the Sun* and several Silver Honorable Mention awards. He is also the author of over thirty short stories and several forthcoming novels, including the highly anticipated horror novella *And The Moon Is Full And Bright,* the dark suspense novel *Family Tree,* and the near-future political cat-and-mouse novella, *Election Day.*

Join his mailing list for limited edition story art, early access to new releases, and periodic FREE short stories.

Join the mailing list: nizthomas.com/newsletter

*9 7 8 1 9 6 4 7 6 5 0 0 6 *